Starborn Descendants

BRADLEY McKIBBEN

Paper back ISBN-13: 978-1-963272-57-4
Hardcover ISBN-13: 978-1-963272-58-1

ShelteringTree.Earth, LLC Publishing
PO Box 973, Eagle Lake, FL 33839

Did you enjoy this book?

We love to hear from our readers.

Please visit the author and illustrator at
ShelteringTreeMedia.com

About the Cover:
Artist: Bradley McKibben
Title of Piece: Milky Way Union
Location of Piece:
https://bradmckibben.wixsite.com/bradleymckibben

STARBORN DESCENDANTS

DEDICATION

This book, like all my past and future works, is dedicated first and foremost to my Lord and Savior, Jesus Christ.

I also dedicate this book to my two children, my beloved wife, and my entire family.
With all my love, always.

CONTENTS

PROLOGUE   vii

1 A PILOT'S DEBUT   1

2 CELESTIAL LAUNCH   5
3 WINGS OF WAR   10
4 THE ENGINEER'S TOUCH   15
5 CADET MEMORIES   22
6 PROMOTION   32
7 UNCHARTED ANOMALIES   38
8 FRACTURED COMMAND   49
9 GUARDIAN OF ANDRONYX   61
10 LYSARA, THE XENO-SPECIALIST   69
11 GALACTIC GRANDEUR   74
12 THE CALL OF THE VOID   84
13 THE GELYTHERIAN ACCORD   102
14 ROGUE PLANET   116
15 SOS   122
16 SURVIVING TORAK-9   125
17 O'BRIEN'S RESCUE   132
18 A SOLDIER'S RECOVERY   137
19 THE DATE   140
20 ECLIPSE RIFT   145
21 DIPLOMATIC DISASTER   152
22 THE SHROUDED TRUTH   156
23 IN HONOR AND LOSS   163
24 WAR   182
25 THE FRONTIER BATTLE   186
26 CALL TO ARMS   198
27 A BRIEF RESPITE   203
28 THARA'S RETURN   207
29 APOPHIS   213
30 GOODBYE, CADMUS   218
31 HELLO, MWU NERAK   232
32 THE BATTLE OF THE THREE SUNS   238

33 VANGUARD'S REST   249
34 COMMANDER   258
35 MAJOR FRIENDS   265
36 LIBERATION   273
37 TRAITORS   286
38 THE NIGHT BEFORE   297
39 ZENITH PRIME   333
40 A WELCOME ALLY   349
41 TERMS OF SURRENDER   354
42 PEACE   359
43 HAASE'S LEGACY   365
44 XELORON'S DOWNFALL   370
45 NEW BEGINNINGS   384
    DISCUSSION GUIDE   389
    ABOUT THE AUTHOR   393

PROLOGUE
The Birth of the MWU

The universe has always been a repository of mysteries, harboring secrets in the far reaches of space, well beyond the understanding of even the most advanced civilizations. Humanity, driven by relentless curiosity, long gazed at the stars, crafting myths and stories to fill the void of their ignorance. The dream of discovering other life forms seemed a distant fantasy—an aspiration consigned to speculative fiction. This long-held wonder became reality in the year 2385 with the reception of a deliberate, intelligent transmission from deep space—the Signal.

This moment marked humanity's first contact with an interstellar alliance known as the Milky Way Union (MWU). The Signal contained a mathematical sequence, unmistakably intelligent, and an invitation to join a coalition that had existed for millennia. The MWU was a federation of thousands of species united under shared principles of unity, diversity, and discovery. Its mission was to foster peace, cooperation, and collective advancement among civilizations. Earth's initial response was cautious—balancing excitement with the sobering weight of interstellar diplomacy. The MWU's representatives, arriving in an awe-inspiring fleet of advanced starships, laid out the terms of Earth's potential membership: access to galactic resources, technology, and knowledge in exchange for a commitment to shared goals.

The alien fleet, a spectacle of technological prowess, hovered silently in Earth's orbit. These ships, immense in scale, cast long shadows across cities as they loomed above. Their designs defied human understanding, with structures seemingly composed of living metal and adorned with glowing symbols that shifted like liquid light. Representatives from civilizations far older than Earth's addressed humanity, their advanced translation technologies seamlessly bridging linguistic gaps. They conveyed the MWU's purpose: not as conquerors, but as partners offering unparalleled opportunities.

In time, the MWU became universally known by its acronym, pronounced "mew," evoking a sound both soft and melodic. This pronunciation symbolized the harmony and cooperation the Union sought to foster across the galaxy, and it resonated with reverence and familiarity among its members.

After years of deliberation, humanity chose to accept the invitation. This decision followed intense debate among governments, scientists, and philosophers, weighing the risks and benefits of joining a galactic alliance. The MWU's origins, stretching back nearly 100,000 years, revealed a galaxy once rife with conflict. Early civilizations, unaware of each other's existence, grew in isolation until expanding empires clashed over resources. These ancient wars devastated entire planets and their inhabitants. Out of this chaos emerged visionary leaders who proposed cooperation over competition, leading to the MWU's foundation. The coalition was built on treaties, shared resources, and mutual benefits. Initially formed by war-weary civilizations, the MWU expanded over millennia, bringing countless species into its fold—some willingly, others through persuasion or demonstration of the Union's technological superiority.

Earth was a fledgling member among a coalition of thousands of species, each vastly different from the next. For humans, the sheer diversity of alien life was overwhelming, spanning forms and cultures far beyond anything imagined in science fiction. To make sense of it all, humanity coined the term *exoform* - a practical catch-all for any sentient life originating beyond Earth. Among MWU pilots, space was often called the void—not because it was literal emptiness, but because of the way it swallowed light, sound, and certainty. It was a term born of reverence, not science.

It was simple, efficient, and distinctly human, encapsulating their struggle to comprehend and classify the galaxy's vastness. It was simple, efficient, and distinctly human, encapsulating their struggle to comprehend and classify the galaxy's vastness.

The MWU's guiding principles emphasized unity as a shared responsibility for the galaxy's stability, diversity as a source of strength through the blending of cultures and knowledge, and discovery as a means to advance collectively. Unity was not simply about political alignment but about shared responsibility, ensuring peace through collaboration rather than domination. Diversity was celebrated as a core strength, with the MWU's vast network of exoforms contributing unique perspectives, technologies, and histories. Discovery, meanwhile, remained at the heart of the MWU's mission, driving its members to explore uncharted regions of space and unlock the universe's secrets.

Earth's integration into the MWU heralded a technological and cultural renaissance. Humanity, once limited to its solar system, gained access to hyperlight drives and terraforming technologies, accelerating space travel and colonization. Mars and other planets became habitable, and Earth's scientists worked alongside these exoforms to advance artificial intelligence, medical technologies, and space-time manipulation. In just a few decades, humanity's fleet included fighter-class vessels, freighters, and massive galactic-class vessels that served as mobile cities.

The MWU's technological advancements extended far beyond these. The Union's catalogue of space phenomena included mapping wormholes, black holes, and regions of dark matter, providing humanity with unparalleled insights into the galaxy's structure. Terraforming technology allowed for the transformation of barren planets into lush, habitable worlds, unlocking new opportunities for exploration and colonization. Entire planets were dedicated to agricultural innovation, ensuring none within the MWU needed to fear scarcity. Additionally, medical fleets traveled across the galaxy, delivering advanced care and eradicating diseases that had plagued civilizations for centuries. The MWU's mastery of space-time manipulation not only facilitated instantaneous communication but also revolutionized transportation, enabling faster-than-light travel with remarkable efficiency.

Diplomatically, Earth evolved into a hub of interstellar interaction. The establishment of the MWU's annual summit on Earth symbolized humanity's growing influence. Initially a pivotal meeting to avert conflict, the summit became a cornerstone for shaping Union policy and fostering unity. Humanity's contributions to AI and diplomacy earned it respect within the coalition, despite early skepticism from more established members.

The MWU's ideals were not without complications. Maintaining unity among thousands of exoforms required constant diplomacy and compromise. Smaller member exoforms sometimes felt overshadowed by larger powers, and universal policies often clashed with cultural traditions. For example, some resented the MWU's perceived imposition of its values, while others accused it of stifling technological progress.

Externally, the MWU faced resistance from factions that rejected its vision of unity. Some saw the Union as overreaching or imperialistic, while others prepared to wage war against it. These tensions strained the coalition, highlighting the fragility of interstellar peace. Rumors of war grew louder, with rival factions amassing fleets and resources to challenge the Union's dominance. The MWU's efforts to maintain peace required delicate diplomacy and strategic compromises, often forcing it to prioritize one crisis over another.

By the year 3024, humanity had become a vital member of the MWU, contributing significantly to its diplomatic and technological endeavors. Earth had transformed into a thriving hub of interstellar commerce and research. However, internal tensions within the MWU and external threats from rival factions threatened the coalition's stability. Humanity's journey into the stars continued, balancing the pursuit of discovery with the need for caution in an ever-changing galaxy.

Cultural adaptation was another challenge for humanity.

Earth's cities became melting pots of interstellar cultures, with alien ambassadors, traders, and travelers mingling with humans. The exchange of ideas and traditions enriched human society but also introduced complexities in communication and governance. The MWU's motto—Unity, Diversity, Discovery—served as a guiding principle, reminding humanity of its role in the galactic community.

1 A PILOT'S DEBUT

Connor O'Brien stood in front of the imposing MWU Academy building, its gleaming metallic facade reflecting the bright midday sun. The academy was the pinnacle of Earth's space program, a place where the best and brightest were trained to join the ranks of the MWU. Today, after four years of rigorous training and countless hours of study, Connor had finally graduated. His first mission as an MWU pilot was just around the corner, and the reality of it all was starting to sink in.

The academy grounds were abuzz with activity, recent graduates mingling with instructors, families congratulating their loved ones, and the occasional high-ranking officer striding purposefully through the crowds. Connor adjusted the snug collar of his skintight uniform, its pristine white fabric with gold trim a testament to his achievement. The material, sleek yet comfortable, fit him like a second skin, emphasizing the athletic build he had honed through years of intense training.

Connor's parents couldn't attend the ceremony, but a nearby holographic booth flickered to life with their call. His mother's voice came first, brimming with pride. "Connor! Oh, my handsome boy, that hair of yours—always so perfectly styled. You've managed to look both dashing and disciplined at the same time."

Connor chuckled, brushing his hand through his dark, neatly groomed hair. "Thanks, Mom. It's the result of years of your advice about presentation."

His father joined the call, his broad smile filling the frame. "Look at you, son. Top of your class and looking sharp. You remind me of myself back in the day—when I was fit and could still outrun your mother."

"Before I could outrun you," his mother quipped with a grin.

Connor laughed, feeling warmth in the moment. "Thanks, Dad. I wish you both could've been here."

"We're there in spirit," his father said. "And, son, we couldn't be prouder."

After a few minutes of conversation, the hologram flickered and faded, leaving Connor smiling as he stepped away. A group of fellow graduates approached; their faces filled with excitement.

"O'Brien, top of the class!" one of them shouted, pulling him into a brief celebratory hug. Another graduate raised a holographic camera, and they posed for a quick picture, their triumphant smiles captured against the academy's grand backdrop. With congratulatory pats on the back, the group dispersed, leaving Connor to reflect on the day's significance.

He didn't linger long. Commander Harris's familiar voice cut through the hum of the crowd. "O'Brien," the commander called, his tone sharp but approving.

Connor turned and snapped to attention. Harris, a tall and imposing figure with a face weathered by years of service, approached with purpose. His uniform bore the insignia of Commander, a rank reserved for captains of galactic class ships.

"You ready to show the galaxy what you're made of?" Harris asked.

"Yes, sir," Connor replied, his voice steady.

Harris nodded, his sharp eyes scanning the bustling courtyard. "Take a look around. What do you see?"

Connor studied the sea of uniforms. The insignia denoted

clear hierarchies: Crewman stripes for those who had completed basic training, silver bars for Ensigns, and gold stars for Pilot First Class. Higher ranks displayed elaborate symbols that shone under the sunlight, while Galactic Class officers wore insignias that radiated authority.

"I see dedication, sir," Connor said. "And years of effort realized."

"Good answer," Harris said, a faint smile tugging at his lips. "But let's see how well you know your stuff. Tell me about the ranks."

Connor straightened. "The ranks start with Crewman, for those who've completed basic training and take on general duties. Those who pursue advanced pilot training graduate as Pilots, while Pilot First Class is their first promotion. Above them are Ensigns, who command smaller teams or vessels. From there, ranks progress through Sergeant, Lieutenant, Captain, and finally Commander, who lead galactic class spacecrafts."

Harris gave a satisfied nod. "And the ships?"

Connor responded with confidence. "Fighter class crafts are about ten meters long, designed for speed and agility. Freighters are cargo vessels, ranging from twenty to over fifty meters in size. Cruisers offer comfort and amenities, often compared to compact one-bedroom apartments within fifteen meters, but they lack heavy defenses. Protector class spaceships are massive, over a hundred meters long, with shielding capabilities to guard fleets or stations. Galactic class ships, the largest, exceed fifty kilometers in length and serve as mobile cities, housing tens of thousands of beings with full facilities."

Harris clapped him on the shoulder. "Your first assignment just came in. You'll be escorting a freighter to a distant station. It's straightforward, but don't get complacent. Space can be fickle."

Connor's chest swelled with excitement. "Understood, sir."

As Harris walked away, Connor turned toward the launch pads, where his ship was waiting. The Cadmus stood gleaming in the sunlight—a sleek fighter-class with a silver-white hull and gold accents. Measuring ten meters, its slender wings extended outward, ready to cut through the stars. The engines emitted a soft hum, almost like a heartbeat, as if it shared his anticipation.

Connor approached and ran a hand over the smooth metal surface, feeling a surge of pride and responsibility. This wasn't just a ship—it was his ship. Every line, every edge, promised adventure.

2 CELESTIAL LAUNCH

"**You ready** for this? First mission as an official pilot. You nervous?" One of the engineers asked, walking up beside him with a smirk.

"Nervous?" Connor laughed, unable to tear his eyes away from the spacecraft. "More like excited. This is what I've been waiting for." His heart raced at the thought of sitting in the cockpit, feeling the hum of the engines, and breaking through the atmosphere into the vast expanse of space.

The Cadmus was a marvel of engineering - small enough to be quick and nimble, but large enough to carry the necessary equipment for extended missions. Its narrow wings flared out gracefully from the body, tipped with thrusters for maximum agility in deep space. The cockpit was built into the central frame, just ahead of the twin engines that powered the ship. Connor had spent weeks studying the specs during training, imagining every aspect of how it would handle. Of course, he had flown in them a few times for hands-on training but doing this on his own and for his first official mission was overwhelming.

He glanced around the bustling hangar. Dozens of personnel were preparing for their missions, checking ships, running diagnostics, and issuing last-minute commands. But none of these registered fully. All that mattered now was the Cadmus.

He approached the ladder leading up to the cockpit. Climbing up, Connor settled into the pilot's seat, the controls comfortably fitting beneath his hands as if they had been tailored to him. He could feel the quiet hum of the engines vibrating beneath him, even though they hadn't powered up yet.

As he slid the cockpit canopy closed over his head, sealing himself inside, everything outside became a muffled hum. The digital display lit up around him - holographic controls, navigation charts, communications links - all flickering to life as the Cadmus booted up its systems. The interface was intuitively advanced and supremely user-friendly.

He keyed the comms. "Cadmus here, requesting launch clearance."

The voice of the flight control officer came through almost immediately. "Roger that, Cadmus. You're cleared for takeoff. Coordinates for your rendezvous point with the freighter have been uploaded to your nav system. Safe flying, O'Brien."

Connor's grin widened as he adjusted the thrusters. "Thanks, Control."

With a flick of his wrist, the Cadmus lifted off the ground, hovering smoothly above the hangar floor. The hangar doors slowly peeled open in front of him. As Connor engaged the forward thrusters, the ship glided out of the hangar, the sunlight gleamed off its metallic hull.

He quickly ascended through the atmosphere, the familiar pull of Earth's gravity lightening as he broke through the clouds and into the upper atmosphere. Then, in a moment that always left him breathless, the blue sky gave way to the black void, scattered with distant stars.

Space!

Connor had always been mesmerized by it, even as a kid. The endlessness of it, the silence, the beauty. No matter how many training simulations he'd run, nothing compared to actually being here. In the vastness of the cosmos, where the only thing separating him from oblivion was the craft's hull, Connor felt more alive than ever. The stars glittered like diamonds on black velvet, and the sheer scale of it all - the galaxies, the nebulae, the endless horizon - was humbling.

He decelerated the Cadmus down to cruising speed, the engines humming smoothly as the ship glided through the void. The freighter he was tasked with escorting was already enroute to a distant MWU space station, and his job was to ensure its safe passage through an area known for pirate activity. It was a fairly routine mission, but for Connor, it was everything. His first mission. His first real test as a MWU pilot.

As he cruised toward the rendezvous point, he took a moment to simply enjoy the flight. The feel of the spacecraft beneath him, the way it responded to the slightest touch of his hand, was intoxicating. The Cadmus was fast - faster than anything he'd been in before - and it felt like an extension of himself, perfectly attuned to his reflexes and instincts.

"Rendezvous point in five minutes," his onboard AI chimed in.

Connor glanced at the nav display, confirming the AI's report. Sure enough, the freighter was just ahead, a massive, lumbering spacecraft compared to the nimble Cadmus. It was built for transport, not speed, and he could already see why it needed an escort. Out here, in the silence of the inky darkness, freighters were easy targets for pirates and smugglers.

The freighter loomed ahead, its bulk casting a shadow over the stars behind it. Connor activated his comms. "Freighter Juno, this is Pilot Connor O'Brien of the MWU. I'm your escort for today's trip. Do you copy?"

A moment later, a gruff voice crackled through the comms. "This is Captain Graves of the Juno. We read you loud and clear, Pilot O'Brien. Thanks for the company."

"Wouldn't miss it," Connor replied with a grin.

The freighter moved slowly but steadily, and Connor took up his position, circling the larger ship in wide arcs, scanning for any signs of trouble. Space, for all its beauty, was also dangerous. Pirates, rogue asteroids, and even gravitational anomalies could appear without warning. Connor's job was to ensure none of that got in the way of the Juno's delivery.

As he patrolled the area, Connor couldn't help but marvel at the view. The stars stretched on forever, uninterrupted by the usual noise and chaos of planetary life. Out here, it was just him and the void - a quiet, infinite expanse that both soothed and thrilled him.

"Approaching the asteroid field," Captain Graves' voice cut through the comms. "All fighters, keep your heads on a swivel."

Connor snapped out of his reverie, checking his instruments. He presumed the other fighter ships that were part of this mission were doing the same. The asteroid field was a well-known hazard in this sector, and it was the perfect spot for an ambush. Pirates often hid among the larger rocks, waiting for freighters to pass through before striking.

He pushed the Cadmus forward, weaving gracefully between the scattered asteroids as he scanned for any sign of ships or weapons. A silent drum of urgency throbbed inside, the familiar rush of adrenaline building as he entered combat mode. So far, nothing was out of the ordinary; just the silent drift of rocks rumbling through the void.

And then - there it was. A blip on his radar.

"Got something," Connor muttered into his comms, narrowing his eyes as he adjusted the ship's course. His sensors had picked up a small, fast-moving vessel hiding among the asteroids. Pirate, no doubt.

"Juno, we've got company," another fighter called out over the comms. "Stay behind the fighters and prepare for evasive maneuvers."

"Roger that," Captain Graves replied.

Connor's fingers danced over the controls, his body tensing

as the enemy ship came into view. It was a small, ragtag fighter, clearly not MWU-grade, but dangerous enough in the right hands. And whoever was piloting it seemed to know their way around an ambush. The pirate ship darted between the asteroids, trying to close the distance between them and the freighter.

"Not on my watch," Connor muttered, pushing the Cadmus into a dive, cutting off the pirate's path.

The pirate ship fired first, lasers slicing through the blackness. Connor dodged easily, the Cadmus responding to his commands like it was reading his mind. He fired back, the twin blasters on his wings lighting up as they locked onto the target.

The pirate ship exploded in a burst of light, debris scattering into the asteroid field. Connor let out a breath he hadn't realized he was holding.

"Pirate neutralized," he reported. "All clear, Juno."

"Nice shooting, Pilot O'Brien," Captain Graves replied, the anxiety in his voice easing. "Let's keep moving."

Another fighter pilot commended Connor for his quick reaction, as another jokingly told him he got lucky for getting the pirate first. The comms shared a couple of laughs at that last comment.

Connor may have taken care of one rogue pirate, but he knew to remain vigilant, scanning the area as they passed through the asteroid field and emerged on the other side. His first mission was definitely *going off without a hitch.*

Connor took a look around his cockpit for a moment, grinning to himself.

"Good job, old girl," he whispered. "I think we're going to get along just fine."

3 WINGS OF WAR

The black void of space stretched out endlessly before him, dotted with glowing stars and distant galaxies. It was beautiful, and it felt like a dream come true. He'd always dreamed of being here - out in the open expanse, surrounded by the majesty of the cosmos.

Ahead of him, the freighter Juno lumbered slowly through the void, its massive bulk shimmering under the starlight. The contrast between his nimble, sharp-edged fighter and the bulky transport was striking, but he knew the freighter's contents were valuable and needed protection. He wasn't the only fighter ship on the mission, but he felt like a lone escort, with the responsibility for the Juno's safety falling on him. He gripped the controls tightly, the muscles in his arms tense but steady.

"All clear," Connor muttered to himself as his scanners showed no immediate threats. He allowed himself a brief moment to marvel at the stars, their twinkling lights reflecting off the Cadmus's canopy.

Suddenly, the cockpit alarm blared, snapping him out of his reverie. Red lights flashed across the control panel as the ship's AI blurted out in its calm, monotone voice, "Hostile entities detected. Multiple unidentified vessels approaching."

Connor's heart leaped in his chest. His hands flew across the console, tapping into the ship's scanner to get a better look at the incoming threats. Sure enough, several small, sleek ships were heading straight toward them, their weapons systems already armed.

"Pirates," Connor growled, his pulse quickening. This was no drill - this was a real, life-or-death situation.

Without a moment's hesitation, Connor powered up the Cadmus's weapons systems. The familiar hum of the ship's energy cannons filled the cabin, sending a rush of adrenaline through him. His training kicked in - every maneuver, every lesson from the MWU Academy came flooding back. He had been at the top of his class for a reason, and now it was time to prove it.

"Cadmus, prepare for combat," Connor commanded his ship, his voice steady despite the apprehension building in his chest.

The first pirate ship fired a volley of plasma rounds, streaks of glowing energy tearing through the cold void. Connor's instincts took over as he yanked the controls, the Cadmus spinning to the side with graceful precision, narrowly avoiding the incoming fire. Every adjustment of his ship was smooth and calculated. The other fighter crafts were handling their respective targets.

"Too slow," he muttered under his breath as he lined up his sights on the nearest pirate vessel. His finger hovered over the trigger for a split second before he squeezed it, unleashing a barrage of energy blasts that slammed into the pirate vessel's shields. The enemy's shields flared bright blue under the impact, but they held.

Connor didn't give them a chance to retaliate. He rolled the Cadmus to the side, dodging another round of plasma fire from a second pirate ship. He wove through the enemy formation with ease, his vessel's speed and agility unmatched by the bulkier pirate vessels. He looped around behind one of the enemies, locking onto their engines.

"Got you," he said with a smirk, firing another volley of energy rounds. This time, the pirate's shields flickered and failed. The blast tore through the hull, and their vessel erupted in a vivid burst of orange and blue light. Connor watched as fragments spiraled into the void. One down, several more to go. The other fighters seemed far less experienced, choosing to stick close to the Juno rather than breaking formation to go on the offensive. Mercy wasn't an option—the pirates had attacked without warning, leaving Connor no choice but to act.

But the pirates weren't going down without a fight. As Connor wove through the chaos, two of the enemy ships broke off and attempted to flank him, their plasma cannons firing in unison. Connor gritted his teeth as he pushed the Cadmus to its limits, twisting and turning to avoid the onslaught of fire. The proximity alarm blared, warning him of how dangerously close the shots were getting.

"Come on, come on," Connor muttered as he narrowly avoided another blast. His hands moved with lightning speed, making split-second decisions that kept him one step ahead of the pirates.

Suddenly, one of the enemy ships managed to score a direct hit on his shields. The Cadmus jolted violently, warning lights flashing across the console as his shield levels dropped.

"Damn it!" Connor cursed, his heart pounding in his chest. The impact had been strong, but his ship was still in the fight. He couldn't let them take him down - not on his first mission.

Pushing the Cadmus to full speed, Connor darted between the pirate ships, using the freighter as cover. The pirates, eager to take him down, followed closely, their weapons blazing. But Connor was too fast for them. He looped around the freighter, using its massive bulk to his advantage, and then swung out from behind it, catching the pirates off guard.

He fired another volley of shots, this time taking out one of the pirate ships with a well-aimed blast to its cockpit. The ship disintegrated into a fiery explosion, leaving only one left. Connor's confidence surged. He was in control now.

With quick, precise movements, he dispatched the remaining pirate. The last spacecraft tried to flee, but Connor was on it in an instant as his vessel blazed through the void like a comet. He lined up his shot, his finger poised on the trigger.

"Goodbye," he murmured, his voice tinged with a mix of regret and resolve. The weight of taking a life pressed briefly on his chest, but duty was clear: the pirates had left him no choice. As he fired the final shot, the pirate ship erupted in a burst of flame, its wreckage scattering into the void like a grim reminder of the cost of survival.

The space around him was quiet once more; the threat was eliminated. A surge of exhilaration coursed through him as he flew the Cadmus in a victory lap around the freighter. His first real battle, and he had come out on top—alone. The other fighters either cheered him on over the comms or stayed stoically silent, their reactions underscoring the same truth: they had chosen to remain close to the Juno, prioritizing defense over taking the offensive. Connor's boldness had made the difference, and the quiet acknowledgment from his peers spoke louder than their cheers.

But as he circled the freighter, a sinking feeling gnawed at him. Something wasn't right. The freighter had taken several hits during the skirmish, and now that the fight was over, the damage was apparent. The once-sleek surface of the transport was marred with scorch marks, and parts of its hull looked dangerously close to breeching.

"Juno, this is Pilot O'Brien," Connor called over the comms, his voice tinged with concern. "You took some heavy damage during the attack. Are you able to continue?"

There was a pause before the Captain Graves responded, his voice strained. "We're still functional, but we've sustained significant damage to our systems. We'll need repairs before we can complete the journey."

Connor frowned. This wasn't good. The freighter couldn't make it to the space station in its current condition, and without reinforcements or these new pilots stepping it up, they were sitting ducks for any other hostile forces that might be lurking in the area.

Just as Connor was considering his options, a familiar voice crackled over his comms.

"Hey, buddy! Need some help?"

Connor's eyes widened in surprise. "Ambryst? What the hell are you doing out here?"

Ambryst, a cherished friend from the academy, chuckled. "Looks like I'm your knight in shining armor today. I picked up the distress signal and thought I'd swing by."

Connor couldn't help but smile. Ambryst was a skilled pilot, and his presence was a welcome relief. But more than that, Ambryst was an alien - an exoform that resembled Earth's axolotls, with smooth, purple skin, external gills, and large, inquisitive eyes. His exoform was known for their dexterity and quick reflexes, and Ambryst was no exception.

"Good to see you, Ambryst. I could use the help," Connor admitted. A few of the ashamed fighters murmured into the comms. "The freighter's in bad shape. Think you can lend a hand?"

"Of course," Ambryst replied, his voice cheerful. "Let's get to work."

4 THE ENGINEER'S TOUCH

Connor rested his fingers on the Cadmus' controls, savoring the momentary peace. The adrenaline from the fight still hummed faintly in his veins, but the stillness of the cockpit brought a calm satisfaction. The pirates were gone, and the freighter was safe—for now.

A crackling voice broke the quiet. "Cadmus, this is Captain Orlin of the Juno. We've sustained significant damage in that skirmish. I need you to dock and assist with repairs. We're shorthanded on engineers. Report to the docking bay immediately and help our Chief Engineer Thara. She'll get you up to speed."

Connor raised an eyebrow. Assist in repairs? That wasn't his job - he was a pilot, not an engineer. He opened the comms, preparing to protest, but the captain's voice cut him off before he could speak.

"And no more victory laps, pilot. This isn't a circus."

Connor gritted his teeth, a flare of annoyance shooting through him. Was that what this was about? A punishment for his little display? He'd saved their skins and this was the thanks he got?

"Understood, Captain. Heading there now," Connor replied, trying to keep the irritation out of his voice.

As Connor maneuvered the Cadmus into the bay and secured

the docking clamps, he couldn't help but wonder what kind of shape the interior was in. Ambryst landed just next to him.

With the press of a button, the cockpit canopy hissed open, and Connor hopped out onto the deck of the docking bay. He adjusted his suit, feeling the slight stiffness in his joints from the strain of battle. He was used to combat, but prolonged dogfights like the one he'd just endured always left him a little sore.

As he descended the short ramp from his ship, he glanced over at Ambryst arguing with a dock crewmember about making sure his spacecraft was well tended to.

Connor's chuckle faded as he watched Ambryst press a palm against the side of his small, silver-blue fighter, whispering something in his native tongue. It wasn't the first time Connor had seen him do it—every time they docked somewhere new, Ambryst would take a moment to speak softly to his ship, like it was a living thing. As he turned back to Connor, he grinned and said, "No gills, no glory!" with a wink, before striding off.

Most humans might have laughed at the ritual, but Connor had learned better. He once asked Ambryst about it during their training at the Academy.

"The vessel has a soul," Ambryst had said, his wide violet eyes blinking slowly. "Not like yours or mine. But it remembers. Every pulse, every panic. It remembers how you treat it."

Back then, Connor had dismissed it as superstition. Now, after so many missions, he wasn't so sure.

Ambryst stepped back from the ship, his usually smooth and laid-back demeanor subdued. The gills at the sides of his neck fluttered—always a sign of distress in his species, like someone sighing through their skin. Connor wondered what was bothering him.

Beneath the surface of Ambryst's jokes and swagger was something deeper. He had once told Connor about the wars on his homeworld, how his people—water dwellers—had been displaced when the oceans were siphoned away by colonizers seeking mineral-rich sea beds. He rarely talked about it, but sometimes, when things got quiet, Ambryst would stare too long at a bulkhead like he was watching waves that weren't there.

Connor made a mental note to check in with him later.

Connor let out a light chuckle. A figure approached him, moving with a deliberate pace. Connor squinted through the low light of the bay, his eyes adjusting to the gloom. This stood apart from any exoform he had ever encountered. She appeared to be made entirely out of coral-like formations. Her skin - or was it an exoskeleton? - was a vibrant mix of blues, greens, and purples, with intricate, branch-like patterns crisscrossing her limbs. Her face was more humanoid, with two large, luminescent eyes and a series of ridges along her brow that glowed faintly. Her arms ended in slender, dexterous fingers; each one tipped with a delicate coral-like growth.

She stood before him, her posture straight and unyielding. Connor's instincts told him that this was someone not to be trifled with, despite her smaller frame.

"You must be Connor O'Brien," she said, her voice surprisingly smooth and clear, with a musical undertone. It had the kind of accent he'd never heard before, soft but with a sharpness that suggested a keen mind.

"That's me," Connor said, keeping his tone neutral. "And you are?"

"Thara," she replied, her large eyes studying him intently. "I'm the chief engineer of this ship. I've been told to supervise your assistance with the repairs."

Connor frowned. "No offense, but I'm a pilot, not a mechanic. You really think I'm going to be much help here?"

Thara didn't smile - if her exoform even did smile - but there was something in her gaze that hinted at amusement. "Captain's orders are captain's orders. Besides, there's more to repairs than just tinkering with machinery. I could use an extra pair of hands."

Connor exhaled slowly. He had no desire to be stuck on this

freighter, fumbling around with wrenches and circuits while pirates could be lurking in the next star system. His place was in the cockpit, flying the Cadmus. But orders were orders.

"Fine," he said, trying to keep the irritation out of his voice. "Lead the way."

Thara turned and motioned for him to follow. As they moved deeper into the ship, the damage became even more apparent. The corridors were dimly lit, with flickering lights overhead, and the air smelled faintly of burnt wiring and coolant. Several panels had been blown off the walls, exposing twisted wires and scorched circuitry.

"Pirates got you good," Connor commented as they passed another corridor with a collapsed section of the ceiling.

"They were more aggressive than usual," Thara replied without breaking stride. "Their attacks are becoming more coordinated. I've been tracking patterns across different sectors, and it's not random anymore. There's a method to their raids."

Connor glanced at her. "You think they're organizing?"

Thara nodded. "Something's changed. We used to be able to fend off smaller groups easily, but lately, they've been hitting us harder, more strategically. It's concerning."

They reached the ship's engine room, where the real damage was. The large, central engine core was still humming but sparks shot from several exposed wires, and the surrounding systems were offline, their consoles dark. Debris littered the floor, and it was clear that some of the engine's outer casing had been severely damaged in the attack.

Thara approached the console, her coral-like fingers moving quickly across the controls. She frowned at the readings, her glowing eyes narrowing.

"This is worse than I thought," she muttered. "We'll need to patch the primary fuel lines and reroute power to the auxiliary systems if we want to get this ship moving again."

Connor folded his arms, watching her work. He wasn't used to taking orders from anyone outside of his flight instructors, let alone someone like Thara, but he could see that she knew what she was doing. He respected competence, and she certainly had that.

"Alright," Connor said, rolling up the sleeves of his flight suit. "Tell me what you need me to do."

Thara shot him a glance, surprised. "You're serious?"

Connor shrugged. "Look, I'd rather be in my ship flying patrol, but since I'm stuck here, might as well make myself useful."

Thara studied him for a moment, then nodded. "Fine. We need to replace the fuel conduit in that section of the engine." She pointed to a part of the engine core where several thick, blackened tubes were sparking. "The conduit's been fried. I'll handle the power re-routing, but I need you to pull the old conduit and install the new one."

Connor walked over to the damaged section and examined it. The conduit was a mess, its surface charred and cracked. He grabbed a nearby set of tools, his hands feeling slightly awkward around the equipment. He hadn't worked with engineering gear since his academy days, and even then, it was more theory than practice.

He yanked the damaged conduit free, sparks flying as it came loose. Thara didn't even look up from her work at the console, but Connor could feel her watching him out of the corner of her eye. He grabbed the new conduit from a nearby supply crate and carefully aligned it with the slots, sliding it into place.

"Done," Connor said, standing up and wiping his hands on his flight suit. "What's next?"

Thara glanced at his work and gave a satisfied nod. "Now we need to realign the power flow. There's a junction box in the next room that's offline. I'll need you to manually reset it while I run diagnostics from here."

Connor followed her instructions, moving into the adjacent room. The junction box was tucked away in a corner, its cover hanging loosely. He pried it open, revealing a mess of wires and circuits. He grumbled to himself as he listened to Thara's instructions and carefully began resetting the system. It took longer than he had hoped, but eventually, the power began to hum through the circuits, the lights flickering back on.

"Power's flowing," Connor said.

"Good," Thara replied. "Just a few more adjustments and we should be operational."

By the time they had finished, the ship's core systems were back online, and the Juno was running on auxiliary power. It wasn't perfect, but it was enough to get them to the nearest repair station without breaking down in the middle of nowhere.

Connor wiped the sweat from his brow as he rejoined Thara in the engine room. Ambryst was awaiting Connor with a friendly wave as he was listening to another engineer give out repair orders of his own.

Despite the tension between them at first, they had worked well together. He had to admit - she was skilled, far more than most engineers he had worked with in the past.

"Not bad, flyboy," Thara said, her tone neutral but with a hint of approval. "You've got some decent hands for a pilot."

Connor smirked. "I'll take that as a compliment."

Thara's large, glowing eyes met his. "I suppose we make a pretty good team."

"Yeah," Connor said, surprising himself. "I guess we do."

He nodded to her, a gesture of respect and camaraderie, but the motion seemed lost on Thara. Her exoform likely had different customs for such things. Still, there was a mutual understanding between them now - a sense of camaraderie forged in the fires of battle and necessity.

Connor checked the time on his wrist display, realizing he had spent far more time on the freighter than he'd planned. He tapped his commlink. "This is O'Brien. Repairs are done. I'm heading back to the Cadmus."

As he made his way back toward the docking bay, he glanced over his shoulder at Thara, who was already back at work on another system. He might not understand her completely, but he knew one thing for sure - if he ever needed help in a tight spot again, Thara was someone he could rely on.

With a final look, Connor climbed back into the Cadmus and fired up the engines. He quickly sent a message to Ambryst asking if he was almost finished, with no response. "He must still be busy I suppose." Connor said out loud as his ship lifted off. He rejoined the security formation around the freighter, his thoughts lingering on the strange, coral-like engineer.

5 CADET MEMORIES

The pirate skirmish felt like a distant memory, though Connor's mind was far from at ease. His hands rested on the controls, but his thoughts wandered. The soft hum of the Cadmus' engines filled the cockpit, but it was the quiet that seemed to amplify his memories - the ones he hadn't thought about in a long time.

He gazed out at the stars, the distant glow of nebulae barely visible on the horizon. It was peaceful, almost serene, but something about the stillness brought him back to a time before the Cadmus, before he was the confident pilot he was now. A time when everything was uncertain - the academy, his first step into the unknown.

Connor had grown up in the heart of Indiana, in the quiet town of Greenfield. It was the kind of place where everyone knew each other, and life moved at a slower pace. The air always smelled of freshly tilled soil in the spring, and in the summers, the fields stretched on for miles, a sea of green and gold swaying under the bright midwestern sun.

Greenfield wasn't the sort of place people left. Most residents stayed, growing up to take over family businesses, farm, or work at the few factories that dotted the outskirts. Connor's father, Henry O'Brien, owned a small auto repair shop that had been passed down for generations. His mother, Laura, taught at the local high school, where Connor had spent most of his teenage years half-listening to lectures about Earth's role in the MWU.

The Union had always fascinated him. Earth had been a member for almost a century, and yet, to many in Greenfield, it still felt like something distant - something that happened to other people. To them, space travel, alien alliances, and the MWU's grand projects were just things seen on the news, not something anyone participated in. But Connor had always been different. He had an insatiable curiosity about the galaxy beyond Earth. He'd spend hours at night, lying on the roof of his family's home, staring up at the stars, imagining what it would be like to leave Indiana behind and explore the farthest reaches of space.

His father didn't understand it. To Henry O'Brien, the MWU represented everything that was wrong with the world - too much change, too much reliance on alien technology, and too little appreciation for the simple life they had in Greenfield. He had always hoped that Connor would one day take over the family business, keeping the O'Brien name and legacy alive in their small town.

"You've got good hands, son," his father would say, watching as Connor worked on an old engine, grease smeared across his fingers. "You could do a lot of good right here in Greenfield. No need to go flying off to the stars."

But that wasn't Connor's dream. He enjoyed working with machines, sure, but his heart was set on something bigger. He wanted to fly - wanted to see the universe, experience things no one in Greenfield had ever seen before. The MWU Academy was the way out. It was his path to the stars, even if it meant leaving his old life behind.

The day he told his parents about his decision to apply to the Academy, his father had been silent, the lines on his weathered face deepening as he listened. His mother, on the other hand, had smiled softly, her eyes full of pride.

"Are you sure about this, Connor?" his father finally asked, his voice heavy with concern. "Once you're out there, you can't just come back when things get tough. The galaxy isn't like Greenfield. It's complicated."

Connor nodded. "I know, Dad. But I need to see it for myself."

His father sighed, wiping his hands on a rag. "I just don't want you to lose yourself out there."

"I won't," Connor promised, though he wasn't entirely sure what that meant at the time.

Connor's first day at MWU Academy had been overwhelming. The Academy itself was a sprawling complex. The buildings towered above him, their sleek, modern designs glinting in the sunlight, constructed from materials so unusual they seemed wholly otherworldly to Connor. Alien architecture mingled with human designs, creating a strange but beautiful hybrid of cultures. The towering spires and sprawling corridors were filled with recruits from every corner of the galaxy. Some were human, like Connor, but most weren't. There were towering reptilian exoforms with sharp claws and elongated limbs, insectoid creatures with multiple sets of eyes, shimmering, gelatinous beings that moved in a fluid dance as they communicated through flashing lights, and many more. It was both awe-inspiring and terrifying.

Connor had always been comfortable in Greenfield, where everyone was familiar, and the rules were simple. But here, at the Academy, everything felt foreign. The technology, the languages, and the very air felt different. It was a shock to the system, and for the first few weeks, Connor struggled to keep up. The physical training was intense, but it was the mental strain that almost broke him. He found himself constantly surrounded by exoforms that had spent their entire lives preparing for this. Some had been flying ships since they could walk, while others had already served in their home world's militaries before joining the MWU.

Connor, by contrast, felt like a fish out of water. His

background as a small-town kid from Indiana didn't seem to mean much here, and he quickly realized that the things he thought he was good at - combat, and problem-solving - were skills everyone here had. Many were better than him.

There were days when Connor considered quitting. The pressure was immense, and every time he stepped into a flight simulator, it felt like the controls were mocking him. His first attempt had been disastrous. He had crashed within minutes, sending his simulated ship spiraling into the side of a space station. The instructors had been unimpressed, and his fellow recruits had been even less forgiving.

"You suck, O'Brien. You'll never get off Earth at this rate," one of the other human recruits had sneered after the sim. "Stick to fixing cars, farm boy."

But Connor wasn't the type to give up easily. As the weeks passed, he started to find his rhythm. He spent every free moment in the simulator, learning the nuances of the controls, studying flight maneuvers, and pushing himself harder than he ever had before. Slowly but surely, his scores began to improve.

It wasn't just the flying, though. The MWU Academy wasn't just training pilots - it was training leaders. The instructors drilled into the recruits the importance of teamwork, discipline, and understanding the bigger picture. The MWU was a massive organization, spanning hundreds of worlds and uniting thousands of exoforms. It wasn't just about flying ships or fighting enemies - it was about maintaining peace and order across the galaxy. Every recruit, whether they were a pilot, engineer, diplomat, or something else, had to understand their role in that grand design.

Connor found himself growing into that role. He still struggled at times, but he was no longer the overwhelmed farm boy from Greenfield. He was a recruit in the MWU, and with each passing day, he became more confident in his abilities.

One of the turning points came during a simulated combat exercise. Connor had been assigned with a squad of other recruits including his best friend Ambryst, tasked with defending a colony from a simulated pirate attack. They had planned their strategy carefully, but when the exercise began, things quickly spiraled out of control. The pirates overwhelmed their defenses, and within minutes, the colony was in chaos. Ambryst hollered through the comms, "No gills, no glory!" as he charged toward the failing shield generators.

Connor had panicked at first, but then he remembered something his father had taught him back in Greenfield: when you're in a crisis, you don't freeze up; you focus. You find the problem and fix it.

At that moment, something clicked for Connor. He took charge of the squad, rallying the recruits and coordinating their counterattack. It wasn't perfect - there were plenty of mistakes along the way - but they managed to fend off the pirates and save the colony. When the exercise ended, the instructors were impressed, and for the first time, Connor felt like he belonged.

As his thoughts continued to drift back to his days at the academy, one memory stood out clearly—the first time he laid eyes on the standard-issue MWU spacesuit. He had been captivated by its sleek design, instantly recognizing it as more than just equipment. Even now, the vivid image of the suit pushed aside the focus of his current mission for a few fleeting moments. He remembered that moment well—the awe and excitement that washed over him, and how that fascination had only grown as he learned about the suit's bioengineered capabilities.

He stood in front of the gleaming white suit, displayed prominently in the locker bay of the MWU's orbital station. Even dormant, the suit's systems were operational, a testament to its advanced design.

It was a stark contrast to the older models he had studied in history modules—rigid, impractical, and clunky, designed more for brute survival than any real versatility or agility. This suit, however, was almost the opposite: a second skin that clung closely to the body, emphasizing both form and function. The white fabric, accented with the MWU's signature gold trim, shone under the soft lighting of the station, a symbol of the Union's unity and technological prowess.

The suit could vary in design and size depending on the exoform wearing it. For humans, like Connor, it resembled a one-piece bodysuit, covering him from neck to toe, perfectly tailored to his physique. But he had seen other exoforms in their own versions - some with extended limbs, others with additional compartments or breathing apparatuses to accommodate different biological needs. The suit was nothing if not adaptable, a testament to the MWU's mission of inclusivity and cooperation across the galaxy.

But the suit's beauty lay far beyond its outward appearance. Every part of it, from the sleek material to the intricate circuitry hidden beneath the surface, was designed with both survival and combat in mind.

Connor gently ran his hand down the arm of the suit, thinking about its most impressive feature—the Data/Holographic Display Projector. As soon as the suit was powered on, the wearer had access to a galaxy's worth of information. With just a simple command or gesture, the suit could project detailed holograms from the wrist or arm, displaying star maps and mission data, or even projecting full-sized holographic decoys to confuse and mislead enemies. The suit's near-AI system constantly scanned and retrieved data from the MWU's vast network, keeping the wearer up to date with the most recent intelligence and tactical information. Whether in the heat of battle or the calm of deep-space exploration, the suit was a tactical marvel.

Connor tapped the small interface on the suit's wrist, watching as a holographic display flickered to life. A star map of the nearby system appeared, spinning slowly in front of him. With a swipe, he dismissed the image, smirking to himself at the sheer convenience of the system. A galaxy's worth of knowledge was right at his fingertips.

Perhaps the most critical feature for galactic cooperation was the suit's Auto-Translator. The Union was a vast melting pot of exoforms, each with its own languages, dialects, and communication methods. The suit eliminated the language barrier entirely. When Connor donned the suit, a small, flexible wire automatically attached itself to his skin, linking him to the suit's linguistic systems. The suit could instantly translate any spoken or written language from across the galaxy, allowing him to communicate seamlessly with alien allies, no matter how complex their speech. When Connor spoke, the suit's tiny audio output, disguised as a small hole in the fabric, would translate his words into any language necessary, broadcasting it to anyone within a fifty-foot radius - or farther, if he raised his voice.

The suit's ability to adapt to the harshest environments was another feature Connor had come to rely on. Adaptive Environmental Shielding was more than just an added bonus - it was a lifeline. The suit could automatically adjust to protect its wearer from extreme temperatures, radiation, and hazardous conditions that would kill a human in seconds. Whether it was the blistering heat of a sun or the cold, crushing pressure of an icy moon, the suit created a micro-environment, ensuring Connor was kept safe from harm.

A smile touched his lips as he remembered his last training mission when the suit's Atmospheric Synthesizer had activated, forming a glowing blue force field over his face in the middle of a firefight on an oxygen-deprived asteroid. Within milliseconds of detecting a hostile environment, the suit had sprung into action, synthesizing breathable air and filtering out toxins. It did more than protect, it adapted instantly, keeping him alive without so much as a pause. It was the epitome of precision and innovation.

Connor's gaze moved to the lower part of the suit where the Medical Nanobots resided. He had never had to rely on them personally, but he'd seen what they could do. The suit contained a reservoir of microscopic nanobots that could immediately disinfect wounds, repair minor injuries, and stabilize the wearer in case of serious trauma. In the chaos of battle, the bots could keep someone alive long enough for proper medical attention, which, in more dangerous missions, often meant the difference between life and death.

As he picked up the helmet, the suit's Internal HUD, or Heads-Up Display, came to mind. The visor projected a 360-degree view, showing vital information like oxygen levels, shield status, mission objectives, and environmental hazards. The atmospheric synthesizer's data could double up with the HUD, showing detailed information about air quality and potential toxins. In combat scenarios, the HUD could lock onto targets, track enemies, and relay real-time data to Connor, enhancing his awareness.

He slid the helmet into place, the visor activating instantly, and the familiar array of data danced before his eyes. Oxygen, check. Gravity field, active. Mission status, ready.

There were times when combat or labor required more than just speed and agility. For those moments, the suit could deploy its Retractable Exoskeleton, a lightweight frame that extended around the wearer's body, enhancing strength and endurance. Connor had used it once during a mission where he had to lift heavy debris to free a trapped crew mate. The exoskeleton had given him the extra strength to lift several tons, but it came at a cost - draining the suit's power quickly. The exoskeleton was usually reserved for emergencies, as it depleted the suit's power in just a few minutes and needed significant time to recharge.

Another feature Connor found particularly useful was the Gravitational Stabilizers. In a galaxy filled with planets of varying gravitational pulls and zero-gravity environments, having the ability to stabilize his personal gravity field was a game-changer. Whether he was walking on the outer hull of a ship or the surface of a low-gravity moon, the suit could simulate Earth's gravity, ensuring Connor never lost his footing.

Hidden within the suit's sleek exterior were compartments for the Modular Tool System, which held small, detachable tools that Connor could use for repairs, hacking into systems, or even combat situations. Depending on the mission, he could swap out the tools for different configurations, ensuring he was always prepared for whatever challenges lay ahead.

Lastly, the suit's Data Uplink and Download capability was essential in the field. With a simple command, Connor could connect directly to ships, terminals, or data hubs, allowing him to download mission-critical information or upload data without the need for external devices. It made communication and coordination during operations seamless and efficient.

Connor took a deep breath, running his fingers over the suit's smooth fabric one last time. It was more than just clothing - it was survival, a finely tuned piece of technology designed to keep him alive and efficient in the most dangerous environments in the galaxy. With this suit, he wasn't just a pilot - he was an extension of the MWU itself, a symbol of its power, adaptability, and endless pursuit of knowledge.

Back in the cockpit of the Cadmus, Connor shook his head, pushing the memories aside. Though the Academy days weren't far behind him, they already felt like another chapter of his life— intense and transformative. They had shaped him, forged him into the pilot he was today. And now, here he was, on his first real mission, flying alongside a freighter, defending it from real pirates. It wasn't a simulation anymore. This was the real thing.

As the Cadmus continued its journey alongside the Juno, Connor's thoughts returned to the present. Ambryst had finally gotten out of repair duty and rejoined the security detail next to Connor. They were nearing their destination, and soon the mission would be over. It had been a long trek, filled with more challenges than he had expected, but he had made it through. The freighter was still in one piece, and so was he.

The commlink crackled to life, and the familiar voice of Captain Orlin came through.

"Pilot O'Brien, we're approaching the station. You're

cleared to return to base once we dock."

"Understood, Captain," Connor replied, a small smile tugging at the corner of his mouth.

As the freighter began its final approach to the space station, Connor guided the Cadmus into position. The journey was almost over, but for Connor, it was just the beginning. He had proven himself today - not just to the MWU, but to himself.

As the freighter Juno completed its docking procedures, Connor received his final orders to return to the MWU base. The mission, though eventful, was a success, and now it was time to head back to Earth to formally conclude his first assignment. With the Cadmus prepped and ready, the stars stretched out before him as he eased the ship away from the station, setting a course back toward the MWU headquarters.

6 PROMOTION

The main hall of the MWU station was vast, its high ceilings illuminated by soft, artificial starlight that glowed, designed to mimic the starfields that lay just beyond the walls of the station. The hall was packed with beings from all corners of the galaxy, a sea of faces - some human, many not - all watching with quiet anticipation. This was a significant moment in the MWU, a promotion ceremony held only for those who had proven themselves in the field. And today, Connor O'Brien was one of those being honored. He stood near the front of the stage, flanked by a few other newly promoted officers. He felt a mixture of fulfillment and unease. While the formalities of the ceremony were a routine part of life in the MWU, for Connor, this felt deeply personal. After his successful defense of the freighter Juno and his leadership in the aftermath, he had been deemed worthy of the rank of Pilot, First Class.

He glanced around at the others who stood next to him. Most were seasoned officers, some with decades of experience, while others were, like him, newly minted heroes of their respective battles. He was the youngest in the group, a fact that wasn't lost on him. The hall was filled with high-ranking officials from multiple exoforms, many of whom Connor couldn't even identify. One, a tall and insectoid figure with chitinous armor, stared at him from across the room, its multiple eyes blinking in an irregular pattern. Next to the insectoid stood a translucent, gelatinous being that shimmered softly, its form constantly shifting. Connor hoped to have already seen Ambryst but knew his close friend wouldn't miss this.

As the ceremony progressed, Connor stood at attention, his arms rigid at his sides, heels together, and gaze fixed forward. He listened as the MWU officials spoke about duty, bravery, and the responsibility that came with rank. Every word resonated with him, though his thoughts wandered. He thought about where he'd started - Greenfield, Indiana - about his family, the life he had left behind. But most of all, he thought about the Academy, about the struggles and victories that had brought him to this moment.

"- and in recognition of his outstanding bravery and leadership, Connor O'Brien is hereby promoted to Pilot, First Class," the voice of the presiding officer boomed, pulling him out of his reverie.

Connor blinked, snapping to attention as the officer gestured for him to step forward. His pulse quickened but he kept his expression calm and steady, even as a small smile threatened to break through. He stepped up to the stage, standing in front of the officer, who was a tall, imposing human with graying hair and sharp eyes.

The officer affixed the new insignia to Connor's uniform - a silver pin shaped like a winged emblem, signifying his new rank. The officer gave him a brief, approving nod.

"You've earned this, O'Brien," the officer said quietly, his voice carrying the weight of experience. "Of course, more will be expected of you now."

Connor nodded solemnly. "Yes, sir."

As he stepped back into formation with the others, the ceremony continued, but the weight of his new rank had already settled on his shoulders. Pilot, First Class wasn't just a title - it was a responsibility. He had more to prove now, and the missions ahead wouldn't be as forgiving as his first.

Later, after the ceremony had concluded and the newly promoted officers had dispersed, Connor found himself wandering the halls of the station, his mind still spinning from the events of the day. He had congratulated a few of the other officers and exchanged pleasantries, but now he needed space. The station, despite its enormous size, was busy, and Connor felt like a small piece in the larger machine.

As he walked, a familiar voice called out to him.

"O'Brien! Still basking in the glory of your promotion?"

Connor turned to see Ambryst, his close friend, heading toward him. The alien's smooth, purple skin glistened under the artificial lights, his external gills flexing as he moved. His wide, amphibian-like eyes blinked slowly as he gave Connor an exaggerated grin.

"Ambryst," Connor said, smiling despite himself. "You know me too well. How are you doing?"

"Better now that I'm not stuck on some boring transport route," Ambryst replied with a chuckle. "You made quite the name for yourself. First mission and already a promotion? What's your secret?"

Connor rolled his eyes, but he couldn't help but feel a swell of pride. "It wasn't all me. The pirates weren't exactly organized. The other fighter pilots there did their part too. Afterwards, I had to help Thara with some repairs. Do you remember her?"

"Ah, yes, Thara. The chief engineer, right? I've heard stories about her. Brilliant mind. Terrible social skills," Ambryst teased, his voice thick with amusement. "As for those other pilots, I read the reports. Bunch of, how do you humans say, bums if you ask me. I get they thought at the moment they were doing what was right, to disengage in combat and focus on protecting the freighter but-" Ambryst shrugged his shoulders with a nod as he let the sentence fall off.

Connor smirked. "Well, as for Thara, she's - efficient. Not much for small talk, though. And don't blame those other pilots.

You said it, they were just doing what they believed to be right in the moment."

Ambryst laughed again, his voice echoing down the corridor. "Well, now that you're all important and such, I imagine you'll be off doing bigger and better things soon. But before you fly off to save the galaxy, how about we grab a drink? I've got a bottle of Garthish nectar stashed away."

Connor glanced at his comm. He had a briefing in a couple of hours for his next mission, but he figured a drink wouldn't hurt. "Sure. But just one. I've got new responsibilities now, remember? And I've got to meet my new commanding officer later."

Ambryst slapped him on the back, a bit too enthusiastically. "That's the spirit, O'Brien! Let's go celebrate your big day."

Several hours later, after a drink and a few rounds of reminiscing with Ambryst, Connor found himself standing outside the briefing room. He had a slight buzz from the Garthish nectar but was otherwise clear-headed. He stiffened a little and took a deep breath before stepping inside.

The briefing room was small but well-lit, with holographic displays projected along the walls. Lieutenant Jacqueline Haase stood at the head of the room, her sharp features and stern demeanor commanding attention. Known as one of the toughest officers in the MWU, she exuded a no-nonsense attitude and demanded the highest standards from her subordinates. Strict but fair, she wasn't afraid to shout when necessary but always acknowledged good work. Wasting no time on pleasantries, she got straight to the point.

"O'Brien," Haase said as he entered. "Take a seat. We need to discuss your next mission. No time for meet and greet."

Connor sat down, his posture straight and attentive. The holographic display shifted, showing a series of star systems and tactical maps. The details of his next mission came into focus, and his stomach tightened as he realized the gravity of what lay ahead.

"We've been monitoring an area in space that has recently been showing signs of increased cosmic radiation. For now, intelligence is suggesting it's an anomaly and that we need someone to go investigate. That's you, O'Brien." Haase explained, her tone matter-of-fact.

Connor frowned. "Of course, but is there any other information?"

Haase's eyes narrowed. "We're not ruling anything out. Your promotion puts you in a position to handle more sensitive operations. Your mission is to gather intel, identify the source of this anomaly, and report back. Got it?"

Connor nodded, already running through the logistics in his head. It was an interesting mission, one that would require him to be careful and resolute.

"I won't let you down, Lieutenant," Connor said, his voice firm.

Haase studied him for a moment, then nodded. "I know you won't. But remember, O'Brien, this isn't just about flying anymore. You're a leader now. Everyone in the MWU will be looking to you to succeed. Don't lose sight of that."

"I understand."

Haase dismissed him with a wave of her hand, and Connor stood up, already feeling the weight of the mission on his shoulders.

Back in his quarters, Connor reviewed the mission details once more, his mind buzzing with both excitement and apprehension. He was ready for this - he had worked hard for this - but the responsibility was new, heavier than he had expected.

With a sigh, Connor stood up and made his way back to the hangar, where the Cadmus waited for him. The day had come and gone and now it was nearly midnight. The stars outside seemed both inviting and ominous, as they always did, promising adventure but also danger. He had survived his first real mission and earned his promotion, and now, the stakes were about to get higher.

Connor ran his hand along the sleek surface of the Cadmus, feeling the cool metal beneath his fingers. As the engines of the Cadmus roared to life and the hangar doors opened, revealing the infinite blackness of space, Connor took a deep breath and guided the ship heavenward.

7 UNCHARTED ANOMALIES

The ship's console flashed repeatedly as the Cadmus approached the surface of the Tier 4 planet below. Connor frowned, glancing at the warnings lighting up on his display. Radiation spikes. Gravitational distortions. The surface might look deceptively peaceful from orbit—lush with captivating flora, teeming with unknown fauna, and blanketed in thick clouds of gas and dust—but he wasn't fooled. This planet wasn't a Tier 4 for no reason.

"Cadmus, explain the Tier classification system," Connor said, his voice steady but curious. If he was going to land here, he needed to know exactly what he was dealing with.

The ship's AI responded instantly, its tone calm and precise. "Planetary tiers are classifications based on environmental hazards and the presence of sentient life. Tier 1 planets are considered safe, with minimal hazards and established populations of sentient exoforms. Tier 2 and Tier 3 planets have increasing levels of environmental danger, with Tier 3 often requiring specific technology to survive. Tier 4 planets, like this one, are characterized by extreme conditions—erratic gravity, high radiation levels, or toxic atmospheres—and no known sentient exoform presence as determined by MWU exploration efforts."

"So, this place is officially labeled 'wild and dangerous,' but no one knows exactly what's out there," Connor muttered, his eyes narrowing at the dense, swirling clouds covering the planet.

"That is correct," the AI continued. "Further classifications within each tier are assigned using letter designations, based on more detailed environmental and biological assessments. However, this planet has not been explored sufficiently to determine its full classification."

Connor stared at the planet's surface as it loomed larger in the viewscreen, a dense mix of strange rock formations, thick forests, and jagged mountain ranges. "A Tier 4 mystery," he murmured, gripping the controls as the Cadmus began its descent.

As the Cadmus broke through the atmosphere, the ship rattled slightly, its systems compensating for the pressure and gravity fields. Connor kept his hands steady.

"Cadmus," Connor asked, a thought tugging at the back of his mind, "is it possible the MWU database is wrong about this planet? That it could even be a lesser-tiered world?"

"Yes," the AI replied without hesitation. "That is entirely possible. The MWU's data on this planet is based primarily on long-range scans and preliminary observations. No official exploration missions have been conducted here, leaving much of its environment and hazards unverified."

Connor exhaled, his grip on the controls tightening. "So, it's either safer than expected - or worse."

"Affirmative," the AI said calmly.

Connor nodded to himself as the ship steadied, the terrain below becoming sharper and more defined.

The Cadmus landed smoothly on a plateau overlooking the anomaly's epicenter. Connor stepped out into the environment, his suit immediately adjusting to the planet's atmosphere. The Atmospheric Synthesizer engaged as the HUD displayed a faint blue glow over his visor, ensuring he had breathable air. The wind whipped at the jagged rocks around him, but the landscape was eerily silent.

As Connor began his descent toward the epicenter, strange waves continued to undulate from deep within the forest below. The trees here were tall and spindly, their bark resembling obsidian, glistening in the waning sunlight. The ground beneath him was uneven, covered in an abundance of vegetation. His gravitational stabilizers adjusted his footing on the steep decline.

After several minutes of careful exploration, his HUD began flashing again, detecting movement just ahead. Connor stopped, taking a low profile as he activated his suit's Data/Holographic Display Projector. A small projection of the landscape appeared on his wrist, highlighting an area just beyond the thick cluster of trees. There was movement - life, and not just the wild fauna he'd expected. The MWU's database had no record of sentient life on this planet, yet his suit was picking up signs of structured movement and even signs of rudimentary construction.

Connor crept closer, his pulse quickening as he peered through the trees. There, at the edge of the forest, was something he hadn't anticipated: a small village. His visor zoomed in on the structures, which were crude but functional - huts made of stone, wood, and mud. Smoke rose from small fire pits, and around the village, he could see beings moving about.

His breath caught in his throat. These creatures were humanoid, but their skin was pale gold, almost metallic, reflecting the light like polished bronze. They had long, sinewy limbs and angular faces with narrow, glimmering eyes. Their movements were deliberate and precise, as if they had adapted perfectly to the planet's harsh conditions. Each being wore simple, primitive clothing, and they moved with a quiet grace as they worked by gathering wood, resources, and preparing food, unaware of his presence.

He cautiously stepped forward, still hiding in the shadows of the trees. It wasn't until he reached the village's edge that his HUD began picking up something even stranger. In the center of the village, rising higher than the huts and structures, was a large metallic object. The structure was old, rusted in parts, but still held together. The villagers seemed to revere it, with some gathered around the object, gesturing toward it with a mix of awe and fear.

Connor's heart fluttered as the suit confirmed what his eyes had already suspected: it was a dark matter capacitor! His HUD projected damage indicators onto its surface—fractured panels, exposed circuits, and visible scorch marks. The capacitor was clearly not functioning as intended, with unstable energy readings emanating from its damaged core.

His mind raced. Dark matter capacitors were one of the most advanced pieces of technology in the galaxy, used by ships to store and regulate dark matter energy for long-distance travel or advanced weaponry. They were dangerous, powerful, and always shielded to prevent exactly what was happening here. This one, however, was exposed and leaking dark matter energy into the atmosphere unchecked. His suit's readings showed the waves radiating outward as the source of the radiation spikes and gravitational distortions he had detected earlier.

The capacitor stood like a monolith among the primitive structures; its purpose and danger presumably lost to the villagers. Connor observed the exoforms closely now, noting their simple clothing and coordinated movements. Where had they come from? He had no immediate answer, but one thing was clear: they revered the capacitor as some sort of sacred relic. Perhaps it had fallen from a destroyed ship long ago, becoming a central part of their lives over generations. However it got there, the unshielded dark matter leaking from the device was already causing measurable damage to the environment. What remained unclear was how deeply it was affecting the planet's ecosystem—or the villagers themselves.

Dark matter capacitors, when functioning correctly, were incredibly efficient, storing vast amounts of energy without destabilizing the surrounding area. But when damaged or exposed, the consequences were catastrophic. Gravitational distortion was already occurring, and if the leakage continued, reality shifts could follow—rifts in the fabric of space-time itself. This capacitor could bend light, warp gravity, and disrupt communication for light years around. Connor knew he had to act quickly before the situation spiraled further out of control.

Connor's HUD flickered as he glanced at the villagers again, who remained unaware of the danger their revered relic posed. He needed to find a way to get the capacitor before the anomaly worsened. His HUD began alerting him of waves becoming more frequent and stronger. The radius of distortion was expanding. If left unchecked, the anomaly could stretch far enough to reach neighboring planets, destabilizing entire systems.

His mind worked rapidly. Gravitational distortion, temporal anomalies, and communication disruptions were already happening here on this planet. If the capacitor wasn't contained soon, these phenomena would spiral out of control.

This item was so obviously revered by the villagers, stealing it wasn't an option. At least, not a good one. They'd most likely not tolerate him taking it.

He sighed, shaking his head. Stealing it without at least trying to talk to them didn't sit right with him. No, diplomacy had to come first. He'd show himself, explain the danger, and hope that reason would prevail. Adjusting the settings on his suit, Connor stood up and stepped out from his hiding spot, walking slowly toward the village.

Almost immediately, the villagers spotted him. There was a moment of stunned silence before panic spread. Several males rushed toward him, clutching makeshift weapons - spears and crude blades carved from bone or rock. Their pale gold skin shimmered in the light, but their faces were hard, their narrow eyes wide with fear and aggression. Connor raised his hands, palms open, trying to show he wasn't a threat.

"Wait, hold on!" Connor called out, though he knew they couldn't understand him yet. His Auto-Translator struggled to process their language, the sounds coming through as fragmented syllables in his earpiece. For a few tense moments, he was sure they'd attack, but just as they drew near, a commanding voice rang out.

The men froze, parting as their leader approached. The leader was taller than the others, his gold skin more weathered and his angular face lined with age. His eyes gleamed with some intelligence as he studied Connor, his expression was wary but curious.

The leader spoke, his words slow and deliberate. Connor's translator clicked and whirred, struggling for a moment before finally succeeding. The translation was basic, the language stripped down, but it was enough to understand.

"You - who are you?" the leader asked, his voice tinged with both fear and authority. "What are you? You look - strange."

Connor took a deep breath, lowering his hands. "I'm not here to harm anyone. I come from the stars."

The leader's eyes widened, his expression a mixture of fascination and cautious curiosity. The villagers murmured softly, their voices like a gentle hum as they exchanged glances, their uncertainty palpable. They didn't appear hostile—only deeply intrigued by Connor's sudden presence and his ability to communicate. The leader stepped closer, his gaze intent, as though trying to piece together the meaning of Connor's words. His movements were slow, deliberate, and free of malice, a reflection of the villagers' peaceful demeanor.

"From stars?" the leader repeated, almost in disbelief. "Life-" he said while pointing up, "-up there?!"

Connor nodded. "Yes. I'm from a place far away. But I'm not here to harm you. I came because something from the stars is here, too."

The leader tilted his head, his brow furrowing in confusion. Connor gestured toward the dark matter capacitor in the center of the village.

"That," Connor said, pointing at the large metallic object. "It came from the stars, just like me."

The leader's eyes followed Connor's gesture, landing on the capacitor. His expression darkened immediately. His jaw clenched, and when he spoke again, his tone was sharp, almost defensive.

"That is gift from god," the leader said firmly. "It gives warmth on coldest nights. It brings light in darkest hours. Food grow tall and fast. Without gift, we not survive."

Connor's heart sank as the weight of their words hit him. He hadn't expected them to revere the capacitor to such a degree. To them, it wasn't just a mysterious artifact—it was life itself. The soft glow of its leaking energy illuminated the village at night, serving as a beacon of hope against the darkness. Its strange warmth had undoubtedly protected them through harsh winters, and its radiation, though dangerous, seemed to accelerate the growth of their crops, ensuring they never went hungry.

Connor's eyes swept over the villagers, noting their lean but healthy frames and the abundant fields that stretched beyond the village. They had built their lives around this artifact, adapting to its presence as if it were a natural part of their world. To take it away would feel like stealing their very existence.

"I understand," Connor replied carefully, choosing his words with precision. "I see what it means to you. It helps you survive—it gives you light and warmth. But this gift," he gestured again to the capacitor, "is dangerous. It's harming your world in ways you cannot see. The very thing that helps you now could destroy everything later."

The leader's eyes narrowed, his expression a blend of caution and stubbornness. Connor could see the tension in their stance, the internal struggle between their faith in the sacred object and the weight of his words. He had to tread carefully—reverence like this could not be easily undone.

The leader's eyes flashed with anger. Apparently, the translator was making Connor's point understandable to the leader. "No! No take. It is ours. It gives us life. It is not dangerous."

Connor suppressed a grimace. The warmth they felt was

radiation—the very thing destabilizing the environment. He glanced at the villagers, their simple tools and handmade garments, their reverence for the capacitor evident in every gesture. They treated it as a divine gift, not a piece of advanced technology. To them, it wasn't machinery—it was magic. Explaining dark matter or radiation to a people who had likely never seen the inside of a starship was an impossible task.

"Please," Connor said, his voice steady but urgent. "I know it gives you warmth, but it's also what's causing strange things to happen around your planet. If it stays here, things will only get worse."

The leader shook his head, his expression hardening further. "We will NOT speak this. No more," he said, his tone final. "You say you from stars, but you cannot take what ours. You stay, share your story, or you leave. But you not take god's gift."

Connor knew there was no point in pressing further. The leader wasn't going to change his mind, at least not today. He forced a smile and gave a respectful nod. "I will come back tomorrow," he said, offering a polite exit. "Perhaps we can speak more then."

The leader seemed satisfied with that and gestured for the villagers to stand down. Connor made his way back to the edge of the village, the community watching him in silence as he left. He could feel the weight of their distrust, but he had no choice. As he reached the cover of the trees, he glanced back one last time at the dark matter capacitor looming over the huts.

Seated in the cockpit of his ship, Connor gazed out at the planet's surface, the fading light of dusk casting long shadows. The weight of his decision bore down on him as he asked the Cadmus' AI for an updated analysis on the capacitor. The AI's calm, impartial voice responded, "Deeper scans indicate the capacitor will reach critical failure in approximately two hours." Connor's chest tightened, and his heart sank at the grim confirmation.

Reporting the situation to his superiors had been the right thing to do—it was protocol, after all. He had immediately contacted

Lieutenant Jacqueline Haase, explaining the dangerous circumstances surrounding the dark matter capacitor and its potential impact on the planet and its primitive exoform inhabitants.

Haase's voice had been sharp, almost exasperated. "You were ordered to observe and report, not to make first contact with an unregistered civilization. Do you realize what kind of diplomatic disaster you could have caused? This is an Evolutionary Eligibility Bureau matter now. Your involvement ends here."

Connor's stomach twisted at her tone, but he pressed on. "Lieutenant, I understand the protocols, but the capacitor is leaking dark matter at an exponential rate. The anomalies are intensifying. If this continues, the entire planet — and potentially parts of its solar system — could be destroyed. I'm telling you; we don't have time for bureaucratic delays."

There was a pause on the line before Haase replied, her voice ice-cold. "You are to fly away to a safe distance and remain in your spacecraft until further notice. The EEB will conduct its assessment. Their decisions always take a minimum of twenty-four hours. Do not interfere further, O'Brien, or I guarantee you'll face court-martial. Am I clear?"

Connor clenched his fists, struggling to keep his tone even. "Lieutenant, with all due respect, we don't have twenty-four hours. Cadmus estimates the capacitor's core will destabilize in under two hours. This isn't just about the planet — it's a galactic safety issue."

"You are not authorized to make that call, Pilot O'Brien," Haase snapped. "You will follow orders, or you'll answer for insubordination."

The line went dead, leaving Connor in silence.

He leaned back in his seat, staring at the darkened terrain outside his craft. His mind raced. Following orders was ingrained in him — it was what he had been trained to do, what made him a soldier. But the human part of him, the part that had joined the MWU to protect and serve, couldn't reconcile the idea of sitting idly by while an entire civilization and potentially a solar system were obliterated.

"Cadmus," he said finally, his voice tight, "scan the capacitor again. How much time do we have?"

The AI responded with its usual calm efficiency. "Based on current instability levels, the capacitor's core is projected to reach critical failure in approximately one hour and fifty-six minutes."

Connor closed his eyes, the internal conflict raging within him. His training told him to follow the chain of command, but his moral compass screamed at him to act. There was no time to wait for a bureaucratic decision. These people didn't understand the danger, and no one else was here to save them.

He reopened the comm line to Lieutenant Haase. "Lieutenant, I'm begging you to reconsider. This is a time-sensitive crisis. If we don't act now, it'll be too late. These people will die."

Her voice wavered, just for a moment. "I understand your concern, O'Brien, and I feel for those people — but this is not your call to make." Her tone hardened as she continued, the weight of authority returning. "You are not authorized. Stand down. That is an order."

Connor cut the connection, his hands shaking. His chest tightened as the weight of his decision threatened to crush him. "Is this really what I have to do," he muttered, his voice raw. "I swore an oath — to follow orders, to protect - but how can I just sit here and watch them die?"

He slammed a fist against the console, his breathing uneven. "Damn it!" The words echoed in the quiet cockpit; his frustration palpable. His training told him to comply. But the part of him that couldn't ignore the suffering of innocent lives screamed at him to act.

"I can't just leave them to their fate," he whispered, his voice cracking. His hands trembled as he made his decision, reaching for the control panel. "If saving them means breaking the law, if it means giving up my own freedom, then I'll gladly take the court-martial. I'll take it all. I can live with the consequences — but I can't live with doing nothing."

"Cadmus," he said, his voice firm, "prepare for extraction. We're taking the capacitor."

The AI acknowledged the command as Connor exited the Cadmus and slipped back into the exoforms' village under the cover of night. Moving cautiously, he retrieved the capacitor, its volatile energy safely contained thanks to his suit's advanced resistance systems. With careful precision, he secured the device aboard the Cadmus, ensuring its stability before preparing to depart.

Connor maneuvered the Cadmus carefully as it rose into the atmosphere, the dark matter capacitor secured in the ship's containment unit. He stared at the planet below, his chest heavy with the weight of what he had done. He had disobeyed direct orders, violated protocols, and stolen what the villagers believed to be a divine gift. But he had also saved them—and possibly countless others—from annihilation.

As the Cadmus ascended through the planet's atmosphere, Connor activated his comms and sent a brief message to Lieutenant Haase. His voice was steady but laden with the weight of his decision. "Lieutenant Haase, this is Connor O'Brien. The capacitor has been secured. I couldn't stand by and let it destroy the planet and its inhabitants. I'll accept the consequences of my actions."

Moments later, as the Cadmus broke free into the expanse of space, his comms pinged with an incoming message. The sender: Lieutenant Haase. The subject line read: *Court Martial*.

8 FRACTURED COMMAND

The cold metal of the handcuffs bit into Connor's wrists as he walked down the long corridor, led by none other than his academy friend, Ambryst. The irony wasn't lost on him. Out of all the pilots in the MWU, it had to be Ambryst - the same alien friend who had shared countless drinks and stories with him, who had once teased him about his reckless nature - that now escorted him to a holding cell.

"Come on, Ambryst. You know I had to do what I did," Connor muttered, glancing at his purple-skinned friend. Ambryst's gills quivered slightly with each breath. Ambryst shook his head and said "I get it Connor, no gills no glory, but you still disobeyed a direct command. You're in here because of your own doing, no matter how righteous it may have been." His wide, amphibious eyes fixed ahead, but the cold look on his face told Connor everything. The usual lightheartedness that characterized Ambryst was gone, replaced with an expression of deep worry and sorrow.

Connor's smirk faded. He knew his friend was distraught. Hell, he was too, but what was done was done. They reached the heavy door of the holding cell, its dull metal reflecting the harsh lights of the corridor. Ambryst pressed a button on the control console, the door slid open with a mechanical hiss.

Without so much as a glance, Ambryst guided him inside, uncuffed him, shut the door and walked away. Connor stood there for a moment, staring at the closed door. The silence weighed heavily on him. He let out a long breath and slumped down on the cold bench at the back of the cell.

His thoughts drifted to two hours before this lunacy had begun.

Connor had landed the Cadmus with a sense of urgency. The moment his boots hit the ground, he made a beeline for the command center. His commanding officer Lieutenant Jacqueline Haase was known for her strict adherence to protocol, and this wasn't something that could be swept under the rug. Connor marched straight to her office, practically crashing into the room without waiting for formalities.

"Lieutenant Haase," he started, his breath coming quickly as he gave a full, detailed account of everything that had happened - the dark matter capacitor, the anomalies, the primitive village, and how he'd taken the unshielded device to prevent further harm to the planet and neighboring systems. By the time he finished, his commanding officer's jaw had dropped.

For a long, uncomfortable moment, the room was dead silent. Lieutenant Haase, a stern woman in her mid-thirties with cropped black hair and a razor-sharp gaze, didn't speak. Connor could see her face gradually turning red, and a sinking feeling spread through his gut. "Here it comes," he thought bitterly.

Suddenly, she exploded.

"What the HELL were you thinking, O'Brien?!" she screamed, her voice rising to a pitch that seemed to shake the walls of the small office. Her fists slammed onto the desk, making the various comm devices rattle. "You took it upon yourself to steal a sacred object from an unknown exoform without protocol, without ANY authorization! Are you out of your mind?!"

Connor had expected the blow-up, but that didn't make it any easier. He stood stiffly, enduring the tirade as curse words filled the room, each one sharp as a whip. Lieutenant Haase's face grew even redder, veins bulging in her neck as she tore into him, her words coming fast and furious. Connor could do nothing but stand there, staring at a spot on the wall, waiting for the storm to pass.

After what felt like an eternity of shouting and accusations, Haase finally collapsed back into her chair, breathing heavily. She glared at Connor, her face still flushed, before she barked, "Get the hell out of my office! But don't go far. I'll have engineering take care of that capacitor before you end up blowing all of US up, too."

Connor gave a curt nod and stepped out, the door sliding shut behind him with a hiss. He found a seat in the waiting area outside, dropping into the chair with a weary sigh. His heart still raced with the adrenaline from the confrontation coursing through his veins. He ran a hand through his hair, silently cursing himself for how everything had transpired. But deep down, he knew he had acted on instinct - trying to prevent something catastrophic. It had been time-sensitive, and he had made a call.

After what felt like hours, the door to Haase's office opened. The lieutenant stepped out, her uniform crisp, her expression cold and her tone professional once more. "Follow me," she said flatly.

Connor did as he was told, his gut churning as he realized where they were headed: the Evolutionary Eligibility Bureau. The EEB was responsible for assessing civilizations and planets for potential inclusion in the MWU, and they weren't going to take kindly to his interference with an unregistered exoform.

They entered the sterile, polished halls of the EEB office, the stark contrast from the rough terrain of that primitive planet only heightening Connor's unease. A commander approached Lieutenant Haase - an older man with graying hair and a deep scowl etched into his face. He looked Connor up and down with disdain, then turned to Haase, whispering in a hushed, angry tone that Connor couldn't quite make out.

The commander stormed off, leaving Lieutenant Haase standing there, her head lowered in defeat. She shook her head slowly, letting out a sigh. Connor felt a sinking sensation in his chest as she straightened up, her professional demeanor slipping back into place.

"You are to face a formal investigation and a galactic tribunal for your actions from your previous mission," she said, her voice hard and cold. "Until that time, you will be detained in a holding cell."

Before Connor could even respond, two guards appeared from behind him. He felt his arms yanked behind his back, and the sudden, unfamiliar sensation of metal cuffs clasping around his wrists sent a jolt through him.

He blinked in disbelief, his gaze shifting to Lieutenant Haase, whose stern expression faltered for a moment. She met his eyes, and for the briefest second, there was something there—regret, sadness.

Connor didn't have time to dwell on it. He was turned around to face his escort, and his heart sank as he saw who it was.

"Ambryst," he whispered, shocked. His academy friend stood there, silent, eyes lowered in shame. Connor stared at him, unable to process the fact that it was his friend who had come to take him away. Ambryst didn't meet his gaze, didn't say a word, as he led Connor down the halls of the EEB office toward his holding cell.

Connor snapped back to the present, sitting alone in that cold, silent room, the weight of what had happened pressed down on Connor like a heavy blanket. Connor leaned forward and rubbed his sore wrists, his head hanging low. He understood why his friend had been the one to escort him - protocol, duty - but that didn't make it hurt any less.

He had made his decision. Now he had to live with the consequences.

He glanced around, taking in the sterile, clinical surroundings of the holding cell. It was clean and minimalist, far nicer than any prison he could have imagined, but a holding cell all the same. The pale gray walls and the hum of the faintly glowing lights above did little to ease his growing sense of dread. He bowed his head slightly, the weight of everything settling onto his shoulders. How had things spiraled so quickly? Was this his reality? Or just some nightmarish fever dream?

He had always wanted to be a MWU pilot. It had been his dream since childhood, and now, just two missions in, he was staring down a galactic tribunal - a court of ten judges appointed to determine whether his actions on the primitive planet warranted severe punishment. He grimaced, wondering if he'd ever return to the skies.

A full day passed. Connor had barely slept, his mind racing with guilt, fear, and frustration. He had acted quickly on the planet and made decisions he thought were right, but there was no guarantee the tribunal would see it that way. He replayed the situation over and over in his mind, doubting every choice he had made. But deep down, one thing remained clear—if he were given the same scenario again, he would make the same decision every single time. The dark matter capacitor could have destroyed that planet, killed those villagers, or even spread to other systems. He *had* requested approval from the E.E.B. and his commanding officers, but they had hesitated. If he had waited for them to act, the damage would have been irreversible.

The sound of footsteps broke through his thoughts. A MWU security officer stood at the door, unlocking it with a sharp click before opening it wide. "Get up," the officer commanded. "Follow me."

Connor stood and followed the officer, two more MWU security personnel falling into step behind him. The corridor stretched long and cold before them, the polished metal walls reflecting their every movement in stark silence. As they moved deeper into the heart of the MWU Command Complex, the sterile, mechanical hum of the structure gave way to a solemn stillness. Finally, they arrived at the entrance to the tribunal chamber, a towering set of reinforced doors that parted with a low, thunderous groan.

Inside was a courtroom of impossible scale, built to project authority and sometimes would inadvertently instill fear. The ceilings soared dozens of meters overhead, supported by sweeping columns of dark alloy engraved with the insignias of countless galactic systems. The gallery stands, capable of seating thousands, loomed above like the eyes of a silent jury, though they were empty now, their emptiness somehow more ominous than if they'd been full. The acoustics made every footstep echo like a judgment passed. At the far end of the room, elevated on a wide dais in a commanding half-circle, sat ten individuals cloaked in the formal robes of MWU judicial command: the tribunal.

Connor was guided to a lone chair at the center of the room, a simple desk before him. The security officers sat him down before retreating, leaving him alone under the scrutiny of the tribunal. His chest tightened as he scanned the faces of the judges. Nine were exoforms, representing different beings from across the galaxy. The final judge, seated near the center, was human. All of them wore the same expression - stern, analytical, and, above all, impartial.

Connor's eyes flickered to the audience in the stands. Lieutenant Haase was there, sitting stiffly, her face blank but her eyes betraying her concern. Beside her sat Ambryst, his usual jovial energy replaced with quiet anxiety. There were others in attendance too - academy friends, officers, commanders, and captains, both human and exoform. Connor recognized the E.E.B. commander sitting toward the back, his arms folded as he watched the proceedings with a scowl.

The first judge, a tall exoform with four arms and dark blue skin, spoke. "We are the tribunal appointed to review the actions of Pilot, First Class Connor O'Brien regarding the unauthorized intervention on Tier 4 Planet Designate XR-317. You will plead your case before us today."

Connor's gaze flicked up at the mention of the planet's designation. *XR-317.* Cold. Lifeless. It didn't suit the vibrant, mysterious world he had seen. If he were ever given the chance, he'd come up with a name that actually meant something.

Each judge introduced themselves briefly, stating their title as Galactic Judge for the MWU. The tension in the chamber grew as they began reading aloud from the official report—one authored by Lieutenant Haase, based on Connor's own submitted account. Connor's stomach twisted as they recounted the timeline: his discovery of the primitive village, the presence of an unshielded dark matter capacitor, and his immediate request for authorization to intervene. The report noted that his request was denied by Lieutenant Haase, citing non-interference protocols. But it also documented his decision to act regardless—removing the capacitor to prevent what he believed would be catastrophic consequences for the planet and its inhabitants.

Once the reading was complete, the central judge turned his gaze toward Connor. "Pilot O'Brien, explain your reasoning."

Connor cleared his throat, feeling the eyes of the room on him. He was nervous, but he knew he had to be honest and confident in his actions.

"Your Honors," he began, his voice steady but with a trace of nervousness. "I acted with the best intentions given the circumstances. When I found the capacitor, it was already destabilizing the environment - radiation, gravitational distortions - it was wreaking havoc on the planet. The exoforms living there didn't even know what they were dealing with. If I had waited to get approval from the E.E.B., it could have taken months for them to assess the situation. By then, the damage might have been irreversible. I chose to act because the risk was too great, not just for the planet but for the neighboring systems."

Connor paused for a moment, his frustration growing as he recalled the red tape of bureaucracy. "With respect to the E.E.B., they didn't even know there was a civilization on that planet. I understood the need for the procedure, but at that moment, there was no time. The dark matter capacitor was a ticking time bomb. I had to make a decision in real-time to protect life. I stand by that decision."

The room was silent for a moment. The judges remained impassive, but Connor could see the faintest flicker of acknowledgment in a few of their expressions. Then, suddenly, the E.E.B. commander stood and walked over to one of the judges. He whispered something that Connor couldn't hear, and the judge nodded before the commander returned to his seat.

The judges began their deliberation, activating a force field around their desks, ensuring their discussions remained private. The room fell into an eerie quiet as they spoke among themselves, leaving Connor alone with his thoughts once more. He watched the shimmering barrier, his anxiety mounting as each minute passed.

Fifteen minutes later, the force field lowered, and one of the exoform judges, a creature with dark orange skin and reptilian features, stood to address the room.

"Pilot O'Brien, we have deliberated. There are varying opinions among this tribunal regarding your actions. One concern raised is that you denied the civilization on that planet the opportunity to evolve naturally - to discover alien life on their terms."

Another judge, this one with glowing white eyes and a soft, chiming voice, added, "However, others believe your actions, though reckless, were logical given the circumstances. You prevented a potentially catastrophic outcome by taking the capacitor."

Each judge voiced their opinion, some in support of Connor's decision, others critical. A few were harsh, calling his actions impulsive and irresponsible. Finally, they turned to Connor and asked for his closing statement.

Connor took a deep breath, standing as he gathered his thoughts. "Your Honors, I never intended for any of this to happen.

I acted because lives were at stake, and I couldn't stand by and watch the situation spiral out of control. If I had the opportunity to do it over, I'd make the same decision. I did what I thought was right to save lives and protect that planet."

His voice gained strength as he continued. "I understand the importance of procedure and protocol, but sometimes, real-time decisions are necessary. I respect the principles of the MWU and I believe my actions aligned with those values. I stand here at your mercy, but I don't regret saving lives."

The room was silent as Connor sat down. The judges once again raised the force field, this time deliberating for only five minutes. When the barrier finally dropped, the central judge stood.

"We have reached a verdict. It was not unanimous, but a majority ruled in favor. Pilot O'Brien, please state the MWU's motto."

Connor stood, his heart pounding as he spoke clearly. "Unity, Diversity, Discovery."

The judge nodded. "These three principles are the foundation of the MWU. As we reviewed your actions, we considered how your decisions reflected these core values."

Another judge continued, "In terms of Unity, you showed compassion for a new species. You could have resorted to violence or taken a more aggressive approach, but you chose diplomacy first. Even when the stakes were high, you valued life above all else."

"For Diversity, you demonstrated respect for the different ways of life. You didn't immediately take the capacitor, but instead, you tried to reason with them, attempting to bridge the gap between your worlds."

Finally, the judge's voice softened. "And for Discovery, you reminded us that even with all our resources and knowledge, the galaxy is vast, and we sometimes miss things. You discovered a new civilization, and for that, the majority of this tribunal is in your favor."

The judge concluded, "Out of ten judges, eight were in favor of your actions, recognizing that you upheld the values of the MWU while responding to an overwhelming situation."

All ten judges stood. The lead judge looked down at Connor with a steady gaze. "This tribunal judges that you are hereby cleared of all charges and fully reinstated as a pilot within the MWU. This tribunal is dismissed."

Connor let out the biggest sigh of relief of his life, slumping back into his chair, barely able to contain the flood of emotions that threatened to overwhelm him. From the stands, Ambryst shot a fist into the air in celebration. Lieutenant Haase gave a small, satisfied smile, nodding her head at Connor. His friend, and some of his old academy classmates, clapped and cheered in support.

Connor caught the eye of the E.E.B. commander, who glared at him, shook his head, and stormed out of the courtroom. Connor chuckled softly, shaking his head as the concern finally left his body.

"Guess I'll have to skip sending him a thank you card," Connor muttered, cracking a grin before leaning back into his chair, grateful to be free.

As the tribunal adjourned and the crowd began to disperse, relief flooded Connor's chest, but it was quickly followed by exhaustion. He stepped down from the podium, his boots clicking against the pristine floor of the massive chamber. Before he could take another step, he was greeted by Lieutenant Haase.

She approached slowly, arms crossed—not in confrontation, but in thought. Her eyes met his, and for a beat, neither spoke.

"I owe you an apology," she said finally, her voice low but genuine. "You made the right call, even if you had to go around me to do it. I was - playing it safe. And that could've cost lives."

Connor gave a faint smile. "We both did what we thought was right. I don't envy the weight of your decisions any more than mine."

Her stern features softened. "You've got guts, O'Brien. Reckless guts, but guts all the same."

He chuckled. "I'll take that as a compliment."

Just then, Ambryst stepped in from the side, a familiar glint in his wide, amphibious eyes.

"You're lucky you're still breathing," he said, trying to maintain a stern tone, though the corners of his mouth twitched upward.

Connor stepped forward and pulled his friend into a quick embrace. "You know me: reckless, stubborn, impossible to kill."

"Still a pain in my gills," Ambryst muttered, but the warmth in his voice made it clear the friendship had weathered the storm.

Lt. Haase cleared her throat. "Actually, Connor, there's one more thing. Planetary Classification wants your input."

Connor blinked. "Mine?"

"They've agreed to let you name the planet. You were the first to make peaceful contact, and after this incident, the MWU wants to acknowledge that. Consider it a rare honor."

She glanced at her datapad, tapping in a few commands. "Please bring up the planet at coordinates: right ascension 11h 33m 21.73s, declination 50° 44' 28.27"—designation XR-317."

He looked thoughtful for a moment. "Anything is better than what it was being called. XR-317. Awful."

Haase raised an eyebrow.

"Sanctus," he said finally. "It felt—sacred. Those villagers treated that capacitor like a divine relic. They didn't need war or tech. They just needed peace. Sanctus means sanctuary."

She gave a small nod. "I'll submit it. It's a good name."

As she confirmed the submission, Haase's tone shifted slightly. "Now that you're no longer awaiting judgment, Command has your next assignment ready."

Connor blinked. "That was fast."

"We don't waste time," she said. "You'll be overseeing the return of the now-shielded capacitor to Sanctus. Diplomatic transport. We're trusting you to make it right."

Connor's eyes widened slightly, then a slow smile formed. "You're giving me my ship back?"

"Temporarily," she smirked. "Under strict protocol, and with a science team onboard to monitor planetary impact. You're not off the hook, O'Brien... but you're trusted."

He straightened, the weight of guilt finally giving way to a sense of purpose. "Then I won't let you down."

9 GUARDIAN OF ANDRONYX

Sanctus shimmered beneath the Cadmus as it broke through the upper atmosphere, the jungle canopy still veiled by thick clouds and violet mists. Connor stood at the rear bay, watching through reinforced glass as a pair of MWU drones descended gently toward the valley where the primitive village lay hidden. Suspended between them was the dark matter capacitor—now fully encased in a radiation-sealed containment shell, harmless and humming softly.

"I still think the name's a bit dramatic," Ambryst said over comms from the cockpit. "Sanctus? Really?"

Connor smirked. "It fits. A sacred place, spared by good timing and bad decisions."

The drones vanished into the fog below, and with them, any lingering weight on Connor's conscience. The capacitor was returned. The villagers were safe. The planet would remain undisturbed—observed from a distance, protected by law. He was finally ready to move on.

Before he could turn away, his comm chirped. A crisp, urgent voice came through.

"Pilot O'Brien, priority one orders just came in. A distress beacon's been activated near the Wastes of Halcyon-7. Command needs you en route immediately. Launch coordinates are already inbound. This one's classified."

Connor tapped the side of his comm and nodded to himself. "Copy that. On my way."

Heart pounding in anticipation, Connor sat in his cockpit as he approached the planet Andronyx, an important MWU colony that had come under threat. This would be Connor's third mission, but it felt like the stakes were higher than ever.

Andronyx was more than just another colony - it was a thriving hub of commerce and culture, home to both humans and a variety of alien species under MWU protection. The planet was vital for the Union, its location making it a strategic asset for trade routes and alliances. But recently, they'd received intel about an impending attack. A group of renegade ships, disillusioned with the MWU's ideals of unity, were planning to launch an assault on Andronyx. These renegades, a scattered fleet of a few dozen ships, were a frequent thorn in the Union's side. They operated outside the law, refusing to join the Union or abide by its principles.

As the Cadmus neared the planet's orbit, Connor caught sight of the rendezvous point on his radar. A cluster of MWU fighter ships was waiting, their silhouettes visible against the backdrop of Andronyx's vibrant light purple and green surface. Connor's heart raced, knowing he'd be flying with some of the best pilots the MWU had to offer. His comm buzzed to life as one of the pilots hailed him.

"Cadmus, this is Lieutenant Zara Kinara, commanding officer for this operation. Welcome to the fight," a voice crackled through his headset. Her tone was firm and confident - the voice of someone who had seen her fair share of battles.

"Copy that, Lieutenant," Connor replied, his hands steady on the controls. "I'm ready for whatever comes our way."

"Good to hear," Zara responded. "We've got reports of a fleet approaching from the outer rim of this system. Intelligence suggests they'll be here within the next hour. Our job is to protect Andronyx at all costs. No renegade gets past us."

Connor swallowed hard; his mind focused on the task ahead. He joined the formation with the other MWU fighters, his ship gliding effortlessly into position just outside the planet's orbit. From his vantage point, he could see Andronyx below - a beacon of life and civilization, completely unaware of the chaos that was about to unfold in the cold void of space above them.

As the minutes ticked by, the stress became clearer. Every pilot was on high alert, their eyes scanning the stars for any sign of the enemy. Connor's hands hovered over the controls, ready to spring into action at the first sign of trouble.

Then, it happened.

"Multiple bogeys inbound!" Lieutenant Kinara's voice rang through the comms as the radar screen lit up with blips. The renegade fleet had arrived.

Connor's heart leaped into his throat as the ships materialized from the darkness, a ragtag fleet of a few dozen vessels, most of them in rough shape. These weren't sleek, well-maintained ships like the MWU fighters - they were battered, rusted, and barely holding together. But there were enough of them to cause real damage if they broke through.

"Renegade fleet, this is Lieutenant Kinara of the MWU. You are attempting an unlawful attack on an MWU-protected planet. Stand down, or you will be destroyed."

For a few tense seconds, there was silence.

Then, a voice crackled back through the comms. "We do not recognize the authority of the MWU," the voice hissed. "Andronyx will be freed from your corrupt rule or destroyed for agreeing to join you. Your choice."

Connor gripped the controls tightly, his jaw clenched. He knew how this was going to end.

"You've made your choice," Lieutenant Kinara replied coldly. "All pilots, prepare for engagement."

Connor's ship shuddered as his weapons systems powered up, his targeting reticles locking onto the incoming ships. There was no more room for diplomacy. The renegades had chosen violence, and now the MWU pilots would defend the planet at all costs.

"Engage!" Kinara shouted, and the battle began.

Connor's fighter shot forward, his hands moving instinctively as he twisted and rolled through the chaos of battle. The stars around him lit up with the glow of energy blasts and missile trails, the silence of space punctuated by the violent collisions of ships. His HUD flashed with warnings as he narrowly avoided incoming fire, his reflexes kicking into overdrive.

The renegade ships may have been in poor condition, but they were fast and aggressive, swarming the MWU fighters with reckless abandon. Connor's targeting system locked onto one of the smaller ships, and with a squeeze of the trigger, he unleashed a volley of laser fire. The ship exploded in a ball of fire and debris, then disintegrated into the blackness of space.

"Got one," he muttered to himself, already lining up his next target.

Around him, the battle raged. MWU fighters darted between the renegades, their superior technology and skill making quick work of the disorganized enemy fleet. But for every ship they destroyed, another seemed to take its place. The renegades were determined to press their attack, no matter the cost.

"Stay focused, everyone," Kinara's voice cut through the comms. "We're thinning them out, but we can't afford to underestimate them!"

Connor weaved through the chaos, his eyes darting between the enemy ships and his radar. He saw a larger renegade vessel closing in on one of the MWU fighters, its weapons charging for a direct hit. Without thinking, Connor dove toward the ship, his fingers dancing across the controls as he fired a barrage of missiles. The missiles struck the renegade ship dead on, causing a massive explosion that sent debris scattering in all directions.

"Thanks for the assist, Cadmus," one of the MWU pilots

called out.

Connor grinned, his confidence growing with every successful strike. They were winning. Despite the initial rush of the renegades, the MWU pilots tore through them with ruthless precision. The renegades had clearly miscalculated. Faced with the Union's overwhelming response, they were now paying the price.

One by one, the renegade ships fell. Some were obliterated in fiery explosions, while others lost power and drifted aimlessly into the void. A few pilots broke formation and retreated, perhaps recognizing the futility of their attack.

"Do we pursue?" Connor asked over the comms, his ship still locked onto one of the fleeing vessels.

"Negative," Kinara replied. "Let them run. They've learned their lesson. We're not here to start a war - just to protect Andronyx. We won't gun down scared dogs running away with their tails between their legs."

A few humans chuckled into their comms, as the exoform pilots shared some confused looks, not understanding the reference.

Connor eased off the throttle, watching as the few remaining renegades disappeared into the darkness of space. The battle was over.

"Good work, everyone," Kinara said. "Andronyx is safe. Let's head back to base."

Connor took a deep breath, allowing the adrenaline to ebb away as his ship turned back toward Earth. The stars seemed a little brighter now, the sense of accomplishment settling in. They had protected the colony and proven the strength of the MWU once again.

Back on Earth, Connor disembarked from the Cadmus, his body still humming with the afterglow of battle. Lieutenant Haase met him at the hangar, her arms crossed, but this time there was no anger in her eyes - just pride.

"Well done, O'Brien," she said, her voice firm but warm. "Here at base, we were monitoring and listening in on the comms.

You've proven yourself in combat and shown dedication to the Union. You even helped other pilots out there when you were being fired upon. And because of that, I have some news for you."

Connor raised an eyebrow, curious.

"As a Pilot, First Class, you've demonstrated bravery, leadership, and courage in the line of duty. With special permission from your commanding officer, me of course, you're now eligible to lead your own squad," Haase explained, a rare smile tugging at the corners of her lips. "Congratulations, Connor. You'll have your own team. Welcome to the rank of Squad Leader."

Connor blinked, momentarily stunned. "Squad Leader? I'll have my own team?"

Haase nodded. "That's right. You'll be able to pick three pilots under your command. Your team will be known as the O'Brien Squad."

Connor's heart swelled with pride and excitement. Leading his own team? It was more than he had ever expected so early in his career. And he already knew exactly who his first pick would be. He excused himself with a proper salute to Lieutenant Haase and took off.

He found Ambryst in the pilot's lounge, sipping some strange neon-colored drink that was likely an alien specialty. The purple-skinned pilot looked up and grinned when he saw Connor approaching.

"Let me guess," Ambryst said, setting his drink down. "You're here to ask me something important. Or stupid" He laughed.

Connor chuckled. "You got me. How'd you like to join the O'Brien Squad?"

Ambryst laughed even louder, his gills fluttering. "Did you even have to ask? Of course, I'll join your squad, buddy!"

With a wide grin, Connor clapped his friend on the back. "Good. You're my first pick."

Over the next few days, Connor carefully selected two more

pilots to join his squad. He hadn't known them personally before, but both had outstanding records and came highly recommended.

The final pilot Connor chose was Threx, though he ironically went by the human name Tyler. The alien moved toward the briefing table, the overhead lights refracting off his crystalline, yellow-hued skin. His body shimmered like living quartz, each shift in posture throwing slivers of color across the wall. It was mesmerizing—alien, but grounded in a kind of restrained grace.

Connor nodded toward him. "Still don't get why you chose the name Tyler."

Tyler's second pair of arms folded across his chest while the upper ones rested casually at his sides. "Easier for your kind to pronounce than Threx'sat-Hylorian'kav."

Connor raised a brow. "Fair. But Tyler?"

"It was the name of a human soldier I respected," Tyler said. "Died saving a group of civilians during a supply raid. The name, it carries weight."

There was a pause, then Connor gestured at the shimmering facets of Tyler's forearms. "Your species always built like that? I've seen you lift cargo like it's nothing. Thought the first time was a fluke."

"We adapt to environment. Crystalline physiology. High tensile strength. Two hearts, distributed neural clusters. Efficiency evolved out of necessity."

"You ever stop sounding like a damn science journal?"

Tyler's eyes gleamed faintly—amusement, maybe. "Sometimes. When it matters."

Connor smirked. "You always that quiet in a squad?"

Tyler stepped up to the terminal and placed his palm against the clearance scanner. "Why waste words when actions speak clearly?"

Connor tilted his head. "So why even join the squad? You could've stayed with your own people."

Tyler turned slightly. "Because the galaxy doesn't fix itself.

And sometimes, silence enables ruin."

Connor watched as the scanner flashed green and the door hissed open. The Threx didn't wait for praise or acknowledgment—just stepped through like he belonged there. And honestly, he did.

As the final member of his squad confirmed their assignment, Connor felt a deep sense of fulfillment. He was a leader now and with his squad at his side, there was nothing they couldn't face.

Before they left for their next assigned mission, the four of them agreed to meet at a bar to blow off a little steam - something Connor suspected he'd be doing often with these three in the future.

10 LYSARA, THE XENO-SPECIALIST

Connor stepped into the dimly lit bar on Earth. The cool air was a welcome reprieve after the long days of training and preparation that had consumed him lately. He scanned the room, his eyes adjusting to the soft lighting that bounced off the polished wooden surfaces and the bottles lining the shelves. It wasn't an upscale place by any means, but it had a warm, cozy atmosphere—perfect for off-duty pilots and officers looking to unwind.

At a small table near the back, Ambryst sat nursing a drink that glowed faintly in the dark—one of those neon-colored concoctions he always favored. His wide, amphibious grin stretched across his face as he waved Connor over. Beside him sat a woman whose presence radiated composed strength. Her slender frame moved with effortless poise, and her lavender skin shimmered beneath the low lights, accentuating the sharp lines of her sleek uniform with a distinct X on her chest, marking her as a Xeno officer of high rank and capability. Long, dark hair framed a face that was striking—angular, elegant, and unmistakably exoform. But it was her eyes that commanded the room: twin pools of silver, luminous and unreadable, as though they held knowledge she hadn't yet chosen to share.

The contrast between her humanoid features and those

beautiful shimmering eyes made her appearance both familiar and strikingly alien, embodying the blend of unity and diversity that the MWU valued so deeply.

"Connor!" Ambryst called out, his voice bubbling with its usual energy. "I want you to meet a good friend of mine - Lysara. Figured you two should meet. Might come in handy for you in the future, considering your knack for finding trouble."

Connor chuckled, sliding into the seat across from them. "Nice to meet you, Lysara," he said, extending a hand. "Ambryst here says you're the best in the business when it comes to alien technology."

Lysara smiled warmly and shook his hand, her grip firm but gentle. "I wouldn't say the best, but I've been around long enough to know my way through a few systems."

Connor took a sip of his drink and relaxed into his chair. "So, how do you two know each other?" he asked, glancing between Ambryst and Lysara.

Ambryst grinned. "We crossed paths on a mission a while ago. I was helping with a transport job on a remote planet when the cargo ship's systems were completely fried. I thought we were stranded, but this genius here swoops in and saves the day, recalibrating the ship's engine core with nothing but a handheld device and a few scraps of wiring."

Lysara laughed softly, waving a hand dismissively. "It wasn't that impressive. The ship was old - just needed a little fine-tuning."

Connor raised an eyebrow, intrigued. "Sounds pretty impressive to me."

As the conversation drifted toward mission stories and shared laughs, Connor couldn't help but notice the ease with which Lysara fit into their dynamic. Her presence was calming, and she had a natural way of making others feel comfortable. As the evening wore on and their drinks dwindled, the conversation became more personal.

"So, Lysara," Connor began, leaning forward. "How'd you end up as one of the MWU's most sought-after Xeno Officers? I mean, alien tech isn't exactly something you stumble into."

Lysara's smile faded just a little, her silver eyes reflecting a touch of sadness as she considered the question. She set her glass down, taking a deep breath before speaking.

"It's… not exactly a simple story," she admitted, her voice soft. "I was born on Celtrix Prime, a planet known for its advanced technology. It's an aquatic world, mostly oceans with these massive floating cities. My family was part of the engineering class - brilliant minds, all of them. My father was a master engineer, and my mother specialized in communications systems."

She paused, her gaze distant. Connor and Ambryst sat quietly, giving her the space to continue.

"I grew up surrounded by technology," she continued. "From the moment I could walk, I was tinkering with anything I could get my hands on. My parents encouraged it - said I had a gift for understanding machines, especially exoform tech. But things on Celtrix Prime weren't as perfect as they seemed. There was unrest, conflict over how much influence the MWU should have on our world."

Connor listened intently, sensing the weight of the story Lysara was about to tell.

"When I was fifteen, there was an uprising," she said quietly, her voice thick with emotion. "A group of rebels opposed to the MWU tried to sabotage one of our floating cities, claiming that the Union was taking away our independence. They hacked into the city's systems and triggered a catastrophic failure. Everything began to collapse - our home, the city's infrastructure, all of it."

She paused again, her eyes glistening with unshed tears. "My parents tried to stop it, to fix the systems and stabilize the city. But it was too late. The city fell into the ocean, and they didn't make it out."

The silence that followed was heavy, the weight of her loss

pronounced. Connor felt a lump rise in his throat as he saw the pain Lysara carried beneath her calm exterior. He could feel the struggle in her voice - the burden of surviving such a tragedy.

"I was one of the few who made it out," she continued, her voice steadying. "After that, I didn't know what to do. But I knew one thing for sure - I wanted to use my skills to help others, to prevent something like that from happening again. I joined the MWU as soon as I was old enough, and I trained as a Xeno Officer, specializing in alien technology. I've been working ever since to bridge the gap between different exoform and their tech, making sure no one is left vulnerable."

Connor sat back, impressed by her resilience. Lysara had turned her pain into something powerful, using it to help others and protect those who couldn't protect themselves. He understood that kind of drive—the need to prove oneself, to ensure that no one else suffered the way he had.

"That's an incredible story," Connor said respectfully. "I'm sorry for what happened, but it sounds like you've made a real difference since then."

Lysara offered him a small, grateful smile. "It hasn't been easy, but I like to think I'm helping in my own way. The MWU has given me the resources to do that, and for that, I'm grateful." Lysara fumbled with a napkin on the table for a moment.

Connor nodded, feeling a bond forming between them. "I have a feeling I'm going to need your expertise in the future. You've got the kind of skills that can make or break a mission."

Lysara blushed slightly at the compliment, her silver eyes softening. "Well, if you ever need me, you know where to find me."

Ambryst, who had been quietly sipping his drink, suddenly chimed in with a playful grin. "Oh, he'll need you, alright. Connor's got a habit of getting into trouble he can't get out of on his own."

Connor laughed, shaking his head. "I wouldn't call it trouble - more like unforeseen complications. But yeah, Lysara, I have a feeling our paths are going to cross a lot more often."

Lysara smiled, the faint blush still lingering on her lavender skin. "I look forward to it, Connor. I'm always up for a challenge."

The three of them fell into easy conversation after that, sharing stories about their missions, their experiences, and their thoughts on the MWU. It was a calm, relaxed evening, a welcome change from the intensity of the missions that often defined their lives. Connor found himself enjoying Lysara's company more and more, not just because of her impressive skills but because of her resilience and the way she had channeled her past into something meaningful.

As the night wore on, they finished their drinks, and the conversation began to wind down. Lysara looked at Connor, her expression soft and sincere. "Thank you," she said quietly. "For listening. I don't talk about my past much, but it feels good to share it with people who understand."

Connor met her gaze, feeling the weight of her words. "Anytime. We're all in this together, after all."

Lysara smiled, her silver eyes gleaming in the dim light. Ambryst, always the jokester, couldn't help but wink at Connor with a mischievous grin. "I knew the two of you would hit it off."

Connor rolled his eyes but couldn't suppress a grin. "Always playing matchmaker, aren't you, Ambryst?"

Ambryst laughed, raising his neon-colored drink in a mock toast. "It's a gift, my friend. It's a gift."

As the three of them stood to leave, Connor felt a sense of camaraderie settling over them, a bond that would undoubtedly grow stronger as time went on. Lysara had proven herself to be more than just an expert in alien tech - she was someone Connor knew he could trust, someone who understood the weight of responsibility they all carried. And as they stepped out into the cool night air, he couldn't help but feel that this was the beginning of something important.

11 GALACTIC GRANDEUR

Connor stood at the massive docking bay on Earth, waiting for the transport shuttle that would take him to one of the MWU's greatest marvels - a Galactic Class ship! He had been on plenty of ships during his time as a pilot, from nimble fighter crafts like his Cadmus to larger freighters. But a Galactic Class ship was in a league of its own, a proverbial floating city in space that served as the heart of many MWU operations.

He had seen the images during his academy training, witnessed the schematics in briefings, and listened to stories from seasoned officers who had been aboard these giants. But nothing could truly prepare him for the sheer magnitude of seeing one in person. The Galactic Class ships were so large they couldn't be constructed on planets - gravity would tear them apart. They were built piece by piece in space, where their size had no limits.

As Connor found himself aboard the shuttle to the Galactic Class ship, his mind turned over the oddness of his current mission. His commanding officer had personally requested that he visit one of the MWU's Galactic Class ships - the MWU Vanguard - and take stock of its inner workings. It wasn't the type of order he was used to receiving. His typical missions involved action, immediate objectives, and clear reasons. This, however, was different. Haase hadn't explained much, just that he was to explore the ship, see how it functioned, and take note of its operations. It wasn't a standard reconnaissance mission or a combat drill, which left him puzzled.

Of course, Connor didn't argue. He respected Haase's authority too much to question her directly, but it still nagged at him. Why this? Why now? The request had come out of the blue, and while he was genuinely excited to see the massive Galactic Class ship up close, the vague nature of the order left him with a sense of curiosity. Was there something more to this? It wasn't that passive assignments were out of character for Haase—but he'd hoped for more by now. Connor couldn't shake the feeling that there was something she wasn't telling him, something just out of sight, waiting to be revealed.

As the shuttle approached the shipyard in orbit, Connor leaned forward in his seat, eyes wide as he caught his first glimpse of the MWU Vanguard. It hovered like a behemoth against the backdrop of space, its sleek white hull glinting under the distant light of nearby stars. Its golden accents, the hallmark of the MWU, shimmered faintly across its surface, marking it as one of the Union's crown jewels. His chest swelled with rising tension as the shuttle drew closer, the scale of the ship becoming more apparent with each passing second. It was so massive that it seemed to stretch endlessly in every direction, its size dwarfing any other ship Connor had ever seen.

The MWU Vanguard was larger than some cities, larger than Connor had even imagined. He could see the hangars built into its lower levels, the vast cargo bays, and rows of windows along its towering superstructure. Just seeing it from the shuttle sent a thrill of pride and excitement down Connor's spine. He was a part of something far greater than himself - a protector of the galaxy, even if this time he was only observing one of its most powerful vessels.

The shuttle docked smoothly in one of the hangars and the hatch opened with a soft hiss. Connor stepped out onto the gleaming metal floors, surrounded by the bustling activity of the ship's crew.

Dockworkers, engineers, and pilots moved with purpose.

"Welcome aboard the MWU Vanguard," a crew member greeted him, nodding as she handed Connor a datapad. "We're honored to have you here, Pilot O'Brien. Feel free to explore the ship during your stay. If you need anything, you can contact any of the crew through this datapad. It'll be yours as long as you are aboard the MWU Vanguard! You can also use it as a map of the ship if you ever find yourself lost. Many times, I found myself lost in this ship when I first came aboard!" She chuckled.

Connor shared a laugh and then thanked her, taking a moment to absorb his surroundings. The hangar was massive, stretching out in every direction to accommodate the multitude of smaller ships docked for maintenance or fueling. Fighter craft, shuttles and drones were neatly arranged, and Connor felt a twinge of excitement at the sight of the familiar vessels. But this was just the beginning - he had a whole ship to explore.

Connor's first stop was the Command Center, the brain of the ship. The journey up to the upper decks took him through wide corridors lined with gleaming walls, each bustling with crew members from a myriad of exoforms. The diversity of the MWU was on full display, with humans, aliens, and AI-enhanced beings working seamlessly together. It was inspiring.

When Connor entered the Command Center, his breath caught in his throat. The room was vast, with a panoramic view of space that made the stars seem like they were within arm's reach. Several officers stood at different stations, monitoring tactical screens, communication arrays, and navigation systems. In the center of the room stood the Command Chair, a raised platform from where the commander could oversee every detail of the ship's operations.

A senior officer noticed Connor's awe and smiled. "First time on a Galactic Class ship?"

Connor nodded. "It's incredible. I knew they were big, but seeing it is something else."

"You get used to it," the officer said with a chuckle. "But it never really stops being impressive. The Vanguard is one of the most advanced ships in the fleet. From here, we coordinate not just this ship, but entire planetary operations. We handle everything from diplomatic missions to deep-space combat scenarios."

Connor spent several more minutes in the Command Center, watching as orders were relayed, and tactical simulations were run. The place where decisions were made that could alter the course of entire star systems. He couldn't help but feel a surge of pride - one day, he hoped to command a ship like this.

Connor then headed toward the Med Bay, a place he rarely visited apart from the occasional routine checkup. As a pilot, it felt oddly out of step with his usual haunts, the sterile air and quiet hum of medical equipment a stark contrast to the bustling flight decks he was accustomed to. But the Med Bay aboard the MWU Vanguard differed greatly from anything he had ever seen. It was enormous and divided into various sections for different medical needs.

There were rows of sterile, brightly lit surgical stations equipped with the latest in medical technology. In one corner, Connor saw a group of doctors working with Medical Nanobots, using them to perform delicate procedures that would have been impossible with traditional tools. Across the bay, crew members were receiving routine checkups or recovering from injuries sustained during missions.

What really caught Connor's eye, though, was the Medical Research and Development Wing. Beyond its transparent walls, he could see scientists working tirelessly on new medical technologies - advancements that would not only help treat injuries but also cure diseases and improve the quality of life across the galaxy. The MWU was as much about discovery and development as it was about defense, and the Med Bay was proof of that.

After leaving the Med Bay, Connor boarded a shuttle that took him deeper into the ship, descending to the vast lower levels where the Hangar Bay and Cargo Bay were housed. Although he had briefly passed through the hangar upon docking, this was his first real tour of the massive space. The Hangar Bay was, quite frankly, mind-boggling in size. Rows upon rows of fighter craft, shuttles, and supply ships were lined up in perfect order. Engineers and mechanics busied themselves maintaining each vessel, some suspended on antigrav platforms to reach the higher parts of the ships.

Connor marveled at the sheer organization of it all. The Hangar could launch thousands of ships at a moment's notice, each one ready for battle or a mission. The Drone Dock was especially fascinating - Connor watched as a group of engineers prepped a fleet of exploration drones, their sleek, insect-like designs ready to be deployed for long-range reconnaissance.

Beyond the hangar was the Cargo Bay, a vast expanse that housed the countless supplies needed to sustain the ship's massive crew. From food and medical equipment to engineering parts and emergency rations, it functioned like a floating warehouse. Yet even here, there was no chaos—everything was cataloged, stored, and monitored with precision. Connor noticed ceiling-mounted security drones quietly hovering along their tracks, their lenses tracking movement. A pair of guards in MWU tactical gear stood near the main access terminal, casually scanning passing personnel with handheld devices. Even with his clearance, Connor's presence drew a brief glance before one of the guards gave a subtle nod, likely confirming his ID through his datapad's signal. He wasn't unwelcome—but he certainly wasn't invisible.

One of the most anticipated stops for Connor was the Engineering Bay. As he stepped into the cavernous room, he was met with the sound of machines humming, consoles beeping, and the steady rhythm of the ship's massive engines. The Inversion Displacement Drive and Dark Matter Chamber were housed here, and Connor could feel the faint vibrations from the powerful engines that allowed the Vanguard to travel faster than the speed of light.

Engineers worked fiercely, monitoring the ship's systems,

performing maintenance checks, and ensuring that everything was running smoothly. Connor approached one of the lead engineers, who gave him a quick rundown of the systems in place.

"The inversion displacement drive is the heart of this ship," the engineer explained. "It allows us to bend space-time, covering vast distances in a matter of moments. But it requires constant calibration, especially when we're traveling through unstable regions of space."

Connor nodded, fascinated by the complexity of the systems. "What about the dark matter? Isn't it dangerous to work with?"

The engineer grinned. "It's like fire - dangerous if handled wrong, but it's what powers our most advanced technology. The dark matter chamber stores and regulates its energy, making sure it doesn't destabilize. As long as we're careful, we can harness incredible amounts of power."

Connor left the Engineering Bay with a newfound respect for the crew that kept the ship running. They weren't just engineers - they were the lifeblood of the Vanguard.

The next few hours were spent wandering through the more familiar areas of the ship: the Mess Hall, where crew members gathered for meals; the Recreation Bay, which had gyms, simulators, and game rooms, even a few of the crew playing a former game of the past called Crypts and Creatures; and the Training Room, where soldiers and pilots practiced combat skills in holo-simulations.

But what truly took Connor's breath away was the Observation Deck. It was located near the top of the ship, with a transparent dome that allowed an unobstructed view of the stars. Connor stepped onto the deck, his footsteps echoing in the silence. For a moment, he was alone in the vastness of space, surrounded by nothing but planets and distant stars.

He stood there, mesmerized by the beauty of it all. The stars seemed to stretch endlessly into the distance, a reminder of how vast the universe truly was. And yet, here he was, a small part of something much larger, something that gave him purpose.

Connor felt a deep sense of pride. The MWU wasn't just a coalition of planets and varying species - it was a beacon of unity, discovery, and progress. And ships like the MWU Vanguard were at the heart of that mission, pushing the boundaries of exploration and defense.

As Connor stood mesmerized by the endless expanse of stars stretching before him, a firm pat on his back snapped him out of his reverie. He jolted slightly, spinning around to find himself face to face with an older man whose uniform bore the distinct insignia of a ship commander. It only took Connor a moment to recognize him. It was Commander Andrew Cornelius Brinson. He straightened up instinctively, transitioning from awe-struck to military discipline as he fell into formation and snapped off a crisp salute.

Commander Brinson laughed warmly, waving his hand in the air. "At ease, Pilot O'Brien. At ease. No need for that right now," he said, his voice gruff but kind. There was an undeniable presence about the man, a quiet strength and authority born from years and years of service. Connor relaxed slightly but couldn't help feeling both honored and a little nervous to be near such a legendary figure.

The Commander stood beside him, his gaze sweeping over the stars with the same admiration Connor had felt moments before. "Amazing, isn't it? I love coming here," Brinson said thoughtfully. "The galaxy is a vast place, so much more than any one person, or even one species, can comprehend. And yet, here we are, trying to bring it all together. That's what we're doing out here - helping the galaxy, one star system at a time. Not everyone's keen on that, though. You know? There are beings out there that see the MWU as a threat, who'd sooner see us wiped out than united. War, sometimes, is the only language they understand." He sighed, rubbing the back of his neck, and for the first time, Connor noticed how his stance faltered—his posture sagging with the quiet fatigue of years spent bearing the burden of command.

Connor listened intently, absorbing every word. Commander

Brinson's tone shifted slightly, becoming more personal as he continued. "I've been at this for a long time, Pilot. And in about five years or so, I'll be stepping down from my command. Time catches up with all of us, but the mission - the Union's mission - goes on. That's what's important. Doesn't matter how old I get, the mission will always be bigger than me, bigger than any one of us." The captain's eyes glimmered with wisdom and contentment as if he had made peace with the inevitable. He gave Connor a gentle smile, then glanced around the deck, almost as if he were saying goodbye to a familiar friend. "But enough of my rambling. I didn't mean to interrupt your stargazing."

""No, no! Not at all, sir," Connor said quickly, standing a little straighter. "It's an honor to meet you, Captain. I've been looking forward to it since I arrived on the Vanguard."

Brinson gave him a crooked smile. "Looking forward to meeting an old man with too many stars on his collar? You must be new."

Connor chuckled, the tension easing from his shoulders. "I figured I'd meet a legend. Didn't expect sarcasm."

"Same thing around here," Brinson said with a wink.

They shared a laugh—genuine this time—and for a moment, the stiffness between them faded. Connor recognized something in the captain's ease and humility that made the title feel earned.

A soft chime came from Commander Brinson's wrist communicator. The Commander glanced down, smiling apologetically. "Duty calls," he said with a wink, excusing himself as casually as if they'd been two old friends chatting instead of a captain and a visiting officer. Connor watched as Brinson walked away, feeling both inspired and reflective after the unexpected conversation. But before the captain left from Connor's view, he turned around and said one last thing: "Your lieutenant, Jacqueline Haase, she's one of the good ones. She asked me personally to allow you an in-depth tour of the ship. I can't say why but I presume the reasoning will be illuminated soon. If you haven't yet, I've given you clearance to check out the AI core room. I highly recommend visiting before you leave." The captain bowed his head ever so slightly and strode on toward his duties.

Connor left the observation deck, heading for the final stop on what barely scratched the surface of the massive ship: the AI Core Room. It was a restricted area, accessible only to those with high clearance—and even then, tightly monitored.

As he approached the reinforced doors, a pair of armed security officers stepped forward. One scanned his ID chip while the other ran a portable biometric reader across his wrist. The scanner beeped green. "Clearance confirmed," the officer said, nodding. "Proceed."

Connor stepped through the checkpoint, the doors hissing open to reveal a narrow corridor lined with surveillance nodes. A hovering drone fell in beside him without a word, clearly his escort for the visit.

The AI Core itself was a marvel of technology—its walls pulsed faintly with streams of encoded data, and a massive column of glowing circuitry ran from floor to ceiling. It wasn't sentient— not in the way humans were—but it could process vast amounts of data and make critical decisions at lightning speed.

As Connor stood before the towering AI Core, watching as its internal lights pulsed rhythmically, he couldn't help but feel awe. This was the future - the cutting-edge technology that allowed the MWU to thrive in a galaxy filled with challenges and dangers.

By the end of the day, Connor had seen more of the MWU Vanguard than he ever thought possible. Each section, from the Med Bay to the AI Core, had its purpose, and its place in the grand design of the ship. And yet, everything worked together seamlessly, a testament to the ingenuity and vision of the MWU and all of its inhabitants. From the humans of Earth to the farthest reaches of the known galaxy.

As he boarded the shuttle to return to his ship, Connor felt a deep sense of motivation. Seeing the Vanguard had opened his eyes to the sheer scale of the MWU's operations, to the incredible potential that lay ahead.

As the shuttle pulled away from the ship, Connor glanced back at the massive structure one last time. The MWU Vanguard hung in space, a symbol of strength, unity, and hope.

12 THE CALL OF THE VOID

The Cadmus hummed quietly beneath Connor as it glided through the dark reaches of space, the stars twinkling distantly like ancient watchers. This mission was a far cry from any other he had ever been assigned. Lieutenant Haase herself had given him the orders to venture into the Void Region - a vast, uncharted expanse where the MWU's maps ended. His orders were clear: explore, document, and survive.

Connor's pulse quickened with a mixture of excitement and nerves. The Void Region was an enigma. Few pilots had ventured into it, and fewer still had returned with more than vague readings or fragmented data. This was his first exploration mission, and the thrill of venturing into the unknown both exhilarated and unnerved him. Exploration missions were different from patrols or skirmishes. There were no clear enemies, no set goals - only discovery, or danger.

In front of him, the stars shifted lazily, far away but seemingly within reach. Around him, in their fighter ships, was his squad - his team. Ambryst, Sailor Grace, and Tyler flew close by, their voices echoing through his comms, cutting through the eerie silence of space.

"Can't believe they sent us out here. The Void's been

uncharted for who knows how long," Sailor Grace's voice crackled through. Her tone was light but carried a tinge of nervous energy.

"Yeah, the mystery's half the fun, Grace," Tyler chimed in, though his voice held a similar edge. "I mean, come on, who doesn't want to explore the unknown?"

Ambryst, always the calm one, offered a measured response. "The unknown can be beautiful, or deadly. Let's hope it's the former."

Connor's grip tightened around the controls, his heart pounding. "It's both," he said, breaking his silence, the excitement in his voice barely contained. "Look, I know this is new territory for all of us. But the Void Region? This is what we trained for. Think about it - we're part of the first MWU team to head out here. Every discovery we make will shape the future of the Union. That's what exploration is about. Not fear, but wonder."

There was a pause before Sailor Grace's voice crackled back through. "You know, O'Brien, you've got a way of making the unknown sound a lot less terrifying and a lot more intriguing."

Connor smirked. "It's what I do. Now keep your sensors sharp and your eyes open. We're flying into territory no one's ever documented. Anything could be out here."

As they flew deeper into the Void Region, the comms fell silent and the only sounds were the soft hums of their ships. Outside, space remained utterly still—cold, vast, and silent. Connor's heart raced with the possibilities. He had studied every possible outcome of deep-space exploration, from strange alien lifeforms to celestial anomalies. But nothing could have prepared him for what happened next.

The sensors on the Cadmus lit up, beeping loudly as a warning flashed across his screen. Connor's eyes widened as the data rapidly streamed in, and his heart skipped a beat.

"Guys, check your scanners," Connor ordered, his voice steady, but his mind racing.

Sailor Grace's voice followed swiftly. "I'm seeing it. A star.

It's going supernova soon. The readings are clear. Damn, that thing's ready to blow."

"It's not just going supernova," Ambryst added, his tone more grim. "I'm looking at the mass readings. This thing's well past the Tolman–Oppenheimer–Volkoff limit. After it collapses, it's going to form a black hole. A big one. Sensors estimate less than 24 hours before detonation."

Connor's stomach dropped as the gravity of the situation hit him. It wasn't unusual for MWU pilots to come across dying stars or supernovas - they were part of the natural cycle of the universe. The MWU documented these events but rarely intervened. After all, what could they do? Even the MWU's advanced technology couldn't stop a supernova or prevent the collapse of a star into a black hole.

"Alright," Connor muttered, half to himself and half to his squad. "We log it and move on. There's no stopping a supernova or a black hole."

Just as he was about to instruct his team to continue, the Cadmus' sensors flared again. This time, the readings were different. Connor leaned closer, his brows furrowed as he studied the data flashing across his screen.

"Wait a minute," he whispered, his voice tense with realization. "There are planets here. Three of them."

"Let me guess," Tyler's voice came through the comms. "They're dead worlds, right? Barren wastelands orbiting a ticking time bomb."

"Two of them, yeah," Connor said, his fingers flying over the controls. "But the third one…"

He paused, and his breath caught in his throat. The third planet wasn't lifeless. It wasn't barren at all.

"The third planet has life," Connor said, his voice tight.

"Say again?" Ambryst asked, disbelief lacing his words.

"Life. A civilization. And not just any civilization - it's like Earth was back in the 21st century. They've built cities, they've achieved light space travel, but they haven't made contact with anything outside their solar system yet. To them, they're alone in the galaxy. Scanners are detecting billions of sentient life forms on the planet!"

"I took some additional scans, sir, primarily on their race. Would you like to hear it?" Tyler said over the comms.

"Let's hear it," Connor said, eagerly awaiting the results.

"These beings, known as the Gelytherians, appear to be humanoid in form—two arms, two legs, upright stance—but they're composed of some kind of energy-based biological structure. Their outer layer gives off a bioluminescent glow, and yeah... they look pretty incredible. Sorry, sir—moving on.

According to planetary scans, their civilization is highly developed. They've achieved light-space travel within their system and have multiple lunar outposts. Economically, they operate on a tech-based system with resource sharing at the core—no signs of large-scale warfare or class-based oppression.

Culturally, they've invested heavily in the arts—broadcasts show orchestral soundscapes, kinetic sculpture gardens, and planetary storytelling rituals. Their education systems are universally accessible, and early scans show an emphasis on community development and planetary stewardship. Honestly, sir... these people matter. They've built something beautiful down there."

Connor's mind raced. The supernova would obliterate their star and the entire system, and then the black hole would devour whatever remained. Based on the planetary scans and intercepted broadcasts, it didn't seem like the Gelytherians had any clue what was coming. In less than 24 hours, their entire world would be torn apart—and unless someone intervened, they wouldn't stand a chance.

"We can't just let them die," Sailor Grace said quietly, her voice cutting through the silence. "Can we?"

Connor rubbed his temples, the memory of his last run-in with the Evolutionary Eligibility Bureau flashing through his mind.

"I've gotten in deep shit with the E.E.B. once already," he muttered. "I really don't want to go through that headache again."

But time was running out. The data was clear - this planet had less than a day before the supernova and black hole destroyed everything. The rest of the universe would continue, and the Gelytherians would be erased, leaving no trace behind.

His mind whirred with the gravity of the situation, and for a few moments, he couldn't form a plan. They were supposed to catalog the anomaly and move on, but how could he just leave billions of lives to perish? His chest clenched with the weight of the decision. He couldn't afford to act rashly, but he also couldn't ignore the ticking clock of impending doom.

The comms crackled to life, breaking the tense silence. "What do we do, Sir?" Ambryst's voice came through, calm but expectant.

Connor didn't have an answer. Not yet.

The silence of space pressed against Connor as he hovered above the unknown planet, his thoughts racing. Ambryst's question still hung in the air, echoing through his mind like a distant bell. The vastness of space outside the canopy of his ship only added to the weight of the decision at hand, an impending crisis that no training could have fully prepared him for.

Connor gave his head a sharp shake, snapping himself back into the moment. He was the leader now - he had to be decisive. "Alright, team," he said firmly, his voice cutting through the eerie silence. "We've got to come up with a plan."

The atmosphere within the squad immediately shifted, his words grounding them all in the reality of the situation. Connor's mind raced with possibilities, but one thing was clear: he couldn't risk repeating the mistakes he had made in the past. His last run-in with the Evolutionary Eligibility Bureau had taught him that, if nothing else, they didn't like surprises. At the very least, he needed to report the situation before acting.

"Patch me through to Lieutenant Haase," Connor ordered,

his voice steady. "And get an officer from the E.E.B. on the line too. They need to hear this."

Within moments, the communication channels were open, and Connor relayed the situation. He detailed the impending supernova, the planets orbiting the star, and the fact that one of those planets housed an intelligent civilization on the brink of destruction. As he spoke, the other side of the comms remained deathly silent.

Connor could sense the silence on the other end of the comms—a stunned pause where no one dared speak. He had just reported a civilization on the brink of annihilation, and now the weight of that revelation hung heavy between them. Billions of lives were at stake, and the countdown had already begun.

Finally, Lieutenant Haase's voice cut through the silence. "Connor, I swear, if there's a disaster waiting in the farthest corner of the galaxy, you're the one who'll find it. This isn't just bad—it's catastrophic. Do you have any idea how many departments I have to wake up for this?"

Connor picked up the strain in her voice—faster than usual, her words clipped like she was barely keeping it together.

"I'm going to have to make calls, O'Brien. A lot of calls. Don't you DARE make contact with that planet yet, understand? DON'T. YOU. DARE." She emphasized each word like a hammer hitting an anvil. "You stay put, observe, and report. Am. I. Clear?"

Connor's shoulders tensed, but he knew better than to argue. "Yes, ma'am. Clear as a Crypthitosos crystal."

The E.E.B. officer chimed in next, his voice tight with anxiety. "Lieutenant, I'll need to get in touch with several departments, as well as the advisory council. We'll need to move fast, but the implications of this are substantial. I'll be back in touch as soon as possible."

The comms went dead, leaving Connor and his squad alone once again in the void. The exchange had lasted only minutes, but it felt like hours. The silence pressed down on him, thick with everything left unsaid. Below, the planet turned slowly, oblivious to the forces aligning against it. Connor tapped his wrist pad and set a personal timer—its glowing numbers counting down the hours, a cold reminder of how little time they had to change fate.

Twenty-three hours, fifty-two minutes. The clock was ticking.

"Now what?" Sailor Grace's voice came through, breaking the silence. "We just wait?"

Connor exhaled slowly, tension still coiled in his shoulders. "For now? Yes. We wait for orders."

Sailor Grace's tone shifted, becoming thoughtful. "I've been scanning the planet's surface. MWU rates them as a Tier 2 Pre-Contact civilization—orbital capability, permanent lunar colonies, but no sign of deep-space communication or contact protocols. From their public broadcasts, there's zero mention of the star's instability. Either they haven't detected it... or someone doesn't want them to know."

Connor grimaced. "That makes it even harder. We've got less than a day before they're gone. We can't just sit here and do nothing."

Tyler's voice joined the conversation, his guttural alien language automatically translated by their suits. "Even if we could save them, they're not ready for the MWU. The Evolutionary Eligibility Bureau wouldn't let them join, not in time for us to save their entire planet."

Ambryst's voice was steady, his expression unreadable. "It wouldn't be the first time something like this has happened. There are stories, you know - planets facing extinction, and the MWU choosing to intervene. Sometimes, those exoforms weren't ready either, but they were saved. They became part of the Union, even if they weren't *eligible* yet."

Connor nodded slowly, absorbing his squad's perspectives.

"I'm proud of you all," Connor said softly. "This was why having a team matters so much. Leadership wasn't just about making decisions - it was about listening to your people, valuing their input, and understanding the full scope of the situation. You're all thinking about the bigger picture. Right now, though, we can't make any assumptions about what the MWU or the E.E.B. will do. We just need to be ready."

Suddenly, the comms buzzed with a flurry of activity, dozens of voices overlapping in a chaotic stream of information. Connor could barely make sense of the cacophony, but he knew it was serious. His squad fell silent as they listened, trying to discern any clear instructions from the noise. Then, as quickly as it had begun, the comms cut out, leaving only a single voice.

"Alright, everyone quiet down," Lieutenant Haase's voice came through, clear and authoritative. "I've muted the rest of the channels for now. O'Brien, I need you to listen carefully."

Connor's blood surged as he leaned forward, focusing entirely on the incoming transmission.

"The MWU is mobilizing a massive operation," Haase began. "We're sending several Galactic Class ships and thousands of freighters your way. The plan is to land on all the major continents of the planet and start evacuating as many of their people as we can. The freighters will shuttle them to the safety of the Galactic Class ships, which can house billions of life forms. "We'll continue rotations until the last civilian is safely aboard."

Connor exhaled in relief, but Haase's next words tempered that feeling quickly.

"There's a problem, though. It's going to take approximately seventeen hours to get enough ships to the planet. That leaves us with only six to seven hours to evacuate a planet full of billions before the star goes supernova."

Connor's hands tightened around the controls, his heart pounding in his ears. The logistics of such a massive operation were staggering. There were so many things that could go wrong - panic, communication breakdowns, structural failures, and even resistance from the planet's governments. And then, there was the ticking clock. If anything delayed the operation, they would lose everything.

Lieutenant Haase's voice grew softer, but her tone was firm. "This is a long shot, O'Brien. But we have no choice. We either save them, or they're gone."

Connor leaned back in his seat, the weight of the mission settling on his shoulders. He knew countless people were listening in on the comms right now, people far above his rank. Possibly even all the way to the top of the MWU! What he said next would set the tone for the operation, and he couldn't afford to falter.

Clearing his throat, Connor spoke with a confidence that belied the nerves coursing through him. "Lieutenant Haase, esteemed members of the MWU listening in, Pilot Connor O'Brien, First Class, along with the O'Brien Squad, ready and awaiting orders. We'll do everything we can to save these people."

He could almost feel the smile on Haase's face trillions of lightyears away as she responded, "Good. Stand by for further instructions, Pilot. This is going to be one hell of a mission."

Connor closed his eyes for a brief moment, gathering himself. The weight of the galaxy pressed on him, but he was ready. Whatever came next, he and his squad would face it together.

The comms sprang to life once more, but this time it was far more organized. Connor could hear the faint murmurs of voices overlapping, occasionally rising in suspense. The gravity of the situation weighed heavily on everyone involved, and it showed in the hurried yet structured nature of the conversations. Despite the structure, there were still moments of chaos - voices overlapping, orders being questioned, logistical challenges thrown into the mix.

Among the many voices, Connor caught a familiar one. Commander Andrew Cornelius Brinson of the MWU Vanguard spoke clearly, his voice carrying the same calm authority that Connor had admired on the Observation Deck. "MWU Vanguard is ready and awaiting orders to depart for the Void Region. We're prepared to assist in the extraction."

The comms buzzed with responses. Some agreed, and others focused on the timeline. A few voices demanded immediate action, pushing for faster deployment, while others raised concerns about the timeframe for such a massive evacuation. Then, one or two dissenting voices broke through the noise, coldly stating that the planet and its people weren't ready to join the MWU and that perhaps they should face the consequences of their extinction-level event alone.

Connor's jaw clenched as he heard these words. The remarks sparked an immediate, unified outcry from others on the comms, voices rising in anger at the callous suggestion. It seemed that nearly everyone was horrified at the idea of standing by while billions of lives were lost. The notion of leaving an entire civilization to die wasn't something the MWU stood for, and the outcry was undeniable.

The comms went silent again, and Lieutenant Haase's voice came through once more, calm but firm. "O'Brien, I've taken you out of that call. We're on a private channel now, just you and your squad." Connor breathed a small sigh of relief. "I've just been given clearance to give you an extremely important task," she continued, her tone leaving no room for argument. "Someone needs to go down to that planet and talk to their leaders. They need to know what's happening, and they need to understand that without the MWU's intervention, they won't survive. You're the one for this mission, Connor. You're there, the closest, and you can speak to them and relay all of the logistics in real-time."

Connor's face soured for a brief moment; the memory of his Galactic Tribunal still fresh in his mind. He had just barely survived the consequences of first contact with an undiscovered exoform, and now here he was, being tasked with something even more daunting. But this time, things were different. This time, he had permission. The weight of the situation shifted from fear to determination, and Connor's expression transformed into a grin of readiness.

"Understood, Lieutenant. I accept the mission," he confirmed. He quickly relayed the orders to his squad, instructing them to accompany him on the ground. "Sailor Grace," Connor added, turning his attention to her, "I need you to find a centralized, highly populated area for us to land. Somewhere we can reach their leaders quickly."

Sailor hummed on the comms as she worked, scanning the planet's surface for suitable locations. After a few tense minutes, her voice crackled back through the headset. "Got it, sir. I've found a large city near the planet's equator. The population density is high, and their government buildings seem to be centered there. I'm sending the coordinates now."

The coordinates flashed across his HUD, transmitted from Grace's system. With a single gesture, Connor locked them in. A nervous flutter crept into his stomach as the Cadmus adjusted its trajectory, but he shook it off.

The squad descended through the planet's atmosphere, the city growing larger beneath them. From above, the streets looked calm—vehicles moved in orderly patterns, and citizens filled public squares and walkways, seemingly unaware of the catastrophe looming beyond their sky.

Connor and his squad disembarked from their ships, standing united as they awaited the arrival of the planet's local authorities. After about 35 minutes, they were met with an armed force - guards wielding what appeared to be stun or lethal weapons, holding the squad at a distance, clearly on edge.

Connor held his ground, steady and alert as the guards kept their weapons trained on him and his squad. Though their features were alien—shifting skin and fluid, unreadable faces—their posture and movements made one thing clear: they were on edge.

Then, a shift in the crowd. Twelve figures emerged, moving with slow precision through the gathering. Their presence alone parted the citizens. Each wore intricately layered robes in vibrant hues, patterns woven with shimmering threads that caught the ambient light. Decorative sashes and metallic crests adorned their chests, each symbol subtly different—likely markers of rank or societal role.

The surrounding civilians dropped to one knee as the twelve approached, heads bowed in reverence. Even without understanding the language, the signs of respect were unmistakable. These weren't soldiers or politicians. These were leaders.

One of the leaders stepped forward and spoke with a clarity that cut through the murmuring crowd. "Who are you, and what is your purpose here?"

Connor swallowed hard, momentarily choking on his breath as he tried to find the right words. This was the moment - everything hinged on how he handled this first interaction. After a deep breath, he straightened himself and spoke. "We are part of an intergalactic organization called the MWU. It is a cooperation of thousands of species across the galaxy, working together to explore, protect, and unite. The Union has pooled our collective resources, technology, and knowledge of the universe to help others - species like yours."

The leaders exchanged glances, their expressions unreadable. Murmurs spread through the group as they deliberated among themselves. After a moment, they turned back to Connor, their voices low but clear. "Why are you here?"

Connor's mouth went dry, and for a brief moment, the weight of their impending fate hit him like a freight train. He lowered his head, shaking it in frustration at the impossible task of delivering such news. But there was no time for hesitation. He snapped back into focus, his voice steady as he addressed the leaders.

"Your star is about to go supernova," he said, his tone grim but direct. "Your planet has less than 23 hours before it's destroyed."

Gasps and murmurs rippled through the crowd, but the leaders remained unmoved. The city's broadcast networks had already picked up on Connor's message, and within moments, alerts flashed across screens and public terminals. Fear spread fast. Clusters of citizens surged through the streets—some panicking, others shouting in confusion—as small riots began to break out. Connor raised his hands, his voice rising above the growing unrest.

"Listen!" he shouted. "We have a plan. The MWU is sending ships - thousands of ships - to evacuate your people. We will ferry you to safety, and once you are secure, we will find a suitable planet for your civilization to rebuild."

The panic subsided somewhat after a time, though the pressure in the air was still heavy. But what struck Connor most was the lack of reaction from the leaders. They didn't seem surprised. They didn't even look concerned.

Connor's brows furrowed in suspicion, and he asked them directly. "You already knew, didn't you?"

The leaders exchanged a brief glance, their faces betraying little emotion. "Yes," one of them finally said, their voice calm, almost detached. "We have known for some time. But we chose not to inform the public. Panic would have only made things worse. We believed it was better to allow them to go peacefully, without fear."

The crowd's reaction was instant. The quiet fear in their faces twisted into anger and betrayal as the realization sank in. Their leaders had known all along and had done nothing. The air was filled with their alien language, buzzing angrily, with accusations flying toward their government.

Connor didn't have time to intervene. He couldn't afford to get involved in this planet's internal affairs. His mission was to save lives, and that was what he intended to do.

Taking a step forward, Connor addressed the crowd once more. "Gather your families, your children. Leave behind what you can't carry - your lives are more important than your possessions. Our ships will be here in sixteen hours to begin evacuating the planet. I am uploading zones to your world leaders and broadcasting stations where you can all wait to be safely transported away from the planet. But please, you need to hurry, especially if you live far from these evacuation points!"

The crowd, still angry but now with a renewed sense of purpose, began to disperse. Connor watched as the masses rushed to gather their loved ones, preparing for the journeys to the nearest evacuation sites.

All twelve leaders approached Connor once more, their faces more solemn now. They bowed their heads deeply in a gesture of respect and gratitude. The one who had spoken earlier stepped forward again, only offering three simple, sincere words.

"Truly, thank you."

The planet's surface was a whirlwind of activity as countless alien residents rushed to designated zones, desperate to secure their place on one of the thousands of freighters coming to save them. The MWU had dispatched an armada of ships, a massive, coordinated effort to evacuate as many of the planet's people as possible before the impending supernova. The hours passed by in a blur of motion, as Connor and his squad threw themselves into the effort, assisting the inhabitants as they packed and gathered their families. The atmosphere was charged with both hope and desperation.

Connor's boots sank into the alien soil as he carried another resident—an older being too frail to walk—toward the ferry zone. He had lost count of how many he'd helped, but the number had to be close to seventy. Around him, his squad moved from group to group, aiding the young, the weak, the wounded. No one was being turned away—not yet. But Connor couldn't help but wonder: if time ran out, would that change? Would the Gelytherians—or the MWU—start choosing who boarded first? And if so… what would that say about them?

The planet's atmosphere hummed with an overwhelming sense of urgency. Entire families rushed past, clutching children and carrying what few possessions they could. The mood was somber, with the only sound of the occasional sobs or cries of fear from the younger residents.

And then, the moment arrived.

A thunderous roar filled the air, reverberating across the entire planet like the sound of a thousand explosions in unison. Connor and his squad looked to the sky just in time to see hundreds—no, thousands—of MWU ships dropping out of warp in the upper atmosphere. Freighters and shuttles descended in perfect synchronization, their engines burning brightly against the darkening sky. Above them, the enormous Galactic Class ships hovered just beyond orbit, barely visible but casting an imposing presence across the heavens. The planet trembled beneath the force of the arrival, and Connor couldn't help but feel a surge of pride as the MWU's rescue operation unfolded before him.

One after another, the freighters touched down in their designated landing spots, their ramps extending to welcome the flood of people rushing toward them. From his vantage point, Connor could see the tears streaming down the faces of the Gelytherians as they realized that salvation had finally come. The scene was both chaotic and beautiful, a symphony of hope amid the impending doom.

For the next several hours, Connor and his squad pushed themselves to the limit. They, along with the MWU rescue teams, did nothing but load, unload, and repeat. The freighters came in waves, ferrying the Gelytherian residents up into space, where the Galactic Class ships awaited them in orbit. The enormity of the task was staggering—billions of lives to evacuate in mere hours—but the MWU moved with remarkable coordination. There were glitches, miscommunications, and moments of chaos, but every crew adapted fast, and the operation surged forward with unwavering momentum.

As the final freighters began to load the last of the residents, the planet's sun began to shift. What had once been a brilliant star, not unlike Earth's sun, now flickered and pulsed with erratic bursts of light. Its surface surged with unstable energy, growing dimmer, then flaring blindingly bright in rapid succession. The change was undeniable, and the fear it ignited in the local population was immediate. Across the planet, people stopped in their tracks, staring upward at their dying sun, their expressions etched with horror and sorrow.

For those in the MWU, the sight was haunting but not unfamiliar. They had witnessed supernovas before and seen the destruction that followed. Still, even the most seasoned officers aboard the freighters and Galactic Class ships hesitated for a moment as they watched the star reach the point of no return. For Connor, the sight was enough to send a chill down his spine, a reminder of just how fragile life in the universe could be.

With the final group of residents safely aboard the freighters, the ships began their ascent into space, leaving the planet's surface behind. Connor and his squad were the last to leave, ensuring that no one was left behind in their area. As the Cadmus lifted off, Connor felt a mix of relief and sadness. They had saved billions, but more than likely not everyone.

The MWU had calculated that they had rescued at least 97.632% of the planet's sentient population - an impressive number, but not perfect. Less than three percent of the population had been lost, either hidden too deep in the planet's wilderness or too far from the evacuation zones to be reached in time. Connor knew it wasn't possible to save everyone, but that didn't stop the bitter taste of defeat from lingering in his mouth.

The final freighters docked with the Galactic Class ships, and the MWU fleet retreated to a calculated safe distance, far enough away to watch the star's explosion without being in harm's way. The majority of the Gelytherians, now safe aboard the massive ships, had one final request: they wanted to watch. They wanted to witness the destruction of their home planet, to see the end of what they had once known.

The Galactic Class ships, including the MWU Vanguard, held their positions, allowing the inhabitants to gather at the respective observation decks. And then, the moment they had dreaded finally arrived. The star, now swollen and unstable, erupted in a cataclysmic explosion. The supernova sent out a shockwave of brilliant light, so bright that even from this distance, it would have blinded the onlookers had the MWU ships not been equipped with protective shields.

The explosion was both beautiful and terrible, a swirling

mass of fiery energy that consumed everything in its path. The residents watched in stunned silence as their planet was torn apart, the pieces of their once-thriving world flung into the void of space. For many, the sight was too much to bear, and tears flowed freely as they mourned the loss of their home. In just a few short minutes, the planet they had known all their lives was gone - obliterated by the power of the supernova.

But the destruction didn't end there. Just as MWU scientists had warned, the star's core collapsed almost instantly, forming a massive black hole. A ripple of distortion pulsed outward as space itself bent in on the collapsing core. What remained of the planet and its surrounding solar system was drawn into the void, stretched and devoured by the gravitational pull, until there was nothing left. There was no sound, only stillness—the aftermath felt impossibly quiet. The residents, the MWU officers, even Connor himself, could only watch in stunned silence as the black hole consumed everything, leaving behind the cold, hollow vastness of space.

Onboard the MWU Vanguard, Connor stood in the observation deck, a young Gelytherian child gripping his hand tightly. The child sobbed quietly, clinging to Connor as though he were the last connection to their lost world. Connor knelt and hugged the child gently, offering what little comfort he could in the face of such overwhelming loss.

A soft pat on his shoulder drew Connor's attention, and he turned to see Commander Andrew Cornelius Brinson standing beside him. The commander gave Connor a gentle smile, his voice low and calm. "This kind of thing - it doesn't just affect these poor people," Brinson said quietly. "It can, and it will, affect you, too."

Connor nodded; his throat tight with emotion. He knew the captain was right. The weight of this mission, the loss of an entire world, would stay with him forever.

Commander Brinson looked out at the stars; his expression thoughtful. "They will rebuild," he said, waving a hand toward the grieving aliens. "They will regain what they've lost. And it'll be us

- the MWU - who will help them along the way." He turned to Connor, his gaze steady. "And we'll be there to help them. You'll be there, O'Brien."

Connor nodded once more, finding comfort in the captain's words. As the engines of the MWU Vanguard hummed to life, preparing to take them away from this place of loss, Connor looked out into the vast expanse of space. He didn't know what the future held for these people, but he knew one thing for certain: the MWU would stand by them, just as they had stood by countless other exoforms across the galaxy.

13 THE GELYTHERIAN ACCORD

Back on Earth once more, Connor began feeling the weight of the past few days settle into his bones. The mass exodus of the Gelytherians was still fresh in his mind - the frantic rush, the fear, and ultimately, the bittersweet triumph of saving countless lives from annihilation. Now, he and his squad were in a strange limbo, waiting for command to give them word on the fate of the Gelytherians.

Ambryst, Sailor Grace, and Tyler stood with him, quietly exchanging words as they waited near the large bay overlooking Earth's lush landscape. The stillness around them was a stark contrast to the chaos they had just left behind. The emptiness of the waiting gnawed at Connor, leaving too much space for his thoughts to wander. The mission had been a success, but what came next for the Gelytherians? Would the MWU find them a new home, or would the bureaucratic machine drag its feet?

As Connor waited to hear from the higher-ups about what the MWU would decide regarding the Gelytherians, a fresh recruit from the MWU Academy approached him.

Connor stood near the debriefing chamber's entrance, arms crossed, trying to tune out the buzz of conversation echoing through the hallway. He was still waiting for word from the higher-ups on the Gelytherians, but his thoughts were interrupted by the sudden presence of someone at his side.

"Sir? Are you Connor O'Brien?"

Connor turned, eyebrows slightly raised. The voice belonged to a young recruit—clean uniform, stiff posture, eyes lit with that mix of anxiety and admiration he remembered all too well. The recruit offered a sharp salute.

"Cadet Arlen Bryce," the kid said. "I've been temporarily assigned to your unit for observational training. Just got cleared to shadow First-Class operatives. It's an honor, sir."

Connor blinked, then gave a small nod. "You've got guts introducing yourself before I ask. That's either brave or foolish."

Arlen grinned nervously. "I've heard about what you did on the Gelytherian mission. Honestly, sir... I don't understand how it all works. Not just the missions, but the MWU itself. The structure. The layers. I've studied it, sure, but it's all... charts and holo-texts. No one ever explains how it feels from inside."

That made Connor pause. He remembered being in Arlen's boots—buried in theory, but unsure how it all fit together in the field. With a sigh, he leaned back against the nearest wall console.

"Alright, rookie. Let's keep it simple, or we'll be here all cycle," Connor said. "The MWU's massive. We're talking thousands of exoforms, millions of personnel, and entire galactic sectors under its reach. It only works because every piece of it fits into a larger system—command, departments, oversight. That structure is what holds the galaxy together."

He gestured to Arlen's insignia. "You're starting in the military branch, same as me. That part's easy—chain of command, mission orders, combat protocols. Commanders run Galactic Class ships—floating cities with enough firepower to vaporize moons. They answer only to the Supreme Chancellors. Everyone below them follows a line of authority that doesn't bend unless it's burned."

Arlen nodded. "And the rest of the MWU? The non-military

parts?"

"That's where most rookies get lost," Connor said. "There's the Administrative Sector—people who handle logistics, resources, crew deployments. Then you've got the Departments and Bureaus. Each one has a specific job—like the Evolutionary Eligibility Bureau? They decide if an exoform qualifies for MWU contact or membership. The Diplomatic Bureau handles peace talks, while Quantum Research messes with faster-than-light tech."

"And the Chancellors?"

"Ten of them. Elected from every exoform in the Union. It's not about species—it's about influence and trust. They vote on major decisions. They can override military decisions, but only as a group. If one steps out of line, the Judicial Division can strip their power through a Galactic Tribunal. I've... sat through one of those. Not fun."

Arlen blinked. "You faced a Tribunal?"

"Long story," Connor muttered. "Point is: the MWU isn't perfect, but it works because every part of it is accountable to the others. That's the glue holding the galaxy together. Doesn't matter if you're a recruit or a Supreme Chancellor—you're part of something bigger."

The recruit nodded slowly, the weight of the explanation sinking in. "Thanks, sir. That... actually makes sense now."

Connor gave a tired smile. "Good. Now keep your ears open and your mouth shut until someone says otherwise. You'll do fine."

He clapped the recruit on the shoulder. "You're part of that now, too. Just remember—every job, no matter how small, fits into the bigger picture. Focus on your role. Trust the system. And if you're anything like I was when I started... you'll figure it out."

The recruit beamed, clearly inspired, and then waved as the recruit ran off toward a classroom. Connor felt a quiet sense of satisfaction.

Before he could linger any longer, a group of Gelytherians approached, their shimmering, multicolored skin glowing softly in

Sol's golden light. They moved with grace, their robes flowing like liquid silk as they neared the O'Brien squad. The dignitaries, clearly leaders of their people, held something in their hands—beautiful medals that glowed faintly, radiating an aura of reverence and gratitude.

The tallest among the Gelytherians stepped forward, his voice soft yet powerful as he spoke. "You have saved our people from certain doom. Words alone cannot convey our gratitude, but we offer you these - medals of honor from our people."

Connor and his squad exchanged glances as the dignitaries placed the immaculate medals around their necks. The medals were unlike anything Connor had ever seen, shimmering with multicolored light, almost alive with a gentle hum. The white cloth bands felt light and comfortable around their necks, and the glow surrounding the medals added a sense of reverence to the moment.

Ambryst was the first to break the silence, a soft chuckle escaping him as he marveled at the craftsmanship. "These are breathtaking." Sailor Grace smiled, her fingers brushing against the glowing medal while Tyler's shimmering skin seemed to resonate with the glow.

After the brief ceremony, the dignitaries offered quiet thanks before excusing themselves, summoned to a private diplomatic session with MWU leadership. Connor and his squad remained behind, still processing the magnitude of the honor. They had helped save a species—and now, their future rested in the hands of others. Somewhere deep within MWU Headquarters, the Supreme Chancellors and high-ranking officials were deliberating on whether to grant the Gelytherians official membership in the Union. All Connor and his team could do now was wait for the outcome, hoping that the voices of the rescued would be heard.

It wasn't long before Lieutenant Haase arrived, walking briskly toward them—flanked by two figures Connor hadn't expected to see together. One was the familiar scowl of the E.E.B. commander, the very officer who had once pushed to have Connor court-martialed. The other wore an official MWU uniform trimmed in black and silver, adorned with insignia even Connor recognized. This was no ordinary officer. This was a Prime Consul—one of the highest-ranking officials in the Union, known for overseeing galaxy-spanning operations from distant capitals. That someone of such stature had chosen to attend the debrief personally meant only one thing: the decision on the Gelytherians was imminent, and Connor's squad was at the heart of it.

Connor straightened up, as did his squad, unsure of what to expect. Haase, the EEB commander, and the Prime Consul exchanged words in hushed tones, discussing something too important to share just yet. Connor watched carefully, his curiosity piqued but his nerves held steady. The EEB commander's disdain for him was obvious, but the presence of the Prime Consul lent a sense of gravity to whatever decision was about to be made.

Lieutenant Haase stepped forward, her expression serious, though Connor caught a flicker of something behind her eyes— relief, maybe.

"The MWU has reached a decision," she said. "The Gelytherians won't just be relocated. They've been granted provisional membership in the Union. Effective immediately."

She let the words settle for a moment. "You and your team didn't just save a species. You brought in a new one."

Connor's heart skipped a beat. The MWU extending membership to a new exoform was no small feat. But Haase wasn't finished.

"However," she continued, "their leadership has been shattered. The previous leaders withheld the truth about their planet's impending demise, causing a crisis among their people. The Gelytherians will need to elect new leaders before they can determine if joining the MWU is in their best interest."

The weight of Haase's words settled on Connor. The future of the Gelytherians rested not only on the MWU's help but also on their ability to rebuild their leadership and their society. The first step had been taken, but the road ahead was long. And for now, Connor could only wait.

A few days had passed since the medal ceremony, held aboard the MWU Vanguard while the rescued Gelytherians remained housed on several Galactic Class ships and temporary orbital habitats. At the time, their former government had already fractured, but surviving cultural dignitaries had come forward to honor Connor's squad with symbols of gratitude on behalf of their people.

Now, with emergency elections complete, the Gelytherians had chosen new leaders—an interim council tasked with representing them in MWU deliberations. Tension hung thick in the air as representatives from across the Union gathered inside a vast conference hall aboard the central diplomatic station. Connor stood near the entrance, scanning the room filled with nearly 200 delegates—humans and aliens alike. These talks would decide more than politics. They would shape the future of an entire civilization.

Members from various divisions were present, including officials from the Departments and Bureaus Division, some higher-ups from the Executive Division, commanders from the Military Division, and countless others. This was a significant diplomatic discussion, and while Connor had not been initially permitted to attend, the Gelytherians had made it a stipulation that he be present. After all, he had been the first to warn them of their planet's impending doom.

As the discussions began, the MWU officials took turns explaining what it meant to join the MWU. Each representative from the different divisions laid out responsibilities, benefits, and even potential downsides. One of the heads of the Interstellar Trade and Commerce Bureau spoke about the economic opportunities and trade benefits that the Gelytherians would gain. The head of the Intergalactic Wildlife Conservation Division assured them that any surviving exoform from their homeworld—flora, fauna, and environmental data—would be protected under MWU conservation protocols, with resources allocated to help recreate and preserve their native ecosystems on a new world.

But then came the delicate subject of risk.

A high-ranking officer from the Diplomatic Relations Council cleared his throat and stepped forward to address the Gelytherian leaders. "It is important to note that while the MWU offers vast resources, alliances, and protections, not all exoforms view the Union favorably. Some believe that our unity and structure threaten their autonomy. While membership is voluntary, joining the MWU can draw unwanted attention. There are factions in the galaxy who see our members as enemies."

The room fell silent as the weight of his words settled over the Gelytherian leaders. They exchanged glances, clearly understanding the gravity of the decision before them. After a moment, one of the Gelytherians, their skin shimmering slightly more brightly than the others, stepped forward to ask a few key questions. Their voices were calm, but the inquiries were sharp.

One of the Gelytherian leaders, robed in deep violet, stepped forward. Their voice echoed calmly through the chamber, translated in real time by MWU tech.

"How will our people be integrated into the MWU? What rights and responsibilities will we hold during this transition?"

A woman from the Department of Cultural Integration stood. Her uniform bore the golden trim of a Sector Director.

"Each new member exoform enters under a ten-year adjustment charter. During that time, your people will retain full self-governance over cultural, educational, and linguistic practices. MWU integration teams will assist with infrastructure, healthcare, and legal protections—but your customs will remain your own. No forced assimilation. Ever."

Another Gelytherian, younger in appearance and wearing a sash marked with spiraling starlight, raised their voice next.

"And what of our identity? Will our history, our beliefs, be recorded or erased? In joining your Union, do we risk becoming a footnote?"

This time, the response came from the Archivist General of the Historical Preservation Bureau.

"Your cultural records—oral, visual, spiritual—will be digitally archived by your own historians, not ours. The MWU guarantees full recognition of your history and sovereignty within our records. We do not erase the past. We preserve it."

A third question followed, sharper in tone.

"What happens if we disagree with the Union? If we find ourselves unaligned with your decisions?"

The Prime Consul stood for this one, her presence quiet but commanding.

"Then you debate, you vote, and you dissent—just as any member world does. No exoform is forced to comply with every directive. But democracy only functions when voices are raised within the system. Should you ever choose to leave, the MWU does not imprison. It negotiates."

A pause. Then came the question that shifted the mood.

"And if we refuse membership?"

The room tensed.

The Prime Consul didn't hesitate.

"Then you remain sovereign. No member species is forced into alliance. However, MWU protection will only extend so far. You would be designated as a Neutral Observing Species. You may not vote. You may not trade in secured MWU sectors. Your children, if born within MWU territory, would not be citizens unless they apply. And you would have no legal standing under our charter if conflict arises."

A hush settled across the chamber. Even Connor, watching from the side, could feel the weight of it. This wasn't coercion—but it wasn't comfort either.

Then came a question no one expected. One of the Gelytherian leaders turned directly toward Connor. "Tell us," they said, their voice steady and clear.

Like most Gelytherians, the speaker presented no distinguishable gender. Their people used neutral pronouns as a cultural norm, a reflection of their fluid, celestial form.

"Why should we join the MWU?"

Connor's heart nearly stopped. The room went dead silent, all eyes turning to him. He swallowed hard, feeling the weight of the question press down on him. His mind raced. Why were they asking him? He was just a pilot, not a diplomat, not an official who could speak for the entire Union. Surely, the others in the room - those with far more experience and authority - should answer this question. He shifted uncomfortably before finally speaking.

"Honestly," Connor began, his voice steady but quiet, "I think you should consult with the officials in this room. I'm just a pilot in the Military Division. My opinions - they shouldn't dictate your future as a whole."

The Gelytherians, however, seemed unimpressed by his humility. "Perhaps," one of them said, a gentle smile on their face, "but you were the first to warn us of our planet's demise. Whether you or anyone else in this grand room likes it or not, we value your opinion. So please, share it."

Connor glanced around the room, his fingers brushing the edge of the Gelytherian medallion still pinned to his uniform. The polished metal caught the light, a silent reminder of the lives he and his squad had helped save. He noticed the stares—some curious, others cold. A few of the higher-ups were visibly displeased with the attention he was receiving, their expressions tight with irritation. Nevertheless, he swallowed his nerves, took a deep breath, and began to speak.

"I haven't served in the MWU for long," Connor began, his voice steady, "but in that time, I've seen firsthand the good it can do. The Union offers protection, resources, and a chance to be part of something larger than yourselves. You gain allies—thousands of exoforms working together for peace and progress. But..." He paused, letting the weight of the next words settle. "As was mentioned earlier, you'll also gain enemies. Some see the MWU as a threat to their freedom. If you join, you'll have to face that reality, too."

He paused, ensuring the Gelytherians had absorbed the full weight of his words. "That said," Connor continued, "I believe the good outweighs the bad. The opportunities for growth, protection, and cooperation far surpass the risks. And, in the end, it's about choosing what kind of future you want for your people. The MWU isn't perfect, but it's a place where you'll have allies—and you won't face threats like the one that nearly destroyed your world alone."

Connor's words hung in the air for a moment, the room still as the Gelytherians quietly considered his remarks. He could feel the sweat building on his brow as he scanned the room, noticing the wide range of reactions from his superiors - some appeared neutral, while others barely hid their displeasure.

Finally, the Gelytherians huddled together, forming a gravity bubble that encased them in silence. Inside, they spoke privately, deliberating their decision. The bubble shimmered, glowing faintly as the leaders conferred in complete secrecy. After what felt like an eternity, the bubble dissipated, and the Gelytherians stepped forward to face the MWU officials once again.

"We have made our decision," the leader said, their voice calm yet resolute. "We will join the MWU."

The silence cracked—first with whispers, then with scattered applause. A few of the MWU delegates began to rise, their hands coming together in measured but sincere approval. Others murmured quietly, less enthusiastic, their faces tight with political caution. Somewhere near the back, Connor spotted Tyler clapping with both hands and one elbow, grinning like he knew this was coming. Sailor Grace gave a slow, deliberate nod, and Ambryst's expression, though unreadable, carried the faintest glint of approval.

As the applause settled and the crowd dispersed into diplomatic murmurs and movement, Connor noticed Ambryst hadn't moved. He was still standing at the edge of the chamber, facing the Gelytherians' delegation—not with tension, but with something quieter.

"You okay?" Connor asked as he approached, lowering his voice.

Ambryst blinked slowly. "They reminded me of us. Back when the ocean still belonged to us."

"You mean your homeworld?"

"A long time ago," Ambryst said. "Before the mining fleets came. Before the waters were drained to feed offworld factories." He paused. "We had a vote, too. To join the MWU. We thought we would be protected."

Connor tilted his head. "You don't think you are?"

Ambryst gave a soft, dry laugh. "I think we are tolerated. Respected, even. But protected? That depends on how useful we remain."

There was no anger in his voice, just memory—saltwater and silence lingering behind every word.

"You believe the Gelytherians made a mistake?" Connor asked.

Ambryst finally looked away from the delegation. "No. I believe they made a choice with hope still in their hearts. And I envy them for it."

Connor exhaled slowly, the tension that had coiled in his chest beginning to ease. The moment hadn't solved everything—but it had landed.

With the Gelytherians' decision to join the MWU now official, the nature of their relocation shifted. What had begun as an emergency humanitarian effort now became a formal resettlement of a member species. The MWU had already identified several viable planets capable of sustaining the Gelytherians' unique biology and culture. Now, planning moved into high gear. Leaders from both sides met in earnest to coordinate transportation, establish infrastructure, and lay the foundations for a new world the

Gelytherians could call home—not as refugees, but as citizens of the Union.

The MWU representatives assured the Gelytherian leaders that the Union would bear the cost of their relocation and the initial setup of their new civilization. One of the officials, an administrator from the Planetary Terraforming and Development Agency, explained how they would terraform parts of the planet to suit the Gelytherians' needs and provide resources to help them thrive in their new home.

Another official from the Cultural Preservation Bureau emphasized that the MWU would work to ensure that their culture, traditions, and way of life would be respected and integrated into their new environment. The Gelytherian leaders, visibly relieved, expressed their gratitude for the MWU's commitment.

"You will not be abandoned," one of the senior administrators reassured them. "The MWU is a collective of thousands of exoforms, working together to protect and uplift one another. You will receive all the assistance needed to ensure your people not only survive but thrive."

Logistics were also discussed: fleets of transport ships, building materials, and the setting up of agricultural and industrial zones on the new planet. The MWU also confirmed they would encourage the Gelytherians to participate in the Union's various divisions, offering them positions in fields such as science, diplomacy, defense, and administration, should they choose to contribute.

Connor sat quietly in the corner, overhearing all of this as the talks continued. These were the nuts and bolts of joining the MWU - necessary discussions about infrastructure, rebuilding, and long-term survival. Though crucial, these boilerplate talks left Connor feeling slightly detached. His mind wandered until he noticed Lieutenant Haase signaling him to leave the room.

He quietly slipped out into the hallway, his boots making soft echoes against the metal floor. As he exited the large room, he spotted Lieutenant Haase standing with a figure he immediately recognized—Commander Edward Martin of the E.E.B., the very man who had once pushed for Connor's court-martial.

"Commander Martin," Haase said, her tone unreadable. "You remember Pilot Connor O'Brien."

Martin gave him a sharp nod. "Unfortunately, yes."

The tall, imposing figure of Commander Martin glared down at Connor. His eyes, sharp and cold, bore into him with clear disdain. Without so much as a greeting, Martin voiced his grievances.

"You've made quite the reputation for yourself, O'Brien," Martin began, his voice icy. "Recklessness. Disregard for procedure. An inability to follow proper clearances or regulations." His words were cutting, dripping with contempt.

Connor stood there, unsure whether to respond or remain silent. Before he could decide, Martin shifted his gaze to Haase, completely ignoring Connor as though he wasn't even present. The commander continued speaking directly to her, outlining matters that were inconsequential to Connor and his squad - administrative updates and procedural reviews.

Connor couldn't help but feel a mixture of frustration and amusement. The only thing this guy had said to him was to berate him, then promptly disregarded him. Typical, he thought.

As the conversation between Lieutenant Haase and Commander Martin came to a close, Martin threw one last sneer in Connor's direction before turning on his heel and marching down the corridor. His presence left an uncomfortable tension in the air.

Lieutenant Haase sighed and turned to face Connor. "Don't mind him, Connor," she said, offering a small smile. "Martin's - well, he's always been like that."

Connor nodded, unsure of what else to say. Haase's expression softened as she glanced at the glowing medal still hanging around his neck, a symbol of the Gelytherians' gratitude for his role in saving their people.

"You did well," she remarked, extending her hand for a

handshake. "Luck and skill, O'Brien. That's what got us here."

Connor smiled, her compliment sending a surge of pride through him. He eagerly shook her hand, feeling the warmth of her gesture. They exchanged a brief, knowing glance - a shared understanding of just how far they had come and how close they had been to disaster.

14 ROGUE PLANET

After spending a good amount of time grounded, Connor and his squad were itching to get back out into the vastness of space. The idle time on Earth had them restless, and the thrill of being on another mission, another adventure, beckoned to them. The stars called to them, and they were ready to answer.

Their next mission was covert, assigned directly by Lieutenant Haase: to locate and apprehend a dangerous alien fugitive hiding out on a rogue planet. According to the intel, this remote and desolate planet was a known hideout for criminals who sought to evade the grasp of the MWU's law enforcement. The mission was classified and would test Connor's leadership and his squad's teamwork to the limit.

The mission briefing had been short. The rogue planet was uninhabited, its surface desolate—marked only by jagged caves, towering mountains, endless deserts, and frozen polar caps. There was no known flora or fauna to speak of, and certainly no sentient life native to it. Still, their intel suggested the planet was currently harboring several alien fugitives. The main target was a notorious alien gang leader who had eluded capture for years. What concerned Connor most wasn't the remote location or even the cold emptiness of the planet - it was the company the fugitive was keeping. Their data showed nearly twenty sentient life forms, all armed and dangerous, residing there as well.

As the Cadmus and the other fighter ships in the O'Brien Squad dropped out of warp speed, the rogue planet came into view. It was a bleak, dead world, hanging in the void with no atmosphere to speak of. The planet's surface was rugged, rocky, and mostly void of any signs of life except for the scattered heat signatures their ships' scanners picked up. These signatures weren't natural - they belonged to the gang.

Connor's comms buzzed to life. "Ready when you are, sir," Ambryst said—his steady tone a clear reminder of the experience he'd earned over the years.

Sailor Grace and Tyler both confirmed they were ready for deployment as well. Connor nodded to himself; his mind focused on the mission ahead.

Grace's voice had come through clear, steady. But behind that calm professionalism was a mind always calculating. Connor had noticed it—how she gripped the edge of her seat for a fraction longer before launch, or how her eyes flicked toward the stars like she was reading them. Sailor wasn't just a pilot. She was raised on windstorms and orbital debris, on a station where every breath was filtered and recycled. She didn't trust open skies. Space, she said once, was only safe when it had walls. Maybe that was why she flew so smooth—because in the cockpit, she controlled the chaos.

"Let's make this quick," Connor replied with determination and excitement. "We've got the intel. We know where they are. Let's stay sharp, execute the plan, and get out of here."

They descended towards the surface of the planet, their ships navigating through the sparse atmosphere with precision. As soon as they landed, the desolate landscape stretched out before them. The heat signatures weren't far, hiding in a cluster of caves near one of the larger mountain ranges. The terrain was jagged, with sharp rocks and uneven ground, but nothing too difficult for their well-equipped squad.

As they advanced, their scanners pinged with activity. "Got movement up ahead," Sailor Grace reported, calm but alert.

Connor led the squad toward the caves, cautiously approaching the entrance. The silence of the planet was eerie - no wind, no rustle of life, just the sound of their breathing through their comms.

They entered the cave system, weapons drawn, scanners sweeping for any sign of movement. The deeper they went, the clearer the heat signatures appeared on their HUDs. Their targets were definitely inside—and it wasn't just the main fugitive. They were dealing with an entire gang.

Suddenly, a flicker of light broke the darkness of the cave— followed by the sharp hiss of something slicing through the air. The cave's thin atmosphere carried the sound just enough for Connor to react. Instinctively, he ducked, and a plasma bolt sizzled past his head, scorching the wall behind him.

"Ambush!" Connor shouted.

Blaster fire erupted in all directions as the squad took cover behind rocks and pillars. The gang members must have heard or seen them land! Plasma bolts and energy rounds filled the air as Connor and his team returned fire. The cave, previously silent and ominous, was now a chaotic battlefield.

Connor darted forward, narrowly avoiding a shot aimed at his head. He fired back, hitting one of the gang members squarely in the chest. The alien collapsed with a grunt, and the acrid scent of scorched ozone lingered in the cave's thin atmosphere.

Ambryst, as always, fought with calculated precision. He moved quickly, firing and taking down two more gang members with expert shots. But then, a loud crack echoed through the cave, and Ambryst let out a guttural shout. Connor's heart sank as he saw his friend's arm blown clean off by a high-powered plasma round.

"Ambryst!" Connor shouted, panic creeping into his voice.

"I'm fine, I'm fine!" Ambryst grunted through the comms, his voice strained but determined. His kind could regenerate limbs over time, much like the axolotl of Earth, but it didn't make losing an arm any less painful. He pressed on, using his remaining arm to keep firing.

Connor and the squad fought their way deeper into the cave. Despite being outnumbered, they used their training and superior technology to their advantage. Sailor Grace and Tyler provided cover fire as Connor advanced toward the strongest heat signature on their scanners—the one matching the gang leader's profile. Their intel had included biometric data and a partial scan, enough for the squad to identify him amid the chaos. The firefight was intense, but Connor's focus never wavered. He was determined to complete the mission.

Soon enough, they were face-to-face with their target: Korvall Dren, the notorious gang leader from the fractured desert world of Rhexor Prime—a planet that had openly rejected MWU membership for decades. Korvall, a towering, muscular alien, bristled with vicious spikes down his back and bore the snarl of someone who had nothing but contempt for the Union. His four eyes gleamed in the dim cave light as he locked eyes with Connor. Without a word, he charged.

Connor barely had time to react before the alien was on him. The two clashed in hand-to-hand combat, the leader swinging wildly as Connor blocked and countered with sharp, precise strikes. His training at the MWU Academy kicked in as he ducked, dodged, and landed blows of his own.

The gang leader struck first, launching a heavy punch that Connor narrowly ducked. The wind from the blow grazed his cheek. Connor countered with a sharp jab to the alien's side, his knuckles slamming into tough, jagged skin. The brute staggered back, snarling, and the fight truly began—brute strength against agility, rage against discipline.

The fight intensified, each move a dangerous dance of strength and skill. The brute swung again, this time with a powerful backhand meant to knock Connor off balance, but Connor anticipated the move. He rolled beneath the strike, using the momentum to sweep the alien's legs from under him. The massive outlaw crashed to the ground with a thunderous impact, but he was quick to recover, kicking up dirt as he scrambled back to his feet. Connor barely had a moment to breathe before his opponent lunged again, locking them both in a brutal grapple. The alien's immense strength threatened to overpower him, but Connor shifted his weight, using agility to break free, driving an elbow into his ribs before spinning away.

Panting heavily, Connor wiped a bead of sweat from his brow, though the inside of his helmet was already damp. The alien wasn't finished yet. Roaring with fury, he charged with both arms outstretched, aiming to crush Connor in a bear hug. Connor sidestepped at the last second, letting the brute's momentum carry him forward, then delivered a precise strike to the back of his neck. The alien dropped to his knees, dazed. Connor seized the moment, driving a swift kick into his chest and sending him sprawling.

Connor stood over him, breath ragged, muscles tense. Through the visor's tactical readout, he saw the target's vitals dip—rapid heartbeat slowing, motion subsiding. The fight was over.

The fight was brutal, but Connor wasn't alone. His squad had his back, and after a few more grueling minutes, they managed to subdue the remaining gang members and their knocked-out leader. Of the nearly 20 gang members, 13 had been killed in the firefight. Connor hadn't wanted to kill anyone, but he knew the job. It was either them or his squad, and he had chosen to protect his team.

In the end, they took seven gang members into custody. The squad used compact stasis cuffs—MWU-standard restraints that locked the prisoners into temporary paralysis, preventing resistance without harming them. With their fighter ships designed for single pilots, Connor had the squad secure the prisoners in a reinforced alcove deeper in the cave, setting up a temporary containment field from their portable deployment kits. Once the perimeter was stable,

Connor contacted the Galactic Law Enforcement Agency (GLEA), and within minutes, they had a transport ship en route to collect the detainees. The mission had been a success—but it had tested every inch of Connor's leadership and pushed his team's resolve to the edge.

As they waited for GLEA to arrive, Connor reported back to Lieutenant Haase. "Mission complete," he said, exhausted but relieved. "We've got seven in custody, and the rest - well, it's done."

"Good work, O'Brien," Haase replied over the comms, her voice firm but approving. "This one will reflect well on your squad. Get back to base once GLEA takes over."

With the mission behind them, the O'Brien Squad boarded their ships and prepared to leave the barren planet. As they lifted off, Connor glanced back at the desolate landscape below, feeling a mixture of relief and pride. They had done their job and done it well. Despite the intensity of the mission, they had come out victorious.

Ambryst, even with his arm missing, cracked a grin as they ascended back into space. "Well, that was fun."

Connor chuckled. "Fun, huh? Let's try to avoid losing limbs next time, yeah?"

The squad shared a few laughs as they left the rogue planet behind, their bond stronger than ever as they celebrated their hard-earned victory.

15 SOS

The cold, barren landscape of Torak-9 stretched endlessly before Connor as his ship, the Cadmus, drifted down through the planet's murky atmosphere. This was a Tier 4 Category X planet, a harsh and unpredictable world, known for its wild ecosystems and lack of sentient life. It wasn't a place anyone willingly visited, but when a long-range SOS signal had been picked up, its origin from a MWU ship that had gone missing nearly a decade ago, someone had to go.

Connor was used to high-stakes missions, but this one had felt strangely low-key compared to the dangerous galactic conflicts he often faced. That was why he had reassigned his squad to another mission of higher importance. In his mind, this SOS investigation would be more of a simple search and rescue, or worst-case scenario, an exploration of an old wreckage. But as the Cadmus descended toward the surface, a slight unease tugged at the back of his mind.

After setting the Cadmus down on a plateau, Connor stepped out into the air. His boots sank slightly into the soft, rocky terrain. The atmosphere here was thick, the planet's low visibility adding to the eerie feeling of isolation. The swirling winds kicked up dust that almost seemed to hum with the energy of the planet. His suit automatically adjusted to the atmospheric conditions, and Connor activated his internal HUD, scanning the area for any signs of life or wreckage.

Suddenly, a deafening roar broke the stillness of the air. Connor froze, his pulse quickening as his HUD immediately began blaring with warnings. Movement registered on the edge of his radar, something massive, approaching rapidly from the left. Connor's instincts kicked in as his heart raced. He whipped around just in time to see a behemoth alien beast charging straight toward him from behind a jagged outcropping.

The creature was colossal, standing nearly three stories tall with thick, scaly skin that glistened under the faint light of the planet's sky. Its four legs were muscular, built for speed and power, and its head was crowned with a series of bone-like protrusions that extended down its spine, giving it a terrifying silhouette. Rows of serrated teeth jutted from its gaping maw, and its eyes glowed faintly in the dim light - a predator of the highest order. Its roar vibrated the very ground beneath Connor's feet.

Without thinking, Connor bolted into action. The beast was faster than it looked, and Connor had to dodge a swiping claw that smashed into the rocky ground where he had just been standing. His breathing was quick, and adrenaline pumped through his veins as he sprinted toward the tree line in the distance. The beast was gaining on him, its heavy footfalls shaking the ground with every step. Connor's mind raced, searching for options. There was no way he could fight this thing - not alone.

As he dove into the thick of the trees, his body crashed through the underbrush. He rolled behind a large tree, panting heavily. The beast let out another guttural roar of frustration, and Connor could hear it stalking the edge of the forest, its massive form too large to maneuver through the tightly packed trees. He stayed still, his breathing shallow, praying the creature would lose interest.

Minutes passed, and finally, the sounds of the beast began to fade as it slunk back into the distance. Connor let out a shaky breath, but his relief was short-lived. In the distance, he heard a terrible sound - the metallic screeching and crunching of metal. His heart sank as he realized what the creature had found: the Cadmus.

Peeking from his hiding spot, Connor watched in horror as the behemoth tore into his beloved ship. Its claws raked across the hull with terrifying strength, leaving deep gouges in the plating. The screech of stressed metal filled the air as the creature battered the vessel, thrashing and snarling as if trying to dominate a foreign object it didn't understand. Connor could only watch helplessly as sparks flew and panels buckled, his once-pristine fighter buckling under the relentless assault.

After what felt like an eternity, the beast finally seemed satisfied with its destruction. It let out one last roar before turning and lumbering away into the distance, disappearing over the horizon. Connor cautiously emerged from the trees, approaching the wreckage of the Cadmus. His heart sank as he surveyed the damage. The ship was utterly inoperable - its engines destroyed, its hull shattered, and its communications equipment torn to shreds. He was stranded.

Connor took a deep breath, assessing his situation. He had limited supplies, no ship, and no guarantee that the Cadmus's automatic distress beacon had survived the assault or was strong enough to penetrate the planet's dense atmosphere. Torak-9 loomed around him—vast, hostile, and unforgiving—and the chances of surviving long enough for a rescue felt slim. He would have to rely on his wits, his training, and whatever sparse resources the planet had to offer.

Steeling himself, Connor knew the mission had taken a dangerous turn. His own survival was now tightly bound to completing the objective. If the distress signal they'd detected was real, there might still be survivors—or at the very least, answers. He scanned the landscape once more, the winds howling around him as the shattered remains of the Cadmus lay in ruin. With no ship and limited supplies, Connor set off into the unknown, determined to find the source of the signal before this desolate world claimed him.

16 SURVIVING TORAK-9

Connor O'Brien was no stranger to adversity, but the endless trials of Torak-9 were beginning to gnaw at his spirit. Each day seemed to bleed into the next in a harrowing battle for survival. Torak-9 was every bit as deadly as its classification - a Tier 4 Category X planet, desolate, hostile, and unforgiving. Nothing about it seemed designed for sentient life, least of all human life. It felt as though the planet itself was determined to kill him.

His wrecked ship, the Cadmus, now sat in disrepair, its metallic shell twisted and shattered after the vicious attack from the behemoth creature that had ravaged it on his first day. His once sleek, trusty spacecraft was nothing more than a crumpled shelter, offering meager protection from the planet's unrelenting environment. Every passing day, he would inspect the damage, but deep down, he knew the ship wouldn't fly again without a full repair crew and a working facility, neither of which he had the luxury of. Still, the Cadmus served as his last connection to the MWU, his only barrier from the planet's savage ecosystem. He used what remained of its systems to send out his own long-range SOS, praying it would reach someone. Anyone.

The first few nights had been the hardest. Sleep was impossible. The sounds of unfamiliar alien wildlife prowled through the darkness. Roars, screeches, and the occasional thumping of massive creatures stomping near his encampment echoed around him. His body, trained to the limits of endurance by years of service, stayed alert through it all. Connor never allowed himself to truly rest, knowing that even a moment of distraction could mean death.

He quickly realized that the food and water supplies he'd packed weren't going to last. His rations were dwindling faster than expected, a bitter reminder that he was stranded on a planet where every source of food and water could be toxic. Torak-9 had its own ecosystem, and his only chance of survival was to integrate into it somehow. Using his suit's environmental scanner, Connor painstakingly identified edible plants, algae, and water sources, all the while dodging or fending off the planet's deadly fauna.

His first encounter with one of the smaller alien predators nearly cost him his life. It had attacked at dawn - a sleek, four-legged creature with a mouth lined with serrated fangs and a tail that lashed like a whip. Its scales beamed in the sunlight, reflecting the barren, red landscape. Connor had barely been able to fend it off with a sharp metal rod he'd scavenged from the wreckage of the Cadmus. He learned quickly that here, on Torak-9, he was just another creature in the food chain.

The days passed, each one a grueling struggle to survive. His suit's power was running dangerously low, and though it provided some essential protection against the planet's harsher elements, he knew it wouldn't last forever. Every sunrise was a reminder of his isolation, of how long he had been waiting for rescue - a rescue that might never come. Yet, Connor held onto hope. His SOS beacon was still active, though he had no idea if it was reaching anyone. He even lost count of the days he was stuck on this nightmare planet.

Torak-9's landscape was no better than its wildlife. The terrain was rough, treacherous even. Jagged rocks, sprawling deserts, and towering mountains stretched endlessly in every direction. Dust storms would sweep across the horizon without warning, forcing Connor to take shelter inside the remains of the

Cadmus. He was trapped in a wasteland, his only company the alien creatures that prowled the skies and scuttled across the scorched earth.

One particularly brutal evening, after fending off yet another predator, Connor found himself leaning against the wreckage of his ship, his chest heaving with exhaustion. The sky had turned a violent shade of purple, a storm brewing on the horizon. The wind howled, kicking up dust and sand that pelted against his helmet and armor, rattling with every gust. Even with his suit sealed, the abrasive particles scratched at his visor, limiting visibility and wearing down his patience. It was on nights like this that he wondered if he would ever see another human face again. His squad, his friends, were out there somewhere—alive, continuing their missions—while he was stranded on this forsaken rock.

As Connor huddled inside the broken shell of the Cadmus, he couldn't help but replay the events that had brought him here. The original SOS signal had led him to this planet - a ship lost for nearly a decade had cried out for help, and Connor had answered. Now, ironically, he was the one waiting for someone to find him. He thought about Ambryst, Sailor Grace, and Tyler, wondering if they even suspected the kind of danger he was in. He even found himself longing to speak with Lysara again. Of all people, the Xeno Officer was on his mind in such a hellscape of a place. He even wrestled with the notion of asking her out on a date if he got off this rock.

Amid his suffering, a new thought began to surface. His scanners had detected a curious reading, something he had overlooked in the chaos of the past few days. It was faint, buried deep beneath the sand and stone, but there was no mistaking it - he was close to the crash site of the missing MWU ship! He had stumbled upon this planet chasing down that ship's distress signal, and now, despite everything, he realized that the downed ship was closer than he had thought.

Hope sparked in Connor's chest. The Cadmus was

unsalvageable, but if he could reach the wreckage of the MWU ship, there might still be a chance - a working part, a power source, or even another emergency beacon he could use to get a faster response from the MWU. It wasn't much, but it was something. He glanced at the horizon, noting the storm rolling in, and steeled himself for the trek ahead.

Connor stood, gathering his few remaining supplies. If he was going to survive, if he was going to get off this planet, he had to find that ship.

Connor's boots crunched over the jagged terrain of Torak-9 as he pressed forward, his mind set on one thing: finding that ship. His body ached from days of fighting to survive, but now a spark of hope pushed him through the exhaustion. He had ventured further from the wreckage of the Cadmus than he ever had before, trekking through desolate landscapes that felt as endless as they were lifeless. He was close. The signal had grown stronger, the faint hum of technology barely clinging to life beneath the planet's surface.

After hours of climbing, ducking, and dodging the occasional predator, Connor finally reached what he was looking for. There, half-buried in a canyon, was the wreckage of a mid-sized MWU reconnaissance vessel—larger than a fighter but much smaller than a freighter. Its hull was torn open, revealing a mangled interior rusted and weathered by years of exposure to the planet's unforgiving elements. Judging by the exterior markings and the layout, it had likely carried a crew of four to six. This was it—the ship that had sent the SOS signal nearly a decade ago.

Connor approached cautiously, pulling out his scanner to confirm. His HUD blinked with the confirmation: this was the source of the distress call. He felt a mix of relief and sadness wash over him. Whoever had been on board had long since perished, their only trace was a fading distress beacon that had summoned Connor to this hostile world.

Stepping into the wreckage, Connor immediately began searching for the ship's logs, hoping to piece together what had happened. The interior was in worse shape than he'd anticipated - parts of the ship had collapsed, and scorch marks marred the walls, likely from the attack that had brought the ship down. As he made his way deeper into the ship, the silence was eerie, save for the occasional creak of settling metal.

After a few minutes of searching, Connor found the ship's command center. The control panels were damaged, but some parts of the ship's systems were still operational. He tapped into the ship's logs, and as they flickered to life, he scanned through the data. The ship had been shot down during what appeared to be a routine survey mission. The attackers? A race he hadn't seen before.

He tapped his wrist to ask the AI database a question. "Can you identify this exoform?" Connor asked, looking at the foreign markings in the logs.

His wrist AI beeped to life, scanning the data before responding. "The exoform identified in the ship's logs is known as the Vorlax. Little is known about them in the public MWU database, but they are a hostile alien faction. Their agenda is primarily anti-MWU, and they've been implicated in several covert attacks. Intelligence reports suggest they've been preparing for open conflict for years."

Connor's jaw clenched. This was the first time he had heard of the Vorlax, but clearly, they had been causing trouble for the MWU long before he ever joined.

Continuing to sift through the logs, he found two video files - the first showing that the SOS was never pressed after the initial crash landing. The pilot hadn't pressed the emergency button. The video, instead, showed that the MWU only recently received the SOS from this ship because a small prey animal accidentally pressed it while seemingly trying to scavenge for food within the command room. This would explain why it took so long for the MWU to receive a distress signal.

The second video file was a recorded transmission from the ship's pilot. Connor hesitated for a moment before playing it. The hologram projected in front of him flickered to life, showing the final moments of the MWU officer. The pilot, bloodied and slumped against the wall of the wreckage, looked barely alive. He was muttering something, but the audio was too garbled to make out.

Then, out of the shadows, several figures emerged - alien, hulking, and menacing. They were unmistakably Vorlax. Their sharp, armor-like skin glistened in the low light, their eyes glowing faintly as they approached the dying MWU pilot. They spoke in a language Connor didn't understand, but the AI quickly translated. The words sent a chill down his spine.

"Such fools, the MWU," one of the Vorlax sneered, crouching down beside the pilot. "Your leaders are so easy to manipulate. A commander feeding us intel right from within your ranks... and you never even suspected."

Connor's blood ran cold. He replayed the words in his mind: a commander feeding the Vorlax intel? Someone within the MWU, high up enough to have valuable information, had betrayed them - betrayed their own people. A primal rhythm stirred as anger and disbelief took over. He watched as the Vorlax laughed, mocking the pilot as he gasped for breath, before leaving him to die alone.

The recording ended, the hologram fading into static, leaving Connor alone in the silence of the wreckage. He glanced down, eyes catching on the remnants the video hadn't shown—torn scraps of a MWU uniform tangled in a twisted support beam, a scorched boot half-buried in the dust. No full body remained, just the echo of someone who had died waiting for help that never came. Connor's fists clenched, a wave of fury and guilt crashing over him. This wasn't just a broken ship—it was a grave. He knelt beside the scattered remains, bowing his head for a long moment. In MWU tradition, every fallen comrade was to be remembered, and Connor silently vowed to report the pilot's name and ensure they were honored properly.

Then his jaw tightened. Someone in the Union had betrayed them. If the Vorlax had a spy inside the MWU, the danger wasn't just here—it was everywhere.

Connor took a deep breath, trying to steady his thoughts. His first instinct was to get this information back to the MWU, but without a functioning ship, he was stuck. Even if the betrayal had occurred nearly a decade ago, the implications were massive— someone had been feeding intel to the Vorlax, and that kind of treachery didn't vanish with time. He needed to find a way to transmit this data, no matter how long it took. The truth had to come to light.

17 O'BRIEN'S RESCUE

How many days had passed since Connor first crashed on Torak-9? He didn't know. His wrist AI had long since stopped counting the hours, and now his days were marked only by the rise and fall of the planet's strange, purple-tinged sun. He had scavenged every bit of the wreckage he could, barely managing to make a shelter out of what remained of the Cadmus. Each day was a new battle for survival against the hostile environment, where every step was fraught with danger - poisonous plants, predatory creatures, and a lack of any reliable food or water.

The SOS beacon he had managed to rig together after his ship was destroyed pulsed weakly into the void of space. He could only hope that someone from the MWU had picked it up and would be on their way. But days turned into what felt like years, and Connor's hope had begun to wither, much like the last few plants he had tried to use for sustenance. His body had grown weaker with each passing day, his energy sapped by the harsh environment and the lack of proper nutrition.

Connor crouched beneath the shade of a jagged cliffside, his throat parched as he tried to sip from his canteen, now filled with the faintly metallic-tasting water he had scavenged from a nearby stream. It wasn't much, and it barely did anything to quench his thirst. His thoughts wandered, bouncing between his desperation to survive and his growing doubts about his future.

Connor spoke into the silence, his voice barely above a whisper. He wasn't talking to anyone in particular - maybe to himself, or perhaps to the universe, seeking some form of comfort.

He mumbled into the silence, as if trying to reassure himself. "If this is the end… you think about your family, your friends. All the people you've helped. The ones you saved. They're what matter." He paused, letting the weight of the words settle in his chest. "I've done enough. I just hope the MWU finds me soon. And if—if I don't make it…" His voice faltered, the thought too heavy to complete. After a moment, he finished quietly, "I just hope they can at least get my body back to my family."

How long could he keep this up? His training had prepared him for extreme conditions, but nothing quite like this. Every muscle in his body screamed in protest whenever he moved, and the hunger gnawed at him constantly. He had become leaner, his normally strong frame now gaunt from the lack of food. His once sharp mind felt clouded, his thoughts sluggish as dehydration and exhaustion took their toll.

Just as he was about to give in to despair, the faintest glimmer of hope appeared on the horizon. A shadow flickered in the sky—steady, deliberate, and far too defined to be a trick of the light or a hallucination. His heart leaped into his throat as he squinted against the harsh sunlight, his vision swimming slightly from the strain.

Suddenly, the unmistakable shape of a massive ship emerged from the clouds - a MWU ship, and not just any ship. It was a Protector Class vessel, one of the largest in the Union's fleet, save a Galactic Class ship. Its colossal frame dwarfed the landscape as it descended with precision, its thrusters kicking up clouds of dust and debris as it touched down not far from Connor's makeshift shelter.

The Protector Class ships were the pride of the MWU, designed for both defense and rescue. Their shields could withstand almost anything, and they could evacuate entire cities if necessary. This one, bearing the insignia of the MWU, was a sight for sore eyes - a beacon of salvation after days of torment.

Connor scrambled to his feet, stumbling heavily as his body struggled to respond. He waved weakly toward the ship, his voice barely a rasp as he tried to call out. The hatch opened, and a group of MWU personnel hurried out, their medical uniforms bright against the barren landscape.

They reached him quickly, their faces a mixture of relief and concern as they assessed his condition. One of the medics, a young woman with kind eyes, gently placed a hand on his arm as they guided him toward the ship. A familiar face met him onboard: Lieutenant Haase herself. Connor could see her eyes were puffy, clearly she had been crying heavily recently.

"Finally! We finally found you, O'Brien. Thank God! You're safe now. We're going to get you home."

Connor barely managed to make a nod at his commanding officer's words, his body sagging with exhaustion as they all helped him aboard the ship. As soon as he crossed the threshold, the weight of the past few days finally hit him. His knees buckled, and the medics caught him before he collapsed completely. They laid him gently on a stretcher, their voices calm and reassured as they began their work.

One of the officers returned a few minutes later, holding a secure data capsule.

"Sir," he said to Lieutenant Haase, "we recovered this from the downed MWU ship. It was still intact in the secondary archive core."

Connor, half-lucid on the stretcher, recognized the device immediately — it contained the recordings. Relief flickered in his eyes as Haase accepted the capsule with a grim nod.

"We'll analyze it back on Earth," she said quietly, her tone tight. "Make sure it's transferred to the Executive Review Channel. Priority one."

The ship's interior was a stark contrast to the hostile environment of Torak-9 - clean, sterile, and humming with quiet efficiency. Connor felt a cool sensation as an IV was inserted into his arm, replenishing the fluids his body had desperately lacked. The medics worked quickly, administering fluids, checking his vitals, and scanning him for any potential alien contagions.

As he lay there, his body weak but slowly recovering, Connor's mind began to wander. He had been so focused on survival that he hadn't had time to process everything that had happened - the destruction of the Cadmus, the alien creatures that roamed the planet, the downed MWU ship he had found, and the damning information about the Vorlax and the traitor within the Union.

The medics wheeled Connor through the corridors of the Protector Class ship, their instruments softly beeping as they monitored his vitals. Around him, the cool sterility of the medical bay replaced the chaos of the planet below. Lieutenant Haase walked silently alongside the stretcher, her face etched with concern. As Connor was lifted onto a diagnostic bed and hooked up to additional monitoring equipment, his thoughts drifted back to the mission that had brought him to Torak-9. He had been sent to investigate an SOS, only to end up sending one of his own. The irony wasn't lost on him—but what gnawed at him now ran deeper: doubt.

For the first time since becoming a pilot—since the very beginning of his MWU service—Connor found himself questioning his future. The weight of his experiences - the near-death encounters, the isolation, the realization that someone within the MWU had betrayed them - pressed heavily on his mind. Was this the life he had envisioned for himself? Was the constant danger, the uncertainty, and the strain worth it?

The soft hum of the ship's engines was soothing, but it did little to quiet the storm of thoughts swirling in his head. He had always been confident in his abilities as a pilot, but Torak-9 had tested him in ways he hadn't expected. The physical challenges were one thing, but the psychological toll was something else entirely.

As the Protector Class ship lifted off from the surface of Torak-9, Connor felt a pang of relief. He was finally leaving the desolate planet behind, but he couldn't shake the feeling that something had changed within him. He was no longer the same confident, eager pilot who had taken on every mission without question. The doubt had taken root, and he wasn't sure how to make it go away.

The ship's commander appeared by his side, a composed look on his face as he glanced down at Connor. "You did well out there, O'Brien," he said, his voice steady. "Not many people could survive what you went through on that planet."

Connor managed a faint smile, but the words didn't bring him the comfort they once might have. The truth was, he wasn't sure if he wanted to keep going like this. Surviving was one thing - living was another.

As the ship sped toward Earth, Connor closed his eyes, letting the hum of the engines lull him into a restless sleep. His body would recover in time, but his mind was another story. The doubts lingered, creeping into every corner of his thoughts. What was next for him? Could he continue on this path, knowing what he now knew?

The next time he opened his eyes, Earth would be in view. Home. But even that didn't feel the same anymore.

18 A SOLDIER'S RECOVERY

The sterile, whitewashed walls of the medical bay felt like a prison, but in comparison to the harsh wilderness of Torak-9, it was a welcome refuge. Connor lay back in his hospital bed, the soft thrum of machines providing a steady rhythm that contrasted sharply with the chaos he had just endured. His body was healing, but his mind was still reeling from everything that had transpired on that hostile planet.

He had been stranded for twelve days, surviving on sparse resources, limited water, and sheer will. Each passing moment had tested him—fighting off predators, scavenging shelter, and clinging to the hope that his distress signal would reach someone. Now, surrounded by the familiar comforts of the MWU's top-tier medical facilities, Connor was grappling with a different kind of weight.

His thoughts churned with the revelation uncovered in the downed MWU ship—the Vorlax soldiers speaking casually about receiving intel from someone within the Union. The recording had played over and over in his mind: their sneering laughter, the mention of a "stupid commander" who'd betrayed them all. It was a ten-year-old message, and yet the implications still burned hot in his mind. If that information had remained buried all this time, who else had suffered because of it? Who else was at risk?

Military protocol had kicked in quickly upon his rescue. As soon as the medics stabilized him, Connor had relayed everything—what he'd found, what he'd seen, and what had been recorded. Haase and a secure MWU intelligence team had personally retrieved the recordings from the wreckage, and the rescue team launched a sweep of the nearby crash site before leaving Torak-9.

Now, Connor sat upright, gently adjusting his position as the IV line tugged against his arm. His wrist AI, now recharged and restored, lay dormant beside him. He was under strict orders to rest, but his mind remained on high alert. The Vorlax weren't just distant aggressors anymore. They had names, faces, and a link to someone high up in the MWU.

A soft knock broke his focus. Lieutenant Haase stepped in, her uniform impeccable, her expression unreadable. Behind her came Ambryst, Sailor Grace, and Tyler. The familiar sight of his squad brought a flicker of warmth.

"Don't get up, O'Brien," Haase said, her tone professional but gentler than usual. "You've earned some rest."

Connor gave a faint nod.

"I know you've got a hundred things you want to say," she continued, holding up a hand. "And you'll have your debriefing session tomorrow. Intelligence is already analyzing the footage you recovered. For now, I'm here on other business."

She stepped closer to the bed, then glanced briefly at the others before returning her gaze to Connor.

"As of this morning, per recommendation from Command and approval from Tactical Flight Division, you've been promoted. Congratulations, Sergeant O'Brien."

Connor blinked. "Sergeant?"

Ambryst grinned and gave a slow clap. Grace beamed, and even Tyler cracked a brief smile, his massive arms folded across his chest.

"Yes," Haase confirmed. "We've adapted traditional military ranking systems for multi-exoform integration. In the

MWU Tactical Wing, sergeants aren't just ground personnel—they lead squads, pilot strike-class vessels, and take point in high-risk operations. You've proven you can handle that."

She paused, letting the words settle in.

"There are limited command slots at every rank. To promote someone, someone else must retire, transfer, or be promoted themselves. One such window opened, and your record—particularly Torak-9—spoke for itself."

Connor exhaled slowly, the weight of the promotion pressing down but not in a bad way. It felt earned. Grounded. Real.

"You survived an incredibly hostile mission, completed objectives, and ensured critical intelligence made it back to us," Haase continued. "You've got leadership potential, O'Brien. And this rank reflects that."

"I… I'm honored," Connor said.

Haase gave a small nod. "Good. Now take the rest of the week for rehab and therapy. Study what you found on the Vorlax. We'll regroup when you're back at full strength. But make no mistake—what you uncovered could shake the very structure of the MWU."

She started for the door, then turned back once more. "Oh—and get used to hearing 'Sergeant.' You've earned it."

The squad followed her out, offering Connor a few last waves and encouraging words. Then the door closed with a quiet hiss.

Left alone, Connor sank into the pillow, the whir of medtech humming softly around him. Sergeant Connor O'Brien. It felt like more than a title. It felt like a responsibility. And there was still work to be done.

He reached for his wrist AI, activating the interface and opening the MWU archives on the Vorlax.

He had a week. He didn't plan to waste a second of it.

19 THE DATE

After about two weeks on Earth, Connor had finally begun to feel like himself again. The physical rehabilitation and therapy sessions had been grueling, pushing his body to recover from the ordeal on Torak-9. His muscles had grown stronger with each passing day, and the aches and pains that once plagued him had dulled to mere whispers. Mentally, he felt sharper too, as if he had emerged from the experience with a renewed sense of clarity and focus. It was good to be back on his feet, though the memories of the planet and its hostile wildlife still lingered in the back of his mind.

Once his strength and clarity had returned, Connor turned his attention to a more pressing matter — his report. He had already submitted a full account of the events on Torak-9, including the disturbing evidence of a traitor within the MWU. Lieutenant Haase had acknowledged the seriousness of the situation but insisted the findings remain classified while the recovered data from the wrecked ship was reviewed. "Give it a little time," she'd told him. "We need confirmation before this reaches anyone else."

"We need to be absolutely certain before we take this any further," Lieutenant Haase had told him during one of their private conversations. "If there's any truth to this, it could shake the very foundation of the MWU. I want to bring in a few trusted people to review the evidence, but I don't want to stir the pot until we know for sure. Give me a little time to dig into this, and I'll let you know what we find."

Connor had understood the need for discretion, knowing full well the seriousness of the accusation. A mole in the MWU was not something that could be taken lightly, and it would be reckless to jump to conclusions without all the facts. He nodded in agreement and requested that she keep him updated with any developments. For now, though, he had to be patient, and he trusted that Haase would handle it carefully.

As much as he wanted to get back out into space, back into the action, he knew that some things needed time to unfold. So, he kept busy by checking in with his squad, making sure they were all ready for whatever mission came next. Ambryst, Sailor Grace, and Tyler were eager to return to duty as well, but Connor had something else on his mind before they could all dive back into the fray.

With a smile tugging at the corners of his lips, Connor told his squad that he had something important to take care of. After everything he'd been through, there was one person who had been on his mind a great deal: Lysara. The Xeno Officer had made quite the impression on him during their last encounter, and he couldn't shake the feeling that there was something special between them. So, with his heart pounding in his chest, he set off to find Lysara and ask her out on a date.

He finally crossed paths with her near one of the local hubs frequented by MWU officers. She was hard to miss, with her pale lavender skin and striking silver eyes that shimmered in the daylight. Connor smiled as they locked eyes, and before he knew it, the words slipped out of his mouth.

"Hey, Lysara, how would you like to go out sometime? Maybe tonight?" he asked, feeling a slight nervousness creep in.

Lysara's eyes widened in surprise, and a faint blush spread across her cheeks. She was taken aback by his boldness but flattered all the same. With a soft smile, she replied, "I'd love that, Connor."

Later that evening, Connor arrived dressed in his finest suit to pick up Lysara, and they began their evening with a Planetary Wildlife Safari. Though they were still on Earth, the experience was immersive — a sleek hovercraft guided them through vivid projections of alien ecosystems, simulating the dangerous beauty of a Tier 4 world. For a moment, Connor tensed, memories of Torak-9 flaring to life. But he steadied himself. This was safe. Controlled. And Lysara's steady presence beside him helped ease the pulse of anxiety as they drifted through the alien wilds together.

As they floated above the simulated alien landscapes, Connor couldn't help but feel a connection growing. Lysara pointed out some of the more exotic wildlife, clearly knowledgeable about their behavior and habitat being a Xeno Officer. He found her expertise fascinating and leaned in, soaking up her every word. They shared easy conversation and laughter as they marveled at the creatures darting beneath them.

The next stop on their date was a Galactic Cuisine Tour. They walked into a massive, buzzing restaurant that prided itself on offering delicacies from across the galaxy. Lysara was excited to show Connor some of her favorite dishes, and they settled at a table surrounded by the scent of exotic spices and strange, unfamiliar aromas. The waiter brought out a plate with something wriggling on it. Connor's eyes widened in disbelief as he cautiously leaned in closer.

"It's not alive, right?" Connor asked with a nervous chuckle, eyeing the wriggling dish.

Lysara giggled. "No, it's just reacting to the sauce. Perfectly safe, I promise."

Connor poked at it with his fork but couldn't muster the courage to eat it. He gave Lysara a sheepish grin. "Yeah, I'm going to pass on that one," he said, pushing the plate away. She couldn't stop laughing at his reaction, her giggles so contagious that Connor couldn't help but laugh along with her. He liked seeing her so relaxed—her laughter felt like music to his ears.

After their adventurous meal—where Connor had eventually found a dish he loved, a sizzling, spice-coated medallion of grilled Zequari root that reminded him of Earth's roasted potatoes with a fiery twist—the night took them to a zero-gravity dance club, where the atmosphere shifted from playful to exciting. As soon as they stepped inside, gravity was disabled, and they found themselves floating. Connor reached out to Lysara, and they floated together, spinning gently in mid-air to the rhythm of the music. Their movements were fluid, unrestricted by gravity, and they danced with a carefree joy that brought them closer.

Lysara floated into his arms, and for a moment, it felt like the world outside didn't exist. The only thing that mattered was the two of them, drifting together in the middle of the galaxy, laughing and smiling. Their closeness felt natural, almost as if they had been dancing together forever.

As the night wound down, Connor had one last surprise planned. He led Lysara to a small pottery studio, a hobby from long ago. It was quaint, a step away from the high-tech world they were used to, but Connor had a feeling it would be a perfect way to end the night. They worked together on a couple's pottery project, their hands gradually coated in clay as they laughed and molded the wobbly shapes into something uniquely theirs.

Connor smiled at the uneven shapes they were molding. "We might not be great at this, but it's a lot of fun."

Lysara nodded, her cheeks dusted with a light blush as she laughed at their clumsy creations. "Who knew making a cup would be this difficult?" she teased.

They laughed as they finished their pieces. The pottery looked far from perfect, but each lopsided curve marked the time they had shared. A soft-spoken instructor, watching from across the room, offered occasional guidance, but for the most part, Connor took the lead. It was a hobby he had dabbled in during his academy days, and now, he found joy in teaching Lysara the basics. It was a small, intimate moment—one that felt natural and effortless.

As the night came to an end, Connor walked Lysara back to her home. They lingered at her doorstep, not wanting the evening to be over. The air was filled with soft jitters, the kind that comes before something important. Lysara stepped closer, her silver eyes shimmering in the dim light, and without another word, they kissed. It was soft and passionate, a kiss that felt like a promise of something more.

When they pulled away, Lysara smiled and handed him her contact on his wrist tech. "Call me anytime, Connor."

He couldn't stop smiling. As he watched her walk inside, he knew that Lysara was someone special, someone he could see himself with for a long time.

20 ECLIPSE RIFT

A familiar excitement bubbled up inside Connor as he stood before the massive bulk of the newly rebuilt Cadmus, his sleek fighter ship. His body craved the adrenaline of his next mission, the thrill of the unknown, and the satisfaction of seeing the stars and planets speeding past the viewport once again. That's not to say that being on Earth now didn't have its perks, now that he was seeing Lysara.

As his squad gathered around him, there was a noticeable buzz in the air. Ambryst, Sailor Grace, and Tyler stood by his side, each of them sharing in the collective excitement for their next assignment. This mission stood apart from anything they had tackled before; the weight of its importance pressed down on them, but it also filled them with a sense of pride. This was no routine patrol, no simple recon mission. They had been assigned to assist one of the MWU's most brilliant minds—a Dark Matter Strategist.

The strategist in question, Doctor Callen Bex, was a renowned physicist specializing in advanced theories related to dark matter and energy manipulation. Connor had heard of Bex before, mostly through academy discussions about his breakthroughs in dark matter propulsion and the complex gravitational distortions caused by the enigmatic substance. There were whispers that Bex's theories could revolutionize intergalactic travel, rendering inversion

145

displacement drives and traditional engines obsolete. Connor, however, knew better than to get caught up in rumors. What mattered now was the mission at hand.

"So, what do you think, boss?" Ambryst's deep, rumbling voice broke through Connor's thoughts. The alien, always quick to share his thoughts, looked eager to get going. "Think we're about to dive headfirst into the unknown? Dark matter is some pretty heavy stuff."

Connor grinned, adjusting his gloves. "You know me, Ambryst. I'm always up for a challenge. But this time, I'm thinking we follow Bex's lead. If we're going into the unknown, at least we'll have a genius guiding us through."

Tyler gave a small grunt of agreement. "Just so long as we don't start messing with reality itself. Dark matter can be unpredictable."

Sailor Grace nodded, her ponytail swaying as she shifted her stance. "I've read some of Bex's work," she chimed in. "His theories are fascinating but risky. We'll have to be careful."

Connor looked around at his squad, feeling the camaraderie that had developed over their missions together. They were a tight-knit group, each of them bringing unique strengths to the table. He was confident that, no matter what they faced, they would handle it as a team.

"Alright," Connor said, clapping his hands together. "Let's suit up and get ready to meet Dr. Bex. We'll find out what we're dealing with soon enough."

The briefing room aboard the MWU Eclipse, a massive Galactic Class ship, was spacious and dimly lit, with holographic displays hovering in the center. Doctor Callen Bex, a Tharnian from the diamond-like moon of Draxelis, stood at the front of the room, his translucent skin faintly glowing as his tall, wiry frame hunched over a holographic console, fingers dancing across the interface.

"Ah, you must be O'Brien and his squad," Bex said, not looking up as they entered the room. His voice was quick and clipped, as though his mind was operating several steps ahead of his words. "Good, good. I'm going to need all the help I can get."

Connor exchanged glances with his team before stepping forward. "Doctor Bex, it's an honor. We've been briefed on the basics of the mission, but we're eager to hear the specifics."

Bex finally looked up from his work, his sharp eyes scanning Connor and his squad with a mixture of interest and impatience. "Yes, well, let's get right to it then. I've been tracking an anomaly in a nearby system - something I believe to be a pocket of destabilized dark matter. It's throwing off gravitational readings and causing fluctuations in nearby star systems. If left unchecked, it could destabilize the region's gravitational balance entirely, possibly even leading to the collapse of several planets."

Connor felt a chill run down his spine at the gravity of Bex's words. The collapse of planets? That was quite the catastrophic threat. The squad fell silent, listening intently.

Bex continued, his hands moving rapidly as he pulled up a three-dimensional model of the affected system. "We're going to need to enter the heart of the anomaly and stabilize it before it spreads. I've developed a containment device - something that should, in theory, siphon off the excess dark matter and reintroduce stability. But the process will be dangerous. The gravitational distortions will be extreme, and there's a chance we'll encounter temporal anomalies."

"Temporal anomalies?" Sailor Grace asked, her brows furrowing. A native of the southern region of Earth, she had always gone by both her first and middle names—a cultural tradition that had stuck with her even in the far reaches of space. "You mean time could shift?"

Bex nodded. "Indeed. Time dilation, reality shifts, even temporal loops. We'll need to stay focused and ensure that nothing interferes with the containment process. Your job is to escort me to the heart of the anomaly, defend the ship from any threats, and ensure I have enough time to activate the device. After that, we'll get out of there as fast as we can."

Connor took a deep breath. This was far more intense than he had anticipated. "Understood, Doctor Bex. We'll get you to the anomaly and make sure you have the time you need. What kind of resistance can we expect?"

Bex shrugged, his focus already returning to his calculations. "Hard to say. The anomaly is in uncharted space, so we don't know if there are any hostile forces in the area. But the dark matter itself will be your primary concern. Ships that have entered the region before have reported severe malfunctions, navigational errors, and sensor disruption."

"Sounds like fun," Ambryst muttered, cracking his knuckles.

Connor smirked. "Alright, squad, you heard the man. Let's get going."

O'Brien Squad stood on the bridge of the Eclipse, watching the stars streak by as they approached the edge of the anomaly. The ship's sensors were already picking up strange fluctuations, the stars ahead bending and warping as the gravitational distortions became more pronounced. Connor sensed the tension building—not just in himself, but in the subtle shifts in posture and quiet glances exchanged among his squad.

"Entering the anomaly's outer boundary," the ship's AI announced. "Gravitational distortions detected. Navigational systems compensating."

Connor glanced over at Bex, who was furiously inputting data into a handheld device. The containment device was ready, but the real challenge was getting it into place. All around them, crew members aboard the MWU Eclipse worked at a frantic pace, each one focused on their critical task while the doctor concentrated on his.

As they entered the heart of the anomaly, the massive ship began to shudder violently. The stars outside twisted and spun in unnatural patterns, and the gravitational forces tugged at the MWU Eclipse from all directions.

"We're in the eye of the storm now," Bex said, his voice tense. "Any ship smaller than a Galactic Class would have already been destroyed! Now, get me as close to the anomaly's core as possible. We don't have much time." Bex commanded the two pilots operating the steering of the hulking ship.

Connor's heart raced as the ship pushed deeper into the dark matter's gravitational well.

With the press of a button from Dr. Bex, the stabilizer deployed from the MWU Eclipse, gliding toward the heart of the anomaly. Energy readings spiked as the containment field activated, causing the ship to tremble under the strain. The stabilizer drifted steadily into place, locking onto the core of the disturbance and beginning the process of siphoning off excess dark matter.

"Stabilizer is in position," one of the MWU Eclipse crew confirmed, watching the readings on the display. "Initiating manual override. Adjusting the output."

The team worked swiftly. Their fingers danced over the control panels as they monitored the stabilizer's energy output. The core of the anomaly was fluctuating; its tendrils writhed, resisting their efforts to bring it under control. The ship groaned under the pressure, and the lights flickered momentarily.

"Doctor, we're experiencing major resistance from the core," another crew member reported over the comms. "We're going to need to boost the stabilizer's power."

"Do it," Doctor Bex's voice crackled back over the line. "We don't have much time before this thing pulls us in."

The MWU Eclipse crew nodded to one another, initiating a power transfer from the ship's secondary engines to the stabilizer. The energy surged into the core, causing the anomaly to flare up one last time before it began to shrink, its tendrils retracting as the stabilizer's field expanded. Meanwhile, Connor and his squad remained on high alert at the secondary defense stations, watching for any sign of hostile interference or system failure. Their role wasn't hands-on, but it was critical—they were the fail-safe.

"We've got it!" Doctor Bex shouted. Relief flooded his voice. "The anomaly's stabilizing."

The holo-display showed the anomaly calming, its swirling mass of dark matter now contained within the stabilizer's field. The energy readings dropped to manageable levels, and the vessel's trembling ceased.

Connor exhaled, his heart still pounding in his chest. "Is it holding?"

A crewmember checked her display and nodded. "It's holding. We're in the clear."

Doctor Bex turned to the crew, his expression tinged with satisfaction. "Excellent work, everyone. The anomaly's been neutralized. Let's get the ship out of here."

The MWU Eclipse's engines roared to life as it began to pull away from the now-contained rift, leaving behind the region of space that had nearly torn itself apart. The mission had been a success, but the tension aboard the starship remained thick—residual nerves and adrenaline still clinging to every crew member who had just stared into the heart of dark matter and lived to tell about it.

Back in the secondary control room, Connor turned to his squad, a tired but triumphant grin on his face. "That was close, but they all pulled it off."

Ambryst let out a breath he'd been holding. "Remind me to never volunteer for another mission involving dark matter anomalies again."

Sailor Grace didn't laugh right away.

She stared at the rift through the viewing pane, its swirling mass now caged behind stabilizer fields. It was quiet now—but too quiet. Like the world had taken a breath and never let it go.

"Grace?" Ambryst nudged her gently with an elbow.

She gave a soft exhale, her voice distant. "Back home, my grandmother used to say places like that were where the universe keeps its secrets. We weren't supposed to touch them. Just... listen."

Silence returned for a beat, broken only by the subtle hum of the Eclipse's systems. Grace tucked a lock of hair behind her ear, then added, "She used to sing during storms. Said the universe couldn't take you if you sang louder than your fear."

Ambryst and Connor exchanged a glance, unsure what to say. But Grace smiled and finally let herself chuckle—small and tired, but real.

"I don't sing much anymore," she said, "but sometimes... I still hum. Keeps the dark from getting in."

Sailor Grace laughed. "I think we've all had enough of those for a lifetime."

Tyler folded his arms, his tone level but pointed. "So what was our role here exactly, if our fighters never left the dock?"

The team lingered on the question for a moment before Connor spoke up.

"We were here in case any external threats showed up near the anomaly," Connor explained, his tone steady. "The Eclipse is powerful, but it's also a target—especially during a mission like this. Our role was to deploy if anything hostile emerged at the perimeter. But inside the anomaly?" He gave a dry chuckle, glancing around. "You heard the doc—fighter-class ships wouldn't have lasted seconds in there."

Tyler nodded at his sergeant's reasoning and stepped back, his quiet presence as steady and unreadable as ever.

As the MWU Eclipse set its course back toward safer space, Connor leaned back in a chair and closed his eyes, grateful for a brief respite before his next mission.

21 DIPLOMATIC DISASTER

Connor O'Brien had been assigned high-profile missions before, but this one felt different. Unease prickled at the edge of his thoughts, a tension he couldn't quite shake. Instead of piloting the Cadmus into hostile space, he'd been pulled into an unfamiliar role—one that blurred the line between military escort and diplomatic aide.

He and his squad—Ambryst, Sailor Grace, and Tyler—had been assigned to temporarily accompany MWU diplomat Brandi Kimbrough aboard the Protector Class vessel Eos. Their orders were specific: provide elite-level security during sensitive peace negotiations with the Zorvakians. While they weren't bodyguards by trade, their recent track record and diverse field experience had caught the attention of MWU brass. This time, the Union needed pilots it could trust—not just to fight, but to represent its values.

Outside, an escort of fighter-class vessels patrolled in tight formation, shadowing the Eos as it traveled to a neutral space station agreed upon for the talks. Inside, armed security teams kept a vigilant watch, while Connor's squad was briefed on protocol, optics, and diplomatic discretion. The MWU hoped to bring the Zorvakians—a powerful insectoid race with a complex warrior culture—into the fold. Success would strengthen the Union's position in the galaxy. Failure… would have consequences.

Once docked, Connor stepped off the Eos with the rest of the delegation, his boots striking the polished floor of the station's reception corridor. The air was filtered and cool, but the silence carried an edge. Everything was too quiet.

The council chamber was circular, with high metallic walls polished to a mirrored sheen. A faint hum vibrated through the floor, likely some form of energy filtration. A long crescent-shaped table separated the two parties—humans on one side, Zorvakians on the other. No refreshments. No aides. Just tension. The Zorvakians stood rather than sat, their tall frames too rigid for standard seating. They said nothing, waiting.

The Zorvakian delegation stood poised, their angular, chitinous bodies gleaming beneath the sterile light. Their mandibles clicked softly as they communicated in low, rhythmic pulses. Connor took his place just behind Kimbrough, alert and observant. Though their presence in the room was meant to be ceremonial, his instincts were sharp, ready for anything.

Brandi Kimbrough entered with an unmistakable air of superiority. Her walk was precise, posture commanding, eyes scanning the room as if evaluating her inferiors. Whatever tension existed before she opened her mouth only escalated once she began to speak.

With an overly confident smirk, Kimbrough began, "I'm sure you Zorvakians have reviewed the MWU's offer. Given your current level of development, you'll find our terms exceptionally generous."

Connor's stomach turned. Diplomatic etiquette wasn't his specialty, but even he knew this was the wrong tone to take.

As the meeting progressed, Kimbrough's tone worsened. When the Zorvakian leader expressed skepticism, she replied sharply, "Even if you do join, don't expect special treatment. If war comes, you'll be on the front lines like everyone else. That's the reality of being part of a galactic union."

Connor bit the inside of his cheek. He glanced at his team—Ambryst's brow furrowed, Sailor tense, Tyler unreadable—but all wore matching looks of disbelief.

The room's tension peaked when Kimbrough rose abruptly. "And if you can't make a decision today," she said, brushing off her dress, "don't expect mercy. The MWU doesn't have time for indecision. You either join us, or you face the consequences."

The Zorvakians erupted in a storm of clicks and hisses. Diplomacy had shattered.

Connor felt a chill crawl down his spine. Even more disturbing than her threats was her phrasing. She kept saying "join me," not "join the MWU."

"We're done here," Kimbrough said, striding toward the exit. "The MWU is leaving."

Connor and his team followed, caught between duty and disbelief. Back aboard the Eos, she stormed onto the bridge and barked, "Fire on the Zorvakian ships. Now."

Every head turned. The weapons officers looked stunned.

"You heard me!" she shouted. "Engage! Or I'll have every one of you reassigned to the deepest hole the MWU has to offer!"

Connor's breath caught. She didn't have the authority to issue combat orders, and everyone knew it. The bridge fell into strained silence.

Then, from somewhere outside, a few of the escorting fighters opened fire—not on the station, but on two Zorvakian crafts preparing to undock. The Eos's weapons remained still, but the damage was done. One starship was destroyed instantly. The other limped away, damaged.

The space station—a neutral zone—had taken a glancing blow during the brief firefight, damaging a docking ring and causing structural collapse on one side. Fires broke out. The damage spread quickly. The emergency containment fields failed. Dozens of civilians—station staff, translators, and diplomatic aides—were lost in the chaos.

Kimbrough folded her arms and smiled. "Take us back to Earth."

No one moved. The crew stared in stunned silence.

Connor stood frozen, the horror settling in his gut like a stone. It hadn't just been a diplomatic failure—it was an atrocity.

When the Eos returned to Earth, Connor and his squad barely exchanged words as they disembarked. Instead, they walked to a quiet bar near the MWU base, needing somewhere—anywhere—to try and process the events.

The booth was quiet. Drinks were poured. No one touched them.

Ambryst finally broke the silence. "That mission wasn't just a failure. It was something else entirely. We were sent to escort a diplomat. Instead, we witnessed a breakdown of everything the MWU stands for."

Sailor nodded slowly. "She was provoking them. Every word, every move—it was like she wanted the Zorvakians to walk away angry. Or worse."

Tyler leaned in, his expression tight. "She wasn't speaking for the MWU. She kept saying 'me.' And I don't think that was a mistake."

Connor rubbed his temple. "She knew exactly what she was doing. This wasn't about peace. It was about division. And she dragged us along for the ride."

They sat in silence again.

"What do we do now?" Ambryst asked.

Connor looked at each of them in turn. "We file our reports. Everything we saw. Everything we heard. No edits. No omissions. If anyone asks us to revise or censor anything—we refuse. The MWU needs to know what happened out there."

They nodded. They didn't toast. They didn't speak again. They just sat, the weight of the mission heavy on their shoulders, and waited to see what came next.

22 THE SHROUDED TRUTH

Connor sat in the quiet of his quarters, the faint hum of Earth's bustling city outside his window barely registering in his mind. It had been days since his return from the mission with the interstellar diplomat, but his thoughts were still plagued by the mysterious encounter with the Zorvakians. Yet, all of that was pushed aside when a notification blinked on his wrist comm, a message from Lieutenant Haase. He had been waiting for this moment. Something told him it wasn't going to be good news.

He tapped the notification, and almost immediately, her face appeared on his holo-display. But it wasn't the usual video call. This time, the transmission was laced with encryption protocols Connor hadn't seen before. Haase's face flickered briefly before stabilizing, and she appeared tense, her eyes darting around her surroundings as if constantly checking for any signs of danger.

"Connor," she whispered, her voice barely above a murmur. "I can't talk long. This has to stay between us."

Connor straightened in his chair, his body tense. "Lieutenant, what's going on? You're not using official channels. Is everything okay?"

Haase's face hardened. "No. It's worse than we thought. I've been able to verify the video logs you sent me from Torak-9. They're authentic—every last detail. The Vorlax, the MWU pilot, and the officer. They referred to him as Captain in the footage, and that lines up. He was the captain of a Galactic Class ship ten years ago." She hesitated, her voice turning cold. "Now? He's a Commander. Still active. Still trusted."

Connor's heart dropped. He knew there was something off about the logs but hearing Haase confirm his suspicions sent a cold chill down his spine. "Who is he?" he asked, his voice low.

Haase leaned in closer to her screen, her eyes filled with fear. "He's one of the Supreme Chancellors now. One of the ten at the very top of the MWU. He's been pulling strings for years, using his influence and power to hide his tracks. I don't know how deep this goes, but I know that I've lost contact with some of the people I trusted to help me look into this."

Connor's fists clenched. "They've gone missing?"

Haase nodded. "It's more than that, Connor. They're gone. Disappeared. Erased. These were people I've worked with for years, who had their own lives and families. They wouldn't just vanish like this without leaving some trace. Someone's covering their tracks, and I'm scared I might be next if I'm not careful. I've dug too deep, and now they know. I'm certain they're watching me."

The weight of her words settled heavily on Connor. If what Haase was saying was true, then the corruption wasn't just isolated to a rogue commander feeding information to the Vorlax - it went all the way to the top. The MWU, the institution that Connor had served and believed in, had been compromised by someone with vast authority. His mind raced, trying to process the implications. This was bigger than anything he had ever encountered. Connor began making wild assumptions in his mind, mostly whether it was just this one supreme chancellor or if there were more involved.

"What do we do, Lieutenant?" Connor asked as his voice was tight with concern. "If this guy is that high up, we're going to need more than just a few logs and suspicions to bring him down. We're talking about one of the ten most powerful individuals in the galaxy."

Haase's eyes darted again, and she visibly flinched at a sound off-screen. She was paranoid and with good reason. "I don't know yet, O'Brien. I honestly don't. I'm in hiding, for now, trying to lay low. But the deeper I go, the more dangerous this becomes. If they know I'm onto them, then it's not just me in danger. You, your squad, and anyone associated with this... they'll be targets. You need to be careful."

Connor's jaw clenched. The thought of his team, Ambryst, Sailor Grace, and Tyler, being put in harm's way because of this made his blood boil. "Then we take this straight to someone who can do something. We can't just sit on this, Lieutenant."

Haase shook her head, her face filled with sorrow and frustration. "It's not that simple. We don't know who we can trust. The Supreme Chancellors hold immense power, and they control everything - the military, the administrative, and the executive divisions. We take this to the wrong person, and it could all be swept under the rug, or worse, we all disappear. No one will even know we existed."

Connor remained silent, the gravity of her words sinking in. He had known the MWU was vast and powerful, but this... this was something else entirely. "So what do we do?"

Haase swallowed hard, her eyes flickering with uncertainty. "For now, we wait. I need to gather more evidence, and I need to reach out to those who I still believe I can trust. I'll be in touch when I have more, but for now, stay low."

She was terrified, more so than he had ever seen her. If she thought this was the best course of action, then he had to trust her.

A sudden noise, louder this time, made Haase's eyes widen. "I have to go," she whispered hurriedly. "I'll contact you in an hour. Stay safe."

Before Connor could respond, the holo-call cut off, leaving him in the dim light of his quarters, his mind racing with everything he had just learned. One of the Supreme Chancellors - the people who governed the entire MWU - was a traitor, feeding information to their enemies, the Vorlax. And now, both he and Haase were caught in the middle of it.

He stared at the blank screen for a long moment, his heart pounding. He needed to get some air, so he decided to take a walk to a nearby park to wait for Haase's call.

Connor sat in a quiet park near the MWU building, the sprawling green space offering a momentary escape from the chaos swirling around him. The peaceful surroundings did little to calm the storm brewing inside him. Lieutenant Haase's call from earlier still played in his mind on repeat. The urgency in her voice, the fear in her eyes - it was haunting. She had promised to call him back within the hour, but now the hour had come and gone.

With each passing minute, the apprehension inside him grew. His mind raced with scenarios. Was she in danger? Did someone intercept the call? Every possibility seemed worse than the last. After the call, he had immediately messaged his squad to meet him at their usual spot in the park—somewhere public, but quiet enough to talk. The longer the silence stretched, the heavier the weight on his shoulders became. His thoughts were interrupted by the familiar sound of approaching footsteps. Turning, he saw his squad walking toward him.

Connor stood to greet them, trying to maintain his composure. "We need to talk," he said, his voice low. "There's something big going on, and I'm not sure how much time we have to figure it out."

Ambryst was the first to speak. "What's happening, boss? You look like you've seen a ghost."

Connor hesitated. He had always been the kind of leader to be upfront with his squad, and this time would be no different. They deserved to know. "Lieutenant Haase - she called me earlier. She confirmed the video logs from Torak-9, the ones about the commander working with the Vorlax. It's worse than we thought. That commander is now a Supreme Chancellor, one of the top ten people running the entire MWU."

His words hung in the air like a lead weight, and his squad's eyes widened in shock.

"No way," Sailor Grace whispered, her hand going to her mouth. "A Supreme Chancellor?"

Connor nodded grimly. "It gets worse. Lieutenant Haase said some of the people she trusted had gone missing. She thinks they were taken, or worse. She told me she's in hiding now, trying to stay under the radar. She's scared and she thinks she's next."

A heavy silence followed, and it was Sailor who broke it. "This is bad. This is really bad, Connor. I almost wish you'd never stumbled across this. Look at everything it's doing now - people disappearing, Lieutenant Haase in hiding, a Supreme Chancellor involved in this mess."

Tyler crossed his four large arms. "We're in deep, Sergeant. And it's not just us. The entire MWU could be at risk if this gets out."

Connor's jaw clenched. "I know. And we don't even know the full scope of it yet."

Ambryst, ever the optimist, tried to offer some perspective. "We've faced tough situations before, Connor. But this - it feels different. It feels like we're up against something way bigger than any of us."

Connor could only nod. His team's concern was valid, and it mirrored his thoughts. But despite the overwhelming feeling of helplessness, he knew one thing for sure: they couldn't give up. They owed it to Haase, and to themselves, to see this through.

The minutes dragged on, the hour mark passing by. Then two hours. Connor's mind began to whirl with increasing urgency. Where was Lieutenant Haase? Has something happened to her? His gut twisted in knots at the thought of her being caught, or worse.

Connor stood abruptly, his resolve hardening. "We can't sit here doing nothing. She's out there, and we have to find her. She said she'd call back, but if something went wrong, she might need help."

His squad nodded, ready to act.

"I want us to fan out and monitor the city," Connor said. "No uniforms, no attention. We don't go looking in obvious places—she said she's in hiding for a reason. But if she's nearby, she might leave a trail. We check secure comm points, watch for anything out of the ordinary. She'll reach out when it's safe."

Tyler, ever pragmatic, pointed out the obvious. "Sergeant, sir, Earth is a big place. She could be halfway across the world by now. We could spend days searching and still find nothing."

Connor clenched his fists. "I know. But I don't believe she'd run that far. If she's in danger, she'd stay close, waiting for help. We have to try."

The squad started with what tech they had—pinging Lysara's last known comm signature, sweeping the city's encrypted MWU channels, and scanning for biometric traces in secure zones. They even tapped into traffic cams and civilian surveillance feeds, hoping for a match. But she'd covered her tracks well—too well. With every digital trail cold, they finally resorted to legwork, spreading out across parks, streets, and buildings in hopes of spotting anything out of place. Hours passed. Every lead was a dead end. With the weight of failure hanging over them, the squad regrouped back at the park.

Connor's frustration was palpable. His fingers tapped restlessly against his thigh as he scanned the city skyline, his mind racing. "We've got nothing. She could be in hiding, or-."

His voice trailed off, but the implication was clear. They all feared the worst.

"I'm going to make a call," Connor said suddenly, breaking the heavy silence. "I know someone in the Galactic Law Enforcement Agency. He might have access to arrest records. It's a long shot, but maybe they've picked her up for questioning."

Connor stepped away from his squad and initiated the call. His academy friend, now a lieutenant in the GLEA, answered after a few rings. The conversation was brief and filled with hushed tones. Ambryst, Sailor Grace, and Tyler stood a few paces away, watching intently, though they couldn't hear what was being said.

When the call ended, Connor lowered his head and let out a long, frustrated sigh. He turned to his squad, his expression one of grim resignation.

"Well?" Sailor asked, her voice tight with anticipation.

Connor sank onto a nearby bench, the weight of the revelation pressing down on him. His voice was cold and flat when he finally spoke. "Lieutenant Haase has been arrested."

The squad exchanged shocked glances. "Arrested? For what?" Tyler asked, his glassy-skinned features hardening in disbelief.

Connor closed his eyes for a moment before answering. "Intergalactic treason."

The words hung in the air like a death sentence, each of them understanding the gravity of what that charge meant. Intergalactic treason was one of the highest crimes in the MWU - punishable by death or life imprisonment.

Sailor sat down beside Connor, her expression hollow. "What - what do we do now?"

Connor stared at the ground, the weight of the situation pressing down on him. For once, he didn't have an answer. They were up against something much bigger than themselves, and now, Lieutenant Haase was in the center of it all. They were left in stunned silence, not knowing what to do next.

23 IN HONOR AND LOSS

Connor left the debriefing room in silence at first, his fists clenched at his sides. His squad followed close behind, still trying to process what they'd heard. The shock hadn't worn off yet—but beneath it, frustration simmered. Lieutenant Haase—the one person they trusted—was now being held in custody, charged with intergalactic treason. As the hallway stretched ahead of them, disbelief gave way to rising anger. It felt like everything was unraveling at once. Connor's jaw tightened. He wanted answers—answers no one seemed willing to give.

The hallways of the Galactic Law Enforcement Agency felt colder than usual as they made their way to the holding area. The sterile environment, the unflinching guards, and the pervasive air of quiet authority only amplified the worry gnawing at his insides. Connor's mind spun in a hundred directions. What had they done to her? Why had they arrested her? Had her investigation into the Supreme Chancellor sealed her fate?

"She's in there, right?" Sailor Grace asked, her voice edged with concern as she glanced at the rows of locked doors. It was clear the situation was gnawing at her too.

Sailor's fingers flexed at her sides, the movement barely perceptible. Growing up on outposts where command decisions meant the difference between survival and silence, she had learned early to trust authority—but only to a point. Lieutenant Haase had earned her respect by listening, not just commanding. Now, seeing her locked away without explanation twisted something in Grace's gut. She hated this kind of quiet—the kind that screamed betrayal before anyone dared say it aloud.

Connor nodded, though his lips remained in a tight line. "Yeah. They're allowing me to see her. The rest of you will have to wait outside."

Ambryst placed a hand on Connor's shoulder, his usual optimistic demeanor replaced with something somber. "Watch yourself in there. We don't know who's listening."

Connor gave him a tight nod before stepping forward, letting the guards guide him to the visitation room. They scanned him, thoroughly checking for any contraband or hidden devices, before letting him inside. The door clanged shut behind him, and for a brief second, the silence was deafening.

Across from him, sitting in a steel chair, was Lieutenant Haase. Only she didn't look like the strong, commanding officer he had known. She looked beaten - exhausted. There were deep bags under her eyes, her lips were dry, and her wrists were bound in electronic cuffs. Connor's breath caught in his throat. It was clear they had tortured her for information. Anger bubbled up inside him, but he forced it down. He needed to stay focused.

"Lieutenant-" he started, but she immediately shook her head, her eyes wide, almost pleading.

Connor blinked in confusion, watching as Haase motioned subtly with her head, gesturing behind him. His brow furrowed as he glanced over his shoulder. There, on the far wall, was a small camera, its red light blinking steadily. It was recording everything. They were being watched.

Connor's mouth went dry as the realization hit him. He couldn't ask her anything - couldn't speak openly here. They were monitoring every word, and whatever Haase had been through, she wasn't going to risk saying anything that could make her situation worse.

"Lieutenant Haase, I-" Connor stammered, unsure of what to say next. But once again, she shook her head.

This time, she raised a trembling hand, putting a finger over her mouth - a silent plea for him to stop asking questions. Her eyes conveyed what her mouth couldn't. She wasn't safe here. They weren't safe here.

Connor's jaw tightened. His instinct was to help her, to figure out a way—any way—to get her out of this mess. But how? The cell was monitored by cameras, and a uniformed guard stood just inside the door, subtly shifting his stance as he listened in. Every word, every glance, was under scrutiny. Connor's mind raced, but he knew there was nothing he could say here—not without putting her in even more danger.

The silence in the room felt stagnant. Connor wanted to scream, to demand answers, but Haase's eyes bore into him, her silent plea for him to stay quiet holding him in place. After a few agonizing seconds, the guard's earpiece buzzed to life. The order was clear.

"Time's up."

Connor's heart dropped as Haase stood slowly, her movements sluggish and stiff from whatever they had done to her. She glanced at him one more time, her eyes filled with unspoken words and fear.

"I'll figure this out," Connor whispered, his voice barely audible, hoping the camera wouldn't pick it up.

She didn't respond. Instead, she allowed herself to be escorted out of the room, her expression never changing, but Connor could feel the weight of her fear. The door clanged shut behind her, leaving Connor standing alone, anger and confusion battling within him.

As he left the room and rejoined his squad, they could see it in his eyes. Something was horribly wrong.

"Well?" Ambryst asked, his voice barely concealing the suspense. "What did she say?"

Connor shook his head, trying to piece together everything. "She didn't. She couldn't. They're watching everything. She wanted me to stop asking questions."

Sailor Grace frowned, crossing her arms. "You mean - she's being monitored?"

"More than monitored," Connor replied, his voice heavy. "It looked like she'd been tortured. Whoever's behind this is trying to get information from her, or to make sure she hasn't given any information to anyone else perhaps. But she's holding back."

Tyler's topaz-like form gleamed in the dim lighting, his tone low and tense. "We can't leave her there, Sergeant."

"I know," Connor agreed, his fists clenched at his sides. "But right now, we don't know who's watching us. We have to play this smart. Whoever is behind this - they're powerful. More powerful than any of us could have imagined."

Sailor Grace shivered. "This is getting worse by the minute. What do we do now?"

Connor looked out at the empty corridor, his mind swirling with possibilities, none of them good. "We need to tread carefully. The wrong move could get us all arrested, or worse."

Connor's mind was still racing from his visit with Lieutenant Haase. He and his squad had barely made it back to their base near the MWU building when the world seemed to tilt on its axis. He felt the ground shake beneath his feet, an unsettling tremor that rattled through the entire city. His squad was close by, all of them aware of the anxiety lingering after Haase's cryptic warnings, but none of them could have anticipated what was about to unfold.

Suddenly, the sky above them lit up in a violent cascade of fire. Explosions rocked the area around the MWU's headquarters, sending shockwaves that could be felt for miles. The deep rumble of heavy weapon fire echoed overhead, and Connor's heart dropped.

"Sergeant!" Sailor Grace called out, running toward him.

"Look!"

Connor barely had time to process the words before he looked up, and his stomach twisted at the sight. Fighter crafts were locked in battle above the Earth, blazing trails of destruction through the sky. Whoever was attacking them was well-equipped, and they were relentless.

"Zorvakians? They'd probably want some payback after that idiot diplomat did what she did!" Tyler growled, his voice having an intense rigidity as he looked skyward.

Connor's eyes narrowed. "I don't know. But whoever it is, they've come prepared."

The sound of low orbital explosions thundered across the sky, and they watched as several MWU fighter ships broke formation to engage the enemies in quick, deadly bursts of fire. For a moment, it seemed like the battle might stay in the skies above, but Connor suspected differently. This may not just be an aerial assault - there could be more coming, most likely headed straight for them.

"They're targeting the MWU building!" Ambryst shouted, pointing to the flashes of light and streaks of missiles hurtling toward Earth.

Connor swore under his breath. "There's no time to get to our starships."

Without hesitation, he turned to his squad, adrenaline pumping through his veins. "We can't make it up there in time, and they've already started the assault. Stay grounded, and we'll defend the MWU building at all costs. We can't let them breach it."

Ambryst, Sailor Grace, and Tyler all exchanged determined glances before nodding, following their sergeant's lead without question. They knew what was at stake. The MWU building wasn't just a symbol of the Union's power and cooperation; it housed crucial information, high-ranking officials, and the systems that kept the MWU running. If the attackers got through, the consequences would be catastrophic.

As the security alert flared red across the corridor, Connor retrieved his sidearm from the check-in station without hesitation.

"Weapons free," Connor barked. "This isn't a drill, squad. We hold the line here in case this attack gets on the ground."

Ambryst wasted no time grabbing his rifle from his back and checking the energy levels on it before nodding to Connor. Sailor Grace and Tyler were already moving into defensive positions, using the exterior walls and structures surrounding the MWU building for cover. The streets were eerily silent—too silent. Most of the city's civilians had already been evacuated to underground shelters when the first warnings hit, leaving an unnatural stillness behind. Above them, the distant booms of the ongoing space battle rumbled like distant thunder. It was the calm before the storm, and Connor could feel it in his bones.

As they hunkered down, Connor's mind whirred. Who would dare attack the heart of the MWU? The timing was too suspicious. Haase's arrest, the information about the Supreme Chancellor, and now this? The pieces were falling into place, but the picture they formed was nothing short of horrifying.

"Incoming!" Sailor Grace shouted, snapping Connor out of his thoughts.

A ground force. Several vessels roared overhead, dropping black-armored figures into the dimly lit streets below. The city was cloaked in night, and the attackers used it to their advantage, moving with sharp, deliberate coordination as they advanced on the MWU building. As one turned its head, the squad caught a clear glimpse— gleaming obsidian exoskeleton, serrated limbs, and glowing green eyes. Vorlax. No question. These weren't just foot soldiers; they were biologically engineered weapons of war, bred for destruction.

"Contact! Open fire!" Connor commanded.

His squad didn't need to be told twice. Ambryst was the first to fire, his rifle unleashing a barrage of plasma bolts that blazed through the dark. Sailor Grace followed suit, using a nearby column for cover as she picked off enemies with expert marksmanship.

Tyler, with his natural strength, had swapped his rifle for heavier ordinance - a shoulder-mounted launcher that sent shockwaves through the street every time he fired.

They weren't ordinary soldiers. Even in the chaos, Connor recognized the telltale obsidian sheen of their exoskeletons and the eerie green glow of their multifaceted eyes.

Vorlax.

The enemy wasn't just at their doorstep—they were already inside the city.

The enemy soldiers returned fire, their blasts sharp and unrelenting. Energy crackled through the air, slamming into walls and scattering debris. Connor dropped one after another as they advanced, determined to breach the MWU perimeter.

"They're trying to flank!" Ambryst yelled over the din of battle.

Connor saw it too - small groups of soldiers breaking off from the main force, circling around to breach the building from the sides. He cursed under his breath. These weren't mere raiders or rebels; these were elite troops, sent here with one goal in mind: to take down the MWU.

"Tyler, cover the left flank! Sailor, watch the right! Ambryst, stay with me - we're pushing them back!" Connor shouted.

His squad sprang into action, their movements swift and efficient as they repositioned to defend the building from all sides. The enemy was relentless, but Connor's squad held their ground. Every time one of the black-armored soldiers got close, they were met with a hail of firepower that left them crumpled on the ground.

Explosions echoed in the distance as more fighters engaged in low-orbit battles, but Connor focused on the immediate threat. He gritted his teeth, pulling the trigger on his rifle again and again, the recoil barely registering as he aimed at the approaching soldiers. For everyone they took down, two more seemed to replace them.

"We can't let them breach the perimeter!" Connor shouted, his voice hoarse with exertion.

"They won't!" Sailor Grace snapped back; her voice filled with determination. She fired a shot that took down a soldier who had been creeping along the outer wall, aiming for the entryway.

Connor grunted in approval. "We're not losing this. Not today."

The fight was brutal, but the O'Brien Squad fought like they always had - together, with precision and trust. The enemy forces were skilled, but Connor and his team had been through too much, and seen too many battles to let them win. As they held their ground, the enemy forces began to falter, the initial surge slowing as more of their soldiers fell to the squad's relentless defense.

"Squad, regroup! Let's finish this," Connor ordered, his voice filled with fierce determination.

As the last of the enemy forces fell back and the squad stood victorious. Adrenaline coursed through him as he surveyed the wreckage around them. The battle above still raged, but for now, they had defended this part of the MWU building. Connor and his squad knew that other grounded pilots, as well as the entire MWU building's security and staff, were defending the building in other areas, and seemingly winning the fight as well.

Connor's breath came in short, sharp gasps as the dust began to settle from the initial waves of attackers. His squad had fought valiantly, their movements fluid and practiced, but the respite was brief. There was no time to dwell on their momentary success, no time to savor the fact that they had pushed back the first onslaught. They barely had a moment to catch their breath before a new sound rumbled through the streets - a distant hum that slowly grew into a deafening roar.

From the edge of the horizon, ships descended, sleek and black, like shadows blotting out the faint light of dawn. They were larger than the dropships from before, and the sight of them caused a chill to run down Connor's spine. These were warships, and they weren't here for negotiation or posturing - they were here for war. The ground trembled as the ships lowered into the atmosphere, and out of them, spilling like a tide of darkness, came more troops. But this time, it wasn't just soldiers. It was something far worse.

"It's not the Zorvakians, it's the Vorlax!" Ambryst breathed, his voice filled with grim realization. His normally calm, axolotl-like face now showed signs of stress.

Connor had read reports about the Vorlax but had never come face-to-face with one. Now, he saw them with his own eyes - and they were every bit as terrifying as the stories had described. The Vorlax were a towering exoform, each standing over eight feet tall. Their exoskeletons were made of a gleaming, obsidian-like material that shimmered in the light, almost organic in its smooth, armored design. Their long, serrated limbs ended in sharp claws, and their faces - if they could even be called faces - were featureless, except for the myriads of multifaceted eyes that glowed an eerie shade of green all over their heads. Their mouths, lined with razor-sharp mandibles, clicked and chattered, emitting a high-pitched sound that grated on the nerves.

They were a perfect blend of biological terror and tactical precision.

"By the stars," Sailor Grace whispered, her voice filled with disbelief. "There's so many of them."

Connor clenched his jaw. This was worse than he could have anticipated. The Vorlax weren't just skilled fighters; they were relentless. They acted with a singular focus, working together in perfect, brutal harmony. He'd read that even a single Vorlax could overwhelm a soldier with ease—and now, he believed it. An entire wave of them? It was going to take everything they had to survive this.

"They just keep coming," Tyler growled, his voice vibrating in a low hum as his golden skin flickered with tension. His extra pair of arms flexed as he prepared himself for the onslaught, gripping a massive weapon in each hand.

The Vorlax poured into the city streets, wave after wave, their numbers seemingly endless. They moved with terrifying speed, their claws tearing into pavement as they charged the MWU building with a singular purpose. The first line of MWU defenders barely had time to react before being overwhelmed by the sheer ferocity of the assault.

"Hold the line!" Connor shouted, his voice carrying over the din of battle. He swung his rifle up and began firing, his plasma bolts striking the Vorlax at their joints, trying to find weak points in their otherwise impenetrable exoskeletons. It took precision - shooting at the wrong angle was useless, as the bolts would simply ricochet off their armor. But Connor was a skilled marksman, and he took down one after another, though it was like emptying a bucket into the ocean.

The squad fought with everything they had. Sailor Grace, quick and agile, darted between cover, picking off Vorlax with pinpoint accuracy, her laser shots finding the gaps in their armor. Ambryst, with his superior strength and quick reflexes, engaged them in brutal hand-to-hand combat, using a combination of martial arts and sheer power to bring down the insectoid enemies. Tyler, the towering alien with his four arms, wielded heavy plasma cannons, each shot thundering through the streets as he blasted apart groups of Vorlax, scattering their broken bodies into the air.

But no matter how many they killed, more Vorlax swarmed from the dropships. It was as though they were an unending tide, bent on overwhelming the defenders through sheer numbers.

"Why are they so focused on the MWU building?" Sailor Grace asked through gritted teeth, pausing to reload her rifle. She ducked behind a pillar as one of the Vorlax's deadly energy blasts missed her by inches, scorching the ground where she had just stood.

"Maybe they want something," Connor muttered, firing off another series of shots. "This isn't a full-scale invasion. They're here for something specific—and it's inside that building."

"That means they want something or someone inside the building," Ambryst added, grappling with a Vorlax that had leaped over the barricade and lunged at him. He twisted the creature's arm with a sickening crack before finishing it off with a blow to its thorax.

"Which means we have to hold them off," Connor said, determination steeling his voice. "The building's sealed, but if they get close enough—they'll tear through it."

The battle raged on, with the Vorlax forces relentlessly pressing forward. Connor's squad worked in perfect coordination with the other MWU soldiers, creating a makeshift defensive perimeter around the building. They used everything at their disposal - plasma rifles, grenades, energy shields, even their fists when it came down to it. The Vorlax, though superior in numbers, struggled against the tactical precision of the MWU forces. The defenders knew the terrain, knew the building's weak points, and they used that to their advantage.

Updates continued to pour through Connor's comm—reinforcing what they already knew. The attack was still localized. But judging by the resistance, whatever the Vorlax were after, they weren't leaving without it.

"Focus all efforts on the MWU building," a voice crackled through the comms. It was a directive from command, confirming Connor's worst fears. "We need all ground forces to defend the headquarters at all costs."

"Got it," Connor muttered, signaling to his squad. "We can't let them get through us."

Wave after wave of Vorlax descended upon them, their guttural language filling the air as they charged. The ground was slick with the remains of fallen soldiers - both MWU and Vorlax alike. The once-pristine streets of the city had been reduced to rubble, smoke, and fire casting eerie shadows as the battle raged on.

"They're trying to flank again!" Sailor Grace shouted, pointing toward a group of Vorlax attempting to circle the building's east side.

"Enemy movement at grid Delta-Six," Connor called out into the squad comms. "They're breaching left—attempting a side entrance."

A burst of static crackled in his ear as Lieutenant Vashir's voice came through the central command channel. "Acknowledged, Sergeant O'Brien. Redirect Bravo-Twelve and Echo-Four to reinforce your position. Flanking maneuver authorized."

"Copy that," Connor replied. He turned to his team. "Ambryst, Tyler—take the north corridor and establish a crossfire with Echo-Four. Cut off that breach attempt. Sailor, you're with me. We'll hold the front approach and coordinate suppression fire with Bravo-Twelve."

He adjusted his visor display, tagging enemy positions in red. "Remember, hit the joints. Pass it on to any unit you cross paths with."

Tyler and Ambryst sprinted into action, their weapons blazing as they intercepted the Vorlax flankers. They screeched in rage as they were met with fierce resistance, but the O'Brien Squad wasn't backing down.

Connor could feel the exhaustion setting in. His body ached from the hours of fighting, but he refused to stop. He fired round after round, his hands moving almost on autopilot as he defended the main entrance to the building. The Vorlax may have been stronger, faster, and more numerous, but they didn't have the one thing the MWU had - unyielding resolve.

Orders from command were already coming in—multiple squads were moving to secure exits and reinforce the inner corridors. But one flank was still exposed.

"I see them," Connor called out, activating his comms. "Squad Six, the enemy is advancing toward the side entrance. Ambryst, Tyler—intercept and redirect them. Sailor, you're with me—we'll hold the line here until backup arrives."

Finally, after what felt like an eternity of fighting, the tide began to turn. The Vorlax forces thinned out, their dropships slowing and retreating as the assault began to falter. The remaining units were being pushed back, their once-overwhelming numbers now dwindling under the coordinated resistance of MWU forces.

But even as the final wave was driven back, Connor knew this wasn't over. The Vorlax wasn't the type to retreat without reason, and the fact that they had attacked the MWU building so specifically meant that something larger was at play.

The O'Brien Squad held their position near the MWU headquarters, spent but unyielding. Around them, the battle still crackled with energy blasts and shouted orders, but the Vorlax numbers were visibly thinning. MWU forces were regaining control.

The reports over the comms confirmed that the majority of the Vorlax attack ships had been destroyed. Explosions lit up the upper atmosphere as MWU fighters swept through the remnants, blasting apart the last stragglers. Fiery debris streaked across the sky like meteors, crashing into distant parts of the city and sending up plumes of smoke and dust. For a moment, it looked like the worst was finally over.

Another large Vorlax vessel had managed to break through the MWU's defenses in space. It was descending fast, firing indiscriminately on the city below. Connor's breath caught in his throat as he watched the craft's energy cannons target civilian buildings, destroying entire structures in a matter of seconds.

The ground shook beneath his feet as one particularly large building was hit, sending a cloud of smoke and debris billowing into the sky. Connor's heart sank as he recognized the building. It was the MWU's holding facility - the prison where Lieutenant Haase had been detained. His eyes widened in horror.

"No," Connor muttered, barely able to hear his voice over the chaos. "No, no, no!"

Sailor Grace noticed the look on his face and followed his gaze to the crumbling building in the distance. "Isn't that-?" she began, but Connor was already moving, sprinting toward the wreckage with a desperate intensity. The rest of the squad followed without question; their exhaustion forgotten in the face of this new horror.

The Vorlax ground forces had been either eliminated or captured, leaving only scattered resistance. The starship responsible for the prison strike veered away from the battlefield as MWU fighters descended from orbit in pursuit. Despite their efforts, the vessel broke through and escaped into the upper atmosphere.

The cityscape was littered with debris, and the streets were filled with the sound of blaring alarms and sirens. The smoke was thick, choking the air as Connor pushed forward, his heart pounding in his chest. He knew the building well - he had been there not long ago to see Haase, to try and speak with her, and now the entire structure was a smoldering ruin.

As he approached the site, he could see the full extent of the devastation. The prison had collapsed in on itself, huge chunks of concrete and steel piled high, still smoking from the blast. Fires raged where parts of the building had ignited, and MWU personnel were already rushing toward the wreckage, doing their best to search for survivors. But it was clear to Connor that there would be few, if any.

"Lieutenant Haase was in there," Connor whispered, barely able to speak as the reality of the situation hit him like a physical blow. His legs felt weak, and he stopped in his tracks, staring at the rubble as if hoping against hope that somehow, Haase would emerge unscathed from the destruction.

Ambryst put a hand on Connor's shoulder, his expression grim. "There's no way anyone could've survived that."

Connor didn't want to believe it, but he knew Ambryst was right. The building was gone, reduced to little more than a smoking heap of debris. Even if Haase had somehow avoided the worst of the explosion, there was no surviving the collapse of a structure that large. The Vorlax had struck a fatal blow, and they had taken Haase with them.

"She didn't deserve this," Sailor Grace said softly, her voice shaking with emotion. "She was trying to help us, to expose the truth-"

Connor swallowed hard, his mind racing with memories of Haase. She had been his commanding officer, someone he had trusted, someone who had fought alongside him. She had put her life on the line to uncover the truth about the Vorlax infiltration within the MWU's highest ranks, and now she was gone - silenced by the very forces she had sought to expose.

"They knew," Connor whispered, his voice trembling with a mix of anger and sorrow. "They knew she was a threat. That's why they targeted this building. This wasn't random."

Tyler nodded in agreement. His yellow sparkling skin flickered with an ominous glow as he looked toward the wreckage. "They wanted to eliminate anyone who knew too much. Haase was too close to the truth."

Connor clenched his fists, the weight of the moment crushing him from all sides. His squad was right. This wasn't just an attack on the MWU - it was a targeted strike to silence those who could expose the Vorlax infiltration within the Union. Haase had paid the ultimate price for her pursuit of justice, and now they were left to pick up the pieces.

"There's nothing we can do now," Ambryst said quietly, his voice heavy with regret. "Haase is gone."

Connor felt a surge of helplessness wash over him. He had failed her. He had promised to help, and now she was dead, buried beneath the rubble of a building that had once stood as a symbol of justice and order.

"I should've...," Connor whispered, his voice barely audible.

"There was nothing you could've done," Sailor Grace said gently, stepping closer to him. "We couldn't have predicted this. None of us could have."

But it didn't matter. The guilt still weighed on Connor, pressing down on him like the very debris that covered Haase. She had trusted him with the truth, and now she was gone.

The sound of sirens and distant explosions faded into the

background as Connor stood in silence, staring at the wreckage. His mind raced with thoughts of Haase, of the conspiracy she had uncovered, of the commander who had betrayed the MWU. He had to honor her memory. He had to finish what she had started.

The battle had finally ended. The skies above Earth were once again calm, and the remnants of the Vorlax fleet had been either destroyed or captured. But for Connor and the O'Brien Squad, the victory felt hollow. The air was thick with dust and smoke, the aftermath of a brutal attack that had shaken the MWU to its core. Bodies of MWU soldiers, civilians, and Vorlax alike littered the city, a grim reminder of the price they had paid.

A fierce rhythm pulsed beneath his ribs as he and his team silently decided in unison to search through the wreckage. Every second felt like an eternity as they lifted debris, calling out her name in the slim hope that she somehow survived, desperately hoping for a miracle. Tyler, with his immense strength and four powerful arms, was moving the largest of the debris, tossing boulders aside as if they were weightless. His focus was unwavering.

"She has to be here," Sailor Grace muttered, her voice trembling as she sifted through smaller pieces of rubble. Around them, MWU medics and rescue teams worked tirelessly, scanning for life signs and pulling survivors from the wreckage. A few prisoners and guards had been found—injured, dazed, but alive. But Haase hadn't turned up. "We can't let her be one of the names on the missing list," she added, desperation tightening her voice.

Connor's throat was tight, and his chest ached. The dust from the rubble stung his eyes, but the burning sensation was nothing compared to the fear gnawing at him. Every instinct screamed at him to keep looking, to not give up until they found her. He knew the odds, but he refused to accept the worst.

"Come on, Haase," Connor whispered under his breath, his hands trembling as he pried open a shattered piece of the building's framework. "Please."

Suddenly, Tyler let out a sharp grunt, lifting a massive slab of concrete with all four arms. Beneath it, in the dust and debris, lay Lieutenant Haase. Her body was still, her once fierce and determined eyes closed forever. Tyler alerted his sergeant and squad and they all came over to see.

Connor's wrist pad, along with the rest of his squad's, immediately confirmed the devastating truth. The life signs reading came back flat. She was gone.

A heavy silence fell over them. Tyler gently set down the boulder and took a step back, his head hanging low. Sailor Grace covered her mouth, tears streaming down her face as she turned away, unable to look. Ambryst stood frozen, his large, purple axolotl-like eyes wide with disbelief.

Connor dropped to his knees beside Haase's lifeless body. His chest felt like it had been crushed, and for a moment, he couldn't breathe. He reached out with a trembling hand, brushing a strand of her dark hair away from her face. Her uniform was torn and covered in dust, her skin pale. She looked so fragile, so small, lying there in the wreckage of the building she had once protected.

"I'm so sorry," Connor whispered, his voice barely audible. "I should've done more. I should've protected you."

But it was too late. There was nothing he could do now.

They had lost her.

For a few moments, none of them moved. The world around them seemed to blur as they stood there, consumed by grief and disbelief. Haase had been more than just their commanding officer. She had been a friend, a mentor, and someone who had fought tirelessly to uncover the truth. And now, she was gone, taken from them by the very forces she had sought to expose.

After what felt like an eternity, Connor slowly stood, his heart heavy with the weight of his failure. The Vorlax had taken more than just lives today - they had taken someone irreplaceable. Later, they would discover that it wasn't just Lieutenant Haase being held here, but also those who she had included in the investigation. Those that had gone missing after they helped her confirm the

Torak-9 reports. Connor and his squad shook their heads in frustration at how coincidental this all felt.

Days passed in a blur. The city was in a state of shock and mourning as the MWU worked tirelessly to rebuild what had been destroyed. The fallen were laid to rest with honor, their graves marked by solemn ceremonies attended by countless soldiers, friends, and loved ones. Lieutenant Jacqueline Haase's funeral was no different. It was quiet, dignified, and filled with so many who had respected and admired her.

Connor and his squad stood together by her freshly packed grave, the silence between them speaking louder than any words ever could. The weight of their grief was prominent, shared among them as they each grappled with the loss in their own way. Sailor Grace wiped away a tear, while Tyler stood stoic, his face unreadable. Ambryst bowed his head, his hands clasped tightly in front of him as if in silent prayer.

As the silence lingered, Ambryst finally broke it with a soft murmur, half to himself, half to the memory of those they lost: "No gills, no glory…"

Connor stood at the front of the group, staring at the gravestone that bore her name. The pain in his chest had dulled over the days since her death, but it was still there, a constant ache that he knew would never fully fade. Haase had been more than just a superior officer - she had been a beacon of strength and integrity in the MWU. And now, without her, the future seemed uncertain.

His thoughts were interrupted by the sound of approaching footsteps. He turned to see a man in a crisp MWU uniform walking toward them. Captain Dorian Kendall, his new commanding officer, was a middle-aged man with a kind but serious expression. He had taken over Haase's role, and while Connor respected him, the change was bittersweet.

Kendall gave Connor a nod of acknowledgment as he approached, his gaze briefly shifting to Haase's grave. "I'm sorry for your loss," he said quietly, his voice filled with a guarded kind of sympathy. "Lieutenant Haase was an exceptional officer—no matter what accusations were made. Some of us never believed them."

Connor nodded in silence, unsure of how to respond. He appreciated Kendall's words, but they didn't change the reality of the situation. Haase was gone, and nothing could bring her back.

"I'm proud to have you as part of the team, O'Brien," Kendall continued, his tone respectful. "I know this is a difficult time, but we need to move forward. The MWU relies on leaders like you. That's why I am promoting you to Lieutenant. Effective immediately."

The words struck a chord with Connor. Lieutenant O'Brien. The title felt foreign to him, a reminder of the responsibility he now carried in Haase's absence. It was a role he hadn't asked for, but one he would accept with the same professionalism and dedication that Haase had instilled in him.

As Kendall walked away after a few more kind words for Haase, Connor turned back to the grave, his heart heavy with both grief and resolve. His squad stood beside him, united in their shared pain and their determination to honor Haase's legacy. Together, they would face whatever challenges lay ahead.

For now, though, they remained silent, standing side by side as they paid their final respects to the woman who had led them, fought for them, and gave her life for the truth.

The wind whispered softly through the cemetery as they stood there, mourning in quiet solidarity.

24 WAR

Connor sat in the expansive meeting room of the MWU headquarters, surrounded by a myriad of high-ranking officials, strategists, and representatives from nearly every division of the MWU. The room was filled with the soft hum of discussion, punctuated by the sharp, low tones of disagreement. Tensions were running high, and it was no wonder. The recent attack by the Vorlax had left everyone on edge, and the MWU was now trying to decide if it was an isolated incident or a prelude to full-scale war.

The vast room was adorned with holoprojectors that displayed maps of galactic sectors, star systems, and neutral zones. A large table dominated the center of the room, occupied by the highest-ranking individuals in the MWU. Around the perimeter, officers like Connor sat, observing, listening, and waiting for their turn to speak. He had been called in, not as a major player in these discussions, but as a witness to the events on the ground. His squad had seen firsthand the brutal efficiency of the Vorlax, and his input was valued - at least by some.

The debate about the Vorlax's intentions was fierce. On one hand, several of the commanders and diplomats were adamant that this was not an isolated act of aggression but a calculated move by the Vorlax to test the MWU's resolve. They argued that the precision and coordination of the attack indicated that it was not the work of rogue individuals but a sanctioned assault from the Vorlax leadership.

On the other hand, there were voices of caution, urging restraint. The MWU had faced situations before where factions within their own had acted out of line without the approval of their entire government. These officials argued that if they retaliated with full military force, they could escalate the situation into an all-out war that neither side potentially wanted. The Vorlax, an exoform that was new to the galactic stage, might not have fully grasped the consequences of their actions. A few voices even hinted that it might have been a misunderstanding - though those voices were quickly drowned out by the more hawkish members of the MWU.

Connor listened intently, his eyes flicking from speaker to speaker. He could sense the frustration in the room, the way people were eager to act but didn't want to be the ones responsible for sparking a galaxy-wide conflict. His thoughts were conflicted. He had seen the destruction and chaos the Vorlax had wrought during their assault on Earth. They were brutal and efficient, but he wasn't sure if it had been an act of war or a group of extremists within their species.

After hours of back-and-forth debate, the discussion finally began to move toward a resolution. The Supreme Chancellor, a hulking alien from a distant system, leaned forward from his seat at the head of the table and spoke in a deep, resonant voice that immediately silenced the room.

"We cannot act without certainty," the Supreme Chancellor said, his voice calm but authoritative. "But we cannot ignore the threat the Vorlax pose. The attack on Earth, whether sanctioned by their government or not, must be addressed. However, war should be our last resort."

This was him. Connor didn't recognize the Chancellor from the Torak-9 holotapes—those recordings had only hinted at a high-ranking traitor. But now, seeing the Supreme Chancellor up close, his instincts screamed confirmation. This was the one. Xeloron. The alien who had orchestrated everything from behind the scenes.

He had a towering presence, his void-scored exoskeleton shimmering with a dim, icy-blue hue—a side effect, it was said, of surviving prolonged exposure to dark matter currents in the Void Region. His ceremonial robes, white with intricate gold trim, flowed with regal elegance. The markings etched into his armored form pulsed faintly with each movement, casting eerie shadows across the floor. It wasn't just his appearance that unnerved Connor—it was the way he held himself. Calculating. Composed.

Xeloron was the embodiment of power cloaked in secrecy. And for now, Connor could only play along.

Nods of agreement rippled through the room, though there were still a few grumbles of discontent. The Chancellor Xeloron continued, "I propose we send a battalion to a neutral zone. Not to engage, but to meet. We will request an audience with the Vorlax leadership and demand an explanation. If they refuse, or if they escalate, we will be prepared."

The room buzzed with murmurs of approval. The plan was a compromise - a show of strength without an outright declaration of war. The battalion they would send would be large enough to intimidate but not so large as to appear as an invasion force. It would consist of a galactic class ship, almost 100 protector class vessels, and hundreds of fighter class ships - a formidable force by any measure.

One of the military commanders, a grizzled veteran who had seen more battles than most, stood and addressed the room. "We need to be ready for anything. The Vorlax are unpredictable, and we don't know how they'll respond."Then we need contingency plans in place. If the Vorlax escalate, we can't afford to be caught unprepared—especially in a zone this unstable."

Connor agreed with the commander. The Vorlax had proven themselves to be a dangerous adversary. Their attack on the MWU had been swift and devastating. Even with the MWU's military might, this situation was volatile.

As the meeting drew to a close, the plan was finalized. The MWU would send their battalion to the neutral zone, but they would hold their fire unless provoked. A message would be sent to the Vorlax leaders on their home planet, Zenith Prime, requesting a diplomatic meeting to discuss the recent events. If the Vorlax agreed to the talks, the MWU hoped they could avoid further conflict. But if they refused—or worse, if they attacked—the MWU would be ready to deploy its full forces and engage in open warfare.

Connor left the meeting with mixed emotions. He had hoped for more definitive action, but he also understood the need for caution. The last thing anyone wanted was a war that could engulf the galaxy. As he met up with his squad outside the meeting room, he could see the same uncertainty reflected in their eyes.

"What do you think, boss?" Ambryst asked.

Connor sighed, running a hand through his hair. "I think we're in for a long ride. But for now, we wait and see. Let's hope the Vorlax are willing to talk."

Sailor Grace nodded, her brows furrowed in thought. "And if they're not?"

Connor glanced back at the massive doors of the meeting room, where the future of the galaxy had just been decided. "We do what we were trained to do. We fight."

25 THE FRONTIER BATTLE

Gazing out at the endless expanse of space as a battalion of nearly 400 starships prepared to make the jump to the neutral zone was something Connor had never imagined he'd witness. The glow of the instrument panel bathed his face in a soft blue hue, the steady hum of the vessel's engines pulsing beneath his skin like a second heartbeat—so familiar now it barely registered. He was back in his element; space missions always stirred something deep within him. Yet, this one felt different. It carried a gravity and urgency that no previous deployment had matched.

The armada was vast, stretching out before him in an impressive formation. The MWU Sentinel, the Galactic Class ship at the center of it all, was a behemoth, its silhouette casting a long shadow over the smaller crafts like his. Surrounding it were the Protector Class ships, nearly a hundred of them, their shields shimmering as they powered up. Around them, like swarming bees, the fighter ships buzzed—hundreds of them, each ready for whatever this encounter with the Vorlax might bring.

Connor took a deep breath, his mind wandering. The mission ahead was a delicate one: a show of force without the intent to engage - at least not unless provoked. But the Vorlax had already proven themselves capricious, and if things went south, Connor knew that every one of these starships would be thrown into the chaos of battle. He didn't want that, and neither did his squad. Yet, they were prepared for it.

His comms buzzed to life, and the familiar voice of Ambryst crackled through. "You ever seen a battalion this big before, boss?"

Connor smirked, flipping a switch on his panel to open the comms to the rest of his squad. "Not up close, no. I've heard about them, and seen the schematics, but being a part of it? This is something else."

Sailor Grace's voice came in next, a touch of awe in her tone. "It's massive. Almost overwhelming. Can't help but wonder if the Vorlax are going to see this and back off, or if it's just going to provoke them even more."

"That's the main question, isn't it?" Tyler chimed in, his voice deep and calm, as it always was. "They don't seem like the type to be intimidated easily. We've seen what they're capable of. This battalion might just be the challenge they've been waiting for."

There was no fear in Tyler's voice, but Connor had flown with him long enough to recognize the weight beneath his calm. Tyler didn't speak about his homeworld often, but when he did, there was always mention of what war had cost the Threx. Not land. Not territory. But balance. Harmony shattered by decades of orbital skirmishes and silent sieges. "My people once built cities out of resonance," he'd told Connor during one long patrol. "Music, light, and mathematics—woven into shelter. Then came the first cannon."

Now, standing on the edge of another war, Tyler didn't speak out of fear. He spoke out of memory.

Connor frowned at that. Tyler wasn't wrong. The Vorlax had attacked the MWU building on Earth with ruthless precision. The idea that they'd be intimidated by this show of force felt naive, but it was the best shot they had. The MWU had to at least try to resolve this diplomatically, but the reality was clear: they were prepared for war.

"Whatever happens, we stick together," Connor said, his

tone firm. "We're not out here to pick a fight, but if it comes to that, we'll be ready. Let's hope it doesn't go that way."

There was a brief silence over the comms as his squad took in his words. It was strange, Connor thought, how much responsibility now rested on his shoulders. He had always been a capable pilot, but leading his squad into situations like this had tested him in ways he hadn't anticipated. He wasn't just responsible for himself anymore - he had Ambryst, Sailor Grace, and Tyler depending on him, just as much as the entire MWU was depending on this battalion to maintain the fragile peace that still existed.

Sailor Grace broke the silence. "What do you think the Vorlax want? I mean, why go through all of this? What's their endgame?"

Connor leaned back in his seat, staring out into the stars. It was a question that had been on his mind for weeks now, ever since the first attack. The Vorlax were a mystery, their motives unclear. They had once entered the initial stages of joining the MWU, but progress had stalled—and now, their actions seemed to contradict any desire for peace. It was as if they were playing a game, testing the MWU, seeing how far they could push without breaking the tenuous peace.

"I don't know," Connor admitted. "They're a proud exoform, that much is obvious. Maybe they see the MWU as a threat to their way of life, or maybe they just don't trust us. But whatever it is, it's bigger than just a skirmish on Earth. They're planning something, and I don't think it's going to stop here."

Ambryst snorted. "You think this is just the beginning?"

Connor sighed. "I hope not. But we have to be prepared for it. The Vorlax are playing a long game, and we're just now starting to see the pieces move."

The weight of his words hung in the air. They all knew what was at stake. The Vorlax weren't just another rogue faction - they were a formidable force with the potential to disrupt the entire galaxy's balance of power. The MWU couldn't afford to underestimate them.

As the battalion neared the jump point to the neutral zone, Connor's fingers danced across the controls, making final adjustments to his vessel's systems. The hum of the engine grew louder as the starship prepared to leap through space.

"We'll know soon enough what the Vorlax are planning," Connor said, his voice steady.

With that, the signal came from the lead vessel, and the entire armada surged forward into the jump. Each vessel's onboard FTL drive engaged in perfect synchronization, guided by a fleet-wide navigation protocol that calculated micro-second delays to avoid overlapping trajectories. The coordination allowed hundreds of ships to enter hyperspace in staggered bursts—tight, efficient, and collision-free. One by one, the fleet vanished from known space, heading into the unknown.

The vastness of the neutral zone stretched out before the MWU battalion as they dropped out of hyperspace. It was a region known for its isolation—an unclaimed expanse of deep space, dotted only by distant stars and the occasional drifting asteroid cluster. The perfect place for diplomatic talks, or—Connor thought darkly—for an ambush.

The battalion of nearly 400 starships hovered in formation, an imposing force ready for anything. At the center, the massive Galactic Class ship Sentinel anchored the formation, its hull bristling with weaponry and reinforced shielding. True to its name, it stood watch over the fleet like a guardian of old. Around it, the Protector Class ships held their positions, prepared to intercept any threat. Fighter ships, including Connor's squad, patrolled the perimeter, their pilots tense and alert. Everyone knew the Vorlax were unpredictable—and no one was taking any chances.

It wasn't long before the Vorlax vessels appeared on the horizon, their jagged, angular forms cutting through space like silent predators. Their hulls were forged from a matte-black alloy with an uncanny ability to distort nearby light, giving them a blurred, shadowed appearance that made tracking them a challenge. As they approached, Connor could see the sheer scale of their fleet—smaller than the MWU battalion, but still a force to be reckoned with.

"They're here," Sailor Grace's voice came through the comms, friction evident in her tone. "Do you think they're here to talk, or are we about to be in the fight of our lives?"

Connor narrowed his eyes, watching as the Vorlax crafts moved into position, their formations precise and disciplined. "We'll find out soon enough," he replied, though he didn't feel hopeful. The Vorlax didn't seem like the type to negotiate in good faith, but the MWU had to try. Diplomatic resolution was always the first priority - war was the last resort.

Inside the Galactic Class ship, the MWU command and diplomatic teams were already preparing for the discussion. Connor knew from previous briefings that there had been much debate over what approach to take. The Vorlax had shown no remorse for their actions on Earth, and even if those who attacked had been rogue, the Vorlax leadership bore responsibility for what had happened. The MWU had to make it clear that there would be consequences - yet they also had to avoid provoking an all-out war.

As the Vorlax ships came to a halt, the comm channels crackled to life. The voice of the elected MWU diplomat, a calm and confident woman named Ambassador Talia Nyx, filled the airwaves. She had been chosen to represent the MWU in this delicate matter, her years of experience in intergalactic relations making her the best candidate for the task.

"This is Ambassador Nyx, representing the MWU," she began, her voice steady. "We have come here today to discuss the recent attack on our forces and the violation of our peace. While we understand that the Vorlax may or may not have sanctioned this attack, the actions of your people have consequences that cannot be ignored. We are here to negotiate the terms of restitution and ensure that such aggression does not happen again."

There was a brief silence on the Vorlax side before a voice

came through - harsh, guttural, and dripping with disdain. "You presume much, Ambassador," the Vorlax leader hissed. "We do not recognize the authority of the MWU. Your so-called 'laws' and 'consequences' mean nothing to us. We will not atone for what you consider a transgression, because we do not see your Union as anything more than a pathetic collection of weaklings grasping at power."

Connor clenched his fists in his cockpit, feeling the nervousness in the air rise. The Vorlax was as defiant as ever, refusing to take any responsibility for the attack. He could feel the frustration building across the battalion, the pilots and crew waiting on edge for what would come next.

Ambassador Nyx didn't waver. "The MWU is a coalition of thousands of species, working together for the betterment of the galaxy. We do not seek power - we seek peace. Your refusal to acknowledge our authority does not absolve you of the actions taken by your people. We demand accountability."

Another silence. Then, the Vorlax leader's voice returned, colder than before. "We do not care for your demands, Ambassador. The Vorlax do not bow to anyone. If the galaxy is to have a true authority, it will not be your Union. The Vorlax will rule, and you will disband - or face annihilation."

Connor's heart skipped a beat at the sheer audacity of the statement. The Vorlax weren't just refusing to cooperate - they were issuing an ultimatum. Disband the MWU? Surrender the galaxy to Vorlax rule? It was unthinkable. He could only imagine what was going on in the command center aboard the Galactic Class ship.

Ambassador Nyx's voice sharpened. "That isn't happening. The MWU will not disband, and we will not submit to your threats. We are here to discuss terms, but if you refuse - "

She didn't get to finish. The Vorlax comms cut out abruptly, and without warning, their crafts sprang into action. The first volley of plasma bolts erupted from the Vorlax fleet, streaking across the void of space toward the MWU battalion.

"ALL SHIPS! WEAPONS FREE!" came the voice of the MWU fleet commander over the comms, and the battle erupted in full force.

Connor's instincts kicked in as he pulled his fighter craft into formation. Plasma bolts and laser fire filled the space around them, the dark void now alight with the chaos of battle. The Vorlax had made their choice - they had chosen war.

"Squad, stay tight!" Connor called out as he maneuvered through the incoming fire. "We knew this was a possibility - now it's time to fight."

Sailor Grace's voice crackled over the comms. "Looks like the Vorlax aren't in the mood for talking after all."

Connor gritted his teeth as he swerved to avoid a plasma blast. "No, they're not. But we're not backing down either." He locked onto a Vorlax fighter, sending a volley of laser fire into its hull and watching as it exploded into a bright burst of light.

The MWU battalion was holding its ground, but the Vorlax were fierce opponents. Their vessels were fast and heavily armored, and they fought with the precision of a well-trained military force. Connor and his squad weaved through the battle, taking down enemy fighters one by one, but the Vorlax just kept coming.

"They're relentless," Tyler growled as he tore through a Vorlax starship with a volley of fire. "How many of these things do they have?"

"Doesn't matter," Connor replied, his focus razor-sharp. "We'll take down every last one if we have to."

The battle raged on, the MWU battalion holding the line as best they could. But Connor knew that this wasn't just about winning a fight. This was the beginning of something much bigger - something that would shake the very foundation of the galaxy.

The Vorlax had declared war.

The space around the neutral zone erupted into a chaotic dance of destruction. The silence of the cosmos was shattered by the thunderous roars of weapons fire, the brilliant flashes of plasma bolts and laser beams cutting through the darkness as the MWU and the Vorlax clashed with everything they had. Connor could barely hear his thoughts over the endless chorus of alarms, explosions, and the frenzied comms chatter filling his cockpit.

"O'Brien Squad," Connor barked into his comms, "Don't break formation!"

His squad members responded with affirmations, their voices tense but determined. Ambryst's fighter cut through the blackness like a blade, rolling out of the way of incoming fire while returning blasts of his own. Sailor Grace's starship was a whirl of speed and precision, moving as if she could anticipate where the Vorlax was going to fire next. Tyler's multi-limbed alien form worked the controls of his craft effortlessly, each shot he took hitting its mark with devastating accuracy.

The Galactic Class ship in the center of the MWU formation loomed like a fortress, its countless turrets and weapon emplacements lighting up as it unleashed a volley of missiles and energy blasts at the Vorlax fleet. The Protector Class ships spread out around it, forming a defensive screen, their shields flaring up with each incoming hit but holding strong against the relentless assault. The smaller fighter crafts like Connor's danced around them, striking at the Vorlax attackers with speed and precision.

"We've got a swarm coming in from the left!" Tyler shouted over the comms. Connor glanced at his radar, his eyes narrowing as he saw the cluster of enemy fighters closing in. He yanked the controls to the left, his fighter ship arcing through space as he angled himself to intercept.

"I see them," Connor replied. "Ambryst, with me! Sailor, Tyler, keep them off our backs!"

"Roger!" they responded in unison.

Connor's starship tore through the vacuum of space, weapons blazing as he targeted the lead Vorlax fighter. It was a sleek, menacing craft, its black hull shimmering with an eerie purple light. Connor squeezed the trigger, sending a barrage of laser fire into the vessel's side. The Vorlax fighter tried to evade, but Connor's aim was true; it erupted into a brilliant explosion.

"Got you," Connor muttered, but his victory was short-lived as more Vorlax fighters surged forward to take its place.

The conflict intensified, each second stretching into eternity. Massive Vorlax warships traded devastating blows with the MWU's Galactic Class vessel, the shields of both titans flaring with each impact. One of the Protector Class ships took a direct hit from a Vorlax missile, the explosion ripping through its hull and sending it spinning out of control before it erupted into a fiery ball of debris.

"We lost the MWU Arcturus!" a voice shouted over the comms, filled with anguish. "We lost - "

"Focus!" Connor yelled, cutting the pilot off. "We can't help them now! Hold formation and stay locked in!"

He barely had time to process the loss as another Vorlax fighter streaked toward him, its weapons blazing. Connor rolled his craft to the side, feeling the heat of the energy blasts as they missed his hull by inches. He twisted his fighter around, unleashing a volley of his own that tore through the enemy craft, leaving it a burning wreck drifting into the void.

All around them, starships were fighting, dying, and exploding into brilliant fragments of light. The space around the battleground was now a graveyard of shattered metal and glowing embers, the remains of both Vorlax and MWU vessels drifting in the weightless abyss.

"Why aren't they falling back?" Sailor Grace yelled, her voice tinged with fear. "We've taken down so many of them!"

Connor's console lit up with a burst of sensor alerts, and his HUD began painting dozens—no, hundreds—of new contacts flooding into the sector. They hadn't warped in from a jump point; they'd been hidden behind a cloaking field, lying in wait just beyond standard sensor range. Now, they emerged in force—sleek Vorlax warships with light-warping hulls that made them almost invisible against the void. The scale was staggering—well over a thousand ships, all converging on the MWU fleet. It hadn't been a skirmish. It had been a trap.

"Oh no..." Connor whispered, his heart sinking as the realization hit him like a hammer. "It's a trap. They were waiting for us to commit."

The Vorlax vessels executed a coordinated encirclement, emerging from multiple vectors to surround the MWU battalion in all three dimensions. Escape wasn't just difficult—it was rapidly becoming impossible. With the Vorlax occupying the high and low planes of approach as well as lateral flanks, the MWU fleet was compressed into a dense defensive posture. The comms erupted in chaos as officers shouted orders, scrambling to adapt to the sudden, multi-axis assault.

"All units, fall back! Retreat! RETREAT!" the voice of the fleet commander shouted, panic evident even through the static. "Get out of there now!"

The MWU battalion broke formation, the once-organized fleet now scrambling to escape the Vorlax ambush. Connor pulled his fighter around, his heart pounding as he searched for an opening.

"This is bad, real bad!" Ambryst's voice crackled over the comms. "We're not going to make it out!"

"Yes, we will!" Connor snapped, refusing to accept defeat. "Stay close! Stick together! We'll cover each other!"

O'Brien Squad tightened their formation, weaving through the chaos as they attempted a breakout along a narrow corridor between converging Vorlax vectors. Explosions lit up the void around them, shrapnel spinning weightlessly through space, while the screams of fallen pilots crackled through the comms like ghosts in the dark.

"Protector Class vessel down! We lost the MWU Taurus! The Lexington is taking heavy fire - "

The reports of destroyed starships came one after another, each one a punch to Connor's gut. He could barely keep track of how many had fallen. All he knew was that they had to keep moving, and they had to survive.

A quiet storm stirred within him as he veered hard to avoid a blast that tore through a friendly fighter. His HUD lit up with warning indicators, but his eyes locked onto something beyond the fray—an energy surge pulsing from deep within the Vorlax fleet. It wasn't a weapon discharge. It was something else.

Far ahead, towering over the battlefield, was the MWU Sentinel, the Galactic Class Ship that had led the charge. It was the symbol of strength and unity, the very heart of the mission. But now, it was under siege. Vorlax crafts swarmed it like hungry predators, their weapons pounding against the Sentinel's shields. The ship's defenses flickered, the once impenetrable shields now cracking under the relentless assault.

Connor's breath hitched as the starship began to buckle. A series of explosions erupted across the hull, sending debris spiraling out into the cold expanse of space. Flames licked across the massive vessel, and in that moment, time seemed to slow. The Sentinel, a starship that had housed thousands of MWU members, was breaking apart.

And then, with a thunderous roar that seemed to shake the very fabric of the universe, the MWU Sentinel exploded in a massive, blinding light. The shockwave rippled across the battlefield, forcing Connor's vessel to shudder violently as he shielded his eyes. Chunks of the once-majestic vessel hurtled outward at high velocity, their trajectories locked in motion—endless, unstoppable. The sight punched a hole in Connor's chest. The Sentinel was gone. And with it, the battle.

"We need to clear the blockade!" Tyler shouted, his voice strained with effort as he dodged enemy fire.

"Cut through here!" Connor ordered, banking hard to the right as he spotted a gap between two Vorlax warships. "Don't stop! Keep going!"

They shot forward, weaving between the enemy vessels, the barrage of weapons fire intensifying around them. Connor's fighter shook with the impact of glancing blows, his shields flaring as they absorbed the damage, but he refused to slow down.

And then, they were through. The stars opened up before them, and the surviving MWU ships, battered and bloodied, surged into open space, racing away from the Vorlax ambush.

"We did it! We're clear!" Sailor Grace cheered, but the victory felt hollow in Connor's ears.

"Not all of us," he murmured, unable to tear his eyes away from the battlefield behind them. Out of the 400 starships that had made the journey, only a fraction remained. The Vorlax fleet loomed in the distance, like a black cloud blotting out the stars, and Connor knew that this battle had only just begun.

The survivors regrouped as best they could, their engines burning as they fled toward Earth. The losses were staggering—only 73 crafts remained. Through the comms, Connor heard the strained voices of fellow pilots: some silent, others barely holding themselves together. Even without seeing their faces, he could feel the weight of their fear and grief pressing in from all sides as they prepared to jump back to safety.

As the stars streaked by in the endless tunnel of hyperspace, Connor took a deep breath, trying to steady his shaking hands. He glanced at his squad's comms channel, hearing nothing but exhausted breathing.

"What now, Connor?" Ambryst asked, his voice hoarse.

Sailor Grace's voice came through, barely a whisper. "You think this means war?"

Connor's jaw tightened, his mind replaying the moment the Vorlax had turned on them, their demands, their contempt. He took a moment to gather his thoughts, then finally replied with a grim certainty.

"Yes. I believe so."

The silence that followed his words was deafening.

26 CALL TO ARMS

The MWU gathered in the grand assembly hall, a vast space with walls adorned with the banners of countless planets. The usual murmur of diplomatic discourse had given way to a charged silence. Today was not a day for routine debates or trade agreements. Today, the fate of the galaxy hung in the balance.

Connor O'Brien, alongside Sailor Grace and Tyler, stood among the ranks of officers and delegates, their eyes fixed on the central podium. The anticipation was like a physical weight, pressing down upon all who awaited the historic announcement.

Supreme Chancellor Xeloron, his regal robes reflecting the gravity of the moment, rose to address the assembly. His voice, when it broke the silence, was resonant and solemn. "Esteemed representatives of the MWU, we are convened in an hour of unprecedented peril. The Vorlax, with their relentless aggression and blatant disregard for galactic law, have left us with no alternative. It is with a heavy heart that I affirm the Milky Way Union is now at war. The Vorlax have made their position unmistakably clear—and we must respond with unity and resolve."

A ripple of reaction swept through the hall—a mix of resolve, disbelief, and rising tension. The Chancellor continued, recounting the coordinated Vorlax strikes that had ravaged MWU colonies and shattered their diplomatic envoys—acts that left thousands dead and signaled, without ambiguity, that the Vorlax had chosen war. "These were not isolated incidents," he said, voice steady but grim. "They were a calculated attempt to destabilize our Union and dismantle the peace we've built across the stars." Despite the galaxy's access to instantaneous communication, the Council had insisted on assembling in person—an emergency summit designed not only for political formality, but to ensure that no signal could be intercepted or manipulated. The weeks that followed the neutral zone battle had been filled with fractured attempts at diplomacy, growing casualty reports, and mounting pressure from member worlds demanding unified action.

Connor, seated among the honored witnesses, felt a knot in his chest. He knew what no one else in this chamber did—not yet. He had seen Xeloron speak with the Vorlax. He had proof of the betrayal. But without a secure channel or corroboration, exposing the Chancellor now, in front of the entire council, could jeopardize everything. Timing mattered. He just hoped it wouldn't come too late.

As the Chancellor spoke, holographic displays around the room lit up, showing maps of the galaxy with territories marked in stark colors - those under MWU protection and the expanding red that signified Vorlax encroachments. "This is not merely a defensive war," Xeloron declared. "It is a war to affirm our right to exist in the cosmos without fear."

Connor's gaze was drawn to the strategic displays. Each point of light represented a battlefield, a community, and lives at stake. He felt the weight of his responsibilities as a pilot and a protector clasped tightly in his chest. Beside him, Sailor adjusted her glasses—augmented lenses calibrated for real-time data overlays—her expression set in a determined line, while Tyler's translucent structure caught the light, casting prisms on the polished floor.

The assembly was then briefed on the strategic preparations for the war. Generals and admirals took to the podium, presenting the plans for mobilizing the MWU fleets and the logistical support that would be necessary to sustain a prolonged conflict. They spoke of forming alliances with neutral systems, enhancing space fortifications, and increasing the production of warships and armaments.

"Every sector, every planet, every individual under the banner of the MWU must contribute to our collective defense," urged Fleet Admiral Petrell, a seasoned tactician whose face bore the scars of previous conflicts. "We will coordinate our efforts across all divisions - military, scientific, and diplomatic - to ensure that our response is swift and decisive."

Connor listened intently, aware that the coming days would physically and mentally test him and his squad in the worst kind of ways. As the meeting progressed, detailed plans and tactical data flowed in streams of light and numbers. He could see the paths that lay ahead, fraught with danger but necessary for survival.

As the war council concluded, the room erupted into a symphony of voices. Plans needed refining, units required briefing, and every ship in the fleet had to be battle-ready. Connor's squad moved together through the crowd—a unit bound not just by duty, but by experience and a shared determination to stand firm against the encroaching darkness.

"This is what we've trained for," Connor said to his squad as they headed toward their ship, the weight of the council's decision driving each step. "We fight not just for the MWU, but for the future of all peaceful beings in the galaxy."

As the war council dispersed and the clatter of hurried preparations filled the halls of the MWU central command, Connor O'Brien and his squad found a quiet corner, a rare oasis of calm amid the storm of activity. Sailor Grace leaned against a bulkhead, her brow furrowed in thought, while Tyler's multifaceted eyes reflected a deep, unspoken worry.

"What are we really dealing with here?" Sailor's voice was a whisper, barely audible over the hum of the station. "I mean, with the Supreme Chancellor... Do you think he could actually be involved with the Vorlax?"

Connor's jaw tightened at the question. The idea had been gnawing at him ever since they uncovered the video of the MWU pilot's final moments—proof that the betrayal reached all the way to the top. There was no more doubt. Supreme Chancellor Xeloron had colluded with the Vorlax, and the knowledge sat in Connor's chest like a burning weight he couldn't put down.

"I've been thinking about Lieutenant Haase," Connor said, his voice low and tense. "She tried to warn us about the corruption at the top—said the Chancellor was steering things in a way that didn't add up. And what did they do? Silenced her. Locked her away."

Tyler shifted uncomfortably, his topaz-like form catching the light with a glitter. "Yes, and wasn't it convenient how that holding area was destroyed during a Vorlax raid? Almost like someone wanted to ensure those voices were permanently silenced."

The gravity of their conversation hung between them like a thick fog. Sailor pushed off from the wall, her expression grim. "If there's truth to it, we're not just fighting a war against the Vorlax. We're up against elements within our own ranks. That's a dangerous path to tread, Connor. If you think of exposing this, it could mean risking everything - our careers, our lives."

Connor felt the weight of her words. He remembered Lieutenant Haase vividly: a brave officer with unshakeable integrity, her career and life ruined because she dared to speak the truth. Could he risk the same? The thought of being imprisoned - or worse, killed - for exposing potential treachery was paralyzing. Yet, the alternative, staying silent, could jeopardize the entire war effort, costing countless lives.

"I know the risks," Connor finally said, his voice firm. "But if the Chancellor is indeed working with the Vorlax, we have to bring this to light. It's not just about us or the MWU - it's about every life in the galaxy being at stake."

Sailor nodded, her face set in a mask of resolve. "Then we need solid proof. Something incontrovertible. We can't just go on suspicions or we'll end up like Haase."

Pragmatic as always, Tyler chimed in. "We should start by accessing the secure communications logs. If there's any direct contact between the Chancellor and the Vorlax, it'll be there. But it's going to be heavily guarded."

Connor agreed. "We'll need to be stealthy. It's risky, but it's our best shot at finding the evidence we need." He paused, looking between his trusted squad members. "Are you with me?"

Without hesitation, both Sailor and Tyler nodded. "Always," Sailor replied, her voice steady.

"Then let's prepare," Connor said, a sense of determination steeling his voice. "We're not just going to fight this war on the front lines. We're going to fight it in the shadows, too. For Haase, the MWU, and the galaxy."

27 A BRIEF RESPITE

After the harrowing ambush and the war council's grim declaration, Connor found himself back on Earth—not for strategy meetings or combat drills, but to attend Ambryst's medical debriefing. The alien pilot had only recently returned to active duty after being captured and tortured by the Vorlax weeks prior, and Connor had insisted the squad regroup to check on him before their next deployment. It was a rare moment of pause amid the chaos of war.

Lysara joined them at the medbay, not as a bystander, but as a Xeno Officer consulting with the medical team on Ambryst's unique physiology. Her insight had proven vital before, and she continued to earn her place among the crew—not just beside Connor, but within the mission itself. Their personal connection was still fragile, new, but she had become one of the few voices that could steady him when the weight of leadership grew too heavy.

As they left the hospital wing, the four of them—Connor, Lysara, Sailor, and Tyler—walked in silence beneath the twilight sky. For once, they had no orders. No targets. Just each other. And in the quiet between missions, Connor realized how much that mattered.

Later that evening, Connor and Lysara met again—just the

two of them—at a quiet spot in the heart of the city. It was a small café with warm lighting and a relaxed atmosphere, perfect for two people who needed an escape from the burdens of duty. Connor couldn't help but smile as Lysara approached, her lavender skin glowing softly in the ambient light. She wore a simple, elegant dress that flowed as she walked, and her silver eyes shimmered as they met his. For a moment, the weight of everything—war, battle, the future—seemed to disappear.

"You look stunning," Connor said, his voice filled with quiet admiration.

"And you clean up pretty well yourself, soldier," she teased back, her smile warm and genuine.

They started the night with easy conversation, deliberately avoiding the heavier topics that usually weighed them down. They talked about mundane things—favorite foods, awkward childhood stories, cultural misunderstandings that had ended in laughter instead of lectures. Lysara shared a memory of her first time piloting a small scout ship as a child and how she accidentally hit the thrusters too hard, launching herself into open space before a much angrier senior officer reeled her in.

After dinner, they walked through a quiet park, talking beneath the stars. As they reached a small bridge over a stream, they stopped, their hands finding each other naturally. Connor looked down at her, his heart uncharacteristically nervous. This felt different. Real.

"I don't know how I feel about all of this," Connor said softly, holding her gaze. "But I do know how I feel about you."

She smiled, silver eyes reflecting the moonlight. "I feel the same," she whispered.

They kissed, tender and hesitant at first, then with growing certainty. That night, they returned to her apartment, and for the first time in what felt like forever, Connor allowed himself to let go of everything else. They spent the night together, tangled in warmth and quiet conversation until sleep finally pulled them under.

The next morning, Connor awoke to Lysara's soft breathing against his chest. Her hair spilled across his arm like a silken curtain, and for a long moment, he simply watched her, letting himself feel the rare peace.

When he moved to get up, she stirred. "Mmm... what time is it?"

Connor glanced at the clock. "We've got a few hours before we need to be anywhere."

She rolled onto her side with a lazy smile, eyes still closed. "You know, you look cute when you sleep."

He chuckled. "Yeah? You snore."

Her eyes snapped open as she grabbed a pillow and smacked him with it. "I do not!"

"You totally do," he grinned, catching the pillow and tossing it aside. "But it's cute."

They laughed, easing into the morning like two people who'd forgotten what it felt like to breathe freely. Eventually, Lysara rested her head against his chest again, the moment turning quieter.

"Connor... what are we going to do about this war?" she asked softly, her fingers drawing slow circles on his skin.

He sighed, staring at the ceiling. "I don't know. It feels like everything's hanging by a thread."

"Do you think we can stop it before it gets worse?"

"I want to believe that," he said quietly. "But after everything we've seen... I'm not sure."

They lay in silence for a while longer before finally rising. As they dressed, Lysara turned to him, her expression softer, more vulnerable.

"So... what are we, Connor?"

He stepped close and gently cupped her cheek. "You're my gal, of course," he said with a wink.

She laughed, cheeks flushed, silver eyes bright. "Yes. I am."

He kissed her forehead, and as he left the apartment, she

stood in the doorway, smiling after him. When the door closed, she whispered again, this time to herself, "Yes. I am."

Outside, Connor walked into the morning light. The peace wouldn't last, and he knew it. But for once, he allowed himself to hold onto the good—if only for a moment longer.

28 THARA'S RETURN

It had been weeks since the Vorlax ambush, and Connor was still trying to wrap his mind around everything that had happened. The MWU had suffered heavy losses, and the growing feeling of unease throughout the galaxy weighed on everyone. War was no longer looming—it had begun. With each passing day, the Vorlax grew bolder, their attacks more calculated and ruthless. Though the MWU had mobilized, launching coordinated countermeasures across key sectors, there remained an unshakable sense that the Vorlax were always one step ahead.

There was a restlessness in Connor's chest, a feeling that things weren't moving fast enough. The MWU needed to act decisively if they were going to have any chance of coming out of this war intact. But right now, they were in defensive mode, trying to pick up the pieces from the last ambush.

The war had shifted everything—there was no such thing as downtime anymore. But while awaiting a data pull from the internal investigation unit assigned to decrypt Xeloron's private communications, Connor had been ordered to stay low-profile and off active duty until the inquiry progressed. Restless and caged, he wandered the city under unofficial watch. He was sitting at a café, nursing a lukewarm drink and trying not to spiral, when he heard a familiar voice behind him.

"Connor O'Brien. Still brooding, I see."

He turned around to see Thara, the alien engineer he'd met during one of his earlier missions. Her vibrant green, coral-like skin shimmered in the sunlight, and her wide, luminescent eyes caught the light with an almost mischievous glint. She stood confidently, dressed in casual gear, but Connor knew better than to underestimate her. Thara was one of the sharpest minds in the MWU—she'd pulled off a near-impossible repair that had saved his squad once, and he hadn't forgotten it.

"Thara," Connor smiled, motioning for her to sit down. "I didn't expect to see you here. What brings you to Earth?"

She sat down across from him. "Well, I'm not here to exchange pleasantries. I've got something big. Something that could possibly turn the tide of this war."

Connor's brow furrowed, leaning in. "Go on."

Thara glanced around, checking to make sure they weren't being overheard. "We've intercepted encrypted Vorlax communications," she said quietly. "There's talk about a weapon - something that's already been developed. I don't know the full details yet. The encryption was too complex for us to crack entirely, but from what we've gathered, it's dangerous. Extremely dangerous."

"A weapon?" Connor's mind raced. "What kind of weapon?"

Thara shook her head. "What little we do know is…staggering. We do know that it was made by the MWU and its project name was Apophis, cleverly named after the serpent god of chaos in ancient Egyptian mythology. The problem is most of the details are redacted. Top secret stuff, apparently. We're working with scraps of information here, but the Vorlax are putting a lot of effort into finding it. But the most damning piece of information is the weapon's secondary title."

Connor was on the edge of his seat. He could barely handle the suspense.

"They said that it's a planet destroyer." Thara let the words linger in the air until Connor spoke up.

"You...you have to be joking Thara. There isn't something that could simply destroy an entire-" he was cut off by Thara swiftly raising her hand in the air for him to stop.

"Yes. Connor...yes. It's exactly what I said it was. At least, based on what little information wasn't redacted."

Connor sat back in his chair, absorbing the information. "Wait—so the MWU developed this... Apophis, and now the Vorlax have it? Or was it always theirs?"

Thara shook her head. "That's the thing—no one's sure. The files on it are almost entirely redacted, even at my clearance level. All we know is that it was part of a black project buried deep within MWU R&D. Then it disappeared from the logs. Now, intel suggests the Vorlax are using something with a matching energy signature."

Connor frowned. "So either we lost it... or it was never really ours."

"Exactly," Thara said, lowering her voice. "And the only people who might know the truth? They're either dead—or deliberately not talking."

"Well, that's the strange part," Thara said, her voice dropping even lower. "Like I said, The MWU has records of this thing but it's heavily redacted. What's more concerning is that it seems as if someone in the MWU is deliberately keeping this information under wraps. I have my suspicions about who might be involved."

Connor's stomach turned. He didn't need to ask who she suspected - it was the same person he had been silently investigating since the discovery on Torak-9. Xeloron, the Supreme Chancellor, had been feeding information to the Vorlax for years. It wasn't a coincidence that the MWU had incomplete data on a Vorlax weapon that could be a game-changer.

"I'm guessing we're both thinking of the same person," Connor said grimly.

Thara nodded, her expression serious. "If Xeloron's fingerprints are on this, that would explain why the files are so thoroughly erased. Not just redacted—gone. Whole records wiped clean from the MWU network. And given his access, he could've buried it deep enough that most wouldn't even know to look."

Connor narrowed his eyes. "And who's looking?"

Thara hesitated for a moment, then leaned in. "A small group of us—engineers, analysts, and a few high-clearance officers who still believe in what the Union was meant to be. We've been quietly comparing flagged anomalies in the archives. Last week, a data fragment linked to an off-grid facility—unlisted in any current deployment maps—pinged a match to an old test site. We think that's where the Apophis is now—either being refined, or worse, activated."

Connor's eyes lit up. "Where?"

"A planet in the outer regions," Thara said, pulling up a holographic map from her wrist device. "It's called Zekara-5. The planet itself is a wasteland. No sentient life, and barely any atmosphere, but it has a few scattered research facilities. It looks like the perfect place to hide something dangerous."

Connor leaned forward, studying the map. "So we know where it is. What's the plan now?"

"That's where you come in," Thara said. "The MWU has already assigned a team to investigate the facility—but they don't know what they're walking into. The official records have been scrubbed, and most of Command believes Apophis is a myth or a defunct prototype. I pulled some strings and got you and your squad added to the mission roster. Your orders are straightforward: infiltrate the site, confirm whether Apophis exists, who controls it now, and what stage of development it's in. Then get out. No heroics. We can't risk exposing this before we understand what we're dealing with."

Connor nodded slowly, his mind already running through the logistics. "What kind of resistance are we expecting?"

"Hard to say," Thara admitted. "The planet isn't heavily guarded, from what we can tell. It's remote and not exactly a strategic stronghold, but since the Vorlax knows of a weapon that can turn the tide of this war, you can only hope they haven't figured out where it is. Regardless, I'm confident it's nothing you and your team can't handle."

Connor stood up, his decision made. "We'll leave in the morning," he said, determination in his voice.

"Good," Thara replied, standing as well. "I'll send the mission details to your wrist AI. But Connor - be careful. If Xeloron is involved, this could be bigger than just one mission. This could be the turning point of the entire war."

Connor didn't need to be told twice. This mission was critical. They weren't just chasing rumors—they were tracking a weapon that could shift the balance of power in the galaxy. And if Xeloron had already given the Vorlax access to it, then the MWU wasn't just at war—they were already outmaneuvered.

That night, as Connor briefed his squad on the mission, the weight of the responsibility pressed down on him. Sailor Grace, Tyler, and Ambryst listened carefully, their faces serious as they processed the information.

"Sounds like we're diving headfirst into another mess," Ambryst remarked, his tone half-joking, though his eyes were serious.

"We've done that before," Sailor Grace said, though there was antipathy in her voice. "But this… if there really is a weapon that is powerful enough to…" she trailed off in her thoughts.

"Then we'd better secure it—or destroy it—before the Vorlax can turn it on us," Tyler said, his voice gruff but resolute.

Thara gave a curt nod. "Exactly. Officially, Apophis was shelved years ago—most of Command believes it never left prototype stage. Unofficially, someone moved it off the books, and every breadcrumb points to that hidden facility. Our job is to get eyes on it, confirm who controls it now, and make sure it can't be used against the Union."

Connor nodded. "This isn't just another mission. We're walking into the unknown, and we need to be ready for anything. But we're the O'Brien Squad. We've dealt with worse, and we'll get through this. Our objective is simple—gather proof, find out who's really behind Apophis, and expose the truth to the parts of the MWU that still give a damn."

The next morning, with their fighter ships prepped and ready, the O'Brien Squad departed Earth on a classified heading. Starliners streaked past their cockpits as they punched into deep space, each of them silent, focused. Their destination was Zekara-5—a shadowed world buried in restricted charts, rumored to house the weapon that could end civilizations.

29 APOPHIS

The stars flickered beyond the canopy, distant and uncaring, but Connor barely noticed them. His mind was locked on the mission ahead—and everything it didn't add up to. The MWU hadn't ordered this operation through official channels. Thara had pulled strings, using her network of loyalists to bypass red tape and quietly get O'Brien Squad inserted into the mission. Officially, they were reinforcing a dormant research site. Unofficially, they were hunting a weapon that had been hidden—maybe even stolen—from the Union's darkest corners. Apophis. A name scrubbed from every system but whispered among those who knew better.

As Connor piloted his fighter toward the distant planet, unease gnawed at the edges of his focus. The mission brief had been intentionally vague—only a handful of top brass knew what they were truly after. But rumors had already leaked through the MWU ranks. This wasn't some forgotten piece of surplus tech. It was an experimental beam emitter—designed for destruction on a planetary scale.

The O'Brien Squad flew in tight formation around the Cadmus; Sailor Grace's voice came over the comms, cutting through the silence of the cockpit.

"You think we'll actually find something down there? I

mean, it sounds like one of those ghost stories the old pilots tell," she said, her voice carrying a note of skepticism.

"It's real," Connor replied, his tone firm. "Whatever it is, command wouldn't send us out here if it were a wild goose chase."

Ambryst chuckled, his tone lighter than it had been in weeks. "Well, I hope it's not some superweapon that blows up in our faces the moment we touch it."

Tyler grunted in agreement. "If it's as dangerous as they say, it shouldn't be in anyone's hands. Not even ours."

Connor didn't respond immediately. Tyler's words hit a little too close to home. The idea of wielding a weapon capable of planetary destruction was unsettling, even to him. The MWU was supposed to be about unity and peace, but this mission seemed to contradict everything they stood for.

The planet Zekara-5 loomed ahead, a desolate wasteland with a thin atmosphere and a surface that appeared barren save for a few scattered research facilities. According to scattered intel and signal anomalies gathered over the past month, one of those outposts likely concealed the weapon's location—an underground stronghold hidden beneath layers of natural rock and artificial interference.

As they descended through the planet's atmosphere, the eerie silence of the place unnerved Connor. There was no sign of life, no vegetation, no fauna. Just a dead world, devoid of any warmth or hope.

They landed near the coordinates, the Cadmus' landing gear sinking slightly into the dust-covered surface. The O'Brien Squad disembarked, weapons at the ready as they approached the facility. The structure was massive, with thick metal walls and a towering entrance that loomed over them like a fortress built for extinction.

Inside, they were met with cold, sterile hallways lined with darkened terminals and machinery that hadn't been touched in years. The place had an eerie stillness to it like it had been abandoned in a hurry.

Tyler took point, his four arms steady on his weapon as he advanced with practiced precision, every movement crisp and controlled.

"This place is a ghost town," Sailor muttered, her voice echoing slightly in the empty corridors. "Where's the weapon?"

Connor tapped into his wrist AI, pulling up the schematics they'd been given. "According to the data, it's further in. An underground vault, heavily shielded. And a ghost town is a good sign. Means the Vorlax might've not gotten here before us."

They cautiously moved through the facility, descending into the lower levels until they reached a massive blast door. Ambryst worked quickly, hacking into the security systems while the rest of the squad stood guard, their eyes scanning every shadow. The absence of automated defenses was unsettling—either someone had disabled them, or they were waiting to activate until it was too late.

The door groaned open with a loud hiss, revealing a vast chamber beyond. In the center stood the weapon—an enormous beam emitter, its scale alone enough to make Connor's pulse quicken. It loomed on a reinforced platform, its sleek, angular frame built with such precision it felt less like machinery and more like a creature waiting to strike.

Connor's breath caught in his throat. Seeing it up close was different—terrifying. The beam emitter hummed faintly with energy, its core glowing with an ominous, pulsing light. This wasn't just a weapon. It was a promise—one built to end worlds without warning.

"This is it," Sailor whispered, her eyes wide with awe and fear. "This is the weapon that could end the war. Or a planet."

But as Connor stared at the emitter, a sense of dread washed over him. The idea of using something so destructive went against everything he believed in. The Vorlax might be enemies, but they weren't all soldiers. They had families, children, and innocents who had nothing to do with the war.

"Are we really going to use this thing?" Ambryst asked, his

voice low and uncertain.

Connor shook his head. "That's not our call. Our orders were clear—get in, confirm the weapon exists, and report back. But..." He hesitated, his eyes narrowing as he studied the emitter. "This thing... it's too dangerous. Even for us. Imagine if the Vorlax got their hands on it."

Sailor nodded grimly. "They could wipe out entire systems. They'd use it without hesitation."

Connor clenched his fists, torn between his duty and his conscience. This weapon had the potential to destroy Zenith Prime, the Vorlax home world, but at what cost? Millions of innocent lives would be lost. It wasn't a decision he could make.

"We need to report this to command," Connor said finally, his voice filled with resolve. "Let them know what we've found. They'll decide what to do with it."

Tyler grunted in agreement. "Better they keep it locked up than let it fall into Vorlax's hands."

Connor nodded, but a part of him still felt uneasy. The MWU was already on edge with the Vorlax, and this weapon could push them over the brink. Was it worth it? Was there any justification for using something so barbaric, even in the face of war?

They secured the weapon, sending a detailed report back to MWU command. Hours passed as they waited for a response, the weight of their discovery pressing down on them like a heavy shroud.

Finally, the orders came through. The higher-ups had decided to retrieve the weapon but not to use it - at least not yet. The MWU's leadership was struggling with their moral battles, torn between the need for a decisive victory and the knowledge that such a weapon would change the face of warfare forever.

A rather large freighter ship was ordered to tow the weapon back to Earth, where it would be stored securely under the highest level of protection. The decision not to use it was a relief to Connor, but he knew it was only a temporary solution. The weapon existed, and as long as it did, the temptation to use it would always be there.

As the O'Brien Squad prepared to leave Zekara-5, Connor took one last look at the beam emitter. Its dark, looming presence was a reminder of the horrors of war, of how easily technology could be twisted into something monstrous.

He turned away, leading his squad back to their ships.

30 GOODBYE, CADMUS

After completing the reconnaissance mission for Apophis, Connor made his way to the Void Admiral's flagship, the MWU Endless Horizon. He now sat in the briefing room, listening intently as Void Admiral Cassius Morrow detailed their next mission. Morrow was a tall, imposing figure, his face creased with the wear of countless deep-space campaigns. His reputation preceded him: a master of deep-space operations and one of the MWU's top tacticians when it came to uncharted territories.

Seated around the table were several other officers. To Connor's left was Lieutenant Sira Nyven, a sharp-eyed communications specialist known for decrypting alien dialects mid-battle. Across from her sat Commander Jalen Rhys, a seasoned combat strategist whose cybernetic arm bore the scars of old border wars. At the far end, silent but focused, was Dr. Klyen Vestra, a xenoanthropologist brought in for his expertise on ancient alien civilizations.

Morrow's eyes scanned the room, assessing the group before him.

"Your mission is simple in theory," Morrow began, his voice steady and commanding. "We're going to strike at the heart of the Vorlax supply network. Without these supply lines, their war machine will sputter. This operation is one of many covert efforts designed to undermine them behind enemy lines. If you're successful, the Vorlax will be reeling."

Connor exchanged glances with his squad. Ambryst gave him a quick, confident grin—the same one he'd worn back at the Academy, as if danger were just another training simulation. Beside him sat Sailor Grace, calm and composed, her fingers hovering near her datapad, already calculating strike routes and fallback plans. Tyler, seated on Connor's other side, wore his usual stoic expression, the kind that hid the fact he was a demolitions expert with a reputation for being unnervingly calm under fire. That calm wasn't bravado—it was ritual. Before every mission, Tyler mentally constructed the blast in reverse. Not the detonation itself, but the aftermath. The silence. The cracked stone, the drifting debris, the echo of force long spent. He believed that if he could picture the ruin clearly, he could control the chaos leading to it. "Destruction is math," he once said to Connor. "But survival... that's art."

Connor didn't fully understand it. But watching Tyler now, still and centered as the Admiral spoke, he knew the Threx wasn't just thinking about the mission—he was already shaping its end.

They all knew what was at stake. The Vorlax were relentless, and cutting off their supply lines would deal a significant blow to their war machine. It wasn't going to win the war overnight, but it would buy the MWU some much-needed time.

Admiral Morrow continued, "You'll be entering uncharted territory. Deep space. No maps, no intel beyond what we've managed to intercept from Vorlax communications. We know where their supply lines are, but the area surrounding them is a black hole of information. You'll need to rely on your instincts, and of course, your stealth. We can't afford to let them know we're coming."

Connor nodded. Deep-space operations always carried an extra layer of risk. No one knew what might be waiting out there.

"Understood, Admiral," Connor said, his voice resolute.

"Good. You leave in four hours," Morrow replied before dismissing them with a wave of his hand.

Four hours later, Connor and his squad launched from Earth aboard their fighter ships, joining the larger MWU stealth fleet already en route to the outer sectors. While the fleet was tasked with engaging supply convoys and disrupting Vorlax logistics across multiple points, Connor's team had a more surgical objective: to infiltrate a key outpost believed to be coordinating regional supply routes. The cold, vast expanse of space stretched out before them as they sped toward the uncharted region where the Vorlax supply lines lay vulnerable.

The journey was quiet, the only sound in Connor's cockpit being the faint hum of the ship's systems and the occasional chatter between his squad members. Sailor Grace's voice crackled over the comms.

"You ever think about how crazy this is? We're flying into the unknown to hit supply lines that barely show up on scans. No one even knows where they're pulling resources from—but something out there is keeping their war machine running."

Ambryst chuckled, his voice carrying a hint of nervousness. "Yeah, but when have we ever done anything easy?"

Connor smirked but kept his eyes on the void ahead. "This is what we signed up for. We hit them hard, disrupt their operations, and get out. Keep your heads on straight, and we'll be back on Earth before you know it."

Tyler simply grunted his agreement.

As they neared the coordinates provided by deep-scan intelligence, the vast darkness of space seemed to press in around them. This stretch of uncharted territory—flagged only weeks ago by intercepted Vorlax signal bursts—differed from any region Connor had flown through. The area was dense with swirling nebulae and scattered asteroid clusters, but it was the artificial patterns that stood out: trails of energy signatures, thermal wake echoes, and half-cloaked refueling depots tucked into the shadows of celestial debris. It wasn't definitive proof, but it was enough to suggest a hidden supply corridor. Still, the atmosphere was unnerving. As their ships weaved through the field, Connor couldn't shake the feeling that they were being tracked—whether by Vorlax scouts or automated sentries, he couldn't be sure. But there was no time for fear. They had a mission to complete.

Connor led his squad in a sweeping formation as they broke off from the main fleet, following coordinated instructions from MWU command. Their target was in sight: a massive Vorlax freighter, flanked by a cluster of smaller cargo ships and two escort craft. Recent intel gathered from long-range scans and decrypted Vorlax transmissions had marked this convoy as a high-priority target—believed to be transporting fuel cells, modular weapons systems, and rations toward the front lines. Disrupting it could stall several battalions and buy the MWU time to regroup.

"Remember the plan," Connor said over the comms, his voice steady. "We hit them fast, and we hit them hard. No hesitation."

The squad broke formation, diving toward the Vorlax ships. In a flash, the space around them erupted into chaos. Connor's ship darted between enemy fighters, his lasers slicing through the void like solar flares ripping across a star's surface. The Vorlax, caught off guard by the sudden assault, scrambled to defend their freighters, but it was too late.

Ambryst and Sailor Grace took out the smaller ships with precision, while Connor and Tyler's ships hammered the freighters with heavy firepower, disabling their engines and rendering them defenseless. Explosions lit up the void as the supply lines crumbled under the O'Brien Squad's relentless attack.

"First target neutralized," Tyler reported, his voice calm despite the intensity of the battle.

"Good work," Connor replied, already eyeing the next group of supply ships.

They moved swiftly from target to target, dismantling the

Vorlax supply network piece by piece. These convoys weren't front-line battlegroups—they were slower, lightly escorted logistics vessels, never meant to engage in direct combat. Each time, the Vorlax scrambled to mount a defense, but they were no match for the MWU's precision strikes, timing, and intelligence. Backed by real-time fleet coordination and stealth tech, Connor's squad disabled ships before the enemy could regroup. Within an hour, the mission was nearly complete.

Connor took a deep breath as the last freighter exploded in a bright flash of light. They had done it. The Vorlax supply lines were in shambles—multiple convoys destroyed, their logistical routes severed before vital resources could reach the front lines.

"Mission accomplished," Connor said over the comms, his voice filled with a mixture of relief and joy. "Let's head back."

As they turned their ships toward home, the enormity of what they had done began to sink in. The Vorlax would feel this loss. And while it wouldn't end the war, it would give the MWU a fighting chance. For now, that was enough.

Connor couldn't help but wonder how many other missions like theirs were unfolding across the stars. He knew his team wasn't the only one targeting the Vorlax's logistics. The MWU had likely dispatched dozens of strike squads deep into contested space, all relying on speed, stealth, and precision to erode the enemy's war machine. It was a game of chess now, and every move—every hit—mattered.

Back at the MWU command center, Connor stood in silence, still processing the gravity of his recent missions. His squad's destruction of the Vorlax supply lines and their daring retrieval of the experimental weapon had made a significant impact on the looming war. The victory came with an added responsibility—a weight Connor felt growing heavier with each passing day.

It was in the midst of these thoughts that Captain Dorian Kendall called him into his office. Connor, always focused and professional, entered the room, his posture stiff but his expression betraying a hint of curiosity. The Captain sat behind his desk, his eyes sharp and observant. He gestured for Connor to take a seat.

"Connor," Kendall began, "I've been following your progress closely. Your last two missions have made waves across the MWU, and your leadership has not gone unnoticed. Your quick thinking and decisiveness have saved lives, crippled Vorlax operations, and given us an edge in this war. You've done well."

Connor nodded, not entirely sure where this conversation was headed but grateful for the recognition. He had poured his heart and soul into every mission, and hearing his superior acknowledge that effort meant a lot.

"Which is why," the Captain continued, leaning forward with a serious expression, "I'm promoting you to Captain."

For a moment, time seemed to freeze. Connor blinked, trying to wrap his head around what he had just heard. Captain. The word echoed in his mind. He'd worked for years before and during the academy to one day rise through the ranks, but he hadn't expected this moment to come so soon. The title carried immense weight - responsibility not just for his squad, but for an entire Protector class ship and a crew of fifty. This was no small jump in rank. This was a life-changing, career-defining moment.

The Captain, sensing Connor's inner turmoil, gave a rare smile. "I know it's a lot to take in. But this is well-deserved, O'Brien. You've earned it. And you'll be taking command of the MWU Nerak, one of our finest Protector class ships."

Connor exhaled, feeling the rush of both excitement and anxiety. The Nerak - a ship he had only heard about in passing conversation, a massive Protector class vessel that was the cornerstone of the MWU fleet's defense operations. It was built to withstand intense battles and project its shield across entire fleets, protecting smaller ships. The crew aboard such ships were some of the best in the MWU, and now Connor would be responsible for them.

"Thank you, Captain," Connor said, his voice steady but still carrying a hint of awe. "It's an honor."

Kendall nodded. "You're ready for this, Connor. The promotion wasn't my decision alone—it went through the proper channels. But I signed off on it because I believe in your capabilities. Your squad is going to grow from three to fifty. No more flying solo in those fighters for you, O'Brien. You'll have a crew that depends on you, and they'll follow you into Hell if you command them to. You need to be ready to lead them, Captain."

Captain. The word still felt surreal, but Connor nodded once more, standing as he prepared to leave. "I'll be ready, Captain."

As he walked out of the office, his mind was already racing with the responsibilities and challenges ahead. Commanding the Nerak would be a monumental task. But before he stepped into that role, there was something Connor needed to do—one final goodbye to the ship that had been his home for nearly two years: the Cadmus.

A few hours later, Connor stood in the hangar where the Cadmus was docked. His heart ached as he approached the sleek fighter, the ship that had carried him through countless missions. The Cadmus had been more than just a tool of war; it had been a symbol of his growth, his victories, and even his losses. They had shared a bond, the kind only a pilot can have with their ship.

Running his hand over the smooth hull, Connor sighed deeply. "One last spin, old girl," he murmured to the Cadmus, his voice laced with affection.

Climbing into the cockpit, he took a deep breath and powered up the systems. The familiar hum of the engines felt like an old friend welcoming him back. With a smooth lift-off, Connor guided the Cadmus out of the hangar and into the open sky. Earth stretched out beneath him, a brilliant blue marble suspended in an endless sea of stars. He flew low, skimming the atmosphere, allowing the familiar rush of speed and freedom to fill his senses one last time.

As he soared around the planet, memories flooded his mind - his first mission, the battles against monstrous foes, the dangerous rescues, and the countless moments of survival. The Cadmus had been there through it all. It had been his refuge, his partner in the dark, and now it was time to pass it on.

After a final lap around Earth, Connor slowly brought the ship back to the hangar. As the Cadmus touched down gently, he powered down the systems and climbed out. A young pilot, barely out of the Academy, stood nervously by, waiting for him.

Connor smiled at the fresh-faced pilot, remembering his days of wide-eyed excitement. "Take care of her," Connor said, patting the Cadmus affectionately. "She's saved my life more times than I can count."

The young pilot nodded eagerly. "I will, sir. I promise."

"What's your name, by the way?" Connor asked the freshly graduated pilot.

"Elias, sir. Elias Grant. Uh, sir."

Connor chuckled as he patted the young pilot on the back.

"Nice meeting you, Elias. I'll be seeing you out there."

Pilot Grant nervously crawled into the Cadmus, feeling the controls for the first time. Connor watched as the Cadmus took off, feeling a pang of sadness as it disappeared into the sky. But the sadness was tempered with pride. The ship would continue to serve the MWU, and he was leaving it in capable hands.

Turning away from the hangar, Connor walked toward the docking bay where the MWU Nerak awaited him. The ship loomed large; its massive form was a stark contrast to the nimble Cadmus. The Nerak was built for defense, designed to protect entire fleets with its formidable shields and weaponry.

As Connor approached the docking bay of the Nerak, he paused just short of the ramp, taking a steadying breath. The ship was imposing—sleek, massive, and unfamiliar. According to his orders, he wasn't officially in command until the swearing-in ceremony later that evening. Until then, he was just a visitor.

He keyed into the terminal and requested permission to come aboard. A few seconds later, a voice came through the comms.

"Authorization confirmed. You're clear to board, Lieutenant O'Brien."

Connor nodded, stepping slowly into the airlock, the magnitude of his new role beginning to settle in. He hadn't told Ambryst, Sailor Grace, or Tyler yet. He hadn't even spoken to Lysara. Part of him wanted to hold on to the Cadmus—to the years of missions, battles, and growth.

Before entering the ship proper, he turned back one last time. Outside the observation window, he watched the Cadmus shrink into the distance, its silhouette swallowed by a sea of stars. His chest tightened.

"Thank you," he whispered.

He snapped back to reality and stepped off the docking platform onto the MWU Nerak for the first time as its commanding officer. The sheer scale of the ship took his breath away, even though he had been aboard other Protector Class vessels before. This one was different. This one was his.

He paused for a moment, soaking in the sight of the massive corridors stretching out before him. The air smelled sterile, the polished steel of the bulkheads glistened under the overhead lights, and the hum of the energy core resonated through the walls—deeper and more powerful than the familiar purr of the Cadmus. This wasn't the quiet pulse of a lone fighter. It was the heartbeat of a warship, alive with systems, crew, and responsibility.

As he approached the inner corridors of the Nerak, two armed security officers stood at attention, their stances firm beneath sleek MWU armor. One stepped forward, holding out a scanner.

"Authorization?"

Connor presented his ID chip. The officer scanned it, and a moment later, his expression shifted.

"Welcome aboard, Lieutenant O'Brien. You're expected."

The doors slid open, and Connor nodded his thanks before stepping inside.

As he walked deeper into the Nerak's corridors, Connor

couldn't help but compare it to his old ship, the Cadmus. The contrast was stark. The Cadmus had been small and nimble—a one-seater designed for speed and stealth, with barely enough room to stretch his legs after long missions. Every nook and cranny had been essential, every panel familiar. There had been no space for comfort, only survival and precision.

This, however, was something else entirely.

But the Nerak, with its towering ceilings, wide hallways, and vast rooms, was an entirely different beast. It was a flying fortress, designed to protect entire fleets with its massive energy shields and advanced weaponry. Connor marveled at the difference. He'd gone from piloting a ship barely the size of a school bus to commanding something as large as a small town!

His footsteps echoed in the expansive hallways as he made his way to the MWU Nerak's command deck. Along the way, he passed various crew members, all diligently carrying out their duties. They saluted him as he walked by, some with the stiff formality of soldiers, others with the casual respect of those who already knew him from past missions. Connor acknowledged each one with a nod, still adjusting to the idea that he was now in charge of all of them.

"Captain O'Brien," a voice called out from ahead. Sailor Grace, always quick on her feet, was standing just outside one of the ship's larger rooms, her signature purple glasses perched on her nose. She flashed him a grin as he approached.

"Sailor," Connor greeted her with a smile. "What do you think?"

"It's huge," she replied, spinning around with her arms outstretched to emphasize the vastness of the ship. "Feels like you could get lost in here."

"Don't remind me," Connor chuckled. "I'm still trying to wrap my head around the fact that this is my ship now."

She nudged him playfully. "Well, Captain, it suits you. And don't worry—you'll have it all memorized soon enough."

Connor smirked. "Still strange hearing that out loud."

She shrugged. "Stranger things. After all, Ambryst's now a Lieutenant, Tyler's on rotation for special weapons ops, and I've somehow become your senior systems officer."

"Guess we're all moving up," Connor said quietly, the weight of that truth settling over him. "Just hope we don't forget where we started."

Connor smiled but said nothing, taking a moment to appreciate the camaraderie. Sailor Grace had been with him since his earliest missions, and her presence reminded him of how far they'd come. She was like a younger sister—sharp, loyal, and unshakably steady in a crisis.

Life aboard a Protector Class ship wasn't like the smaller crews they'd trained with—there were no civilians here, no families. Just fifty military personnel, all under Connor's command, each assigned a precise function in the ship's operations. Sailor had been promoted to Senior Systems Officer, taking over for Lieutenant Elias Grant, who had transferred to the Aletheon.

No matter how vast the Nerak felt, Connor knew he wasn't alone. His squad had risen through the ranks with him. They weren't just comrades. They were his foundation.

Connor felt the subtle shift in momentum as the Nerak began its ascent into orbit. From the bridge, his senior officers were already executing the scheduled launch sequence—standard protocol while he completed his orientation rounds. He smiled at the thought of watching it all unfold soon from the command center.

As they continued down the corridor, Connor's eyes scanned the various doorways leading to different sections of the ship. The Nerak had everything he could ever imagine needing: a Med Bay for treating injuries and illnesses, a massive Cargo Bay that could store enough supplies to support a fleet for months, and even a Recreation Bay complete with gyms, lounges, and virtual reality rooms to help the crew unwind during long missions.

"It's a far cry from the Cadmus," Connor said, shaking his

head in disbelief. "Back on the Cadmus, I had just enough space to breathe and not much else."

Sailor laughed. "Yeah, I remember. You were practically folded in half when you got out of that thing after a long mission."

She smirked. "I wasn't much better in the Wraith. That cockpit felt like it was built for a contortionist."

Connor chuckled at the memory. "It wasn't exactly the most spacious ship in the fleet, but she got the job done." He paused, his tone softening. "I'm gonna miss her."

She nodded, understanding the sentiment. "But now you've traded up to a flying fortress. Look at this place, Connor. It's got everything! You've earned it."

He nodded in agreement and said "We've earned it. All of the O'Brien Squad."

They arrived at the Command Deck, a massive circular room filled with holographic displays, communications terminals, and control stations. In the center was the captain's chair, overlooking the entire deck like a throne in the heart of the ship. From here, Connor would be able to monitor everything that happened on the MWU Nerak, issue orders, and communicate with the rest of the MWU fleet.

He walked slowly toward the command chair, running his hand along the sleek surface of the control panels. Commander Halen, the acting bridge officer, stood at attention beside it.

"Captain Connor O'Brien," Halen said, his voice crisp. "Per MWU Command Directive 77-A, I hereby transfer operational authority of the Nerak to you. All systems and crew await your orders."

Connor nodded. "Transfer acknowledged."

Halen stepped aside, and only then did Connor take the seat. As he sat down, the weight of his new role settled over him. This wasn't a cramped fighter cockpit anymore—this was a Protector Class command deck. A crew of fifty depended on his judgment, and the mission ahead would test every decision he made.

This was where he belonged now.

The command deck was buzzing with activity as officers worked at their stations, but as Connor sat in the captain's chair, the noise seemed to fade into the background. He glanced at the large windows in front of him, offering a stunning view of the stars. It was a sight that never got old - the vastness of space stretching out in every direction, filled with endless possibilities and dangers.

Connor leaned back in his chair and smiled. "Well," he said to himself, "looks like I've traded my cramped little cockpit for a throne." He chuckled softly.

As if on cue, Ambryst appeared at his side, his axolotl-like features twitching in amusement. He gave a small nod toward the command chair but waited until they stepped into the captain's ready room before speaking.

"Throne, huh? Don't get too cocky, Captain," he said with a grin.

Connor chuckled. "I'll try not to let it go to my head."

The formality dropped just enough between them in private—two friends navigating a new chain of command, still anchored by old trust.

Connor laughed. "You're right, you're right. But for now, I think I'll enjoy the view."

The squad gathered around him on the command deck, each one of them marveling at the sheer size of the Nerak. Tyler glanced around with a look of approval. "This ship is strong. It will protect us well."

Sailor Grace chimed in, "And it's got more than enough room for all of us, that's for sure."

Connor smiled, feeling a sense of joy in his new ship and crew. Ambryst coughed a little and asked a question he was embarrassed to say.

"So, are we still going to fly in our fighters or…?" He let the question die off as Connor chuckled.

"No, Ambryst. I'll have you three close by. Here on the

bridge with me."

Ambryst and Sailor Grace looked at each other and shared a high five with some silent cheers as Tyler gave a half smile, presumably also keen on sticking together.

31 HELLO, MWU NERAK

Connor stood on the bridge of the MWU Nerak, staring at the looming, infinite darkness of the Void Region. The ominous expanse stretched before them, familiar yet deeply unsettling. It had been months since Connor's last foray into this forsaken part of space, and as he gazed into the void, memories of their previous encounters flooded his mind.

He smirked slightly, shaking his head. "Back here again," he muttered to himself. "I guess this place never gets easier."

His squad members—Lieutenant Ambryst, now in charge of tactical operations; Sailor Grace, serving as senior systems officer; and Tyler, reassigned to special weapons integration—were stationed at key positions around the bridge, each locked into final preparations.

They knew what was coming. The Vorlax had regrouped in this remote sector, amassing a strike fleet in the wake of the MWU's recent sabotage of their supply lines. Though that operation had crippled their logistics, it hadn't stopped them—it had only made them more dangerous.

Now, the Nerak's mission was to thin their ranks and reclaim territory lost in the early years of the war. Dozens of colonies had already fallen. Millions displaced. And with the stolen prototype weapon still under analysis—and the identity of the traitor still unknown—every move the MWU made carried risk.

This wasn't the first step. It was the next blow in a long and costly war. And Connor knew they couldn't afford to miss.

Connor pushed the comm button on his chair. "Crew, this is Captain O'Brien. Remember why we're here in the Void Region. Command has tasked the Nerak and other ships with overtaking a secluded Vorlax fleet. This will be a serious win for us—and for the war.

Remember your training. Breathe. Stay calm. We're all in this together. And we can win this."

He released the comm, his voice steady but laced with anticipation.

Connor then asked the bridge if they were ready.

Ambryst gave a sharp nod from his post at the weapons station. "Locked and loaded, Captain."

Sailor Grace, stationed by the communications hub, ran a final check on the system, making sure the rest of the fleet was in sync with them. "All systems go, Captain. Command is ready for the signal."

Tyler stood at the rear console, monitoring the weapons systems with his usual quiet focus. Though he rarely spoke, Connor could sense the tension in him. This wasn't just another mission—it was a full-scale assault, and they all knew what was at stake.

"Good. Let's show the Vorlax what we're made of," Connor said, his voice dropping to a more serious tone.

He tapped the comm. "Nerak, prepare to engage."

The fleet, consisting of several dozen ships, moved in formation as they approached the Vorlax fleet formation hidden within the vast blackness of the Void Region. Their sensors, still a marvel of MWU technology, barely managed to detect the faint energy signatures of the enemy ships.

The MWU Nerak took the lead, its sleek, shielded exterior gleaming as it pierced the stillness of space. As they neared the

Vorlax ships, a heavy tension settled over Connor's chest. This was a dangerous game they were playing—one misstep, and the entire crew could be torn apart by the vicious forces lying in wait.

"Captain, they've spotted us!" Sailor Grace's voice rang out suddenly. "Enemy ships powering up weapons!"

"Engage now!" Connor barked, and with a swift motion, the MWU Nerak surged forward, followed by the rest of their fleet. The first barrage of plasma blasts shot from the Vorlax ships, barely missing them by mere inches.

"Fire at will, Ambryst!" Connor shouted, gripping the armrest of his command chair as the ship shuddered with the force of their retaliatory strikes. The main cannons of the MWU Nerak lit up the void, sending beams of energy slicing through the darkness. Explosions bloomed like brief stars as Vorlax fighters were obliterated in the initial assault.

"Enemy ships returning fire!" Tyler called out from his position, his four arms rapidly working the controls to adjust their shields. "Shields are steady!"

The battle quickly descended into chaos. Plasma bolts and laser beams crisscrossed the blackened skies, lighting up the Void Region in flashes of red, blue, and gold. Fighter ships on both sides weaved through the carnage, trying to get a tactical advantage over their opponents. The Vorlax, known for their relentless assaults, wasted no time in launching wave after wave of ships toward the MWU fleet.

"Keep them in your sights! Don't let them break our line!" Connor ordered, watching as Ambryst expertly targeted the incoming Vorlax fighters, shooting down several in quick succession.

"Their shields are strong, but they won't hold forever," Ambryst grunted. "Just gotta keep hitting them."

"They're trying to flank us!" Sailor Grace warned. "Three ships coming in from the starboard side."

"Keep them off our tail!" Connor snapped, spinning his chair toward the tactical display. "Ambryst, redirect fire to intercept. Tyler, shift the aft shields—now!"

"Tyler, reinforce our starboard shields!" Connor commanded, his mind racing as he processed the battlefield. Every instinct and every ounce of training was being put to the test. The Vorlax were strong, but the MWU had come prepared. This battle wasn't just about thinning the enemy's forces—it was about showing them the MWU would not back down.

As the battle raged on, the MWU Nerak led the charge, its weapons blazing as allied ships followed in formation, engaging the Vorlax from multiple vectors. Coordinated MWU squadrons moved in sync, hammering enemy positions with calculated strikes. But for every Vorlax ship they took down, more emerged from the swirling dark, pouring in from the edges of the conflict zone. Connor knew they were facing a heavily fortified fleet—but the sheer number of reinforcements was staggering, and the battle was quickly becoming a war of attrition.

"They're pulling us in deeper," Sailor Grace muttered, her eyes scanning the sensor readings. "This wasn't just a defensive stand... they want us in the center of their formation."

"They're trying to break us apart," Connor muttered, frowning as he studied the tactical display. "Hold formation. If we let them split us, we're done."

Each second felt like an eternity. Alarms blared, shields flared, and the relentless pace of orders, maneuvers, and impacts never let up. Connor's fleet was holding its ground, but the strain was beginning to show—hull breaches, depleted shields, and mounting casualties across multiple ships.

"Connor, we've neutralized most of their support vessels," Sailor Grace reported, her voice tinged with relief. "If we disable their flagship, it'll disrupt their coordination—and we can force a full retreat."

Connor leaned forward, opening a channel to the fleet. "The flagship's at the rear—heavily shielded but exposed if we punch through. Recommend focusing fire there. Without it, they'll lose cohesion."

The MWU Nerak shifted its focus, launching a barrage of concentrated firepower at the Vorlax command ship. The battle reached its climax as both sides fought with everything they had. The Vorlax flagship, heavily armored and bristling with weapons, retaliated fiercely, but the relentless assault from Connor's fleet was too much.

Finally, with a thunderous explosion, the Vorlax flagship was destroyed, sending shockwaves through the battlefield. The remaining Vorlax ships, now leaderless and scattered, began to retreat.

"We did it!" Ambryst cheered, pumping his fist in the air.

Connor allowed himself a small smile of satisfaction. "Don't get too comfortable. We're not done yet," he said, addressing the Nerak crew. "Sweep the remaining enemy vessels. If any attempt to surrender, prepare to take prisoners."

As the last of the Vorlax ships were eliminated, the MWU fleet regrouped. The battle had been a success.

Connor opened a fleetwide channel, his voice steady but proud.

"This is Captain O'Brien. To all MWU vessels—well done. Today, we struck a decisive blow against the Vorlax and reminded them that the Union will not falter. To the brave souls we lost—your sacrifice will not be forgotten. And to those who fought beside me— you've earned more than just victory. You've earned honor. Prepare for retrieval and regroup. O'Brien out."

"Set a course for Earth," Connor ordered, his voice calm but resolute. "We've got a lot of work ahead of us."

The MWU Nerak and the remaining ships turned toward home, leaving behind the shattered remnants of the Vorlax fleet in the cold expanse of the Void Region.

Of the Vorlax crews, only a few surrendered. Those survivors were taken aboard MWU prison ships under high-security containment. Protocol dictated they be transferred to a classified detention facility for interrogation and war tribunal proceedings.

Connor made sure the process was handled with dignity. He knew how the Union treated its enemies would echo far beyond this battle—and possibly shape the wars still to come.

32 THE BATTLE OF THE THREE SUNS

From the command deck of the hulking Protector Class ship Nerak, Connor gazed out at the sprawling barrage of stars, the weight of his recent victory still fresh on his shoulders. After having reported back to command on Earth, the MWU Nerak was immediately tasked with another mission. His ship, along with the fleet under his leadership, was en route to a distant star system far beyond the regular boundaries of MWU territory. This particular system was unique, not just for its three massive suns burning fiercely in the void but also for the isolated exoforms it housed. Only one planet in the system was habitable, and it was home to that species—an outpost of life surrounded by stellar chaos.

Navigating a tri-star system was no small feat. The gravitational push and pull between the three suns created volatile solar tides, magnetic interference, and unpredictable thermal currents. Long-range scans were often distorted, and traditional comms could become unreliable without constant recalibration. The MWU had only mapped a handful of such systems, and none had been considered viable for conflict zones—until now. It was a tactical nightmare, but for the Vorlax, it made for the perfect cover.

The urgency of their mission weighed on him. The Vorlax, ruthless in their pursuit of galactic dominance, had already made contact with the system's inhabitants. An ultimatum had been delivered: join their cause or be wiped out.

The Vorlax's intent was clear. Their goal wasn't just the domination of this one species - they wanted complete control over the galaxy, with the MWU eradicated. The Vorlax believed that the MWU's attempt to unite different exoforms under one peaceful banner was a threat to their expansionist agenda. Their actions had already sparked brutal conflicts across the galaxy, and Connor had been thrown into the midst of this war. Today's mission was different though. It wasn't just about winning a battle; it was about gaining the trust of a species that had no reason to believe in the MWU. If they failed here, the consequences could ripple across the galaxy. One more ally for the Vorlax could tip the scales of war.

As they neared the system, Connor sat in the ship's war room, holographic projections of the alien planet spinning slowly in front of him. His command team gathered around the table, their faces lit by the pale blue light of the holograms. Sailor Grace sat on his right, tapping at her wrist console. Ambryst leaned forward as he studied the projections, while Tyler stood to the side with arms folded.

Connor tapped the console, switching the projection to a rotating schematic of Vorlax ship signatures. "Scans indicate a mix of their standard warship classes: Talon-class interceptors, Maul-class assault cruisers, and at least one Harbinger-class dreadnought. The Talons are quick and maneuverable—used for harassment and flanking. Mauls are brawlers, durable and armed to the teeth. The Harbinger... it's a different beast entirely. Massive, shield-heavy, and equipped with long-range plasma lances. We can't take it head-on. We'll need to isolate and overwhelm it."

"The system's defenses are practically nonexistent," Sailor Grace began, her voice tinged with concern. "They've lived in isolation for so long, they never thought they'd need them."

Connor nodded. "That's why the Vorlax targeted them. An easy takeover."

"But why is this system so important to the Vorlax?" Ambryst asked, leaning forward. "It's so far from their main territory. What do they want here?"

Connor tapped at the controls, zooming in on the planet's topography and the three suns orbiting the system. "It's a strategic location. If the Vorlax can secure it, they'll have a stronghold far behind MWU lines. It could give them the perfect staging ground for launching further attacks into our territory. And if they get these exoforms on their side, it's just one more ally to strengthen their fleet."

Silence hung over the group for a moment. Each of them understood the gravity of what lay ahead. The Vorlax had to be stopped, and this exoform needed to be convinced that the MWU could offer more than just protection—it could offer a future.

Connor turned to his command staff. "The battle's going to be tough. The Vorlax have already made contact with the locals, and we don't know how far their influence has spread on Cyrix-3. But we need to show these beings why the MWU is their best chance at survival. If we can protect their planet, drive the Vorlax out, and give them hope, they'll stand with us instead of surrendering to fear."

"Not entrenched, but definitely positioned," Connor replied. "Their ships are circling the outer orbit, probably trying to intimidate the locals before moving in."

"Preliminary scans suggest a small strike group—ten to fifteen ships, mostly assault cruisers," Connor replied, glancing at the readout. "No sign of a command vessel, so it's likely just a pressure tactic for now."

"And us?" Ambryst chimed in, cracking his knuckles.

"We've got forty ships with us, including the Nerak. It should be enough, but we need to be smart about this. A frontal assault won't cut it. We need to engage strategically, use the suns to our advantage, and strike when they least expect it."

Tyler spoke. "The suns' gravitational pulls could work in our favor. If we can lure the Vorlax ships into the wrong position, the conflicting gravities could tear their formation apart."

Connor nodded. "Exactly. But we'll need precision. The exoforms on the planet will be observing our movements—if not from orbit, then through their own surveillance systems. If we look disorganized, or if the Vorlax overwhelm us, we'll lose any chance at earning their trust."

He turned to face the squad fully. "This is more than just another mission. We're not just fighting the Vorlax today - we're fighting for the future of this species. We have to be perfect."

The room fell silent again, but this time it was a silence of resolve. Each member of the squad understood the gravity of the situation. Their mission was more than just protecting the system - it was about showing the galaxy what the MWU stood for.

As the fleet neared the system, Connor stood on the command deck, watching as the triple suns came into view. Their blazing light reflected off the hulls of the ships in his fleet, painting the void in brilliant hues of orange, yellow, and red. The planet itself was just a small, dark orb in the distance, dwarfed by the massive celestial bodies that dominated the system.

"Everyone, get to your stations," Connor ordered, his voice calm but firm.

Connor's three closest friends and original squad requested to use their fighters for this mission. Connor approved it, knowing they were excellent in their fighters, but made sure they knew not to make it a habit. He needed them in command with him, so he gave permission this once.

The eerie stillness of space fractured as the Vorlax fleet emerged from the system's outer fringes. Dozens of their warships decloaked from stealth fields or dropped out of subspace, as if pulled from the darkness itself. Their sleek, angular designs contrasted against the brilliance of the three suns, casting long, menacing shadows through the volatile light. The faint shimmer of Vorlax energy shields rippled to life—battle-ready. For a breathless moment, all was still. Then, the comms lit up as MWU command began barking orders.

Connor's eyes flicked over the incoming enemy fleet. His mind was clear. This wasn't just any battle. The lives of all beings on the planet below hung in the balance, as did the MWU's reputation as protectors. Failure here would mean losing the trust of a potential ally and giving the Vorlax another foothold in their war against the galaxy.

"All ships, this is Captain O'Brien," Connor's voice echoed through the comms, steady and authoritative. "Form up and prepare for battle. Use the triple sun's gravitational pull to our advantage. We'll use the light and radiation as cover, strike hard, and retreat before they even know what hit them."

The battle began in a flash of light. The Vorlax opened fire first, their energy cannons lighting up the void between them and the MWU fleet. The space between the fleets became a blinding storm of laser fire and missiles, as the Vorlax sought to obliterate the MWU before they could organize a defense.

"Fleet, stay close!" Connor barked as his ship lurched forward, engines roaring. Ambryst, Sailor Grace, and Tyler flanked him, their fighter ships weaving through the chaos with practiced agility. They veered between bursts of enemy fire and the wreckage of fallen ships, executing sharp rolls and tight turns to evade the Vorlax barrage.

The triple suns created a challenging battlefield. Their intense radiation disrupted targeting systems, while gravitational forces pulled unpredictably at every ship. The relentless energy output strained shield generators, causing smaller vessels' defenses to flicker and fail under the stress.

Connor's voice cut through the comms again, this time sharper. "Pull back into the light - they can't target us if they can't see us properly!"

His squad followed suit, expertly navigating their ships to use the blinding glare from the triple suns as cover. Sailor Grace took point, weaving her fighter through the beams of light, forcing the Vorlax ships to misfire and hit nothing but empty space.

"Ambryst, Tyler - take out their rear defenses while they're blind!" Connor ordered.

With swift, precise maneuvers, Ambryst and Tyler dove through the chaos, flanking the Vorlax ships from behind. A barrage of missiles launched from their ships, striking the Vorlax rear lines and crippling several of their vessels. Explosions erupted, sending debris flying through the battlefield. One Vorlax cruiser split in two, its remains spiraling into the gravitational pull of one of the suns.

"Direct hit!" Tyler's voice came through, his normally stoic tone carrying a rare hint of excitement.

The Vorlax responded with a renewed fury, their front lines pushing harder into the MWU forces. Massive cruisers unleashed relentless waves of firepower, their guns trained on the MWU's Protector Class ships. The Nerak shook as several blasts hit its shields.

"Shields at sixty percent," an officer called out from the bridge, panic evident in his voice.

Connor gritted his teeth. "All power to forward shields! We won't let them break through!"

The Nerak's shields flared brighter, absorbing the brunt of the Vorlax assault, but it was clear the Vorlax were prepared for a long fight. One of their massive dreadnoughts moved into position, firing a beam of concentrated energy at the MWU's flanking ships. Several smaller vessels were obliterated in an instant.

"Damn it!" Connor cursed, watching the destruction. "We need to cut off their command ship, or this is going to get ugly."

He scanned the battlefield, his eyes locking onto the Harbinger-class dreadnought—the Vorlax command vessel. Massive and heavily armored, it hung back from the front lines, directing the assault through encrypted command relays. Intelligence had yet to confirm the identity of its commanding officer, but if past encounters were any indication, it would be one of their warlords.

"Squad, with me," Connor ordered, locking in the command ship's coordinates. "We're going straight for the head of the beast."

The three fighter ships of the O'Brien Squad broke formation, weaving through the storm of laser fire as they set their sights on the Vorlax command ship. The closer they got, the more intense the resistance became. Vorlax fighters swarmed them, determined to protect their commander.

Tyler's ship took a glancing hit, causing his shields to flicker, but he powered through. "I'm fine, keep going," he grunted.

Ambryst took out two Vorlax fighters with a well-placed missile, clearing the path for Connor. As they approached the command ship, Connor could see its massive guns turning to face them.

"Now or never," he muttered under his breath. "Everyone, break and evade!"

On Connor's signal, the squad split, dodging incoming fire as they closed in on the command ship. Sailor's fingers danced over the controls, locking onto the bridge's shield array. "Firing now!" she called out. A concentrated burst of missiles streaked toward the target, striking with a force that rocked the dreadnought and sent it into a slow spin as its systems began to fail.

"They're vulnerable!" Sailor Grace shouted. "Now's our chance!"

Connor clenched the armrest as the Vorlax ship's hull began to shatter under sustained fire. "All ships, focus fire on the Harbinger!"

The MWU forces responded immediately, unleashing a barrage of firepower that tore through the Vorlax lines. The Harbinger exploded in a massive fireball, debris scattering across the battlefield. Almost instantly, the remaining Vorlax ships faltered—just as they had in previous engagements. Their formation collapsed without centralized leadership, a glaring weakness Connor now saw as a pattern. He made a mental note: the Vorlax hierarchy was brittle, and striking down their command vessels could be the key to winning this war.

The battle was over, the echoes of explosions still reverberating in Connor's mind as he stood on the bridge of the MWU Nerak. What was left of the Vorlax fleet had retreated, their once formidable presence in this three-starred system now reduced to the distant specks of light disappearing into the void. The aftermath of the fight had left a heavy silence in its wake, broken only by the hum of ship engines and the soft, persistent crackling of damaged systems being restored to order.

Connor exhaled a deep breath, the tension in his shoulders slowly dissipating. The exoforms that called this system home had been saved—for now. As MWU comms officers attempted to re-establish contact with the planet's leaders, Connor hoped their actions had earned trust. The Vorlax had slipped away, presumably regrouping for another attack, and he knew they'd be back. Still, the immediate danger had passed, and the MWU forces were in control.

As the remaining MWU ships regrouped and scanned the starfield for survivors, Connor and his fleet remained vigilant. The exoforms caught in the crossfire had survived with minimal casualties, thanks to the MWU's rapid and precise intervention. Known as the Aurenn, this peaceful and intelligent race was believed to draw spiritual or cultural significance from the three suns that sustained their world—a mystery still being unraveled by MWU xenologists. Until now, they had remained largely isolated, their presence recorded only in fragmented long-range scans and speculative research logs.

"Captain O'Brien," came the voice of one of the MWU diplomats from his commlink, breaking the silence. "The Aurenn leadership wishes to speak with you and the MWU command. We've initiated contact and they've agreed to an immediate diplomatic meeting."

Connor gave a nod, his thoughts already shifting to the next phase of their mission. Protecting the Aurenn from further Vorlax aggression was critical—but their planet's isolation, lightyears from MWU-controlled space, made long-term defense nearly impossible. The Council would need to decide quickly: either establish a permanent MWU garrison here or begin diplomatic talks about relocating the Aurenn to safer territory. But convincing a people so spiritually tied to their homeworld's triple suns would be no simple task.

"They've been through hell," Connor muttered, remembering the scrambled transmissions they'd intercepted— frantic Aurenn voices calling for aid, images of civilians fleeing into the glowing forests beneath the triple suns, desperately trying to evacuate their crystal-domed settlements. They had no defenses, no ships—only hope that someone would answer. Their survival had depended entirely on the MWU's intervention.

The command room buzzed with activity as Connor made his way to the conference deck, where key MWU diplomats awaited the incoming holographic transmission from the Aurenn leadership. His thoughts wandered to the task ahead, one that was just as important as the battle they'd fought: securing a future for the Aurenn.

The meeting took place moments later via hologram, the Aurenn leaders appearing before Connor and the others. The Aurenn had humanoid features, though their skin shimmered with a silver sheen under the lights, a trait that marked them as uniquely adapted to their home world's intense solar radiation.

"We are indebted to you for saving us," said Valak, the chief leader of the Aurenn, his voice calm but edged with the gravity of the situation. "But we know this victory is temporary. The Vorlax will return."

One of the MWU diplomats nodded, saying, "You're right. Your system is remote, and without ongoing protection, you'll be vulnerable. The MWU is prepared to offer you permanent safety, but it will require you to relocate."

There was a long pause as the Aurenn leaders exchanged

glances. The weight of what the MWU had suggested settled over the room. Leaving their home, a place they had lived for millennia, was not a decision to be taken lightly.

"We understand," Valak finally said, his voice filled with a quiet resignation. "We are not blind to the danger we face, and we know we cannot defend ourselves against the Vorlax without your help. If relocation is what will save our people, then we will accept it."

A murmur of agreement passed among the other Aurenn leaders. It was a decision made out of necessity, not desire, but one they accepted with grace.

Connor felt a mixture of relief and empathy for these people. He understood but couldn't relate to the pain of leaving a home behind, of being forced to flee in the face of overwhelming danger. Relocation might save lives, but it wouldn't stop the Vorlax from claiming the system.

"We can't just evacuate them," he muttered. "If we abandon this planet, the Vorlax will turn it into a forward base."

The MWU would need to do more than relocate the Aurenn—they'd have to fortify the system, deploy long-term defense platforms, and ensure the Vorlax couldn't exploit it. Protecting the Aurenn meant holding the line, not just moving it.

"Very well," said one of the MWU diplomats, stepping forward. "We will begin the evacuation process immediately. The MWU will provide the necessary resources and ships to transport your population to a suitable location within our territory. We'll work with your leaders to ensure the safety and well-being of your people during the transition."

The logistics of moving an entire species across the galaxy was no small task, but the MWU had done it before. They had the ships, the resources, and the expertise to make it happen smoothly. Connor's fleet, alongside several other MWU battalions, would assist in the operation, ensuring the safe evacuation of the Aurenn from their home world.

Days passed in a blur of coordinated effort. Massive freighters descended upon the Aurenn home world, loading up entire cities' worth of people, supplies, and cultural artifacts. The Aurenn, for their part, moved efficiently, their long history of cooperation making the evacuation process as seamless as possible.

The sight of the Aurenn leaving their planet was bittersweet. They were being saved but at the cost of their home.

"This is the right thing to do," Sailor Grace said quietly, standing beside Connor as they watched the freighters lift off one by one. "But I can't imagine how hard it must be for them."

Connor nodded. "They're strong. They'll adapt, but I can't help thinking about what they're losing. The Vorlax did more damage than we know."

The last of the Aurenn ships left the planet's surface. The MWU had bought time, but time wasn't enough. The Vorlax were relentless, and their ambition to dominate the galaxy would not be deterred by a single defeat.

As the MWU fleet combined with theAurenn set course for safer territories, Connor stood on the bridge of the Nerak, his mind already racing ahead to the next battle. The success of this mission was undeniable, but it was just a steppingstone in the long, bloody road ahead.

"Prepare for warp," Connor ordered, his voice steady despite the storm brewing in his thoughts.

33 VANGUARD'S REST

Once back in safe territory, the MWU Nerak along with its fleet of fighter ships were tasked to meet up with a Galactic Class ship, the MWU Vanguard, for their next mission. Connor was excited to finally get to work alongside Commander Brinson. Connor and his crew didn't waste any time getting to the rendezvous point, merging into the vast formation of other MWU Protector class ships, cruisers, and fighters, all surrounding the Vanguard.

The cold silence of space stretched endlessly before the MWU's fleet as they prepared to strike a decisive blow against the Vorlax. Hovering among the stars, their ships loomed like sentinels in the void, the flagship MWU Vanguard at the helm, its formidable silhouette cutting through the darkness. Connor sat at the helm of the MWU Nerak, listening to the varying fleet's chatter over the comms.

"Captain, you good?" Ambryst's voice cut through the stream of commands and reports, steady as ever.

"I am," Connor replied, his eyes scanning the tactical display.

Ahead of them, Commander Andrew Cornelius Brinson commanded the MWU Vanguard with his typical unwavering resolve. Connor admired Brinson, not just for his rank or skills, but for his leadership - a man who embodied everything the MWU stood for. It gave Connor confidence knowing Brinson was in command, guiding them through this harrowing operation.

As the fleet advanced deeper into the Vorlax sector, the void twisted unnaturally, as if reality itself were resisting their presence. Cloaking fields? Gravitic turbulence? The MWU couldn't be sure— but the Vorlax had shaped this space to their advantage.

"All units, engage! Weapons free!" Brinson's voice echoed over the comms, calm but forceful.

The battle erupted in a flurry of lights and sound as laser beams, missiles, and plasma streaked across the vast expanse of space. Connor and his crew followed suit with Connor delegating orders to various officers and crew.

"Stay sharp, Nerak! Focus on the bigger ships. We'll let our fighters deal with theirs!" Connor ordered.

The Nerak wove through the chaos of battle, lasers firing with pinpoint accuracy as Vorlax ships fell in rapid succession. Its shielding systems extended outward, casting protective fields over nearby MWU vessels. Explosions rippled across the battlefield as enemy craft disintegrated under relentless fire. Still, the Vorlax pressed on, their fighters swarming like predators in a frenzy.

The Nerak jolted as enemy fire blazed past, close enough to rattle the hull. Connor gripped the armrest, his jaw set and gaze locked on the chaos unfolding ahead. He'd been in a hundred skirmishes, but this—this demanded absolute precision. One misstep, and the entire operation could collapse.

Suddenly, his command deck display flared with a warning. One of the Vorlax's Harbinger-class dreadnoughts had locked onto the MWU Vanguard. Connor's stomach lurched as he watched the enemy vessel unleash a devastating barrage, striking the Vanguard's core systems head-on.

"Protector class ships, get to the Vanguard if you aren't already," Brinson's voice crackled over the comms, resolute. "Stay focused, everyone. We'll hold the line."

Connor gritted his teeth and commanded his pilots to head to the Vanguard for support. Meanwhile, Ambryst was firing upon the dreadnought's fighters in a desperate bid to draw their attention away from the Vanguard.

But the damage had been done. The MWU Vanguard, though still holding strong, had taken a critical blow to its core, and Connor could feel the gravity of the situation weighing heavily on his chest.

The chaos of battle surrounded Connor as the space above the battlefield filled with ships exchanging furious fire. His ship wove through torrents of plasma and laser bursts, its reinforced shielding absorbing the worst of the assault — a testament to its Protector Class design. Even amid the furious combat, Connor's eyes were locked on the MWU Vanguard. The flagship of the fleet — Brinson's pride — had taken devastating hits. Its once-impenetrable shields, even bolstered by support from ships like the Nerak, flickered and then failed, leaving the great vessel vulnerable to the relentless Vorlax barrage.

Explosions rippled along the hull of the Vanguard as the Vorlax ships pressed their advantage, zeroing in on the wounded beast. A direct hit to the starboard side caused a massive rupture, and debris flew out into the void. Connor's heart clenched as he watched the ship stagger in its orbit.

"We have to help them!" Sailor Grace screamed across the bridge; her tone was laced with desperation.

"If we get any closer, we're dead!" Ambryst cut in. "They're swarming that ship like flies."

Connor clenched the armrests of his captain's chair, his knuckles white. He knew they couldn't do anything to stop the assault, but watching the Vanguard slowly fall apart was a blow that hit harder than any enemy fire. Commander Brinson was on that ship - the man who had led them with wisdom and courage. The man Connor had looked up to for so long.

As if on cue, his comm buzzed to life with a familiar voice.

It was Brinson.

"O'Brien," Brinson's voice was steady, though the strain beneath it was unmistakable. The background noise was chaos — alarms blaring, the ship's frame groaning under the pressure. "I don't have much time, son, so please... just listen."

"Commander..." Connor struggled to find the words, his throat tight with emotion. He knew what was coming.

"Connor, you've always been a fighter," Brinson said, his voice tight with strain but clear. "And you're already a Captain, which makes this next part easier. The truth is, we've lost too many good people. Commanders. Admirals. Leaders across the MWU are dead or missing. It's not just about honor anymore—it's necessity. This is war. Promotions are coming fast, and we need strong, steady hands in place. The High Command and I talked before this mission. If something happened to me, the plan was to elevate you. We've seen what you're capable of."

Connor blinked back the sting in his eyes. "Commander, don't say that. We're not done yet. There's still time - "

But Brinson's voice cut him off. "There's no saving us, son. The Vanguard is done. But we're going to take as many of these bastards with us as we can. You hear me?"

The beat of life hammered in his veins as he wanted to scream. He wanted to tell Brinson to hold on, to initiate evacuation protocols — anything. But deep down, he knew it was futile. The damage was done. The Vanguard was a dying giant, and even the escape pods wouldn't make it out in time.

"I...understand, sir," Connor whispered, his voice breaking.

Brinson chuckled — a warm sound that didn't belong in the middle of a warzone. "Good man. Listen closely now. As Commander of this fleet, I'm officially transferring command of the MWU strike force to you, Commander O'Brien. You are now the acting Admiral. Confirm receipt."

Connor swallowed hard. "Confirmed, sir."

"Then you take care of that fleet of yours, O'Brien. They

need you now more than ever."

The comm went silent. Then, in a flash of light that momentarily blinded him, Connor watched in horror as the MWU Vanguard exploded in a massive burst of energy. The shockwave rippled outward, disintegrating several nearby Vorlax ships — and crippling a handful of MWU vessels that had been too close. Protective shielding saved some, but not all.

Connor stared at the display in stunned silence. The loss of the Vanguard was a gut punch—Brinson's voice still echoed in his ears—but there was no time to mourn. The fleet was in chaos, scattered and leaderless. He straightened in his seat and toggled the fleet-wide channel.

"This is Captain Connor O'Brien, acting fleet commander," he said, his voice steady despite the knot in his throat. "Reform ranks. Defensive perimeter around our injured vessels. Target priority is now the Harbinger-class dreadnought. All ships, on me."

There was a beat of hesitation—then acknowledgments began pouring in from across the comms. He could feel it, a shift in the airless void, as ships realigned, captains rallied their crews, and the MWU forces reformed behind him.

Connor leaned over the tactical display, marking Vorlax weaknesses, rerouting fire teams, calling out maneuvers as instinct took over. He didn't need Brinson's rank to lead—only the crew's trust, and he had earned that through action, not title.

Tyler's voice came over the comm. "You heard him. Let's show them what O'Brien's fleet can do."

The formation tightened. Under Connor's command, the fleet moved with renewed precision—interceptors darted into flanking positions while assault ships regrouped into staggered formations, boxing in the Vorlax with relentless pressure. Connor identified choke points in the Vorlax lines and exploited them, redirecting firepower with surgical efficiency. Then, he spotted what Brinson might have missed—a vulnerable gap in the dreadnought's flank where their shield matrix looped. Without hesitation, he called out the maneuver and led the charge through the breach. The Nerak surged ahead, its shielding network extending to protect vulnerable allies, buying them time to strike. The balance of the battle shifted visibly. For the first time, the Vorlax offensive faltered under the weight of unified resistance.

Connor's hand shook as the reality of it sank in. Brinson was gone. The ship that had led the MWU into battle so many times had been obliterated. The man who had been a mentor to him was no more. His eyes blurred as he watched the remnants of the Vanguard scatter into the void, mingling with the twisted wreckage of Vorlax fighters.

"Captain, we need you," Sailor Grace's voice was soft, but it held the weight of the moment. The rest of the MWU fleet had rallied, taking advantage of the chaos the Vanguard's destruction had caused, and they were pushing the Vorlax back.

The battle was slowly turning in their favor. But the cost had been immense.

Connor wiped his eyes and straightened in his seat. He knew what Brinson would want him to do. They still had a mission to complete. And for Brinson's sake, for the sake of everyone who had fallen, he would make sure it was done.

The surviving MWU fleets that had rallied behind the Vanguard were no longer leaderless—they had found purpose in Connor's command. The fleet's coordination and resolve surged as his orders cut through the comms with clarity and confidence. Victory came not from numbers, but from leadership born in the crucible of loss.

Yet when the last Vorlax ship fell silent, the silence that followed was heavier than any battle cry. Connor sat motionless as his ship drifted through the void, surrounded by wreckage and the cold echo of what had been. The stars still flickered, but their light felt dimmer—overshadowed by the sacrifice that had bought them this fragile peace.

The MWU Vanguard was gone. Commander Brinson was

gone.

A numbness had settled over him, one that he couldn't shake. His thoughts were heavy like a weight pulling him down. All around him, MWU ships were slowly regrouping, survivors rallying together to count their losses and patch up the damage. But for Connor, the battle wasn't over. Not really. Not in his mind.

"Commander? We need to go." Sailor Grace's voice crackled through the ringing in Connor's ears. Her tone was soft and sympathetic, but there was an urgency to it. "Everyone's heading to the MWU Sentinel for a debrief."

Connor blinked, snapping back to reality. He nodded to himself, allowing his pilots to adjust his ship's course toward the massive remaining Galactic Class ship. The Sentinel was one of the few surviving larger ships, and now, it had become the refuge for the battered fleet.

As they landed on the deck of the Sentinel, the full scale of the losses began to hit him. Crews moved in every direction, their faces drawn, some smeared with blood or grime. Wounded soldiers were being rushed to med bays, while engineers frantically worked to repair the damaged ships that had barely limped back from the battlefield.

Connor was the last to leave the Nerak, taking a few extra minutes alone on the bridge. When he finally disembarked, he stepped onto the deck with a heavy heart. His squad—Ambryst, Sailor Grace, and Tyler—were already waiting for him. They looked worn, but alive. That alone was a small victory, he supposed. But the loss of the Vanguard and its commander weighed down every step he took.

Ambryst lingered behind the others as they walked.

The corridor lights cast a pale shimmer across his scaled skin, and he paused just long enough to press a webbed hand against the cool alloy wall of the Sentinel. He could feel it vibrating faintly with life—crew scrambling, systems stabilizing, wounds being patched both in metal and in spirit.

He inhaled deeply through his gills, letting the recycled air fill him. But it wasn't the same. Not like home. Not like the warm, salt-rich tides of his birthworld, long consumed by colonial mining fields and chemical war. A place he hadn't seen in decades.

Around his neck, tucked beneath his uniform, the sea-glass pendant hung heavy. He grasped it now, gently, murmuring a prayer in his native tongue—words he hadn't spoken aloud in cycles.

"To the lost, may the waters carry you gently. To the living, may we find the current that leads us home."

He thought of Brinson—of the way the man had stood tall even in defeat. And he thought of Connor, who now carried that weight.

The squad was whole, but the fleet was not. And something inside Ambryst knew it would never be again.

He rejoined the group in silence, his face as unreadable as ever—but behind his calm eyes, a storm churned.

As they made their way to the debriefing room, Connor was pulled aside by a ranking officer. The grim look on the officer's face told him everything he needed to know. Commander Brinson's death had been confirmed, though part of Connor had already accepted it the moment he saw the Vanguard explode. Still, hearing the finality of it made the grief hit harder, like a fresh wound.

Inside the Special Operations Team Room, the atmosphere was heavy with tension and loss. Commanders spoke in hushed voices, discussing the details of the battle, the numbers of the dead, and the extent of the damage. But Connor barely heard them. His mind was elsewhere — back in the final moments of the Vanguard, hearing Brinson's calm, resolute voice telling him to carry on the fight.

They were victorious today, but at what cost? Was this truly a victory when so many had died, when the Vanguard had been lost in a blaze of sacrifice? The MWU had won the battle, yes, but the losses felt like a defeat in his heart. And worse, several Vorlax ships had escaped.

In a quiet moment after the debrief, Connor found a secluded corner of the ship and leaned against the wall, closing his eyes. His body ached from the adrenaline and exhaustion, but it was his mind and his heart that were the most weary. He thought of Commander Brinson - his mentor, a friend. The man who had guided him and always believed in him. And now he was gone, taken by the brutal reality of war.

The grief came in waves, washing over him in silence. He had lost people before, but this felt different. This loss cut deeper. Brinson had been like a father figure to him, someone who had always seemed invincible. And now, Connor felt the weight of responsibility, heavier than ever. Brinson had entrusted him with the future of this fight and had believed in him enough to give him those final words of encouragement.

Connor knew he had to honor that trust. He had to keep fighting. But there was doubt creeping in - doubt about the war, about the direction the MWU was heading. Was this endless cycle of battles and loss truly the way forward? Was there no other path?

He opened his eyes and stared out of the window into the vastness of space. Somewhere out there, the Vorlax were regrouping, planning their next move. The fight wasn't over. It wouldn't be over until one side emerged victorious. But Connor wasn't sure anymore what victory would even look like.

Brinson's voice echoed in his mind once again, urging him to carry on. To keep fighting. And he would. He had to. But as he stood there, staring into the stars, he made a silent vow: he would honor Brinson's legacy, but he would also search for a way to end this war with as little bloodshed as possible.

The galaxy couldn't afford to lose more good people like Brinson.

34 COMMANDER

"It feels good to be back on Earth," Connor kept telling himself.

The Memorial Service had been both honorable and devastating. Held in the heart of Union Command, it paid tribute to every soul lost in the battle—Brinson among them. Uniforms were spotless, medals gleamed in the light, and solemn faces filled the rows. Posthumous commendations were presented to grieving families, and flags were folded with care and reverence. Connor had stood in full dress, shoulder to shoulder with high command, offering a few words in Brinson's memory—but words had never felt so small.

Even with Lysara's steady presence beside him, the loss still ached. The ceremony lingered in his mind as he stepped through the MWU's automated doors, boots echoing sharply on the polished floors.

The quiet park he had visited just hours ago seemed a distant memory as Connor stepped through the MWU's automated doors, his boots echoing on the polished floors. The holographic projections of distant starscapes and planetary systems lining the walls only served to remind him of the vastness of the conflict ahead - and the uncertainty that lay before him.

The summons he received had come unexpectedly, cutting

through the brief solace he'd found after the recent string of missions.

The message had been brief and formal, leaving little room for interpretation. A high-command meeting - immediately. It was the kind of meeting that could change a career or end it. As he walked down the long corridors, the murmur of ongoing operations surrounded him - officers rushing to stations, technicians monitoring galactic feeds, analysts poring over endless streams of data from all corners of the galaxy. Today, though, Connor felt detached from it all. The battles, the missions, the victories, and the losses - they were all still fresh in his mind, but today, something else loomed larger.

He was ushered into the briefing room, where the weight of the moment hit him even harder. Around the long, crescent-shaped table sat members of MWU High Command from various divisions. Their expressions were unreadable but their presence unmistakably imposing. They were the architects of the war, the decision-makers guiding the galaxy's future. And now, all eyes were on him.

Connor took a deep breath as he stepped into the room, feeling the cold prickle of anticipation up his spine. He saluted, taking his place in the center, waiting for whatever news they were about to deliver. As the room settled, the lead officer cleared his throat.

"Captain O'Brien," began the officer, his voice calm and steady, but with an undeniable weight behind it. "Your service and leadership during recent missions have not gone unnoticed. Your actions have saved countless lives, and your decision-making under fire has consistently placed the MWU in a stronger position."

Connor swallowed hard, trying to keep his expression neutral, but inside, his thoughts were racing. He knew he'd been effective in the field, but what was this all leading to?

"We've reviewed the circumstances of your field promotion," the officer continued, "and after thorough consideration, High Command has unanimously agreed to confirm your status as Commander, effective immediately."

Connor blinked. For a moment, the words didn't quite register. Commander? His mind reeled, trying to grasp the full weight of what that title meant.

In the MWU, becoming a Commander wasn't just a step up—it was a shift in gravity. It meant authority over not just a crew or a single ship, but entire strike groups, including the Union's most powerful warships.

The promotion had been born in the fire of battle—Brinson's last order—and now it was being made official. The room felt like it was closing in, the air heavy with the permanence of what was being placed on his shoulders.

The officer continued speaking, but Connor's thoughts drifted to Lieutenant Haase. She had seen something in him long before he ever had. Years ago, she'd taken him aboard a Galactic Class ship during what he thought was just a routine orientation. Somewhere in that quiet moment between stars, she had told him, "You're destined for something bigger, Connor. One day, you'll understand."

At the time, it had felt like nothing more than encouragement from a superior officer. But now, standing in this room as his field promotion was being made official, her words echoed with a clarity he hadn't understood—until now.

In his mind, Connor replayed the memories of recent battles - the heat of the fighting, the lives lost, and the crushing weight of command. Could he handle even more responsibility? Could he bear the burden of leading thousands of beings into battle, knowing that every decision he made would carry life-or-death consequences?

One of the senior officers, clearly noticing Connor's hesitation, leaned forward slightly. "We understand this is a significant decision, O'Brien. It's not one we've made lightly. The war is escalating, and we need leaders like you to guide us through the difficult times ahead. And-" the officer's words trailed a little as he looked at the other high-ranking individuals in the room, "-if I'm being candid, we're losing a lot of good people to this war. Those people have ranks and titles and commands that need to be filled by someone."

Connor shifted uncomfortably. The war had already cost him so much—Brinson, Haase, and too many others whose names were now etched into the memorials of the fallen. He thought of the battles ahead—the sacrifices that would be required.

He hadn't dreamed of becoming a Commander. He'd joined the MWU to fly, to protect, to serve from the cockpit of a fighter, not from the command deck of a Galactic Class ship. A floating city. A fortress. A responsibility that felt galaxies away from who he used to be.

But personal desires didn't factor into service. He had sworn an oath—one that demanded obedience, sacrifice, and honor without hesitation. This promotion wasn't a request. It was a call to fulfill his duty. And ready or not, he would answer.

And yet, it wasn't about what he wanted anymore, was it? This was war, and war demanded sacrifices - of time, of freedom, of comfort. Could he say no to a promotion that might allow him to make a bigger difference? Haase had seen it in him, even Brinson saw it. And now, the High Command was offering him the chance to live up to that potential.

The room fell silent, all eyes fixed on him. Connor could feel the weight of expectation pressing in. The title of Commander wasn't just a promotion—it was a seismic shift. He'd be stepping into a role that carried immense responsibility, bypassing years of traditional advancement.

He knew it would raise eyebrows. Resentment among the ranks was inevitable. But this wasn't about popularity—it was about duty. About honoring the sacrifice of those who believed in him. Connor met the gaze of each officer in turn.

Then, with a measured breath, he spoke. "I need time to consider the full weight of what's being asked of me."

The lead officer nodded. "Understood, Commander O'Brien.

But be swift. The war waits for no one."

Connor saluted and left the room, the gravity of his new command pressing down with every step. Outside, the sky was overcast—a fitting reflection of his mood as he walked through the bustling city streets. The path ahead was no longer a question of choice, but of duty. The MWU had placed its trust in him, and now he had to rise to meet it.

Connor took his time with the offer of promotion to Commander. The weight of the decision loomed large after everything that had unfolded recently, and he needed clarity before making such a life-altering choice. The proposal was overwhelming, especially with so much still lingering in his mind. Deciding to sleep on it, he allowed himself a full night's rest.

The next morning, Connor set aside an hour for deep reflection. He knew the responsibility that came with the rank wasn't something to be taken lightly. The prospect of commanding more than just his small fleet weighed heavily on him, but after thoughtful consideration, he found his answer.

Just as he reached his conclusion, his wrist AI buzzed, signaling an incoming hologram call. Almost as if the universe had aligned perfectly, one of the senior officers from the previous day's meeting appeared, asking if he had reached a decision.

Connor had made up his mind, and the timing of the call felt fated. Without hesitation, he stood tall, composed, and responded, "Sir, I humbly accept the role of Commander. I will serve the MWU with dedication and integrity, carrying out my duties with honor for as long as I live."

The call only lasted a few more minutes, with the Officer congratulating Connor and giving him some brief administrative information.

The quiet hum of the MWU headquarters buzzed in the background as Connor stood up to look out the window. The weight of his new title pressed down on him with the mass of a thousand Thrag stones—dense, obsidian-like minerals used by starbuilders to anchor orbital structures. His temporary quarters at HQ overlooked a serene courtyard, with a charming little park in the distance. The stillness outside stood in stark contrast to everything that had happened recently—and the gravity of what lay ahead.

The quiet hum of MWU headquarters surrounded Connor as he stood at the window of his temporary quarters. The garden below was serene, a stark contrast to the chaos and death that had brought him here. The title of Commander weighed on him—he was no longer a pilot in the fight, or a captain guarding the vulnerable. He was a strategic leader now. A decision-maker. A symbol.

He exhaled sharply and turned from the view. The Pinnacle awaited.

Outside in the corridor, officers passed him with stiff nods or careful glances. Conversations stopped when he approached. The promotion had stirred the ranks. He could hear it in whispers—some questioning his readiness, others blaming Lieutenant Haase or Brinson for pushing him too fast. He didn't blame them. He might have done the same in their position.

A junior officer intercepted him near the lifts. "Commander O'Brien," she said, snapping a sharp salute. "Your shuttle to the Pinnacle is prepped and ready."

Connor returned the salute. "Thank you, Ensign."

As the lift doors closed behind him, he let the noise fall away. This wasn't about proving anything to the critics. It was about living up to those who had trusted him—Haase, Brinson, his crew. And for their sake, he would rise to meet this challenge.

When he met with his squad later that day, they voiced their concerns, but in a more supportive manner. Ambryst, ever the blunt one, asked, "How are you going to get them to respect you, Commander? I mean, let's be real, jumping to Commander isn't something people forget easily."

Connor sighed, rubbing the back of his neck. "I know. Trust me, I know. But I didn't ask for this. Command decided, and now it's on me to prove it wasn't a mistake." He looked around at his squad - Ambryst, Sailor Grace, and Tyler - and saw the uncertainty in their faces. But he also saw loyalty.

"We believe in you," Sailor Grace said softly. "But the others, they're going to take some convincing."

Connor nodded. "I don't expect it to be easy. They've been in the trenches just as long as I have, maybe longer. But I'm not here to make friends or ask for their approval. I'm here to do the job."

Tyler, in his usual steady voice, added, "They'll see your worth, Connor. You've led us through enough missions, and you'll do the same for them. But until they see it with their own eyes, don't expect the tension to go away."

Connor appreciated their support. As he left his friends to prepare for their new roles aboard the Pinnacle, he couldn't help but think of Commander Brinson. Tyler would serve as his head of security, Ambryst had been tapped as Chief Tactical Officer, and Sailor Grace would manage communications and serve as liaison to the Union's Xeno Relations division. Each of them had earned their place—but Connor still wondered: would Brinson have handled this promotion with the same steady confidence he always carried? Could he?

Later that evening, Connor finally stepped aboard the MWU Pinnacle for the first time. The massive Galactic Class ship towered above everything he had ever flown before. It was a far cry from other ships he had piloted before.

The scale of his responsibility hit him all at once. As he reached the command deck, he took a deep breath. It was both exhilarating and terrifying. Connor stood there, taking it all in, feeling the enormity of the task ahead. This was his ship now. His crew. His responsibility.

35 MAJOR FRIENDS

Connor strode onto the command deck of the MWU Pinnacle, the doors parting with a soft hiss. Officers stood at attention as he passed, the enormity of the ship reflected in their precise coordination. He nodded at each of them, trying to project the confidence he hadn't fully earned yet.

"Commander on deck," called Lieutenant Vesh, his newly appointed second-in-command—an experienced tactical officer from the Galactic fleet. She handed Connor a datapad without missing a beat. "Latest reports: engineering confirms full system integrity, medical is fully staffed, and security rotations are back on schedule. Also... we've received four formal complaints about the recent promotions. Anonymous, of course."

Connor exhaled through his nose, eyes scanning the bridge. The Pinnacle buzzed with activity—officers relaying orders, navigators plotting movement through the sector's fringes, defense teams drilling formations. Every piece moved like clockwork, and now he was the one responsible for keeping that clock from breaking.

"Thanks, Vesh," he said, accepting the pad. "Schedule a sit-down with department leads tomorrow. I want their candid feedback."

"Yes, sir. And… off the record?" Vesh's voice dropped slightly. "They're adjusting to you. Some faster than others. But your reputation from Torak-9 and Celtrix carries weight."

Connor gave her a grateful nod. "I'll take whatever weight I can get."

As he circled the bridge, he noticed how some officers straightened up a little too quickly, or stole glances when they thought he wasn't looking. He couldn't change how he got here— leaping two ranks in wartime was always going to sting. But he could earn their respect the hard way: by doing the job.

He ducked into the nearby situation room, where tactical maps of ongoing battles flickered across a massive holo-display. Tyler, now officially head of security, stood beside the projection with a cluster of junior officers. He looked up as Connor entered.

"All quiet?" Connor asked.

"Too quiet. Vorlax haven't pushed in this sector for twenty hours. That's either good news… or they're preparing something worse."

Connor nodded. "Keep drills running. Rotate live simulation teams. I want this ship sharp."

"Understood, Commander."

From there, Connor moved through engineering, then medical—introducing himself personally to department heads, asking direct questions, watching how they responded. He didn't bark orders. He asked what they needed. Most answered with respect. A few hesitated. That was fine. Trust wasn't granted by uniform alone.

By the time he reached his quarters that evening, the weight of the day hung in his shoulders. He hadn't been in a cockpit in weeks, hadn't heard the roar of thrusters under his seat or the static crackle of his squad's comms. But this was the battlefield now— meetings, delegation, strategy. And in its own way, it was just as dangerous.

He sat on the edge of his bunk and activated the room's

intercom.

"Computer, open personal channel," he said. "Send to: Officer Lysara."

A soft tone confirmed the connection.

"Hey," Connor began, leaning forward slightly. "I know I've been... tied up with everything lately. But I was thinking—this ship's got room. Lots of it. If you're open to it... maybe you could move aboard. No pressure. Just... think about it."

He ended the message, then leaned back, eyes on the stars beyond the viewport. He couldn't afford many personal moments, not now. But he also couldn't forget what—who—he was fighting to protect.

Taking his place at the front of the room, he turned to face the assembled crew. "I know there are whispers about my command, and even about the decisions I'm making today," Connor began, his voice steady but resolute. "I understand the concerns some of you might have. But this ceremony is about acknowledging three individuals who have proven themselves time and again in the line of duty. I've personally watched them grow into exceptional officers—steady, loyal, and indispensable to the MWU."

He gestured toward them across the crowd. "Lieutenant Ambryst Korrin, Lieutenant Sailor Grace, and Lieutenant Tyler Vance—please step forward."

As the three approached the platform, he continued, "Today, I am officially promoting you to the rank of Captain, effective immediately. You are no longer just squadmates—you are leaders aboard the MWU Pinnacle, entrusted with commanding your own departments and contributing directly to the direction of this war."

The three original O'Brien squad stood, confused, wide-eyed, and shy but willingly stepped up on top of the platform behind Connor.

He continued, "Ambryst Korrin, Sailor Grace, and Tyler Vance have demonstrated unwavering courage, discipline, and devotion to the MWU. They've faced death without hesitation, protected this Union with everything they have, and led with integrity when it mattered most. These promotions are not just acknowledgments—they're responsibilities earned through sacrifice and proven leadership."

He paused, letting his words settle. "We've all lost people in this war. We've seen brave men and women of the MWU fall in battle, and I know many of you carry that weight every day. This war is far from over—and it will take all of us, united and focused, to endure what lies ahead. That's why I've chosen to elevate three officers whose actions under fire have shown not only skill, but the judgment and resilience required to lead. Ambryst, Sailor, and Tyler have stood in the thick of chaos and made the right calls when it mattered most. Their promotions reflect that strength."

Connor's eyes scanned the room, meeting the gaze of several officers who looked less than pleased. He could feel the weight of their judgment, but he stood firm. He had made his choice, and he wasn't going to back down. He would stand by his squad no matter what.

The ceremony itself was brief but meaningful. As Connor pinned the new Captain insignias onto his former squadmates, a quiet pride settled in his chest. They had come a long way since their early missions together—through firestorms, ambushes, and impossible odds. What began as a tight-knit combat unit had evolved into something greater. They were no longer just tactical assets or mission specialists—they were leaders now, each entrusted with shaping the future of the Pinnacle. And together, they would face whatever challenges came next.

As the ceremony ended and the crew dispersed, Ambryst approached Connor with a rare smile. "Thank you, Commander," he said, his voice quiet but sincere. Sailor and Tyler nodded in agreement, their expressions filled with gratitude.

Connor clapped Ambryst on the shoulder. "You earned it," he replied. "Now comes the hard part - proving to everyone on this ship that we four belong!" They all shared some hearty laughs.

Despite the tension that still lingered, Connor felt a weight lifted. He had made his decision, and now it was time to move forward. The Pinnacle was his command, and with Ambryst, Sailor, and Tyler by his side, he felt as though he really could take on the universe.

After the ceremony, Connor sat with Ambryst in the briefing room of the MWU Pinnacle. The recent promotions and the responsibilities that came with their new ranks lingered in the air, but Ambryst's demeanor was calm, though thoughtful. Connor had known Ambryst for a long time and could sense that something was on his mind.

"Commander," Ambryst began, using Connor's newly earned title with the respect it deserved but with the familiarity of their long-standing friendship. "I've got a personal matter I need to take care of. It won't take more than a day - two at the most."

Connor raised an eyebrow but didn't press for details. He had always made it a point to respect the personal lives of his crew, and that hadn't changed even with his recent promotion. He knew that being in the thick of war, constantly on high alert, could take a toll on even the strongest soldiers. Sometimes, taking care of personal matters was as important as any battle they fought.

"Of course, Ambryst," Connor replied with a smile. "Take the time you need. You've earned it." He paused for a moment, then added with a chuckle, "Hell, if you need more than a day, just let me know. The ship won't fall apart without you."

Ambryst chuckled and shook his head. "Still can't believe you're the one giving orders now."

Connor smirked. "Neither can half the crew."

The two shared a quiet laugh, the tension easing between them.

"You haven't changed," Ambryst said, more seriously. "Still leading like you always have—listening first, then acting."

Connor shrugged. "I don't see the point of command if your team can't trust you."

Ambryst nodded, his expression softening. "That's why we follow you."

"Thanks, Connor," Ambryst said, his expression softening. "You're a good friend. It's just something I need to take care of, but I'll be back before you know it. No need to worry."

Connor gave a small nod, though he couldn't help but feel a flicker of curiosity about the personal matter Ambryst was referring to. But he didn't pry. Everyone on the crew had their own lives outside of their duties, and they all had the right to attend to those things without being questioned.

"I'm not worried," Connor responded with a grin. "I know you'll handle it. And when you get back, we'll have plenty more to do. Things are just heating up out there." He motioned vaguely toward the vastness of space beyond the viewport, where they all knew the war against the Vorlax was steadily intensifying.

Ambryst nodded solemnly, his mood shifting slightly as he remembered the reality of the conflict they were still embroiled in. "Yeah, I've got a feeling it's going to get rough before it gets better."

"It always does," Connor replied with a sigh, "but we've gotten this far. We'll keep going."

Connor returned to the bridge and stepped into the operations alcove where Lieutenant Vesh was already reviewing diagnostics with two junior officers. She handed him a small datapad as they walked toward the central console.

"Morning update," she said briskly. "Deck seven's recycling system is fully functional again, tactical systems are synced across all defense arrays… but we're still missing one key player."

Connor scanned the list, immediately catching the gap. "Engineering."

Vesh nodded. "We've got crews running maintenance, but there's no chief overseeing them. It's bottlenecking coordination across propulsion, shielding, and repairs. The ship's too big for scattered supervision."

"I know," Connor said, tapping the pad. "I've been thinking

about that. There's someone I trust—worked with her on the Auren Rift recovery mission. Name's Thara. She's sharp, fast under pressure, and knows how to make alien tech behave better than anyone I've seen."

Vesh raised an eyebrow. "Exoform?"

"Yeah. From the Kelorin system," Connor replied. "She's unconventional, but if this ship is going to survive what's coming, we need more than conventional."

Vesh offered a short nod. "I'll prepare the formal invitation. You want it encrypted and priority flagged?"

"Make it top priority," Connor said. "I want her here yesterday."

Connor turned to Lieutenant Vesh. "Draft and send an encrypted communique to Engineer Thara of the Kelorin system. Offer her the position of chief engineer aboard the MWU Pinnacle— full clearance, immediate transfer authorization."

A The next morning's briefing ended with Connor standing at the front of the operations bay, surrounded by department heads.

"One final item," he said. "Our new chief engineer arrives within the hour—Kelorin specialist, previously attached to the Celtrix Prime relief mission. Some of you may remember her work on the orbital field stabilization array."

There were murmurs among the staff. Vesh, ever efficient, tapped something into her datapad.

"She's already cleared docking protocols," Vesh confirmed. "I'll have Security escort her straight to Engineering."

Connor nodded. "Good. Make sure there's no confusion— she was personally requested. Any questions about her qualifications can be answered by her performance."

An hour later, the main hangar's inner airlock hissed open, and Thara stepped onto the Pinnacle's deck. Tall and wiry, with pale green skin lined with bioluminescent threads along her neck and wrists, she carried no visible tools—just a compact satchel and a calm, deliberate expression. Her compound eyes scanned the bay with quiet focus.

A few engineers nearby paused, uncertain. One of them leaned toward another. "She's... not Union-born, right?"

"No," said Tyler, stepping in behind them. "But she's the one who kept the Celtrix atmospheric shield from collapsing. So unless you can top that, maybe just let her work."

Thara reached the Engineering deck minutes later. Connor met her just outside the main systems hub.

"Chief Engineer," he greeted with a respectful nod. "Welcome aboard."

Thara gave a slight bow, her voice resonant but clipped. "Thank you, Commander. I've reviewed the Pinnacle's schematic packages on the way here. It's impressive—massive redundancy layering, hybridized power grid. Beautiful work. But you've got an unbalanced coolant flow between your central conduits. Likely a feedback delay on the secondary buffer."

Connor blinked, then smiled. "You've been here five minutes."

Thara's lips twitched in a near-smile. "Five minutes too long, then. Permission to begin system optimization?"

"Granted. I'll let Engineering know you're in charge."

As she disappeared into the labyrinth of pipes and control panels, Connor turned to Lieutenant Vesh.

"I want every crew member to see why she's here," he said. "Let her results do the talking."

36 LIBERATION

A shimmering three-dimensional star map hovered in the center of the command room, projecting a rotating lattice of stars, systems, and territories—some still lit with MWU blue, others flickering in the crimson of Vorlax occupation. Connor stood before it, arms crossed, studying the conflict lines with the scrutiny of someone who had spent the last few weeks entrenched in strategic warfare.

He had led dozens of operations since taking command, securing key victories and holding fragile territories. But this mission felt different. Heavier. More personal.

The intercom beeped, and a familiar voice rang out - his communications officer. "Commander O'Brien, Intelligence has sent an urgent report. You need to review it immediately. It's about Brandi Kimbrough, the interstellar diplomat you once had dealings with."

The moment the name "Brandi Kimbrough" was spoken, a wave of annoyance and resentment surged through Connor. Their only encounter had been disastrous—Kimbrough, then a reckless and unpredictable diplomat, had played a key role in the destruction of a neutral space station and the massacre of several Zorvakians. Even then, Connor had sensed something off about her. He had distrusted her instincts, her evasive answers—but now, it seemed her actions had been far worse than anyone had realized.

He pulled up the encrypted message and quickly skimmed through its contents. The intelligence report revealed a chilling truth: Brandi Kimbrough had been leaking sensitive information to the Vorlax. Not just minor intel or logistical details - she had been passing along critical data that was actively hindering the MWU's efforts in the war. Ship movements, supply routes, and even classified operations had been compromised because of her betrayal.

"Damn it," Connor muttered under his breath. This explained the Vorlax's recent precision in their attacks and their ability to ambush MWU fleets with alarming accuracy. The enemy had another insider, and it was someone who had once worked alongside MWU leadership. Worse still, Kimbrough had once been under Connor's protection. He had been assigned to keep her safe, not knowing she was capable of such a colossal betrayal.

Connor clenched his fists as he read further. The intelligence report indicated that Kimbrough was currently in hiding, likely aware that the net was closing in. She had last been spotted in a remote system on the fringes of Vorlax-controlled space—too far from MWU protection, and too dangerous for a full-scale approach.

A mission like this wouldn't call for the full might of a city-class vessel. It required speed, stealth, and precision. Connor would need to take a smaller, specialized craft and lead the retrieval operation himself—with only those he trusted at his side. Brandi Kimbrough wasn't just a traitor—she was a liability the Union couldn't afford to leave unchecked.

He tapped his wrist communicator and summoned his senior officers to the briefing room. It didn't take long before Sailor Grace and Tyler were seated around the large table, their faces filled with concern and curiosity.

"What's going on, Commander?" Sailor Grace asked, her usual calm demeanor replaced with tension.

Connor looked around for a moment, then asked "Where is Ambryst?"

The others looked around, and Tyler said "He must still be gone. He said he had personal matters to attend to."

Connor squinted with a sense of suspicion. It had already been a few days now with no contact from Ambryst. It was something Connor would have to look into later but the immediate focus needed to be Brandi Kimbrough.

Connor took a deep breath. "We have a serious situation on our hands. You all remember Brandi Kimbrough - the interstellar diplomat from the mission to the neutral station?" They all nodded. The memory of that disastrous mission still lingered. "Intelligence has confirmed that she's been leaking crucial information to the Vorlax. Her actions have compromised our entire war effort."

Sailor Grace's eyes widened, her hand instinctively resting on the table as she processed the news. "She's been working with the Vorlax this whole time?"

"That's what the report suggests," Connor confirmed. "And now, our orders are clear: we need to find her and bring her in before she does any more damage."

The weight of the task pressed on everyone in the room. Tyler, ever the practical one, folded his four arms and asked, "Do we know where she is?"

Connor rotated the existing starmap display, zooming in on a dim cluster of systems near the edge of Vorlax-controlled space. "There—she was last seen in this sector. Remote, unstable, and a perfect place to disappear if we don't move fast."

The room fell into a heavy silence as they absorbed the gravity of the mission. They'd be entering hostile territory to capture someone who had once stood beside MWU leadership. Kimbrough's betrayal had already dealt a serious blow—but if they could bring her in alive, there was still a chance to uncover how deep the damage went. She might hold names, patterns, or access points that the Vorlax were still exploiting. The danger was real—but so was the opportunity to stop further sabotage before it spread.

"We'll take the Pinnacle and intercept her," Connor said, his voice steady. "I want our ship prepped and ready for departure within the hour. Make sure we're armed and fully equipped for a stealth operation. We can't afford to alert the Vorlax to our presence."

Sailor and Tyler nodded in unison, both of them trusting in Connor's leadership and the bond they had forged over countless battles.

As they left the briefing room to carry out their orders, Connor remained seated for a moment longer, staring at the star map. Somewhere out there, Brandi Kimbrough was hiding, likely believing she could continue her treachery without consequences.

But she was wrong.

Connor stood up and followed his crew, resolved to see this through. Brandi Kimbrough had betrayed the MWU, but he would bring her in—alive and accountable. Too much had already been lost because of her. He wouldn't allow her to vanish into the shadows again. Not this time.

The shuttleship detached smoothly from the underside of the Pinnacle, descending toward the swirling green mists of the planet's upper atmosphere. From orbit, the world looked sickly—its cloud cover tinged with volatile gases and faint electromagnetic static that shimmered like oil on water.

Inside the shuttle, Lieutenant Tyler led the strike team as his eyes were locked on the terrain below. Connor had given him direct command of the recovery operation—protocol demanded it. As Commander of a Galactic Class vessel, Connor remained aboard the Pinnacle, overseeing tactical support and monitoring from the operations deck.

Tension filled the shuttle. The soldiers onboard wore tight expressions, their fingers flexing around their rifles as they braced for a landing deep in Vorlax-patrolled territory. Somewhere down there, Brandi Kimbrough was waiting—possibly armed, definitely dangerous.

Aboard the Pinnacle, Connor watched their progress through

a live feed, jaw clenched. Kimbrough's betrayal was a wound that ran deeper than he wanted to admit—and recovering her was only part of the solution. He needed answers. He needed to know how far her treachery had spread.

Tyler kept a watchful eye on their surroundings. The alien's four arms, always ready for combat, were tense with anticipation.

"Remember," Connor said, his voice low but firm, "we go in, take out the Vorlax, and bring Kimbrough back alive. We need answers, not more bodies."

The squad of MWU soldiers that accompanied them nodded, weapons at the ready. They moved silently through the dense foliage of the planet, following the heat signatures of the Vorlax troops. Kimbrough had made this remote world her hiding spot, aligning herself with the Vorlax to evade capture. But Connor wasn't going to let her slip away again.

"Over there," Tyler said, his voice a low rumble as he pointed toward a clearing in the distance.

Sure enough, there she was - Brandi Kimbrough - accompanied by ten Vorlax warriors. Their grotesque forms stood in stark contrast to the smooth diplomatic regalia Kimbrough still wore as if she thought herself above the situation she had created. The Vorlax, with their elongated limbs and grotesque array of eyes, looked ready for a fight, their greasy skin shimmering faintly under the planet's weak sun.

Connor signaled for his squad to take positions. They spread out in the dense foliage, surrounding the group of Vorlax. Tyler, standing beside Connor, had his energy rifle at the ready.

"On my mark," Connor whispered into his comm, eyes fixed on Kimbrough, who seemed completely unaware of their approach.

Without hesitation, Connor gave the signal.

The jungle erupted into chaos as the MWU soldiers opened fire, lasers and plasma rounds tearing through the air. The Vorlax were caught off guard and scrambled to defend themselves, but Connor's squad had the advantage. Tyler charged forward, his glassy form a blur of motion as he tore through two of the Vorlax with ease, his four arms giving him the upper hand - literally. He smashed one to the ground with a heavy blow while simultaneously firing his rifle at another.

Connor took down a Vorlax warrior with a well-placed shot, then turned his attention to Kimbrough. She hadn't even tried to run. The smug expression on her face made Connor's blood boil. She had aligned herself with these monsters, and now she was going to face justice.

Within a minute, the Vorlax were dead, their bodies scattered across the clearing. The air was filled with the acrid smell of burnt ozone, and the quiet buzz of the planet's atmosphere returned. Connor approached Kimbrough, who had her hands raised in mock surrender, her lips curled into a sardonic smile.

"Well, Commander," she said with a smirk, "I suppose I'm under arrest now."

Connor's eyes narrowed. "You'll answer for what you've done, Kimbrough."

But as his squad moved to take her into custody, Kimbrough chuckled - a soft, chilling laugh that sent a wave of unease through Connor. "You think you've won, don't you?" she said, tilting her head. "You think this war is about battles and ships, but you're missing the bigger picture."

Connor clenched his fists, his patience running thin. "Enough. You're coming with us."

Kimbrough ignored his words, her voice dripping with malice as she said, "Tell me, Commander, have you spoken to your friend Ambryst lately?"

Connor froze, her words slicing through his thoughts like a knife. He hadn't seen him since the promotion ceremony when Ambryst had asked for time off to handle a personal matter. A cold dread settled in the pit of his stomach as he stared at Kimbrough.

"What did you do?" Connor demanded, his voice hard.

Kimbrough's smile widened. "Oh, dear Ambryst. Such

loyalty, such strength. And yet, right now, he's probably begging for mercy while the Vorlax tear him apart."

A surge of panic hit Connor like a physical blow. He stepped forward, grabbing Kimbrough by the collar of her diplomat's dress. "Where is he?" he growled, fury rising in his chest.

Kimbrough's laughter filled the air, cold and unforgiving. "It's too late, Commander. They have him. He's probably screaming right now. The Vorlax don't show mercy, you know."

Connor's grip tightened, his knuckles turning white. His mind raced, replaying every interaction he'd had with Ambryst over the past few days. Ambryst had said he'd be back in a day or so - no more than that. But that day had come and gone, and now Kimbrough's words echoed in his mind like a nightmare.

Connor snarled, "I swear, if you've done anything to him-"

"Oh, it's not me, Commander," Kimbrough said with mock innocence. "The Vorlax, they've been quite thorough in ensuring your squad feels the full brunt of their hospitality."

Connor's vision blurred with rage, but he forced himself to let go of Kimbrough. She wasn't worth it - not yet. He needed her alive, if only to confirm the truth. But the weight of her words pressed down on him like a suffocating cloud. Ambryst, one of his closest friends and most trusted officers was in danger.

"Get her on the ship," Connor ordered, his voice cold and unyielding. "We're leaving."

As his squad dragged Kimbrough toward the waiting shuttleship, Connor's mind churned with plans. They had to find Ambryst—and fast. Whatever the Vorlax were doing to him, Connor wouldn't let it stand. He'd burn through every system in the sector to bring his friend home.

Hours later, after being interrogated aboard the Pinnacle, Kimbrough finally gave up the location. She offered it without resistance, almost too easily—smiling through every word like it was part of some cruel game. That, more than anything, unsettled Connor. The coordinates matched a known Vorlax outpost hidden in a dense asteroid field—small, isolated, and just far enough from patrol routes to go unnoticed.

Now, as the Pinnacle approached the edge of that field, Connor stood on the command deck, his mind spiraling with rage and desperation. The traitorous diplomat's voice echoed in his thoughts: Ambryst is being tortured. His chest tightened at the image. Every second they delayed was another second his friend might not survive.

"We're almost there," Tyler's voice cut through the silence on the bridge. The alien's calm demeanor was a contrast to the storm raging inside Connor. The Pinnacle's sensors pinged as they closed in on the small Vorlax outpost hidden within a dense asteroid field. It wasn't a major base, just a small cell of Vorlax forces - enough to hold Ambryst captive but not enough to pose a serious threat to a Protector Class ship like the Pinnacle.

"Prepare to launch," Connor commanded, his voice steady despite the turmoil inside. He was going down there himself. This wasn't a mission for subtle diplomacy or cautious planning. This was personal. Ambryst was his family, and the Vorlax would pay.

Within minutes, Connor and his handpicked team—Tyler among them—launched from the Pinnacle in a shuttleship, descending toward the Vorlax outpost hidden on a barren asteroid. Before departure, he issued temporary command oversight to Captain Sailor Grace. It wasn't standard procedure, but Connor trusted her judgment implicitly.

The landing was quick and without ceremony; they didn't have time for subtlety. As the shuttleship touched down on the jagged surface, Connor felt the weight of urgency settle in his chest. This wasn't just a rescue. It was personal.

Connor had known it was a trap the moment Kimbrough gave up the location so easily. The Vorlax hadn't just captured Ambryst for intel—they wanted a response. They wanted him. And now, as the shuttleship touched down on the rocky asteroid, that certainty solidified.

The hatch opened to a barrage of laser fire, slicing through the air with deadly precision. The Vorlax were waiting, their positions already fortified. Connor didn't flinch. He and Tyler surged forward, weapons blazing, storming into the outpost under cover of the squad's suppressive fire. There were fewer enemies than expected—just five or six—but each one fought with the savage precision of an ambush long prepared.

Connor dodged a blast and barreled into one of the Vorlax, slamming the butt of his rifle into its grotesque face. The creature snarled, its many eyes glaring, but Connor's fury gave him an edge. He wrestled the Vorlax to the ground and with a swift motion, ended its life.

Tyler, meanwhile, was a force of nature, his four arms making quick work of two Vorlax soldiers at once. His topaz-like fists shattered bones with each punch, and his speed made him nearly impossible to counter.

But Connor wasn't focused on the broader fight. His mind was laser-focused on finding Ambryst. He sprinted through the narrow corridors of the outpost, his heart thudding as he tore open doors, screaming Ambryst's name, desperate for a sign of his friend. Finally, in the farthest room of the outpost, he found him.

Ambryst was bound to a chair, bruised and battered but alive. Relief washed over Connor like a tidal wave, but it was quickly replaced by anger.

"Connor," Ambryst croaked, his voice weak but defiant. "Took your time I see."

Connor approached quickly, cutting the restraints with a flick of his blade. "I've got you, brother," he said, his voice rough with emotion. "Let's get you out of here."

But before they could move, three more Vorlax appeared, blocking the exit. Connor stepped forward, his body radiating fury. "More?" He chuckled, raising his fists, "Good."

The battle was brutal, but Connor fought with ruthless precision, his rage sharpened by the emergency strength enhancements surging through his combat suit. Every movement was faster, more focused—his blows landing with controlled fury. This wasn't just combat; it was release. A channeling of every ounce of fear, guilt, and frustration he'd bottled since learning of Ambryst's capture. And now, he was taking it out on the enemy— one crushing strike at a time.

One Vorlax lunged at him, but Connor sidestepped and slammed his elbow into the creature's neck, sending it sprawling. Another Vorlax managed to land a hit, but it barely registered with Connor, who retaliated with a flurry of strikes. In the chaos, Tyler had caught up, dispatching the remaining Vorlax with his indomitable strength.

In minutes, it was over. The Vorlax lay sprawled across the corridor, their grotesque forms motionless amid the wreckage. Connor stood panting, his fists still clenched, streaked with Vorlax blood. The outpost had gone silent—nothing but the flicker of failing lights and the shallow breaths of Ambryst echoing in the confined space.

"Are you okay?" Connor asked, his voice softer now as he helped Ambryst to his feet.

"I've had worse," Ambryst replied with a strained smile, though his voice wavered as he shifted slightly, a tremor running through his bruised shoulders. His swollen jaw twitched, and one eye was still half-closed from swelling, but he held Connor's gaze without flinching.

They made their way back to the landing craft, leaving the Vorlax bodies behind. As they ascended into space, Connor sat beside his injured friend, his mind racing.

"Bridge, this is the Captain," he said into his wrist AI.

"Yes, Commander, the Bridge is standing by," replied the soft, yet professional voice on the other end.

"Destroy that Vorlax prison. I want nothing left - scatter its remnants to the farthest reaches of the galaxy."

"Understood, sir. Initiating sequence now," came the

immediate response, unwavering in its execution.

The MWU Pinnacle's colossal weaponry unleashed its power, shaking the entire ship as the barrage of firepower obliterated the prison. As Connor felt the tremor of the attack reverberate through the hull, a small sense of relief settled within him. The destruction of the place that had imprisoned and tortured his friend brought him a much-needed, albeit brief, sense of justice.

Now at the Medbay, Connor realized how quiet of a place it was. It still buzzed with the soft murmur of conversations between doctors and patients, along with the subtle energy of the ship's many systems. Ambryst lay on one of the recovery beds, his breathing steady now as the ship's advanced medical tech worked to heal his injuries. His purple skin, pale and bruised from the torment he'd endured, was already showing signs of recovery. The axolotl-like regeneration traits of his people were a blessing in times like these.

Sailor Grace and Tyler entered the room, their presence filling the small Medbay with warmth and camaraderie. Ambryst turned his head slowly, a faint smile crossing his lips as he saw his friends.

"Well, look who's still in one piece," Sailor Grace said, trying to keep the tone light. But the gravity of what Ambryst had been through weighed heavily on all of them.

"One piece," Ambryst rasped, his voice hoarse from the ordeal. "Barely. But hey, can't get rid of me that easily."

Sailor Grace moved closer to the bedside, her usual sarcasm softened in concern. "You're not allowed to scare us like that again," she said, her hand resting gently on his arm. "We almost lost you, you know."

Ambryst's eyes flickered with a mix of pain and defiance. "They wanted everything—Pinnacle specs, patrol rotations, fleet deployment intel. They tried to crack me. Believe me, they tried."

Tyler, standing at the foot of the bed, crossed his arms, his crystal-like body reflecting the soft Medbay lights. "You held out," he said in his deep, resonant voice. "That's what matters. What did they want from you?"

Ambryst sighed, the weight of the memories pressing down on him. "Information. They wanted me to give up details on the Pinnacle, on the MWU's fleet movements, strategies, anything that could give them an edge in this war." He paused, a flash of delight crossing his face. "But I gave them nothing! Not a damn thing."

Connor felt a swell of admiration for his friend, but also a pang of guilt. "I shouldn't have let you go," he said quietly, shaking his head. "If I had known - "

"Stop." Ambryst interrupted, his voice stronger now. "You couldn't have known. I told you I needed a day to handle something on the outer trade routes—personal business. I thought it'd be quick, in and out. But the Vorlax must've been waiting. They hit my transport just outside the jumpgate—disabled it before I could even signal for help."

He let out a shaky breath. "But what matters is that you came for me. That's all that matters."

Sailor Grace glanced between the two, her brow furrowed. "How bad was it, Ambryst? I mean, they clearly didn't go easy on you."

Ambryst's eyes darkened as he recalled the experience. "It was bad," he admitted. "They used everything they had. Pain stimulators, neural disruptors, even old-fashioned brute force. They wanted me to crack. But every time they asked, I just kept thinking about all of you and the Pinnacle. There was no way I was giving them what they wanted. I wasn't about to betray everything we've fought for."

Connor felt a lump in his throat as he listened. Sailor Grace shed a tear as Tyler nodded his head solemnly. Ambryst had been through hell, and yet, he'd held firm. "You're stronger than any of us, Ambryst," Connor said softly. "None of us would've blamed you if you had given them something. But you didn't. That means something."

Ambryst shifted in the bed, wincing. "It wasn't long… but it didn't have to be. Every hour down there felt like a lifetime. There were moments I didn't think I'd make it. But I kept telling myself— if I broke, they'd win. And I wasn't about to give them that."

Tyler, usually stoic, gave a small nod of approval. "You fought for all of us, even when you were alone."

Sailor Grace smiled, though her eyes were still filled with tears and worry. "We've got your back, Ambryst. You did well. But don't do that again, okay? Well, I mean to say, don't get abducted again. Okay?"

Ambryst chuckled weakly, though it quickly turned into a cough. "Deal. Next time, I'll bring you all with me."

They shared a quiet moment, the four of them united by the bond they'd formed through countless battles and hardships. For all the war had taken from them, it had also forged an unbreakable trust between them.

Connor cleared his throat, his voice steady now. "We'll leave you be for now. You need to rest. Don't worry about anything else right now, just get better."

Ambryst smiled, his strength returning little by little as Connor shook his hand. Then Sailor Grace gave him a long hug, which hurt Ambryst's ribs a little but he didn't have the heart to say anything. Finally, Tyler gave him a slight smile with a nod.

As they left the Medbay, the three of them knew that Ambryst's strength, both physical and mental, would carry him through.

37 TRAITORS

When a mysterious data drive was delivered to the MWU through anonymous channels, Connor—along with several Commanding Officers and MWU Intelligence—was summoned for a classified holographic conference. The anxiousness in the room, despite being mostly hologram, was staggering as MWU Intelligence Officers, clad in their sharp uniforms, stood before him revealing shocking information. The moment Lieutenant Haase's name was mentioned, Connor's heart sank.

Haase, his former commanding officer, had been gathering intel before her death. She had set a timer on a highly sensitive data drive, designed to be delivered to the MWU in case anything happened to her. Haase had predicted the lengths their enemies would go to hide the truth, and this drive, now in the hands of MWU Intelligence, was her final act of defiance against the growing corruption within their ranks.

As the officers elaborated on the findings, Connor's knuckles grew whiter and whiter. The data uncovered widespread infiltration by Vorlax sympathizers - traitors who had embedded themselves across the MWU. The intelligence report detailed years of secret communications, financial exchanges, and covert missions that had allowed the Vorlax to gather key information on the

MWU's fleet movements and strategies. These traitors had sabotaged operations, betrayed key missions, and helped steer the war in the Vorlax's favor.

"Nearly 200 members," one officer reported solemnly, "have been identified as actively aiding the Vorlax. They're spread across different planets, ships, and even within our leadership ranks. We've confirmed that several of these individuals are not just low-ranking officers or bureaucrats. Some of them hold significant power, allowing the Vorlax to influence crucial decisions."

Connor's quarters were silent for a moment, and then the realization hit: the war was never just about the Vorlax. It was about the MWU's integrity, and its ability to protect the galaxy while being undermined from within. Connor felt a wave of frustration and anger wash over him, but his thoughts kept coming back to Haase. Even in death, she had found a way to help him, to help the MWU.

The intelligence continued to unfold the layers of conspiracy, with evidence pointing directly to one of the highest-ranking figures in the MWU: Supreme Chancellor Xeloron. This hulking alien, revered for his vast knowledge and leadership, had been playing both sides, manipulating the war from the shadows for years. Decisions that should have been in the best interest of the MWU were tainted by the influence of Vorlax sympathizers, many of whom had unwittingly become pawns in Xeloron's grand scheme.

Connor's mind raced. How deep did this conspiracy go? How many people he trusted had been feeding information to the Vorlax? He knew the answer was far more complex than he could fathom at this moment, but the MWU's integrity had been compromised on a scale no one had anticipated.

Connor paced back and forth in his quarters, the weight of Haase's revelations still settling over him like a storm. The classified hologram meeting had concluded just minutes ago, but one detail refused to leave his mind: ten traitors were aboard the Pinnacle. It hadn't come from the live briefing—but from the final section of Haase's data drive, which had decrypted itself only after

MWU Intelligence authenticated her death record and inserted the drive into a secure terminal. Haase had planned for this. The drive had been timed, set to unlock in stages, in case she didn't survive. Her foresight had just saved them again.

The names of the ten traitors flickered on the screen before him, each one a shock to his system. People he may have not known for long but still fought alongside. Individuals who had shown loyalty - at least on the surface - but had been secretly aiding the Vorlax. The anger simmering inside him threatened to boil over, but Connor remained calm, knowing he had to act swiftly and decisively. The betrayal wasn't just personal - it was a direct threat to the Pinnacle, and by extension, the MWU's efforts in the war.

Connor hurriedly got to the bridge and sat down in his command chair.

"Captain Sailor Grace, report to the bridge," Connor said firmly into his comm, his voice steady despite the storm of emotions within. Sailor's voice crackled back almost instantly, acknowledging the order.

Within minutes, Sailor arrived at his side, her brow furrowed in concern. She had seen the unease in Connor's face and knew something serious was unfolding.

Connor leaned closer and lowered his voice. "We've been compromised. Ten of our crew members—traitors. They've been working with the Vorlax. We need to act now."

Sailor's eyes widened slightly, but she gave a subtle nod, keeping her face neutral so the rest of the bridge crew wouldn't notice.

"Who are they?"She asked.

Connor glanced at the screen, his fingers tapping a few buttons to share the list with her wrist AI. "Two from engineering, one from communications, three from security, the rest are scattered across various departments."

The betrayal stung, but there was no room for hesitation. These individuals had endangered the entire ship, perhaps even jeopardized missions that had cost lives. The thought made Connor's jaw tighten.

"We'll arrest them," Sailor said, resolute. "We can't let this fester."

Connor nodded, the gravity of the situation fully settling in. "Find Tyler and a small team of security to take with you, too. Round them up. Confine them to the brig." He hesitated for a moment, then added with a grim smirk,"Throw them in with Kimbrough," Connor added with a grim smirk.

Sailor raised an eyebrow. "The diplomat?"

"The traitor," he corrected. "She's still in holding until Intelligence extracts her from our ship. Until then, she's our problem."

Sailor nodded and turned, issuing orders to the security teams. Within minutes, the Pinnacle was abuzz with activity. Officers moved swiftly through the ship, isolating and apprehending the suspected traitors. The Pinnacle's brig, rarely used, was now becoming a holding cell for some of the most dangerous threats to the MWU - those who had been working from within.

Connor watched as his crew did their work, his heart heavy with the knowledge that trust had been violated. He had always prided himself on knowing his crew, but the web of deception spun by the Vorlax had ensnared them all. He couldn't shake the feeling of betrayal, the weight of responsibility pressing down on him harder than ever before.

As the last of the traitors was led to the brig, Connor decided to speak to them as a whole.

Connor paced in front of the row of captured traitors, his eyes scanning each one. His fury simmered just beneath the surface, but he held it together, determined to extract some useful information. The ten traitors - each of them once trusted members of his crew - stood with heads held high, defiant in their silence. It angered him how calm they seemed, as if betraying their own people hadn't weighed on their consciences.

"You really thought you'd get away with it, didn't you?" Connor asked, his voice even but charged with frustration. "Selling out your own to the Vorlax, undermining everything we fought for. What was your price?"

Silence.

The group exchanged looks, their expressions unyielding. One of the traitors, a lieutenant he had once trusted to command a wing of fighters, stared straight ahead, lips tight, offering nothing. Connor stepped closer, locking eyes with him.

"Was it worth it?" Connor continued, leaning in slightly. "Risking everything for whatever promise they gave you? Power? Money? Freedom? Speak."

Nothing.

The quiet stretched on, the hostility undeniable. The only thing breaking the silence was the ten traitor's cellmate Kimbrough, who was giggling at Connor's attempt to crack them. A flicker of frustration crossed Connor's face. He knew he wouldn't break them, not here, not like this. Their loyalty - or rather, disloyalty - was sealed. They had chosen their path, and nothing he said would shake them from their stance now.

Connor exhaled slowly, gathering himself before stepping back. His tone turned cold, cutting through the heavy silence. "Fine. Enjoy the brig while you can. It's only temporary. Your permanent accommodations will be far less pleasant."

His words lingered in the air, sharp and final. The traitors remained silent, but Connor could see the flicker of realization in their eyes - their fates were sealed.

Connor retreated to his quarters. He sat at his desk, staring at the blinking light on his terminal. The data drive from Haase had been his salvation in this dark moment—and a haunting reminder of what she had sacrificed. Branded a traitor and imprisoned before her death, Haase had left behind this final message, a failsafe she must have known would only be discovered if things went terribly wrong.

Until now, no one had believed her.

But the data on the drive was undeniable: names, transmissions, command logs—all painstakingly compiled and timestamped to match classified incidents across the MWU. In death, Haase had cleared her name and exposed the conspiracy that had cost her everything.

Connor leaned back in his chair, the silence of his quarters almost suffocating. His mind raced as he thought about Haase, about the countless lives that had been lost because of the corruption within their ranks. He thought about the war, the endless battles, and the faces of those he had lost. Brinson. Haase. And now, his crew had been infiltrated by the enemy.

He let out a deep breath, running a hand through his hair. "Even in death, you're still helping me, Haase," he whispered, the words barely audible in the stillness of the room.

The data drive had done more than just uncover traitors - it had also solidified Haase's legacy as a true hero of the MWU. She had seen the cracks in their system, the hidden dangers lurking in the shadows, and she had given her life to bring them to light. Connor knew that her death hadn't been in vain, but it didn't make the loss any easier.

Connor turned back to his terminal, ready to draft a report to MWU Command, detailing the arrests made aboard the Pinnacle and his ship's current security status in light of the revelations from Haase's data drive.

The revelations brought to light by Lieutenant Haase's data drive shook the MWU to its core. It was difficult for anyone to imagine that one of the most powerful figures in the entire galaxy, Supreme Chancellor Xeloron, had been operating as a hidden agent of chaos, orchestrating parts of the Vorlax war from within. The carefully curated image of Xeloron as a symbol of galactic unity was now in shambles, replaced by the truth—a leader who had manipulated his people and their allies to serve the ambitions of the Vorlax.

The moment the evidence was confirmed, MWU High

Command moved swiftly. Xeloron was arrested by elite operatives and taken into custody without resistance, stripped of his rank and removed from power.

Connor was summoned back to Earth shortly after the arrests of the approximate 200 traitors within the MWU. Normally, a holographic briefing would have sufficed—but this meeting required more than encrypted transmissions. It required unity, security, and a show of unwavering resolve.

As he stood in the secure briefing room at MWU Headquarters, surrounded by senior officers and intelligence operatives, his stomach twisted as the investigators corroborated every detail of Haase's findings. "It's all true," the lead officer said, barely hiding the disgust in his voice. "Xeloron's been feeding crucial information to the Vorlax. He's been manipulating our decisions, steering us toward certain defeat in key battles, and covertly weakening our defensive strategies."

Connor clenched his fists, anger boiling within him. To know that someone so revered had orchestrated their downfall from within was almost too much to bear. Around him, he could see the same disillusionment reflected in the eyes of those who had once looked to Xeloron as a symbol of unity.

The investigator continued, pointing to a holographic display of evidence - communications between Xeloron and Vorlax commanders, strategies intentionally designed to undermine the MWU's efforts, and cryptic orders from the Supreme Chancellor that led to the unnecessary sacrifice of countless lives.

"How long has this been going on?" Another Officer asked, her voice trembling with disbelief.

The investigator sighed. "Nearly a decade. Xeloron's been embedded in this conspiracy for years, maybe even longer. He's used his position of power to manipulate galactic politics, trade routes, and military movements - all to serve the Vorlax agenda."

Connor felt sick. He thought about the lives lost, the battles that had seemed inexplicably difficult, and the decisions made that had felt wrong in retrospect. Xeloron had been at the center of it all. The war against the Vorlax hadn't just been fought on the battlefield; it had been fought in the shadows of the MWU's highest ranks.

And now, the traitor was in custody.

Supreme Chancellor Xeloron's arrest had been swift and without incident. The moment the evidence was confirmed, MWU High Command with all the other 9 Supreme Chancellor's permission, wasted no time. A team of elite operatives apprehended him in the Supreme Chancellor's chambers, taking him to a high-security facility designed for the most dangerous criminals in the galaxy. Despite his immense power, there had been no resistance - only the cold silence of an individual who knew his time had come.

Even with Xeloron removed from power, the war raged on. The Galactic Tribunal—tasked with charging and sentencing him—delayed the proceedings. The MWU couldn't afford to shift focus now. Too much was at stake. Until then, Xeloron sat in a high-security prison, his authority severed and his silence intact—for now.

The room went quiet as the weight of the revelation settled over everyone. Xeloron hadn't just held office—he was one of the ten Supreme Chancellors, a pillar of MWU leadership. His betrayal cracked the very foundation of the Union. If someone like him could be corrupted, who else had already fallen? What secrets still hid in the ranks?

Connor's thoughts turned to Lieutenant Haase. Even imprisoned and branded a traitor, she had pursued justice. Her final act—activating that data drive—had unmasked Xeloron and saved the MWU. She had known the cost, and she had paid it. Now, the burden to finish what she started belonged to those still alive.

Connor's voice broke the silence. "Haase gave her life to expose all of this. We owe it to her, and to everyone who's died because of this war, to make sure Xeloron and everyone involved in this conspiracy is brought to justice."

The others nodded in agreement, though the mood remained

somber. Xeloron's arrest coupled with the other 200 individuals working with the Vorlax was a victory, but it was only a small one. Winning the Vorlax war would be the real victory.

Connor said "We can't let our guard down now. The Vorlax are still the primary issue here and who knows how many others might have been influenced by Xeloron. We need to finish this war and restore the MWU to what it should be."

The briefing room emptied shortly after, officers and operatives dispersing to handle the aftermath of the revelation. Connor stayed behind for a moment, gazing at the holographic image of Xeloron, now a prisoner of his own making.

"We'll make sure you pay for what you've done," Connor muttered to himself. The shadow of Xeloron's actions would loom large, but Connor was determined to carry on Haase's legacy.

Coming back to the MWU Pinnacle, Connor was surrounded by his senior officers in a large briefing room. The atmosphere was tense, the weight of recent revelations still hanging heavy over them. The room was dimly lit, the only light coming from the holographic display showing the galaxy's star maps and the latest positions of their fleets.

Connor took a deep breath, standing at the center of the room. He knew this was one of the most important meetings he had ever led. The officers, human and alien alike, looked at him with a mixture of anxiety and anticipation. They needed direction, a leader to unify them in the face of not just an external enemy, but also the internal corruption that had threatened everything they stood for.

"We've dealt a significant blow to the Vorlax conspiracy," Connor began, his voice steady but filled with resolve. "Thanks to the bravery of Lieutenant Haase and the sacrifices made by many, we've rooted out traitors in our ranks. But make no mistake - we've got a lot coming our way still."

Connor's eyes scanned the room, meeting the gaze of each officer, including his three friends originally from the O'Brien Squad. He saw the doubt in some of their eyes, the fear in others.

They had been fighting the Vorlax for so long, and now they had to confront the reality that some of their own had been working against them. But Connor couldn't let that paralyze them. He had to keep them moving forward.

"The fact that nearly 200 MWU members were found working with the Vorlax is a stark reminder of how deep this corruption runs," he continued. "Even our own ship wasn't immune. Ten traitors - ten people who stood beside us, who swore the same oaths as we did - were actively working against us."

There was a murmur among the officers, but Connor raised a hand to silence them.

"We can't allow this to tear us apart," he said firmly. "The Vorlax want us divided. They want us weak. But we will not give them that satisfaction. We have to be stronger, and more united than ever. Our loyalty to the MWU and each other is what will see us through this war."

He paused for a moment, letting his words sink in. The officers were listening intently now, their attention fully on him. Connor knew that this was a turning point - not just for the Pinnacle, but for the entire MWU. They had exposed a dangerous conspiracy, but now they had to ensure that their organization didn't crumble under the weight of that revelation.

"I won't lie to you," Connor said, his voice softer now but filled with conviction. "We've taken a hard hit. Losing Supreme Chancellor Xeloron to the Vorlax's influence was a devastating blow to the leadership of the MWU. But we've shown that we can root out this corruption, and we've shown that no one, no matter how high-ranking, is above accountability."

He glanced at Sailor Grace, Tyler, and the others who had stood by him through every victory and setback. Their loyalty—to him and to the MWU—remained unshaken.

Connor straightened his posture, taking on the full charge of his leadership role as Commander of the Pinnacle. "From this moment forward, our focus must be on the war. We cannot let internal strife weaken us. We have to trust each other. We have to stand united. We owe that to those who have sacrificed everything for the MWU."

The officers nodded, the discomfort in the room slowly beginning to ease. Connor could see the resolve returning to their faces. He knew that any rumors or dispersions his officers had about him from being promoted to Commander so quickly were now gone. They were ready to follow him.

"Dismissed," Connor said finally, and the officers began to leave the room, each one returning to their respective duties with a renewed sense of purpose.

But even as the room emptied, Connor remained behind for a few moments longer. He walked over to the large observation window and looked out into the immenseness of space. The stars glittered in the distance, cold and indifferent, but to Connor, they were a reminder of what they were fighting for - the survival of their galaxy, the freedom of its people, and the hope of a better future.

With a final, deep breath, Connor turned away from the window and exited the room. There were battles to be fought, decisions to be made, and a war to be won. He wasn't going to let Haase's sacrifice, or the sacrifices of countless others, be in vain.

38 THE NIGHT BEFORE

Tomorrow was the day - the moment that would determine the fate of the MWU, the Vorlax, and perhaps the entire galaxy. The remaining nine Supreme Chancellors, along with their advisers and countless high-ranking officials, had reached a unanimous decision: it was time to bring the battle directly to the Vorlax home world, Zenith Prime. This would be the final confrontation, the definitive clash between the MWU and the Vorlax exoform, an assault that would either seal victory or bring ruin to both sides. There would be no turning back. The galaxy's future hinged on the outcome of this final strike.

The impending assault on Zenith Prime weighed heavily on Connor's mind as he stood in the large war room at the MWU headquarters back on Earth.

The war room pulsed with urgency as battle plans for the assault on Zenith Prime came into focus. Holographic projections of the Vorlax homeworld rotated above the central table, surrounded by simulations of fleet formations, entry vectors, and defensive grids. Supreme Chancellors debated strategies while military commanders mapped out every phase of the operation, from orbital engagement to ground deployment.

Connor stood among them, silent but attentive. His role was

clear: he would co-lead the initial wave, commanding the Pinnacle and its strike group to pierce the Vorlax outer perimeter. Intelligence projected a 60% attrition rate in the first hour. They were walking into a meat grinder.

He clenched his jaw, eyes scanning the projections as numbers and probabilities flashed in red. This was it. Everything they had fought for was now on the line—every fallen soldier, every scar. Haase's warnings, Brinson's sacrifice—it all led to this. He couldn't afford to drift now.

"Commander O'Brien," one of the Chancellors addressed him, "Your squad will breach Point Apex. The Vorlax are heavily fortified in that sector. Do you believe your crew is ready?"

Connor straightened. "Yes, sir. They've trained for this. They'll hold the line."

The Chancellor nodded and turned to the others, but Connor's mind lingered. This wasn't about bravery anymore. It was survival. For his team, for Lysara, for the future.

He had to make this count.

With a deep breath, Connor finally accepted his role in the mission that had just been assigned. He would co-lead the first strike force in the MWU's final assault on Zenith Prime, commanding the Pinnacle at the front of the offensive. The decision had come moments earlier, ratified by the Supreme Chancellors and military high command. But before departure, Connor needed grounding— something to steady him beneath the weight of war pressing in from all sides. His thoughts turned to Lysara, the Xeno Officer who had become more than just a colleague. Over the past few months, they had grown closer, and she had become one of the few sources of peace in his life.

Later that evening, Connor followed his heart, fervently urging him to Lysara's quarters, where the glow of the city outside cast a soft light into the room. She greeted him with a warm smile, her eyes reflecting understanding before he even spoke. She could see the burden he carried. They sat together, talking softly about the mission ahead, about the weight on his shoulders, and about the things they couldn't change.

That night, they shared more than just conversation. The connection between them deepened in ways Connor hadn't expected. In her presence, he found a moment of reprieve from the war that had consumed his life. The comfort of her touch and the sincerity of her words made him feel something he hadn't felt in a long time - hope. Hope that maybe, just maybe, there was life beyond the war, a future beyond the battles.

As they lay together, wrapped in the stillness of the night, Connor held her close, feeling the warmth of her body against his. The uncertainty of what lay ahead was still there, but for the first time in a long while, it didn't feel so heavy. Lysara rested her head on his chest, and as sleep began to pull her under, she whispered, "No matter what happens, Connor, you're not alone. And I-" she cut herself off, with what Connor could only tell was an embarrassment. But he knew what she was going to say, and so he took the first leap of faith and said it, too.

"I love you too, Lysara."

She turned to him, wide-eyed and flush in the face as he gently kissed her lips. A few tears streamed down her cheeks as they embraced one another.

As they pulled away, he smiled softly, kissing the top of her head, grateful for her presence in his life. As sleep overtook him, he made a silent vow to her and himself. He would fight - not just for the MWU, but for the future they both deserved, a future he wanted with her. Tomorrow would bring war, but tonight, they had each other, and that was enough.

Far below the surface of Earth, beyond the reach of stars and strategy, Ambryst sought peace not in people—but in water. As an aquatic exoform, Ambryst had always drawn strength and serenity from the depths, a place where the sounds of the surface world faded away, leaving only the quiet hum of the ocean currents. Earth was not his home, but it did offer a small piece of it through the specially constructed underwater habitats designed for exoforms like his, who relied on aquatic environments for comfort and survival.

The entrance to the habitat was tucked away in one of Earth's sprawling cities, accessible through a series of tunnels that led deep beneath the ground, eventually opening into a vast, submerged world. The moment Ambryst stepped into the water, he felt the familiar pull of the currents, the gentle embrace of the liquid wrapping around his body as he descended into the depths. His limbs moved effortlessly through the water, the weight of his worries slowly peeling away as he swam further from the surface.

This was his sanctuary.

He wasn't alone in this underwater refuge. Several others of his kind, Ambythians, as they were called, had gathered here for the same reason. Many were warriors, just like him, veterans of battles fought across the galaxy. Others were civilians - scientists, engineers, diplomats - each playing their part in the larger tapestry of interstellar conflict. The reunion was understated, the way of his people. There was no need for grand gestures or overblown greetings. Instead, they greeted each other with a nod or a simple touch of webbed hands, a silent acknowledgment of shared history and purpose.

They swam together, silently at first, moving through the habitat's vast expanse, which was modeled after the great oceans of their planet. Ambryst felt a deep connection to these waters, even though they were artificial. It was in the water that he found clarity, the thoughts of battle, duty, and the uncertainty of tomorrow settling into a quiet rhythm that matched the ebb and flow of the currents around him.

Eventually, the silence gave way to conversation, though it was as fluid and unobtrusive as their movements. The Ambythians exchanged stories - of home, of war, of the countless worlds they had visited during their time with the MWU. For many, the war with the Vorlax had become their defining struggle, and while they fought for the MWU, each had their reasons for standing firm in the conflict. Some fought for honor, others for survival, and a few simply for the hope that one day, the galaxy might find peace.

Ambryst listened more than he spoke. His mind was focused on the mission that lay ahead. Though the waters brought him peace, the weight of what was to come still pressed down on him. The MWU's final assault on the Vorlax planet would be their most dangerous mission yet. He knew the risks. They all did. But here, in the water, surrounded by his people, Ambryst could almost forget the war, even if only for a short time.

At one point, as they glided through the habitat's coral gardens, one of the Ambythian elders approached Ambryst. The elder's eyes were wise, filled with the knowledge of countless years spent in the galaxy's oceans and battles alike. "You've been a strong warrior, Ambryst," the elder said in their fluid, melodic tongue, a language that carried easily through the water. "But remember, strength does not come from the fight alone. It comes from knowing when to let go."

Ambryst nodded, understanding the deeper meaning behind the words. His strength as a warrior had never been in question, but there was more to war than the fight itself. There was a cost to every battle, a toll that weighed on the spirit, and it was in moments like these - surrounded by his people in the quiet of the ocean - that he was reminded of why he fought. It wasn't for glory or conquest. It was for the preservation of life, for the peace that he hoped would one day come.

As the night stretched on, the group continued their journey through the water, their movements synchronized as they swam in unison. For Ambryst, this was his way of preparing for the battle ahead - not with weapons or strategy, but by reconnecting with his element, the place where he felt most at peace. It was in the water that he found the strength to face what was to come.

When the time came for him to leave, Ambryst bid his fellow Ambythians farewell, offering a final touch of hands and a nod of respect. As he ascended toward the surface, the war settled back into his mind, but this time, he felt more grounded. The water had given him what he needed - a moment of calm before the storm.

Back on the surface, as he dried off and prepared to return to the MWU Pinnacle, Ambryst allowed himself one last look at the underwater habitat. He knew it might be a long time before he returned to the waters of his people here on Earth, but the peace he had found there would stay with him.

While Ambryst left the waters behind, high above Earth's orbit, Sailor Grace sat in solitude—finding her own kind of peace, not in motion, but in memory. The room was small, personal yet utilitarian, its walls lined with only the barest of decorations: a few photos of her family and a small plant she had grown from a seedling during her time aboard the MWU Pinnacle.

With a sigh, Sailor Grace sat at her desk, the light from her terminal casting a soft glow across her face. In front of her were the letters she had written to her family, each one carefully crafted with words that carried both love and caution. Her mother, father, and younger brother would receive the first three letters. As she re-read her words, Sailor couldn't help but smile at the fond memories of home, but a part of her also felt a pang of melancholy. This mission, like the ones before it, carried the weight of risk. Every battle they fought seemed to chip away at the certainty of survival, and she wanted to be sure that, no matter what happened, her family would know she was thinking of them.

The letters were written in her usual style - straightforward but heartfelt. She made sure to mention the little things: how she missed the smell of her father's workshop, the comforting sound of her mother's voice, and the mischievous smile of her brother that always made her laugh. The letters held an air of finality, though she dared not think of them as farewells. Instead, she chose to think of them as reminders of the love that anchored her to Earth, the love that kept her grounded no matter how far across the galaxy she traveled.

She sealed the letters with a simple motion, storing them in the comms system, ready to be sent in the event that she couldn't return. Sailor sat back, exhaling deeply as the weight of her thoughts pressed on her chest. There was an undeniable gravity to the situation they faced, and she couldn't deny the part of her that was scared. But Sailor Grace was a soldier, and with that came the acceptance of danger. Tonight, though, she needed something to ease the burden, something to remind her that there was still beauty, even in the uncertainty of war.

She reached for her small notebook, its pages already filled with bits of poetry, scribbled thoughts, and fragmented verses that had come to her in quiet moments like this one. Writing poetry had always been her way of processing the world, of finding meaning in the chaos. The words didn't always flow perfectly, but that wasn't the point. Writing gave her a way to express what she couldn't always say out loud - the fear, the sorrow, and sometimes even the hope.

Tonight, her poetry turned toward the war. Her pen moved across the page in fluid strokes as she wrote about the weight of war and the small, fragile moments of peace that often went unnoticed amid the violence. She wrote about the stars, the immensity of space, and the silence that often came before a battle. Her words were heavy, filled with passion, but they also carried a certain resilience, a belief that, even in the darkest moments, there was still something worth fighting for.

After several verses, Sailor set her pen down, staring at the words on the page. They didn't offer answers, but they did give her a sense of clarity. It was as if putting her thoughts into words had lifted some of the burden from her heart. She glanced at the clock. There was still time before she needed to go to bed, and her mind craved a distraction from the thoughts of war that had consumed her all day.

She reached for the book on her bedside table, a worn anthology of eight short stories that she had been reading on and off for the past few weeks. The familiar characters and their tales had become a comfort to her, a brief escape from the harsh reality of the world she lived in. Sailor thumbed through the pages until she found where she had last left off. The story was about a group of explorers, much like her, venturing into the unknown in search of something greater. The parallels to her own life were not lost on her, but in the story's simplicity, she found solace.

As she read, the restlessness in her body began to melt away. For a short while, she was able to immerse herself in the fictional world, allowing the characters' struggles and triumphs to distract her from the mission looming ahead. The stories reminded her that, no matter how distant or cold space seemed, there were still moments of connection, moments of humanity that could be found even in the darkest places.

Eventually, her eyes grew heavy, and Sailor knew it was time to sleep. She carefully placed the book back on her bedside table, its pages folded neatly to mark her place. As she lay down, pulling the covers over herself, she thought of the war, the battles - they were always there, lingering at the edge of her thoughts. But tonight, in this brief moment of calm, Sailor allowed herself to feel the hope she had written about in her poetry. Tomorrow would come, but tonight, she had her words, her stories, and the love of her family to hold onto.

And that was enough.

Tyler remained aboard the Pinnacle while the others returned to Earth, choosing motion over meditation. For him, the night before battle wasn't for stillness—it was for action, a ritual of movement that kept him centered in the chaos of war.

He made his way to the ship's exercise room, a space designed to accommodate all exoforms on board. The room was massive, with equipment of varying sizes and shapes. Some pieces of equipment were built for human use, others for exoforms far larger or more uniquely shaped than himself. The room was largely empty tonight—many crew members were likely resting before the mission ahead or had gone back down to Earth—but Tyler preferred it that way. The hum of the ship's engines and the sharp clank of weights, as they connected with the floor, were the only sounds that greeted him. It was peaceful in its own way, a stark contrast to the chaos they would face tomorrow.

Without wasting a second, Tyler got to work. Four arms gave him a distinct advantage in these sessions, allowing him to work multiple parts of his body simultaneously. He gripped the largest set of dumbbells and began a steady routine of lifting. His golden body, tough yet flexible, shimmered faintly under the exercise room's lighting as his muscles engaged in repetitive, brutal motions. Every lift, every pull, and every drop of the weights connected him to his purpose - to keep himself sharp, to ensure he was prepared for whatever challenges the Vorlax threw at them next.

The clank of weights hitting the floor reverberated around the empty room as Tyler shifted from one set of exercises to another. Squats, deadlifts, and presses - all were executed with precision and intensity. Sweat poured from his translucent skin, glistening under the lights, each droplet a testament to the strain he was putting on his body. But the ache in his muscles was familiar, almost comforting. In these moments, he wasn't thinking about tomorrow's battle or the possibility of death; he was simply focused, his mind and body working as one.

With each passing minute, Tyler pushed himself harder. He moved to the treadmill, setting it to the highest speed, running with a rhythm that matched the beat of his racing heart. His legs, long and powerful, pounded against the belt in a rapid, thundering cadence, propelling him forward with a force that mirrored his determination. His breathing was heavy but steady. The treadmill's mechanical whine grew louder as Tyler increased the incline, pushing his body to the brink of exhaustion. Yet, there was no hesitation in his movements, no desire to stop. This was how he prepared - not with meditation, but with motion, testing the limits of his strength, his endurance, and his resilience.

After what felt like hours, Tyler finally began to slow down.

His muscles burned, aching with the satisfying pain of a workout well done. His breath came in heavy bursts, his luminous skin drenched in sweat. But in his mind, he was clear, focused, and ready. Tomorrow's mission would be brutal - he knew that. But here, at this moment, surrounded by the clang of weights and the steady thrum of the ship, he felt a sense of peace. He was ready. He had prepared his body and his mind for the challenges ahead.

As he wiped the sweat from his brow, Tyler's thoughts briefly wandered to his squad - Connor, Ambryst, and Sailor Grace. Each of them had their ways of preparing for the mission, and their rituals for finding peace before the storm. Tyler respected that. They were a team, forged through countless battles and bonded by trust. Tomorrow, they will fight together again, just as they always had. And when the time came, Tyler knew he would be ready to protect them, to stand by their side in the thick of battle, just as they had done for him so many times before.

The lights in the gym flickered softly as Tyler finished his workout, his muscles sore but his mind sharper than ever. With a final glance at the empty room, he headed back to his quarters.

39 ZENITH PRIME

The atmosphere within the MWU Pinnacle was charged with a mixture of anticipation and fear. Connor stood at the head of a large briefing room, gazing at the intricate holographic map of Zenith Prime that hovered above the table. His eyes were fixated on the clusters of red dots, representing Vorlax defenses that were scattered across the planet and its surrounding space. The room was filled with a low murmur of officers and crew, whispering to each other in hushed tones. The enormity of the mission before them weighed heavily on everyone.

Connor raised his hand, silencing the room. The hologram zoomed in, revealing massive planetary defense systems, orbital cannons, and a tremendous fleet of Vorlax warships already patrolling the area. His trusted squad members - Sailor Grace, Tyler, and Ambryst - stood closest to him, their eyes following the map, understanding the sheer difficulty of what they were about to face.

"Zenith Prime is not just any planet. It's their capital world, and we know it's going to be fortified beyond anything we've faced so far in this war. Vorlax forces will do whatever it takes to protect their home."

Sailor Grace, ever the strategist, pointed to a sector of the planet's orbit. "We could attempt a flanking maneuver here," she suggested, "but the intelligence reports show that the Vorlax have layered defense systems. Anything we throw at them will have to break through multiple barriers before we can even reach the surface."

Ambryst, whose calm demeanor never seemed to falter, chimed in. "We'll need every ship, every fighter at its best. And even then, we may not make it through without significant losses."

Connor nodded, the reality of their situation sinking deeper. It was one thing to know the risks on paper, but facing them head-on in just a few hours was entirely different. Tyler, who had been quiet during most of the briefing, finally spoke up. "We've beaten the Vorlax before," he said boldly. "But we need a plan that accounts for the unexpected."

Connor appreciated Tyler's confidence, but inside, doubts still gnawed at him. This was different - this wasn't just about skirmishes or covert operations. This was a full-scale war against the heart of the Vorlax empire, the last effort from the MWU to end the war at its source.

With the room growing silent, Connor steeled himself, masking his uncertainty. Connor suddenly received word on his wrist AI from intelligence and the higher-ups who have worked tirelessly in real time to deduce the best war tactics and strategies they could surmise. Connor cleared his throat, turning to the entire Pinnacle assembly. "We're going to follow a two-pronged assault," he finally decided. "Our Galactic Class ships will lead the charge, targeting their orbital defenses first. Meanwhile, all of the fighter ships will engage the Vorlax warships to create a path to the surface. Once those defenses are down, we can land forces directly on Zenith Prime."

The whole Pinnacle crew nodded, ready to bravely follow his lead.

After the briefing, Connor retreated to the bridge of the MWU Pinnacle, watching as the final preparations were made. His fleet was part of an armada - over ten thousand ships strong, including Protector Class ships, Galactic Class ships, and countless Fighter Class vessels. It was the largest offensive the MWU had ever launched, and it felt like the universe was holding its breath, waiting for the moment when it would all come crashing down.

The Pinnacle targeted the planetary turrets with precision, launching devastating volleys that eventually began to cripple the Vorlax defenses. Connor watched with grim satisfaction as several key installations on Zenith Prime were engulfed in explosions, temporarily reducing the intensity of the anti-air fire erupting from the surface toward the MWU fleet.

The launch began. Engines roared to life, and the entire fleet surged forward, leaving the safety of their staging area outside Earth's orbit. The stars stretched into streaks of light as the armada entered hyperspace, racing towards Zenith Prime.

As the massive MWU fleet emerged from hyperspace and took position just beyond Zenith Prime's planetary defenses, a tense silence settled over the command deck of the MWU Pinnacle. Connor stood at the center of the bridge, hands gripping the edge of his console as he stared at the planet ahead. The purple and green hues of Zenith Prime seemed peaceful from a distance, belying the carnage that was about to unfold. His officers waited in silence, their eyes darting between their commander and the planet looming on the holographic displays.

"This is it," Connor muttered under his breath. The attempt at diplomacy had to work - there had been too much loss already. He motioned to his communications officer to open a channel to the Vorlax.

An official broadcast from MWU High Command was sent out across the system, demanding the Vorlax stand down, cease all hostilities, and lay down their arms. The message was stern but offered one final olive branch: if the Vorlax ended the war now, there would be negotiations, peace, and the chance to rebuild.

Connor and his crew held their breath, watching the communications screen as the minutes dragged on. The seconds felt like hours. Then, a response came in.

A Vorlax leader appeared on the screen, his face twisted into a contemptuous sneer. His skin shimmered with the distinct pale markings of his species, his many eyes glinting with malice. The message was brief and cold. The video was being projected to every ship in the MWU, even the headquarters all around the Galaxy. "The Vorlax bow to no one. You have been a pest in our plans long enough. You will get nothing from us except annihilation."

With that, the channel cut off, and the message was clear: there would be no peace.

Connor exhaled slowly, his jaw tightening. "All ships," he commanded, "prepare for battle."

The Vorlax began firing almost immediately after the communication ended as if they had been waiting for this moment all along. The first barrage of fire came from the surface of Zenith Prime - massive planetary installations launching long-range plasma blasts, cutting through space toward the MWU fleet. The sky lit up in bright streaks of light as the Vorlax fleet, hovering in orbit, fired in tandem with their ground forces.

Chaos erupted across the MWU's comms as smaller ships within the fleet attempted to break formation and engage, but the first few minutes were nothing short of a bloodbath. Fighter Class ships were obliterated in quick succession, barely able to dodge the onslaught before being engulfed in fire. Screams of pilots echoed through the comms before being cut off entirely. Several Protector Class ships took direct hits, their shields flickering as they struggled to hold off the bombardment.

"Pinnacle, status report!" Connor barked, his eyes darting across the screens in front of him.

"Shields at full capacity," an engineering officer replied, but the apprehension was clear. "Engaging Vorlax planetary defenses."

The MWU Pinnacle, alongside other Galactic Class Ships, began firing back at the Vorlax orbital defenses. Explosions lit up the sky around them, with both sides trading heavy blows, each struggling to gain the upper hand. As the Pinnacle unleashed its firepower, Connor could see the flickers of Vorlax defenses beginning to falter under the onslaught.

Meanwhile, above the planet, thousands of Fighter Class ships from both sides swarmed like angry hornets, engaging in deadly dogfights. The Vorlax fighters exhibited bizarre, erratic flight patterns that left many MWU pilots scrambling to keep up. They moved unpredictably, swerving in directions that defied conventional combat tactics. The Vorlax ships, jagged and angular, seemed to weave in and out of formation, making them difficult to target.

"Commander, their movement is chaotic," A female pilot's voice crackled through the comms. She was in the thick of the battle, piloting through the madness. "We're losing too many."

"I see it," Connor replied, gritting his teeth as he watched the battle unfold through his command screens. "Stay calm and follow their patterns. They're erratic, but they're still patterns. Get a feel for their movements. We can counter them."

He began coordinating a series of strategic maneuvers, sending fighters in small squadrons to flank the Vorlax ships. Slowly, through trial and error, his pilots adapted to the strange movements of the Vorlax. Bit by bit, the MWU began to regain ground in the battle, taking down more Vorlax ships as they worked together to anticipate their movements.

Amidst the chaos, Connor's voice remained steady over the comms, guiding his pilots through the relentless waves of Vorlax fire. Every decision was critical, every order a matter of life or death.

As the battle over Zenith Prime raged on, the bridge of the MWU Pinnacle was alive with the chaos of war. Explosions rippled across the black expanse of space, illuminating the battle between the MWU and the Vorlax forces. Connor stood at the command center, his eyes scanning the battle reports and tactical displays. His mind raced as the tide of war ebbed and flowed. Amidst the chaos, he spotted a massive Vorlax command ship, larger than anything else in the enemy fleet.

As the hulking command ship veered its ugly design over the battlefield, MWU Command gave the order to take it out, warning that it could disrupt their coordination.

Connor motioned to his crew. "Get me tactical on that Vorlax battleship. I need to know what we're dealing with."

Data flooded the screen, showing the hulking ship's weak points. This ship is a vital brainpiece behind much of the Vorlax strategy. Without its command, a great deal of the Vorlax fleet will be thrown into disarray, giving the MWU a significant advantage. Connor decided.

"I'm leading a strike team to board that ship," he said firmly. "Tyler, Sailor Grace, you're with me. Ambryst, you're in charge while I'm gone."

He wasn't about to send his people into danger without stepping in first himself. That was the kind of leader he had sworn to be—and if taking that ship down meant risking everything, he would lead the charge.

Ambryst gives him a sharp nod, acknowledging the trust Connor placed in him. "Don't worry, sir. I'll hold the line while you're away. Won't wreck the ship, too!"

Minutes later, Connor, Tyler, and Sailor Grace are aboard a small, nimble shuttle, breaking away from the Pinnacle and heading straight toward the Vorlax command ship. Luckily, shuttles were so small compared to most ships that they were virtually undetectable. As they approach, the ship looms larger and larger, its strange, jagged form casting an ominous shadow over the battlefield. Vorlax fighters zip around them, but in addition to their size, the shuttle's cloaking device keeps them hidden from enemy sensors.

The shuttle breaches the hull of the Vorlax ship, its docking clamps locking onto the alien vessel's exterior. As the hatch opens, they are immediately met by a small detachment of Vorlax soldiers. The Vorlax, with their unsettling array of eyes and armored exoskeletons, charged at them, wielding advanced energy weapons and savage blades.

The firefight erupts instantly. Tyler barreled into the fray, swinging two massive energy rifles like clubs. Sailor Grace took cover behind a bulkhead, firing precise shots that took down Vorlax soldiers with lethal accuracy. Connor fought at the front, wielding both blaster and blade, cutting through the alien soldiers as they pressed forward.

The interior of the Vorlax ship is an unsettling fusion of organic and mechanical elements. The walls seem to pulse and breathe, a strange biomechanical symbiosis that feels alive in the most unnatural way. Every corridor they ran through seemed to shift and move as if the ship itself was part of the battle.

"This place is... alive," Sailor Grace muttered as they continued to press forward, navigating the shifting halls.

"Focus," Connor said sharply. "We need to get to the command center. We don't have time to take on every Vorlax in this ship."

The deeper they ventured into the ship, the more intense the resistance became. Vorlax soldiers poured into the halls, and at one point, they were surrounded by a squad of armored warriors. Tyler smashed through their ranks with brute force, using his extra arms to fend off attackers from all sides. Sailor Grace took out several with a well-placed grenade, sending Vorlax bodies flying.

Finally, after a half hour that felt like an eternity of fighting, they reached the command center. It's a vast chamber, filled with alien technology that hums and pulses with energy. At the center stands the Vorlax Commander - a hulking figure even larger than the others. His armor glows with a strange energy, and his multi-eyed face watches them with a menacing sneer.

"You dare invade our sanctum?" the Vorlax Commander growled, his voice echoing through the chamber. "Such a feeble assault."

The Vorlax Commander charged forward, his speed and strength catching Connor off guard. He moved like a blur, striking with inhuman precision. Connor barely managed to block his first strike with his energy blade, but the force sent him skidding across the floor.

"Tyler, Sailor, take the others!" Connor shouts as he faces down the Vorlax Commander alone.

The fight is brutal. The Vorlax Commander is a skilled warrior, moving with the strength of a beast and the precision of a trained soldier. Every strike from his massive blade sends shockwaves through the room. Connor is forced on the defensive, parrying blow after blow as he searches for an opening.

Tyler and Sailor Grace were engaged in their own battles, taking down the Vorlax soldiers guarding the command center. Tyler's fists shattered chitin with brutal efficiency, while Sailor's blaster fire pierced through their armor with deadly precision.

Finally, Connor finds his opening. With a swift maneuver, he ducks beneath the Vorlax Commander's next swing and delivers a devastating upward slash with his energy blade, severing the alien's arm. The Vorlax Commander roars in pain but charges again, refusing to back down. But Connor, with a well-timed spin, drives his blade into the Commander's chest, ending the battle.

As the Vorlax Commander collapsed to the ground, Connor turned to his wrist AI. "We need to overload the engines," he said, moving quickly to one of the control panels. The technology is alien, but with the help of his AI, Connor begins to figure it out. Alarms begin to blare as the ship's engines go critical.

"We're not sticking around to see what happens next," Connor snapped. "Move!"

The team rushed back to their shuttle, Vorlax soldiers chasing them through the halls. Connor yelled at Tyler and Sailor to keep running no matter what. As they reached the docking bay, the shuttle's engines fired up, and they blasted off just as the Vorlax command ship began to tear itself apart. From the safety of their shuttle, they watched as the massive ship exploded in a brilliant burst of energy, taking with it a large portion of the Vorlax fleet.

Sailor lets out a whoop of triumph, and Tyler grins. "We did it," he says breathlessly.

Connor gave them both a nod. "That's one command ship down. But we're far from done." He tapped his wrist AI, watching the data stream. "Let's hope this thing grabbed something useful— schematics, controls, anything. Let's get back to the Pinnacle."

As the shuttle speeds back toward the MWU Pinnacle, the team knows that this victory, while significant, is just one battle in a much larger war.

Once Connor and his team returned to the MWU Pinnacle, the taste of their victory from destroying the Vorlax command ship lingered, but there was little time to celebrate. The moment their shuttle touched down, a massive explosion rocked the ship. Alarms blared, and the screens in the command center lit up with new enemy signatures. The Vorlax have launched a ferocious counterattack, emerging from the nearby asteroid fields where they had been lying in wait.

"Status report!" Connor barked, his heart pounding as he strides to the tactical console.

"Vorlax reinforcements, sir," Sailor Grace reported, her voice tense. "Dozens of them, coming in fast from the asteroids. Looks like they're launching a full-scale counterattack."

Connor's tactical mind quickly races through the possibilities. The destruction of the Vorlax command ship may have triggered this desperate counteroffensive, but this is worse than expected. In minutes, multiple MWU ships are reduced to fiery wreckage. The battle, which had once seemed to be in the MWU's favor, now swings dangerously in the opposite direction.

"We've lost two Protector Class ships already," Tyler announced, his voice grim as he watched the destruction unfold.

The Vorlax have gained momentum, using the element of surprise to tear through MWU forces. Plasma beams and missiles streak across the battlefield, lighting up the void in a deadly ballet.

Connor's mind raced. "Get me a read on those asteroid fields.

We need to know exactly where they're coming from and how many ships are still in reserve."

The sensors update, showing dozens more Vorlax ships emerging from the cover of the asteroids, all converging on the weakened MWU fleet. The realization hits Connor - this was a trap from the start. The Vorlax knew the MWU would target their command ship, and they'd been waiting for this exact moment to strike back.

"Form a defensive perimeter around the Pinnacle!" Connor commanded his fleet, his voice clear and strong despite the chaos. "All fighters, focus on protecting the Protector Class ships! If we lose our shields, we're done!"

The order was quickly relayed, and his fleet began to regroup. Ships scrambled into position, forming layers of defense as the Pinnacle took point, anchoring the center of the MWU forces. Connor's instincts told him that holding the line was their only option for survival.

Despite the coordination, the Vorlax forces were relentless. Their ships darted in and out of the battle like predators, using their erratic flight patterns to confuse and overwhelm the MWU defenders. Every time one wave of Vorlax ships was repelled, another wave seemed to replace it, swarming the MWU fleet with deadly precision. The space around Zenith Prime became a graveyard of destroyed ships, the debris field growing thicker with each passing moment.

"They just keep coming," Sailor Grace mutters, her fingers gripping the console in frustration.

Connor clenched his jaw. He knows they're at a severe disadvantage. The Vorlax have the home-field advantage, not only in numbers but also in the knowledge of the battlefield. This system, right above Zenith Prime, is their territory. For every MWU ship destroyed, the Vorlax seems to have ten more ready to replace it. The MWU, however, is far from home, far from reinforcements, and running dangerously low on resources.

They hadn't expected the Vorlax to recover so quickly. Intelligence suggested Zenith Prime's fleet had been crippled after the last engagement—but the enemy had regrouped faster than anyone anticipated. Maybe the MWU had underestimated their resolve– or maybe they'd been fed bad intel from the start. But now, there was no turning back. This wasn't just a battle—it was a last-ditch attempt to end the war before the galaxy bled out.

"We can't keep this up forever," Tyler grunts as another explosion rocks the ship. "We're outnumbered and outgunned."

Connor refuses to let despair creep in. "We don't need to win this fight outright," he says, his voice low but filled with determination. "We just need to hold long enough to force them into retreat. If we can break their formation, we can start picking them off. But we have to play smart. No more direct engagements unless absolutely necessary."

His crew on the bridge nodded, understanding his strategy. Tyler spoke up, saying "We need to outlast them."

"Exactly," Connor said. "Keep our ships close, let the fighters cover the Protector Class ships, and focus all fire on their weaker vessels. If we can force them into a retreat, we might just survive this."

The command center hummed with tense energy as the orders went out. Other fleet's ships began to pull back into tighter formations, their shields overlapping in a defensive net around the much larger Galactic Class ships. The Vorlax swarmed, but the MWU ships held their formations, blasting through the enemy with pinpoint precision.

Despite their efforts, it's clear that the Vorlax are throwing everything they have at the MWU. Connor watches the battle unfold on the tactical display, his hands gripping the edges of the console. He's never seen the Vorlax this desperate, this relentless. They're fighting like cornered animals, and that only makes them more dangerous.

"Hold steady, all. This situation is still ugly, but they seem frantic," Connor said, keeping his tone confident.

In truth, though, he knew they couldn't win this war through sheer firepower. Outlasting the Vorlax—breaking their morale, not their hulls—was the only real path to victory.

Fires raged on several MWU ships, their hulls cracked, leaking atmosphere and sparking violently from damaged energy lines. The Vorlax fleet, too, was in a state of disrepair, with several of their warships crippled and burning. Amidst this apocalyptic scene, Connor remained focused, his hands clenched tightly around his captain chair's armrests as he analyzed the tactical situation on his screen.

The initial chaos of the counterattack had subsided, and despite the Vorlax's brutal flanking maneuvers, the MWU fleet had finally managed to regain a foothold. The fleet had stabilized. Ship formations tightened, shields were realigned, and defensive maneuvers were more coordinated. Connor's decision to form a protective perimeter around the Pinnacle and the Protector Class ships had saved them from being overwhelmed, but the situation was far from resolved.

"Status report!" Connor shouted, barely above the noise of weapons fire and the explosions that reverberated through the ship.

Tyler's voice came through the comm, steady but grim. "We've taken out three more Vorlax cruisers, but our energy reserves are dangerously low. The Vorlax are matching us, hit for hit. It's like fighting ourselves."

Connor grits his teeth. "We can't afford a stalemate," he said, his mind racing to find a solution.

Connor got on the comms with the other various commanders, and they all saw the same thing. It looked to be an even match - a battlefield littered with debris and the wrecks of both MWU and Vorlax ships. Neither side had the upper hand. For every Vorlax warship they took down, the Vorlax would retaliate by obliterating one of theirs. It was a brutal war of attrition, and it was clear that both fleets were nearing the end of their resources.

"We're evenly matched," Sailor Grace said, her voice tight with frustration as she monitored the fleet's movements. "We take them down, they take us down. Neither side is gaining any real ground. We all see the reports, Commander. It's as if both sides of this war have no upper hand now."

Connor nodded but didn't respond. His mind was working through every tactical option available. He knew the Vorlax were just as depleted as the MWU was. Their wild, erratic attacks were no longer as coordinated as they had been earlier in the battle, and their reinforcements had slowed down, though they hadn't stopped entirely. But the MWU fleet was in a similar state. Every hit they took, every energy cell they burned through, brought them closer to the breaking point.

As both fleets had been reduced to mere fragments of their original might, the barrage of fire gradually slowed, eventually fading into silence. The relentless combat came to a halt, with both sides crippled, their numbers drastically reduced and ships in desperate need of repair. The sudden quiet after hours of brutal warfare was almost unbearable, as if the void itself mourned the devastation.

Connor surveyed the scene. His gaze fell on the scattered pieces of galactic-class ships, protector-class vessels reduced to ash, and fighter ships left in shambles. It was hard to quantify the losses, but Connor could feel the weight of everyone pressing down on him. These were not just numbers - they were lives, people he had sworn to protect. He gripped the edge of his command chair, taking a deep breath.

"Order the fleet to regroup," Connor said, his voice carrying the sorrow of the losses but also the determination of a leader. "I want every remaining ship in my fleet to send in damage reports. Get our medics to the worst-hit areas. We'll do what we can to help the survivors."

As the crew scrambled to follow his orders, the Pinnacle itself was being patched up. Technicians and engineers worked tirelessly, trying to restore power and stabilize the ship. Though still operational, the Pinnacle had taken heavy damage during the fight. Its shields were flickering, and several weapons systems were offline. But it wasn't just the Pinnacle; nearly every MWU ship had suffered substantial damage.

Reports began flooding in from other commanders. Connor's heart sank as the gravity of the situation became clearer. Fleet after fleet, report after report, delivered grim news: their numbers were dwindling, and they were dangerously low on essential resources like fuel and ammunition.

One of the Galactic Class commanders, Captain Dorian, appeared on Connor's screen, his face etched with exhaustion. "Commander O'Brien," he said gravely, "We've lost nearly sixty percent of our fleet. The MWU as a whole are outnumbered, and even with the Vorlax pulling back for now, I don't see how we can push forward."

Connor nodded slowly. "I've seen the same on our end, Commander. Other commanders are saying the same thing, too. Our forces have been devastated. But we can't retreat. If we leave now, we lose everything we've fought for."

Dorian sighed but nodded in agreement. "What do you propose we do? Command back home isn't responding. Presumably, they're trying to think of a plan themselves."

Connor was silent for a moment, thinking. They needed time - time to repair, time to regroup, time to figure out their next move. But the Vorlax wouldn't give them that. Not willingly.

Suddenly, a new message appeared on the comms. Admiral Kershaw, one of the ranking MWU commanders, delivered more bad news. "Commander O'Brien, we've just detected movement on Zenith Prime's surface. The Vorlax... they're regrouping. Our scouts report that they've restocked their resources and are beginning to ascend back into space. This break in the fighting - it was just a tactical retreat. They're coming back, and they've got reinforcements."

Connor's mind raced. The Vorlax, with the home-field advantage, had simply used the lull in the battle to restock and recharge. Now, they were about to unleash the rest of their strength.

Connor clenched his fists. The situation had gone from dire to nearly impossible.

The comms line opened again, this time with Commander Asher, another Galactic Class ship captain. "We're out of options, everyone," Asher said gravely. "We can't hold them off. If they launch another full-scale attack, we'll be obliterated. We need to retreat."

Connor shook his head. "We can't retreat, not now. The entire mission - no, the entire war - depends on what happens here. If we fall back, the Vorlax will sweep through the galaxy."

"But we're out of ships, out of resources - hell, we're barely holding together!" Asher said, his voice rose in desperation. "We'll be nothing but target practice if we stay."

Connor understood the desperation in his fellow commander's voice. They weren't just losing ground—they were losing hope. Yet, retreating wasn't an option. Not now.

As the senior commanders began deliberating over the comms, Connor's thoughts surged like a storm. The situation was bleak, but there had to be a way to at least buy them more time.

"We're going to have to fight defensively," Connor said, interrupting the frantic discussion. "We pull our forces back, create a defensive perimeter, and hold them off for as long as we can. We may not be able to defeat them head-on, but we can outlast them. We can make them bleed for every inch of space they take."

Connor continued his argument, "Think about it, if we turn and run, they have a tactical advantage against us. They could figuratively stab us in the back. If we retreat and still manage to get back to our respective headquarters, they could follow each of us and destroy what little defenses those worlds have."

The other commanders were silent for a few moments. Then, one by one, they signaled their agreement—some with nods, others with subtle gestures unique to their exoform physiology: a flick of a tail, a low-frequency pulse, a shift in bioluminescence. It wasn't a solution, but it was the best they had. Connor could tell he'd given them the worst-case scenario—and they all understood what it meant. They might very well be the last line of defense for countless planets depending on them.

"Understood," Admiral Kershaw said. "We'll set up the defensive perimeter. O'Brien, you'll take command of the forward flank—sector Theta. It'll be the hardest hit, but I know you can hold it."

Connor nodded. "We'll be ready."

Connor's gaze hardened as he addressed the crew over the shipwide comm. "Prepare for round two, everybody," he said, voice filled with determination. "We aren't done yet."

The MWU Pinnacle began preparing for the next stage of the battle, its crew rallying behind their commander.

40 A WELCOME ALLY

The Vorlax returned to the battlefield with newly repaired ships and more forces than the MWU, and the ominous sight of their reinvigorated fleet sent ripples of nervousness through the MWU ranks. The starry expanse between the two forces seemed like a final line drawn in the sand. Though Connor and his crew had been working around the clock to repair the MWU Pinnacle, along with the other ships in their fleet, they knew their efforts were only temporary solutions. The MWU fleet's resources were depleted, and while they managed to recover some combat capabilities, they were still vastly outnumbered by the returning Vorlax forces.

In the Pinnacle's war room, the holographic projections of the remaining fleets told a dire story - where once the MWU had hoped for a decisive victory, now they were looking at their final stand. The Vorlax were positioned strategically, their ships spread wide in an aggressive formation, surrounding the MWU on multiple sides.

Connor sat quietly as the senior commanders reviewed the finalized battle plan, their tones heavy with frustration and fatigue. Though the strategy was set, doubt lingered in every pause and exchange. The Vorlax's relentless assault made the odds grim, and everyone knew that holding the line would be a miracle—launching a counteroffensive, even more so. Yet despite the bleak outlook, a familiar determination stirred within Connor. This war had already taken so much from him, but he wasn't ready to surrender.

Back aboard the MWU Pinnacle, Connor met with his squad. Sailor Grace, Tyler, and Ambryst stood in silence as Connor spoke, his voice unwavering despite the weight of responsibility.

"We've been here before," Connor said, meeting each of their gazes. "We've fought when we were outnumbered, and we've come out on top. This isn't any different. We're not giving up - not now."

His crew nodded, their faith in him unshaken. They knew the odds, but Connor's leadership gave them a reason to fight.

Subsequently, the Vorlax ships began their final approach, and with the last war cry of determination, the MWU prepared for the last battle. As Connor looked out into the abyss of space, he felt the familiar rush of adrenaline.

As the Vorlax unleashed their devastating assault, pushing the MWU fleet into their planned defensive retreat, an unexpected event shifted the entire battle's momentum. Amid the chaos, Connor's tactical interface blared with a new set of incoming signals - hyperspace readings! The entire MWU watched in disbelief as an entire fleet of ships emerged from the void, thousands of ships surrounding the battlefield from nearly every angle.

Their ships were unmistakable: sleek and insectoid in design, with exoskeleton-like hulls and segmented structures that resembled the anatomy of a bug. Greenish bioluminescent energy pulsed through their cores, giving the vessels an eerie, organic glow as they darted through space. From his vantage point, Connor could see how quickly they maneuvered in tight swarms, coordinating with unsettling precision—like a hive responding to an unseen signal. They moved fast and struck faster, overwhelming their targets through sheer numbers and tightly orchestrated tactics.

It's the Zorvakians! The insectoid race the MWU once thought might never support them due to the malevolent act caused by the traitorous diplomat Brandi Kimbrough. The very same exoform that had every reason to turn against the MWU now arrived as a powerful ally.

For a few moments, the MWU wasn't aware who the Zorvakians were there to help until their command ship sent out the simple but very welcomed message through all communications: "The Zorvakians stand with the MWU!"

"By the stars - " Sailor Grace mutters, eyes wide. Tyler stands stunned, his four arms gripping the nearby console. Ambryst cheered with a fist pump in the air.

Connor was filled with relief as he watched the Zorvakians dive into the battle without hesitation. Their ships, smaller but more agile than both the Vorlax and MWU vessels, swarmed in intricate patterns. Thanks to their hive-like coordination, similar to the Vorlax, the Zorvakians executed complex tactical maneuvers that even the most advanced MWU or Vorlax ships would have struggled to counter. It's as if their entire fleet moved as one mind, every ship in perfect sync with the others.

The insectoid ships formed a protective barrier around the damaged MWU fleet, allowing the larger Galactic Class ships and Protector Class vessels to regroup without taking further damage. Insectoid fighters wove in and out of the gaps between the larger MWU ships, intercepting Vorlax attacks and returning fire with deadly precision. Their swiftness, combined with sheer numbers, made them an ideal complement to the MWU's heavier firepower.

The MWU fleet's commanders, who just moments ago were calculating the odds of a near-impossible victory, now saw hope.

"Get the Zorvakians patched into the tactical net! Let's integrate their formations with ours!" Connor barked into his command interface, a new spark of hope igniting within him. The initial declaration of allegiance had come moments earlier—a resonant pulse from the Zorvakian command relay, simple but unmistakable. Now, with tactical systems linking up, MWU Command moved quickly, syncing the hive-mind's formations with their own. What had seemed like a desperate final stand now began to look like a true turning point.

The Zorvakians don't simply fight - they swarm. Their ships operated in a tight formation, surrounding Vorlax ships and creating confusion with their rapid, erratic movements. Their hive mentality allows them to adapt on the fly, shifting strategies as soon as the Vorlax attempts to counter. The chaos this created in the Vorlax ranks was staggering; their well-organized lines quickly became disrupted.

Ambryst, watching the battle from the command center, lets out a breath of disbelief. "I'll be honest guys, I thought we were dead."

Connor spoke to his officers, saying "With the Zorvakians forming an impenetrable front line, the whole MWU can now shift from defense to offense."

The larger Galactic Class ships, once vulnerable, now refocused their heavy artillery on Vorlax capital ships. Explosions lit up the battlefield as the combined forces of the MWU and Zorvakians pressed on.

As the Pinnacle led a series of strikes, Connor's eyes moved from screen to screen, adjusting orders as the battle fluctuated. The Zorvakians continued to prove their worth, executing swarm tactics that baffled the Vorlax and gave the MWU the time they desperately needed to reassert dominance and control in this battle.

The tide of the battle had finally begun to shift. The Vorlax were no longer the unstoppable force they once appeared to be.

"Focus fire on their command centers! Don't give them a chance to regroup," Connor ordered, his eyes darting between tactical displays and the chaos outside the command window of his ship.

Under Connor's command, the combined forces of the MWU and Zorvakians pressed forward, pushing the Vorlax back towards Zenith Prime.

But as the Vorlax commanders sensed the growing threat of

total defeat, they issued a retreat order. Their ships began to pull back, abandoning key positions and leaving behind several wrecked ships in their wake.

"They're pulling back," Tyler observed from the command deck. "But it doesn't feel like a full retreat."

Connor nodded. "No, they're just regrouping. But we've taken out key positions. They've lost ground."

The Vorlax began a tactical retreat toward the far side of Zenith Prime, their ships pulling into defensive positions as they prepared for their next moves.

Connor's interface lit up with a priority alert, and a familiar MWU identifier flashed across his HUD as multiple commanders chimed in through the tactical net. "We've crippled their primary defenses, and it looks like they're retreating!" one of the captains reported, his voice sharp with cautious optimism.

"I know," Connor replied, his voice steady. "Let's regroup and tend to the wounded."

The final remaining Vorlax ships vanished into the dark void of space, retreating from the safety of their home world's orbit like wounded dogs.

As all of the MWU and Zorvakian ships began to assess and repair damages, the MWU High Command back at Headquarters sent out a message that brought everyone comfort and cheer.

"The war is over! The Vorlax have sent their notice of surrender!"

41 TERMS OF SURRENDER

Connor's heart clenched, not just in victory, but in quiet relief. It was finally over.

"The remaining Vorlax ships have retreated or been destroyed, Commander," an officer reported, her voice carrying a mix of exhaustion and hard-won triumph.

Connor nodded, though his face remained stoic. The planet below was filled with Vorlax, and despite their surrender, they obviously wouldn't be welcoming.

But there was no time to revel in any victory; they needed to secure peace as swiftly as possible.

From Earth, Ambassador Ilyra D'Vaan, the diplomat elected to represent the entire MWU, prepared to deliver a critical message to the Vorlax. Before proceeding, she coordinated with the surviving fleets and the Zorvakian allies, ensuring all parties were patched into the communication. The goal was for everyone to witness the pivotal interaction with the Vorlax leadership firsthand.

"Patch us through," Connor said to a crew member on the bridge. A moment later, the image of a seasoned MWU diplomat appeared on the communications screen, ready to broadcast the message to the Vorlax on the surface of Zenith Prime.

The diplomat's voice was steady, and resolute, as it echoed

across the communication channels of the planet. "To the leaders of the Vorlax, the battle above your world is over. Your fleet has been defeated. Your cities and people are vulnerable. We offer you one chance to negotiate peace but you must stand down, disengage, and cease all hostilities towards the MWU and the accompanying Zorvakian fleets. We are prepared to discuss terms that will ensure the safety of your people."

Connor listened closely as the message was broadcast across the planet. Minutes passed, the suspense thick in the air, until a response filtered through the speakers, laced with static and tension.

"This is the Vorlax High Council," came the guttural voice. "We acknowledge our defeat and are ready to negotiate terms of surrender. Our leaders will convene with your diplomats. We agree to the ceasefire."

Connor exhaled, his grip on the edge of his chair loosening as the weight of the war began to lift. There was hope for peace now, and the road to reconciliation had begun.

The collective fleet floated in silence over Zenith Prime. Below, the once seemingly invincible Vorlax empire now lay exposed—its once-mighty fleet shattered, and its planetary defenses crippled beyond repair.

Contemplating the recent message from the Vorlax, Connor couldn't shake the hollowness that came from their words. He could sense a bitter tone in their dialogue.

The voice of one of the MWU commanders cut through the silence. "The Vorlax are ready. It's time to prepare for our descent."

Within hours, the MWU and Zorvakian forces began preparations for the diplomatic mission that would finalize the Vorlax surrender. Connor joined the commanders from Galactic Class ships—battle-worn leaders representing fleets that had bled to halt the Vorlax war machine. Alongside them stood the MWU's top diplomats, poised not just to negotiate peace, but to shape the post-war future of the galaxy.

Boarding a secure shuttle bound for the Vorlax capital,

Connor glanced out at the smoldering remnants below. This mission was more than an armistice—it was a chance to ensure the Vorlax would never again rise to threaten the galaxy.

The Vorlax capital loomed below, a stark contrast to the towering structures of the MWU's galactic cities. What was once a bustling center of power and authority had become a war-torn wasteland. Even from the skies, Connor could see the scars of the battle. Buildings were crumbling, the streets were deserted, and the remnants of their once-mighty war machines littered the landscape. Connor hated that their planet suffered loss and damage; However, their planetary defenses had to be eliminated, the same as their ships in orbit. This was simply collateral damage of the war that the Vorlax started.

"Prepare for landing," a voice crackled over the shuttle's comms, breaking Connor from his thoughts. He gave a brief nod to Sailor Grace and Tyler, who were accompanying him as part of the diplomatic team. He left his good friend Ambryst in charge of the Pinnacle whilst gone. They were all too aware that while the war might have been won in space, this meeting could easily reignite tensions.

The MWU shuttles touched down in the Vorlax capital with a soft thud, the atmosphere thick with both physical dust and an unseen but unmistakable hostility. As Connor disembarked and took in the sight of the Vorlax city around him, his heart sank. Victory had come but at an immense cost. He couldn't shake the image of all the brave souls who had laid down their lives to get them here.

The other MWU commanders seemed to share his sentiments. One by one, they stepped off their shuttles, each carrying the same burden of grief and loss. They had come to negotiate peace, but for many, it felt as though the galaxy would never truly recover from the devastation the war had wrought.

Sailor Grace whispered softly beside him. "So many lives lost on both sides. Was it all worth it?"

Connor didn't answer immediately, his gaze fixed on the

remnants of the Vorlax defense turrets in the distance. "I hope so," he finally replied, though his voice was heavy with uncertainty.

As the MWU delegation gathered, ready to meet with the Vorlax leaders, the atmosphere was bittersweet. The war had ended, but the scars - both physical and emotional - would take generations to heal. This was a victory drenched in the blood of too many lost lives.

The Vorlax leaders awaited them inside a grand, though heavily damaged, council chamber - a remnant of the once proud and powerful Vorlax empire.

The Vorlax leaders, hulking figures with their many-eyed faces displaying neither warmth nor malice, stood across from the MWU and Zorvakian delegates. Their defeat was clear, but their pride remained intact. The MWU elected diplomats, flanked by military representatives like Connor, began the difficult task of hammering out terms. The focus of these negotiations was not just peace, but the reintegration of the Vorlax into the galactic community - a prospect that seemed both necessary and daunting.

Discussions were heated at times. The Vorlax were a warrior people, and for them, surrender felt like a dishonor. However, the loss of their fleet and the threat of further destruction to their home planet forced them to the table. The MWU and Zorvakians pushed for a permanent ceasefire, disarmament of the remaining Vorlax military forces, and reparations for the many worlds damaged in the conflict. The Vorlax, in turn, sought assurances that their species would not be subjugated or completely dismantled.

Connor watched closely, aware that one poorly chosen word could undo everything they'd fought for—and turn a fragile ceasefire into a fresh wave of bloodshed.

After days of negotiations, an agreement was finally reached. Both sides, though worn and exhausted, acknowledged that this war could no longer continue. The Vorlax leaders signed the ceasefire documents, named the Vorlax Concord, officially ending the hostilities. The war that had ravaged the galaxy for so long was over.

The terms of the surrender included a comprehensive disarmament of the Vorlax fleet, the dismantling of their war factories, and strict oversight by the MWU to ensure compliance. The Vorlax, humbled by their defeat, agreed to these terms, recognizing that their survival as a people depended on cooperation rather than continued conflict.

For the MWU and their allies, the victory was ambivalent. The focus now shifted to rebuilding what had been destroyed. Planets ravaged by the Vorlax and their war needed aid, displaced species required relocation, and the galaxy itself needed time to heal.

The final signatures were penned and the Vorlax leaders retreated to their chambers silently. As much as the victory was worth celebrating, no one did. Not then.

42 PEACE

The MWU wasted no time in launching their post-war recovery efforts. The first priority was to provide aid to the planets most affected by the Vorlax onslaught. Dozens of star systems were requesting help in a variety of ways but most importantly security. Connor had been a part of coordinating the various species affected by the war, ensuring that aid arrived where it was most needed and that the MWU's resources were being used effectively.

Connor spent hours reviewing reports from affected planets, signing off on aid shipments, and planning the logistics of recovery operations. As he read through the documents, images of the destruction kept flashing through his mind - something he knew wouldn't be fixed overnight but still needed to be discussed with someone.

One of Connor's key diplomatic missions was to mend the fractured relationship with the Zorvakians—the insectoid species who had once refused MWU alliance after the assassination of their leaders aboard a neutral space station by the traitor Brandi Kimbrough. The incident had shattered trust. But in the final days of the war, it was Connor's direct negotiations—risking his own life to deliver reparations and a formal apology on behalf of the MWU— that helped reopen dialogue. Combined with the Zorvakians' own strategic interest in stopping the Vorlax, these efforts led them to fight alongside the MWU in the climactic battle.

Connor knew that these hostilities couldn't be ignored now that the war was over. He had personally requested to lead the diplomatic efforts with the Zorvakians, determined to ensure that their fragile alliance would not crumble after the war. His meetings with their leadership were tense at first, the scars of the past conflict still fresh. The Zorvakians had sacrificed many of their own in the war, and though they had fought alongside the MWU, there remained a deep sense of wariness toward the MWU leadership.

As Connor sat across the table from the Zorvakian diplomats, he couldn't ignore the sensation of being watched—hundreds of glinting eyes locked onto him from across the table, unblinking and alien. Each diplomat observed him in silence, measuring whether the MWU was truly worthy of their renewed trust.

Connor's steady leadership began to chip away at the Zorvakians' distrust. During their third diplomatic session, a high-ranking envoy named Xeleth-Kai—whose shimmering carapace darkened with tension each time Connor spoke—finally addressed him directly.

"You stood idle while our leaders were slaughtered," she said, her voice sharp with lingering pain. "Why should we believe this new alliance is any different?"

Connor didn't deflect. He rose, crossed the room, and presented the official MWU reparations order—stamped, signed, and sealed. "Because I've fought to make sure you're at the table this time. Not beneath it."

That moment shifted the tone. From then on, Xeleth-Kai and other Zorvakian delegates began responding with guarded questions instead of accusations. Connor invited them to review aid deliveries firsthand. He accompanied them to supply depots. He made sure Zorvakian colonies were included in post-war recovery briefings.

The talks were still tense, but now they moved forward. Not

because trust was fully restored—but because the MWU had started to earn it back, one honest act at a time.

As Connor walked back from yet another long meeting with the Zorvakians, he reflected on the progress made. It wasn't perfect, and there was still much to be done, but the foundation was being laid for a lasting partnership. The war had nearly torn apart the fabric of the galaxy, but in its aftermath, there was an opportunity to create something stronger. Rebuilding wasn't just about restoring what was lost - it was about creating something better for the future.

After the relentless destruction of the war, the Vorlax—though humbled by defeat—remained a formidable force. The MWU aimed to forge lasting peace, but the path ahead was fraught with complexity. Disarmament protocols, reparations, and future cooperation demanded careful, nuanced diplomacy.

While Connor remained focused on securing compliance from the Vorlax—his presence as a war-tested commander offering credibility—the MWU assigned Dr. Elira Voss, a xeno-specialist and Connor's partner, to lead the parallel negotiations with the Zorvakians. Her deep understanding of interspecies psychology and cultural nuance made her the perfect liaison.

The two exchanged updates frequently, each shaping the fragile future from different sides of the diplomatic divide—Connor through force-tempered pragmatism, Elira through empathetic precision.

Connor entered the Vorlax council chamber, the air thick with antipathy. Seated around the massive, dimly lit table were the Vorlax leaders - scarred veterans of the war, their expressions hard and unyielding. Many still resented the MWU and its interference in their way of life. The challenge now was ensuring that peace was maintained in the long term.

Their capital city had begun the slow process of rebuilding. As Connor looked out the window behind the negotiating table, he could see the skeletal remains of destroyed buildings, now being patched together by the very survivors who had fought so fiercely against the MWU.

Despite their surrender and the many hours afterward that led to the Vorlax Concord, further talks were needed. These were to cement the future of peace. It was clear from the start that this was going to be an uphill battle. The Vorlax leaders, while officially compliant, spoke with guarded words, their mistrust undeniable.

Connor sat quietly at first, listening to the exchanges. The MWU diplomats argued back and forth with the Vorlax representatives, but neither side seemed willing to bend. The stress in the room grew, and it became clear that these peace talks were reaching a deadlock.

Finally, Connor spoke up. "This war has cost us all far too much. The loss of life, the destruction - none of it can be undone. But we have the chance now to ensure that it never happens again. We're not here to subjugate you. We're here to build a future where the galaxy is safe from these kinds of conflicts."

The Vorlax leader, a hulking figure with a face marked by countless scars, narrowed his many eyes at Connor. "Noble words Commander, but we are not fools. The MWU has power over many species, and we do not wish to become just another pawn."

Connor met the leader's gaze, unfazed. "Who said you'd be pawns? The MWU has always been a coalition of equal members, each contributing to the whole. If you choose to see this as subjugation, then we've already failed. We're offering a partnership - one where we can prevent more destruction like this." He motioned out the window to the ruined city below. "We've all lost people. Look around. Look at your planet, sir! At its condition. I've lost friends in this war. But I'm here because I believe that their deaths will mean something if we can stop this from happening again."

The Vorlax leader was silent for a long moment, his eyes shifting to the other Vorlax council members. Eventually, he spoke, his voice softer but still tinged with suspicion. "What you say, it makes sense. But trust is not something that can be rebuilt easily."

Connor nodded. "None of us here expected it to be. But we

have to start somewhere. Please, let's work together to make sure that this peace lasts. That your planet rebuilds and that your young ones have a future to look forward to. I know you don't trust the MWU right now but let me show you that we're committed to making this work."

The discussions stretched late into the night, with Connor serving as a vital bridge between the MWU diplomats and the Vorlax council. Though not officially in charge, his presence carried weight—his combat experience and front-line leadership earning him a rare measure of respect from both sides. The talks remained tense, but slowly, progress emerged. The Vorlax agreed to dismantle portions of their most dangerous weaponry, while the MWU pledged non-interference in Vorlax governance—so long as galactic security standards were upheld.

As the talks wrapped up for the day, Connor felt hope. It wasn't perfect, but there was a chance - just a chance - that this fragile peace could hold. The Vorlax would never be fully trusted by many within the MWU, not for a very long time, but Connor believed that their cooperation could lead to a new era of interstellar diplomacy.

Connor left the council chamber exhausted, but with resolve hardening behind his eyes.

In the weeks following the Vorlax surrender and the conclusion of Zorvakian negotiations, Connor transitioned into a new role—one rooted more in reconstruction than diplomacy. He spent long hours in strategy sessions with MWU leadership and emissaries from dozens of species, helping to shape policies that would govern intergalactic relations in the fragile peace that followed.

While not a formal diplomat, Connor's battlefield credibility and his empathy—honed through the war's devastation—gave his voice weight. He championed transparency, inclusion, and fairness, determined to ensure that no species would feel ignored or sidelined in the galaxy's new chapter.

In one of the final sessions, the council turned its attention to a contentious topic: the Vorlax's future place in the galaxy. Though they had never been part of the MWU, their surrender had reshaped interstellar power dynamics. Connor advocated for a carefully measured approach—offering the Vorlax a path toward peaceful participation in the broader galactic community, but with firm safeguards in place.

"Give them room to recover," he told the council, "but not so much freedom that they can rebuild in secret." His stance echoed a growing consensus: healing would require restraint without humiliation, accountability without domination.

After nearly a year of tense negotiations, reconstruction efforts, and fragile diplomacy, the time had finally come to sign a new intergalactic peace accord. The summit was held on a neutral planet, its atmosphere carefully chosen to symbolize impartiality and hope. Leaders from the MWU, the Zorvakians, the Vorlax, and dozens of other species gathered beneath a shared banner—one that now stood for cooperation instead of conflict.

Connor stood among them, a silent witness as these once-warring factions came together to mark a new chapter in galactic history. Though the scars of war remained, the treaty they signed was more than ceremonial—it was a declaration that trust, though hard-won, was possible.

43 HAASE'S LEGACY

For the first time in a long time, Connor allowed himself to question his career. What had he truly gained from all this? The glory of victory felt somewhat hollow, tarnished by the bloodshed and heartbreak that accompanied it. The friends he had lost, the lives taken too soon - it weighed on his conscience. What was the point of it all if, in the end, it only brought more suffering?

But then, as he looked deeper into the stars, he remembered what they had fought for. The lives they had saved. The worlds they had protected. The galaxy's future. The battles hadn't been in vain. The pain wasn't meaningless. Every life lost had been in service to something greater - a chance for a peaceful galaxy, where species could coexist without fear of annihilation. That was worth fighting for.

He thought of the Zorvakians, who had once been neutral but now stood side by side with the MWU, having decided not only to join but to work within the MWU as well. He thought of the countless worlds that had been freed from the Vorlax threat, the civilians who now had a future because of the sacrifices made. He thought of the first civilization he found and discovered, and how they now have a safe future ahead. These victories, however bittersweet, reminded him of why he had chosen this path in the first place.

"Sometimes I beat myself up too much," he said to himself. The galaxy still needed people like him - those willing to make the hard choices, those willing to fight for what was right, no matter the cost. Whatever thoughts he had of quitting the MWU were quickly thrown out of his mind. He couldn't turn away from his responsibilities. Not after everything.

He had chosen this path for a reason, and despite the pain, he was ready to see it through to the end. His mind was clear. His purpose was set. He would continue his service to the MWU, not because he was obligated to, but because it was the right thing to do. And in doing so, he would honor the memories of those who had fallen, ensuring that their sacrifices would never be forgotten.

With a quiet resolve, Connor turned away from the view of the stars. He smirked as he thought to himself in a not-so-humble way that with him at the helm, it would at least have a fighting chance.

Connor was halfway through a routine debrief with the Zorvakian reconstruction delegates when the door slid open—and in walked Admiral Terros, flanked by two members of MWU High Command. The room stilled.

"Captain O'Brien," the admiral began, voice formal but edged with something more personal, "the Council has reached a unanimous decision. You're being offered command of the Vanguard—a brand-new Galactic Class vessel."

For a moment, Connor said nothing. He hadn't come to this meeting expecting anything beyond resource logistics and cross-species coordination. And now, they were handing him the future.

"Why me?" he finally asked.

Admiral Terros offered a rare smile. "Because no one else has earned the trust of this many factions—or proven themselves when it mattered most."

The ship was a marvel of engineering—surpassing even the most advanced Galactic Class vessels in the fleet. Far more than a warship, it featured expanded medical bays, cutting-edge research labs, advanced AI-assisted command systems, and a dedicated hangar capable of launching multiple Pinnacle-class fighters.

But more than its tech, the ship represented a turning point: a clean slate after years of war. The MWU's offer wasn't just a reward—it was a statement of faith. They believed Connor could help lead the galaxy into a new era of peace and purpose.

For a moment, Connor hesitated. The seriousness of the offer was remarkable but undeniable. Taking command of such a ship would elevate him to a position of even greater responsibility.

But then, in that moment of hesitation, he thought of Lieutenant Haase.

She had always believed in him. Her mentorship had been a guiding force in his life, and her loss had hit him harder than he had ever let on. With that in mind, Connor knew he had to accept. This was the right choice.

However, before finalizing his decision, Connor made a simple yet profound request. He asked the MWU high command to allow him to name the ship the MWU Haase, in honor of his late mentor. He explained that without her guidance, he wouldn't be the leader he is today. Her name deserved to be remembered, not just by him, but by the entire galaxy.

The request was met with silence at first. The high-ranking officers around him exchanged glances, clearly moved by his words. Then, one by one, they nodded in agreement. They, too, had known Lieutenant Haase's dedication and sacrifice, and they understood the significance of the gesture.

"It will be done," one of the senior officers finally said, his voice carrying the weight of authority. "The ship will be named the MWU Haase, and her legacy will live on."

Connor felt a mixture of satisfaction and melancholy wash over him. It was a small tribute, but it meant the world to him. This new ship, this new chapter in his career, would be a testament to everything he had learned under Haase's mentorship. As the meeting adjourned, he walked away with a feeling of closure - and a renewed conviction to lead the MWU into its next chapter. The MWU Haase would be his ship, and through it, he would honor not only Haase's memory but also the ideals they had both fought for.

As preparations were underway for the christening of the MWU Haase, Connor took the rare opportunity to reflect on the journey that had brought him to this point. It was a journey marked by growth, loss, and an unrelenting dedication to something greater than himself. In many ways, standing on the threshold of this new chapter in his life felt surreal. The once-young pilot who had been so eager to prove himself had now risen to command one of the most advanced ships in the galaxy, a ship that bore the name of his greatest mentor. The road to this moment, however, had not been easy.

Connor glanced out at the gleaming hull of the new ship and thought of how far he'd come. From a lone pilot in a one-seater fighter to a commander trusted with the future of peace. Once, his world had been measured in kill-counts and narrow escapes. Now, every decision he made shaped entire civilizations.

He didn't need to be the best at flying anymore. He needed to be the best at leading. And that meant knowing when to fight—and when to forgive.

As the final touches were being made to the ship, Connor walked its halls, marveling at the size and sophistication of the MWU Haase. It was a far cry from the days of piloting single-seat fighters. This ship wasn't just a vessel; it was a city in the stars, a fortress of hope, and a beacon for the future. Thousands would live aboard it, relying on his command and guidance. It was a role he had earned, but one that humbled him more with each passing moment.

The day of the christening came, and as the ceremonial proceedings unfolded, Connor stood on the bridge of the ship, admiring the memory of seeing the words "MWU Haase" on the side of his ship. This ship represented more than just his journey - it was a testament to all those who had fought, bled, and sacrificed for the galaxy's future.

As the captain of this new Galactic Class ship, he wasn't just tasked with maintaining peace but also with shaping a new era for the galaxy - one defined by unity and cooperation among species that had once been enemies. His role had evolved from that of a soldier to that of a leader, a symbol of resilience and hope. And while the battles may have changed, the stakes remained just as high.

With a final glance out, Connor took a deep breath and steeled himself for what was to come. The galaxy had been torn apart by war, but now it was his duty to help rebuild it. The MWU Haase was more than just a ship; it was a promise - a promise that peace, no matter how hard-fought, was possible.

As the ceremony concluded and the crew began to settle into their new roles, Connor stood tall and ready. Ready to lead, ready to inspire, and ready to honor the legacy of those who had come before him. His eyes scanned the vast expanse of space, knowing full well that his destiny, and that of the galaxy, was still unfolding.

44 XELORON'S DOWNFALL

In the aftermath of the war, one event weighed heavily on the minds of billions across the galaxy: the Galactic Tribunal of former Supreme Chancellor Xeloron. This trial, long anticipated by countless species, became the focal point of attention, as citizens from across the MWU's vast expanse eagerly awaited the verdict on his betrayal and treachery. The galaxy held its breath as justice finally began to unfold.

Connor had recently left Earth to take the MWU Haase out for its first voyage, giving himself and his new crew a few days to adjust to the ship. The journey allowed everyone on board to settle into their new roles, familiarizing themselves with the intricate systems of the state-of-the-art Galactic Class ship. The time away gave Connor a chance to bond with his crew and establish the MWU Haase as their home in the vast galaxy.

Upon returning from the voyage, Connor received an invitation to attend the Galactic Tribunal of Xeloron, a momentous event he was eager to witness. Accepting the invitation, Connor was now seated in the gallery of the expansive tribunal chamber, listening intently as the proceedings unfolded, keenly aware of the importance of justice in the wake of the recent war. Happily enough, Lysara had been invited to join and she sat right next to Connor, both of them sharing a quick peck on the lips before the tribunal began.

The Galactic Tribunal convened in an atmosphere thick with tension, the weight of the galaxy's eyes on the room. The courtroom, a sprawling and state-of-the-art facility located within the MWU's most secure sector, was specifically designed for high-profile cases like this one. The architecture was breathtaking, with high vaulted ceilings, holographic interfaces, and vast transparent walls that allowed views of the stars and the vastness of space beyond. But today, the grandeur felt cold, matched by the stern expressions of the ten Galactic Judges who had taken their seats on the elevated platform.

Each judge represented a different species and region of the galaxy, a symbol of the MWU's inclusivity and diversity. Their robes reflected their origins - some shimmering with the iridescent scales of aquatic species, others sleek and metallic, reflective of more technologically advanced civilizations. Though their appearances varied greatly, they all shared a unified sense of purpose: to deliver justice, no matter the power or influence of the accused.

At the far end of the courtroom, the Supreme Chancellor was escorted in. He once cut an imposing figure, his influence commanding respect and even fear. Now, however, the veneer of his former authority had faded. His appearance was disheveled, a shadow of his former self. His once regal robes were replaced with a simple, worn uniform, a stark contrast to the grandeur he had once enjoyed. The weight of his betrayal, and the immense power he had sought to wield, seemed to have drained him. As he was seated in the center of the room, under the watchful eyes of the galaxy, there was no longer any sense of invincibility. Instead, there was a glint of defeat in his gaze, an acknowledgment of the inevitable.

The prosecution wasted no time. Magistrate Thessa Virell of New Vireon, a seasoned legal authority known for her unshakable demeanor, stepped forward to deliver the opening argument. Her voice was steady, sharp, and deliberate as she laid out the damning case against the former Supreme Chancellor.

Around the chamber, holographic displays flared to life—intercepted communications between Xeloron and the Vorlax leadership flickering in the air. These transmissions had been pivotal in unraveling the conspiracy, proving beyond doubt that the Chancellor had been leaking sensitive MWU intelligence to the enemy for years.

The evidence was damning. Though this was only the opening session, interstellar tribunal protocols allowed for preliminary material to be displayed for public transparency. Holographic projections flared to life, showcasing intercepted messages from Xeloron to the Vorlax—outlining MWU fleet movements, defense gaps, and strategic vulnerabilities.

A second display captured footage of covert meetings in dimly lit sectors of neutral space stations, where Xeloron had negotiated with Vorlax envoys. Betrayal had a face now—and it belonged to the man who once called himself Supreme Chancellor.

The prosecutor then revealed the heart of the Chancellor's motivations: an insatiable desire for personal power. From the very beginning, it seemed, he had harbored resentment toward the MWU's collaborative and democratic structure. He had never wanted to be part of a collective organization. Instead, his ambition was singular - he wanted to rule. The Vorlax had offered him exactly that - a promise of control over an entire planet, a dominion all to his own. In exchange, all he had to do was aid in the destruction of the MWU, to ensure its fall from within by weakening it, piece by piece.

The betrayal was deeper than anyone had initially imagined. The prosecutor emphasized that this wasn't just about an alliance with the Vorlax. The Supreme Chancellor had systematically sabotaged the MWU, weakening it from within and allowing countless lives to be lost in the war. The courtroom was silent as the prosecution's evidence painted a clear picture of this monster who was driven not by loyalty or duty, but by a hunger for absolute power.

As the prosecutor concluded the opening argument, the weight of the evidence was clear. The Supreme Chancellor sat motionless, his gaze lowered, as though fully aware that his crimes were too great to defend. The once-mighty leader, who had commanded respect across the galaxy, was now reduced to nothing more than an alien whose ambitions had led to his downfall.

The tribunal chamber still pulsed with unease after the opening session. In MWU courts, traditional dual arguments had long since given way to a unified presentation of evidence—reviewed in real-time by a cross-species judicial panel. Transparency mattered more than legal theater.

The damning revelations of Xeloron's betrayal—his collusion with the Vorlax and naked pursuit of personal power—left the room steeped in silence. All eyes were fixed on the disgraced former leader, now seated at the center of the tribunal, stripped of rank and influence. Whatever he had once been, today he would face justice under a law rebuilt to protect a galaxy, not a nation.

Knowing full well the gravity of his situation, Xeloron leaned forward and demanded his defense. His voice was hoarse but edged with the final flickers of arrogance, as if clinging to a crumbling throne.

"I want Heather Edmands," he rasped. "I know her. I've read the transcripts. I've heard the stories. She's the galaxy's finest Galactic Law Counselor. And she's the only one who can represent me."

According to MWU legal structure, defendants in tribunal-level trials could petition for a change in counsel at any point prior to the sentencing phase—though it was rare. Most legal advisors were appointed in advance by impartial AI selection committees, but Xeloron's request, while dramatic, remained technically valid. The panel of judges paused, deliberated in silence, then gave a single nod. The request would be honored.

Heather Edmands was a name known across the galaxy, synonymous with brilliance and unwavering expertise in the realm of galactic law. Her legal prowess was unmatched, and her reputation for taking on and winning the most challenging cases had earned her respect and, in many cases, fear from adversaries. A decorated defense lawyer with countless victories under her belt, she had defended high-profile clients, navigated the trickiest of legal loopholes, and had a reputation for not backing down.

The tribunal members exchanged glances, intrigued by Xeloron's choice. There was no doubt—if anyone could find even a shred of defense for him, it was Heather Edmands. Her name carried nearly as much weight in legal circles as Thessa Virell's, though their philosophies couldn't have been more different.

As the Galactic Tribunal resumed, one of the ten judges addressed Xeloron directly, her voice firm but measured.

"Under Article 7 of MWU Tribunal Law," she said, "you are entitled to request representation by a certified Galactic Law Counselor. However, if you choose to do so, all future arguments must be made on your behalf by your legal representative. This is to ensure consistency of defense and to prevent manipulation of the tribunal through conflicting narratives."

The chamber fell quiet as the weight of the ruling settled in. Xeloron sat still, eyes narrowing, clearly weighing his chances. Finally, he gave a single nod. "I agree to the terms."

The decision triggered immediate action from the Galactic Tribunal. Within moments, they dispatched a formal subpoena to Heather. The communication sent to her explained the situation and emphasized that the choice to represent Xeloron was entirely her own. Not long after receiving the message, Edmands responded swiftly to the Tribunal, "I'll be there immediately." Her calm but resolute message left the entire courtroom awaiting her arrival with bated breath.

Minutes of tense anticipation hung in the air before the tribunal doors finally slid open—and she entered.

Heather Edmands had been stationed nearby at the request of the MWU Council, her presence on standby in the event Xeloron invoked his right to request specific counsel. Few believed he'd have the audacity to ask for her. Fewer still believed she'd accept.

But here she was—composed, unreadable, and ready to do what no one else would: defend the most hated man in the galaxy.

Heather's presence was commanding without being overstated. Dressed in the sleek, professional attire of a Galactic Law Counselor, her eyes were sharp and focused, taking in the scene before her. She walked with a purpose, her steps echoing in the vast courtroom as she approached the defense stand. Her calm yet authoritative demeanor radiated confidence, as if she had already sized up the entire situation in mere moments.

Xeloron, despite his disheveled appearance, seemed to regain some of his confidence, as if her presence alone was his ticket out of this mess. "Heather," he started, a flicker of arrogance creeping into his voice. "You know why I asked for you. No one is better than you. I want you to represent me."

Heather stood in front of him, her eyes locking onto his. Her silence was unnerving, drawing out the friction as the entire tribunal and gallery watched. Then, after what felt like an eternity, she spoke, her voice calm but laced with steel.

"I don't defend traitors. Or assholes." Heather said, her words slicing through the air like a blade. The firmness in her voice left no room for negotiation. "You're exactly where you deserve to be."

The courtroom fell into stunned silence. Even the ten Galactic Judges—seasoned individuals who had seen and heard it all—looked taken aback by the forcefulness of her rejection. This was Heather Edmands, the woman who had won case after case for some of the most controversial figures in the galaxy, and she had just unequivocally refused the former Supreme Chancellor.

Xeloron's face twisted, his confidence shattering. For a moment, he looked as if he had been physically struck. The very woman he believed would save him had just condemned him without hesitation. His lips parted, but no words came out. The hope that had flickered in his eyes vanished as reality set in - he was truly alone in this fight.

One of the Galactic Judges, an elder from the Narthraxian species, cleared his throat and addressed Xeloron. His voice was deliberate and authoritative. "Given the severity of the charges and the nature of this Galactic Tribunal, and since there doesn't seem to be any alternative legal representation or anyone willing to represent you, counsel will not be permitted at this time. You must defend yourself, as is typically the procedure for tribunals of this scale."

A low murmur spread through the gallery as the full weight of the judge's statement settled in. Not only had Xeloron been refused by the galaxy's greatest legal mind, but now he would be forced to stand alone and argue his case. The irony of it all - once the leader of the MWU, surrounded by advisors and strategists, now left to defend himself without any allies - was palpable.

Heather Edmands, having delivered her powerful line, gave Xeloron one last look before turning and walking out of the courtroom, her stride as confident as when she entered. Her role was complete, and her message had been clear: justice would not be swayed by influence, power, or even desperation.

For a moment, no one moved. Then came the murmurs—soft at first, then rising like a tide as those in the gallery processed what had just happened. Even the judges exchanged glances, their measured composure slipping ever so slightly.

Connor remained silent, arms folded, eyes fixed on Xeloron. He saw the flicker of something new in the man's expression—not arrogance, not defiance, but fear. And for the first time since the tribunal had begun, Connor allowed himself a grim sense of satisfaction.

Xeloron sat back in his seat, eyes hollow, the weight of his impending fate pressing down on him. The courtroom no longer held any hope—only judgment.

The trial intensified as the next round of evidence was presented. Every eye in the massive Galactic Tribunal was fixed on the prosecution, and the air seemed to vibrate with unease. The ten Galactic Judges, their expressions grave, listened carefully as the prosecution detailed one of the most shocking revelations yet: the Supreme Chancellor had orchestrated the first attack on the MWU.

A gasp rippled through the courtroom, the sudden intake of breath from the gallery a stark reflection of the collective shock that followed. Several of the Galactic Judges respectfully asked for everyone to lower their voices. The prosecution continued, her voice unwavering as she laid out the cold, hard truth. It was Xeloron, the very man who had stood at the helm of the MWU as one of its most powerful leaders, who had given the Vorlax their first orders to strike. His voice, his command, had sparked the conflict that would ripple through the galaxy, leaving countless dead in its wake.

"Let the record show," Magistrate Thessa Virell declared, her voice unwavering, "that the order to strike Holding Zone Epsilon—where Lieutenant Haase and over two dozen MWU officers were imprisoned—came directly from the accused. He gave the Vorlax their target, knowing full well it would mean the deaths of his own people."

A ripple of horror moved through the gallery. Connor clenched his jaw, the weight of that memory crashing over him again. This wasn't just betrayal. It was execution—coordinated, cold-blooded, and personal.

Connor, sitting among the audience, felt a jolt in his chest as the name of his former commanding officer echoed through the room. His heart fluttered like a trapped bird as the story unfolded, each new revelation driving the knife of betrayal deeper. The prosecution laid out how Lieutenant Haase and her team had been key to uncovering Xeloron's treachery, their investigation piecing together the puzzle of his clandestine alliance with the Vorlax. They had been on the verge of blowing the entire operation wide open, and Xeloron had known it. To protect his secrets, to safeguard his ambition, he had ordered their deaths.

Connor's hands gripped the armrests of his seat, knuckles turning white as he fought to control his rage. Memories of Haase flashed through his mind—her fierce determination, her loyalty to the MWU, her leadership that had shaped him into the Commander he was today.

Beside him, Elira reached over and gently placed her hand over his, grounding him. She said nothing, but her eyes were locked on him, reading the storm building beneath his surface.

And now, to hear that it was Xeloron—the man who had pretended to serve the same cause—who had been responsible for Haase's brutal murder? It was more than Connor could bear. The betrayal ran deep, not just to the MWU, but to him personally. Haase had been more than a mentor; she had been a guide, someone who believed in him when no one else had.

The prosecution described in excruciating detail how Haase and her allies had been held captive, unaware that their time was running out. Xeloron had given the Vorlax clear instructions: eliminate them. The Vorlax had carried out their orders with ruthless precision, bombing the holding area and ensuring that no one would leave alive.

Haase—the woman who had dedicated her life to the MWU—hadn't just been betrayed. She had been executed, sacrificed as a calculated move in Xeloron's twisted game for power.

A hushed whisper began to spread through the gallery, the shock and horror conspicuous. Even the Galactic Judges, who had maintained their dispassionate expressions throughout much of the trial, exchanged uneasy glances. The weight of this revelation was staggering - the sheer depth of Xeloron's treachery now laid bare for all to see.

Connor's body trembled as he sat in the courtroom, struggling to keep his emotions in check. The room seemed to close in around him, the voices of the prosecution fading into the background as his mind raced. He had long suspected the truth—but now it was undeniable. Haase had been murdered not by chance, not in the chaos of war, but on explicit orders.

She had come too close to uncovering the conspiracy that would later unravel the galaxy's highest seat of power. And now, the world knew it too.

He clenched his jaw, forcing himself to breathe, forcing himself to stay composed. He could feel the eyes of his squad on him, their silent support a lifeline in the storm of emotions swirling inside him. Thankfully, Lysara had been sitting next to him and she gently placed her hand on his. It almost instantly calmed his nerves down as he thanked her for soothing his anger. But the betrayal was almost too much to comprehend. Xeloron had been someone they all trusted, someone who was supposed to protect the galaxy - not destroy it from within.

The prosecution continued, explaining how Xeloron had carefully manipulated events from behind the scenes, using his position of power to orchestrate attacks that would weaken the MWU while strengthening his alliance with the Vorlax. He had been playing both sides from the very beginning, and Haase's murder had been the first domino to fall in his twisted plan.

As the evidence mounted, the mood in the courtroom shifted from shock to outrage. Murmurs of anger and disbelief filled the room, and even the Galactic Judges seemed to sit a little straighter, their expressions hardening. This was no longer just a trial - it was a reckoning.

And for Connor, it was personal.

The courtroom buzzed with antipathy, the final pieces of Xeloron's betrayal falling into place.

Now came the time for Xeloron to finally give his defense. No one in the entire room seemed to care about what he had to say, but the Galactic Judges would be unbiased until they heard everything from both sides.

Xeloron stood in the center of the tribunal, his once imposing figure now gaunt but still commanding attention. His voice started low, almost a growl, as he admitted to his collusion with the Vorlax. "Yes, I worked with them," he spat. "They were my means to an end. While you all bickered over peace and unity, I was building something greater, something this galaxy could respect and fear." His tone sharpened, and he seemed to revel in the horror and outrage that rippled through the audience.

"I wanted power, true power," he said unapologetically, his gaze sweeping the room. "Not to be some puppet chancellor bowing to the whims of a committee. The Vorlax gave me what the MWU could not: the promise of control, the promise of dominion over this entire galaxy." His eyes glinted with malice, showing no remorse for the devastation he had helped orchestrate.

Then, suddenly, Xeloron's voice erupted into a furious shout, his fists clenched at his sides. "You idiots!" he screamed, glaring at the Galactic Judges and the room full of MWU officials. "You think peace with the Vorlax will save you? Do you think you can coexist with a race born for conquest and destruction? Siding with me would have been your salvation! You could have had real leadership, true power! Instead, you grovel for peace - weak, pathetic peace!"

The silence that followed was thick, the tribunal chamber awash with a mixture of shock, disgust, and disbelief at the depth of his betrayal and the magnitude of his unrepentant ambitions. And with that, Xeloron sat back down, presumably finished with his defense.

The courtroom, filled with high-ranking officials, commanders, and spectators from across the galaxy, waited in anxious anticipation for the Galactic Judges' verdict. They were now under the forcefield that allowed them to speak freely without being heard by anyone else.

These ten Galactic Judges, representing the galaxy's most diverse species and regions, sat stoically above the court. Their expressions revealed nothing as they deliberated the fate of the former Supreme Chancellor. Each had been selected not only for their deep understanding of galactic law but also for their unwavering commitment to justice. Now, they held the fate of a traitor who had nearly torn apart the very fabric of the MWU.

For what felt like an eternity, the Tribunal was silent, save for the quiet murmurs of those in the gallery, nervously awaiting the decision. Connor sat in his seat, his emotions battling between relief that justice was within reach and the sorrow that this justice would never bring back the lives lost - especially Haase's.

Finally, Chief Arbiter Yaltren Mos—a towering figure of authority from the harsh courts of Olitherus—rose to speak as the forcefield lowered. The courtroom fell into a hushed stillness. All eyes turned toward the bench, and even Xeloron, the disgraced former Supreme Chancellor, seemed to sit up straighter, though his disheveled appearance still bore the scars of defeat.

"The court has heard all arguments, reviewed the evidence, and weighed the immense gravity of the crimes committed," the head judge began, his voice firm and resolute, carrying across the vast room. "We, the Galactic Judges, hereby deliver a unanimous verdict."

Connor felt his breath catch in his throat, as did many others, as the next words determined the fate of the individual who had betrayed them all.

"Supreme Chancellor Xeloron, for your direct involvement in treason against the MWU, your orchestration of attacks that led to the deaths of tens of thousands of innocent lives, and your role in the murder of Lieutenant Haase and her colleagues, you are hereby stripped of your title, your rank, and all authority within the MWU. Your ambitions of power and conquest have led only to your disgrace."

The words struck the room like a hammer blow. Stripped of his title. Someone who had once stood at the pinnacle of power, guiding the direction of the entire galaxy, was now left with nothing. Xeloron had once seen himself as a ruler of worlds, someone who believed he could manipulate the fate of an entire galaxy for his own gain. Now, all that remained of his once formidable presence was a broken, bitter husk.

The head judge's voice cut through the room again. "Furthermore, you are sentenced to life imprisonment, to be carried out in the most secure facility within the galactic prison system, where you will live out the remainder of your days. You will be held accountable for your betrayal, your lust for power, and the countless lives you destroyed."

There was no applause, no celebration. This was not a moment of triumph - it was a somber reckoning. Xeloron had taken so much from the galaxy, and though justice had been served, the damage he had caused could never be fully undone.

As the guards approached the former Supreme Chancellor, shackling his wrists with glowing restraints, the weight of his defeat finally seemed to sink in. His head hung low, and though his face remained expressionless, a bitter sneer tugged at the corner of his mouth. There was no victory left for him - only the cold, unforgiving reality that his dreams of ruling an entire planet, of seizing power beyond the MWU's reach, had crumbled into dust. He had gambled everything and lost it all.

Connor watched him closely, his eyes fixed on the alien who had been at the heart of so much destruction. He felt a flicker of relief knowing that Xeloron's reign of manipulation was over, but there was no joy in the victory.

As Xeloron was being led away, right before the massive doors of the courtroom would close behind him forever with a heavy finality, he spoke one last time.

"You think this is the end of me?" Xeloron hissed, his voice low but dripping with malice. "Imprison me if you must, but know this - I was never alone. My plans, my vision, they are far greater than you could ever imagine. Even from within the coldest cell, my influence will spread like wildfire." His grin widened as he stepped forward, speaking louder now, his words cryptic but full of menace.

"The seeds have already been sown. You may have taken my freedom, but you've done nothing to stop what's already in motion."

The courtroom grew eerily quiet, his final words hanging heavily in the air like a dark omen. As the guards led him away, the unease lingered. Everyone in the room could feel the weight of his threat - cryptic yet terrifying. Xeloron, even in his downfall, had managed to instill a sense of foreboding that no one could shake. What had he set in motion? And more disturbingly, who was still loyal to him?

With a deep breath, Connor rose from his seat, hugged Lysara, and left the courtroom with his friends.

45 NEW BEGINNINGS

The corridors of the MWU Haase hummed with quiet energy as Connor walked the length of his new ship, taking in the sheer magnitude of the vessel. It was as if the MWU had breathed new life into the galaxy itself when they built it. The Galactic Class ship, massive and majestic, represented so much. It was the embodiment of his mentor and everything she had stood for. The soft hum of the engines felt like her spirit carrying them forward, pushing the galaxy toward a future shaped by cooperation and peace. It was a ship born from tragedy but destined for exploration, growth, and unity. And it was Connor's to command.

Connor heard the familiar sound of footsteps approaching, a smile creeping onto his face as he saw his friends Ambryst, Sailor Grace, Tyler, Thara, and his girlfriend Lysara approaching. Each of them had shared in his journey. They had fought together and survived together, and now they stood on the threshold of something entirely new.

Ambryst, calm and steady as always, gave Connor a nod of approval as he approached. The serene alien had been Connor's rock through the hardest moments of the war, a friend who had seen the worst but always remained grounded. Sailor Grace, with her warm smile and unwavering loyalty, fell into step beside Connor, her brown eyes reflecting the optimism they both felt. Tyler cracked a small grin, his four arms casually crossed. He had proven time and again that his strength was not just physical but emotional, his loyalty unmatched. And Thara, the brilliant engineer, exuded excitement at the thought of discovering new technologies and alien species in unexplored sectors of the galaxy.

But it was Lysara who stood closest to Connor, her presence a quiet comfort. The connection they had built was different - deeper, more personal. As the ship prepared for departure, she gave him a playful nudge, reminding him that the galaxy was vast, but they had each other to face whatever came next.

"Everything set?" Connor asked, looking at his crew - his friends - his family.

"All systems operational. We're ready for launch," Thara confirmed with a gleam in her eyes.

Sailor Grace chuckled. "I hope you're ready to explore some completely uncharted territory. We have no idea what's going on out there."

"Isn't that what makes it exciting?" Lysara chimed in, her voice full of anticipation. "There are entire sections of the galaxy just waiting for us! Who knows what we'll find?"

Connor nodded, feeling the same thrill. This was why they had fought, why they had struggled through the darkness - to reach this moment, where they could forge a new future together. "Whatever's out there, we'll face it as a team."

Ambryst's deep voice added to the sentiment. "As a family! And if things get difficult, we'll handle it, just like we always have."

Tyler flexed one of his arms. "As long as you don't mind me breaking a few things if we have to."

Connor laughed, his heart feeling lighter than it had in years. "You break it, Thara fixes it. That's the deal."

"Just as long as you don't break the ship, handsome" Thara warned playfully, her brow raised.

No one had expected that, least of all Tyler. The ever-stoic alien now seemed to be blushing, something Ambryst then jokingly commented on, saying "I didn't think your species could blush!"

They shared a collective laugh, and for a moment, the heaviness of the war seemed distant.

Connor led his crew to the bridge, where the rest of the command staff were already in place. As they took their positions, the massive viewports displayed the distant stars, promising new adventures. The ship's AI reported all systems were nominal, awaiting the captain's command to embark.

For a moment, Connor stood silently, taking it all in. The MWU Haase was not just any ship. It was a new beginning for all of them. It was a chance to explore, discover, and build a galaxy united by shared understanding and purpose.

He took a deep breath and smiled. "All right, crew. Let's see what's out there. Initiate launch sequence."

A collective cheer went through the whole ship as the engines roared to life.

As they left the confines of known space, Connor looked back one last time at the shrinking Earth with a soft smile, the home they were leaving behind. But there was no sadness - only excitement for the future.

As the MWU Haase soared into the unknown, Connor turned to his crew, the people who had become his family.

"Here's to new beginnings," Connor said softly, his voice full of hope.

Lysara, standing next to him, leaned in with a smile. "To new beginnings!"

And with that, the MWU Haase flew deeper into space, leaving behind the scars of war and venturing into the boundless mystery of the galaxy, where endless possibilities awaited. Connor and his crew, united by loyalty, love, and adventure, were ready for whatever the universe had in store for them.

Back on Earth, in the shadows of his office, Commander Edward Martin, of the Evolutionary Eligibility Bureau, poured over classified reports and encrypted communications as his focus shifted from his duties. His eyes glinted with devilish ambition. As he furiously swiped through top-secret holographic projections, he stopped on one and began to chuckle.

"They have no idea," he said, with a smug look on his face. "But they will."

Commander Martin's expression was cold and calculating as he stood before the holographic projection of Apophis, the planet-killer weapon.

The End

DISCUSSION GUIDE
FOR SMALL GROUPS, CLASSES, OR INDIVIDUAL REFLECTION

1. Leadership and Responsibility:

- Connor rises from a fighter pilot to a fleet commander. How does his leadership evolve throughout the story? What do you think are the qualities of an effective leader in a time of war?

- When Connor reflects on the sacrifices of his crew, how does it influence his decisions as a leader?

2. Moral Complexity of War:

- The book explores the ethical dilemmas of war. What decisions made by Connor or the MU challenged your views on right and wrong in times of conflict?

- Do you think the MWU's actions against the Vorlax were justified? Why or why not?

3. Betrayal and Trust:

- How did the betrayal by Supreme Chancellor Xeloron impact your perception of the MWU? What does this reveal about the challenges of maintaining unity in a diverse coalition?

- Have you ever experienced a situation where trust was broken in a leadership role? How does this compare to what Connor faces?

4. Allegory and Real-World Parallels:

- In what ways do the conflicts and alliances in **Starborn Descendants** reflect real-world political or social issues?

- The Vorlax and Zorvakians represent contrasting approaches to conflict. What do these species reveal about humanity's capacity for both destruction and cooperation?

5. Cultural Diversity:

- The MWU represents a coalition of species with unique perspectives. How did the inclusion of alien characters like Lysara and Tyler enhance the story?

- If you could add another alien species to the MWU, what qualities or values would they bring to the table?

6. Impact of Sacrifice:

- Connor and his crew face personal losses throughout the war. How did these moments shape their characters and the story's trajectory?

- How do the sacrifices of characters like Lieutenant Haase reflect the overall theme of perseverance in the face of adversity?

7. The Role of Technology:

- Advanced technology plays a critical role in the MWU's strategy. How does the depiction of technology in the book enhance or complicate the narrative?

- If you could use one piece of futuristic technology from the story, what would it be, and how would you apply it to your life?

8. Galactic Politics:

- The MWU's struggles with internal corruption and

external threats. What do these dynamics suggest about the challenges of governing on a galactic scale?

- How do you think the MWU's political structure could have been improved to avoid Xeloron's betrayal?

9. Hope and Unity:

- Despite the war's devastation, the alliance with the Zorvakians brings hope. What message does this alliance convey about the importance of unity in the face of adversity?

- How does the concept of unity across species challenge or reflect current societal divisions?

10. The Vorlax as Antagonists:

- The Vorlax are portrayed as a brutal and chaotic force. How did their tactics and motivations shape the MWU's response and the story's tension?

- Do you think the Vorlax could have been negotiated with, or were they destined to be enemies?

11. Themes of Loyalty:

- Connor relies on the loyalty of his crew to achieve success. Which relationship in the story stood out to you as the most compelling example of loyalty, and why?

- Have you ever experienced loyalty being tested in your own life? How did that resonate with Connor's experiences?

12. Personal Growth:

- How does Connor's journey from a pilot to a commander mirror his personal growth? What qualities does he develop along the way?

- How do you think Connor balances his duty to the MWU with his personal relationships, such as with Lysara?

13. Future Challenges:

- The ending hints at new threats, including Edward Martin's mission. What do you think Connor's next adventure will involve, and how will his experiences prepare him for it?

- If you were writing the sequel, what challenges or conflicts would you want to explore?

14. Emotional Resonance:

- Which scene or character arc had the strongest emotional impact on you, and why?

- How did Connor's reflections on his fallen comrades affect your perspective on the costs of war?

15. Universal Lessons:

- What lessons from **Starborn Descendants** can be applied to leadership, teamwork, or personal sacrifice in everyday life?

- How did this book change the way you think about collaboration and unity in the face of overwhelming challenges?

ABOUT the AUTHOR

Bradley McKibben is a neurodivergent writer from Indianapolis, Indiana, whose storytelling explores complex emotions and relationships within imaginative, speculative settings. Born in 1988 in Frankfort, Indiana, as the youngest of four siblings, Bradley grew up immersed in gaming and fantasy worlds, finding solace in creative adventures. As a teenager, he balanced skateboarding with singing in his high school show  choir, nurturing a love for both artistic expression and boundless imagination.

Today, Bradley lives with his wife, Jacqueline, and their two children: Tyler, now 16, and Sailor, age 7. His passion for storytelling has led to the universe he has created in this series.

Bradley's writing reflects his Christian faith and lifelong fascination with fantasy and science fiction. When not writing, he enjoys playing piano and acoustic guitar or cheering on his favorite football teams. With a vision to inspire and captivate readers worldwide, Bradley is dedicated to crafting stories that resonate deeply and ignite the imagination.

Previously Published Books by Bradley McKibben are available through Amazon.com:

Countless Roads: A Collection of Short Stories (2024)

The Angelino Slayer (2024)

SHELTERING TREE

Earth
Publishing

ShelteringTreeMedia.com

www.ingramcontent.com/pod-product-compliance
Lightning Source LLC
Chambersburg PA
CBHW071646260626
47170CB00001B/261